D0056553

NO LONGER PROPERTY OF
ANYTHINK LIBRARIES/
RANGEVIEW LIBRARY DISTRICT

By Lara Adrian

Kiss of Midnight
Kiss of Crimson
Midnight Awakening
Midnight Rising
Veil of Midnight
Ashes of Midnight
Shades of Midnight
Taken by Midnight
Deeper Than Midnight
Darker After Midnight
Edge of Dawn

eBook novella
A Taste of Midnight

EDGE *of* DAWN

Lara Adrian

Delacorte Press | New York

EDGE *of* DAWN

Midnight Breed Series
Book Eleven

Edge of Dawn is a work of fiction. Names, characters, places, and incidents are the products of the author's imagination or are used fictitiously. Any resemblance to actual events, locales, or persons, living or dead, is entirely coincidental.

Copyright © 2013 by Lara Adrian, LLC

All rights reserved.

Published in the United States by Delacorte Press, an imprint of The Random House Publishing Group, a division of Random House, Inc., New York.

Delacorte Press is a registered trademark of Random House, Inc., and the colophon is a trademark of Random House, Inc.

LIBRARY OF CONGRESS CATALOGING-IN-PUBLICATION DATA

Adrian, Lara.
Edge of Dawn / Lara Adrian.
pages cm. — (Midnight Breed Series)
ISBN 978-0-345-53260-2
eBook ISBN 978-0-345-53261-9
1. Vampires—Fiction.   I. Title.
PS3601.D74E34 2013
813'.6—dc23   2012043277

Printed in the United States of America on acid-free paper

www.bantamdell.com

2 4 6 8 9 7 5 3 1

First Edition

Book design by Virginia Norey

For my readers
Come along with me. The adventure continues . . .

Acknowledgments

With thanks, as always, to my family, friends, and staff for all of the love, support, and patience (OMG, the patience!) while I am checked out from real life and happily immersed in my writing.

To my readers in the States and around the world, thank you so very much for your incredible enthusiasm for my books! I am continuously amazed and humbled by your kindness, friendship, and support. (((HUGS)))

To my worldwide publishing teams and support staffs, thank you for helping my books reach their audience, and for the care and effort you put forth to ensure my work is the best it can be.

Special thanks to reader Candice Brady, who generously contributed to a fundraiser held to assist a dear member of the romance community who suffered a tragic loss in her family. Candice's winning bid scored a special "guest spot" in this novel.

EDGE *of* DAWN

JOURNAL ENTRIES

from the private history archives of the Order
Washington, D.C., headquarters

December 26

The year no longer matters; neither does the date. After what's happening right now around the world, my guess is history will soon be explained simply in terms of Before and After. Before mankind realized vampires were real, and *after.* After a power-crazed vampire named Dragos freed scores of the most deadly members of the Breed—savage, blood-addicted Rogues—turning the incarcerated monsters loose on an unsuspecting, and obviously unprepared, human public. Even as I write this, I can hardly believe what I'm seeing.

The carnage is unspeakable. The terror unprecedented. It's hard to look away from the terrible news broadcasts and Internet video pouring into the Order's temporary compound in Maine. Every report brings footage of screaming men, women, and children, hysterical crowds stampeding on darkened streets, none of them fast enough to elude the predators in pursuit. Cities glowing bright with flames, vehicles abandoned and smoking in the ruins, gunfire and misery filling the air. Everywhere, there is bloodshed and slaughter.

Lucan and the rest of the warriors of the Order have mobilized for Boston to combat the violence, but they are barely a dozen Breed soldiers against hundreds of Rogues flooding into major cities all over the globe. By the time dawn rises to send the Rogues back into the shadows, the cost in innocent lives could number easily in the thousands. And the damage left in the wake of all this blood-soaked chaos—the mistrust between the humans and the Breed—may never be repaired.

Centuries of secrecy and careful peace, undone in a single night . . .

Day 345, A.F.D.

It's been almost a year since First Dawn. That's what everyone calls it now—the morning after the Rogue attacks that changed the world forever. First Dawn. What a hopeful, innocuous term for such a horrific moment in time. But the need for hope is understandable. It's critical, especially when the wounds from that awful night and the uncertain day that followed are still so fresh.

No one knows the need for hope better than the Order. The warriors have been fighting for twelve hard months to win back some sense of calm, some semblance of peace. Dragos is no more. The Rogues he used as his personal weapons of mass destruction have all been destroyed. The months of carnage and terror have ended. But too much hatred and suspicion still festers on both sides. It's a volatile time, and even the slightest spark of violence could explode into catastrophe.

In two weeks, Lucan is scheduled to speak on behalf of the Breed before all the nations of the world. Publicly, he will call for peace. Privately, he's warned all of us in the Order that he dreads man and Breed may instead find themselves swept into war . . .

August 4, 10 A.F.D.

Sometimes it feels as if there's been a hundred years of spilled blood and lives during the decade that's passed since First Dawn. The wars continue. Violence escalates around the world. Anarchy reigns in many major cities, spawning criminal activity from bands of rebels and other militants in addition to the relentless killing on both sides of the conflict.

Every day, the Order's headquarters in D.C. receives sobering reports from the leaders of its district command centers now situated around the world. The war grows worse. Blame for the bloodshed is slung from both directions, deepening the unrest and adding fuel to an already raging fire. Our hope for peace between man and Breed has never seemed further out of reach.

And if this is the state of things ten years into this conflict, I am afraid to guess at what that could mean for the future . . .

1

HUMANS.

The night was thick with them.

They choked the dark sidewalks and intersections of Boston's old North End, overflowed from the open doorways of dance clubs, sim-lounges, and cocktail bars. Strolling, loitering, conversing, they filled the near-midnight streets with too many voices, too many bodies shuffling and sweating in the unseasonable heat of the early June evening.

And damned too little space to avoid the anxious sidelong looks—those countless quick, darting glances from people pretending they hadn't noticed, and weren't the least bit terrified, of the four members of the Order who now strode through the middle of the city's former restricted sector.

Mira, the lone female of the squad of off-duty warriors, scanned the crowd of *Homo sapiens* civilians with a hard eye. Too bad she and her companions were wearing street clothes and discreetly concealed weapons. She'd have preferred combat gear and an arsenal of heavy firearms. Give the good citizens of Boston a real excuse to stare in mortal terror.

"Twenty years we've been outed to mankind, and most of them still gape at us like we've come to collect their carotids," said one of the three Breed males walking alongside her.

Mira shot him a wry look. "Feeding curfew goes into effect at midnight, so don't expect to see the welcome wagon down here. Besides, fear is a good thing, Bal. Especially when it comes to dealing with their kind."

Balthazar, a giant wall of olive-skinned thick muscle and ruthless strength, met her gaze with a grim understanding in his hawkish golden eyes. The dark-haired vampire had been with the Order for a long time, coming on board nearly two decades ago, during the dark, early years following First Dawn, the day the humans learned they were not, in fact, the ultimate predator on the planet.

They hadn't accepted that truth easily. Nor peacefully.

Many lives were lost on both sides in the time that followed. Many long years of death and bloodshed, grief and mistrust. Even now, the truce between the humans and the Breed was tentative. While the governing heads of both global nations—man and vampire—attempted to broker lasting peace for the good of all, private hatreds and suspicions still festered in each camp. The war between mankind and Breed still waged on, but it had gone underground, undeclared and unsanctioned but nonetheless lethal.

A cold ache filled Mira's chest at the thought of all the pain and suffering she'd witnessed in the years between her childhood under the protection of the Order, through the rigorous training and combat experience that had shaped her into the warrior she was now. She tried to sweep the ache aside, put it behind her, but it was hard to do. Tonight of all nights, it was next to impossible to shut out the hurt.

And the part of this war that was personal, as intimate as anything in her life could be, now gave her voice a raw, biting edge. "Let the humans be afraid. Maybe if they worry more about losing their throats, they'll be less inclined to tolerate the radicals among them who would like to see all of the Breed reduced to ashes."

From behind her, another of her teammates gave a low purr of a chuckle. "You ever consider a career in public relations, Captain?" She threw a one-fingered salute over her shoulder and kept walking, her long blond braid thumping like a tail against her leather-clad backside. Webb's laugh deepened. "Right. Didn't think so."

If anyone was suited for diplomatic assignment, it was Julian Webb. Adonis handsome, affable, polished, and utterly devastating when he turned on the charm. That Webb was a product of a cultured upbringing among the Breed's privileged elite went without saying. Not that he ever had. His background—along with his reasons for joining the Order—was a secret he'd shared only with Lucan Thorne, and the Order's founding elder wasn't telling.

There were times Mira wondered if that's why Lucan had personally assigned Webb to her team last year—to keep a close eye on her for him and the Council and to ensure the Order's mission objectives were being met without any . . . issues. Since her humiliating censure for insubordination by the Council eighteen months ago, it wouldn't surprise Mira to learn that Lucan had entrusted Webb to smooth out any potential rough patches in her leadership of the unit. But she hadn't worked her ass off, trained to the brink of killing herself to earn her place with the Order, only to throw it away.

It was highly unusual—all but unheard of, in fact—for a female to come through the ranks with the Order and be awarded a place as captain of a warrior team. Her pride swelled to think on that, even now. She'd lived to prove herself capable, worthy. She'd pushed herself ruthlessly to earn the respect of the Order's elders and the other warriors she'd trained with—respect she'd eventually won through blood, sweat, and stubborn determination.

Mira wasn't Breed. She didn't have their preternatural speed or strength. She didn't have their immortality either, something she, as a Breedmate—the female offspring of a *Homo sapiens* mother and a father of as yet undetermined genetic origins—could obtain only through the mated exchange of a blood bond with one of the Breed. Without that bond being activated, Mira and those other rare females born Breedmates would age, and ultimately die, the same as mortals.

At twenty-nine and unmated, she was already beginning to feel the physical and mental fallout of her taxing career choice. The wound she'd been carrying in her heart for these past eight years probably didn't help either. And her "conduct unbecoming" reprimand a year and a half ago was likely more than enough excuse for Lucan to want to reassign her to desk duty. But he hadn't yet, and she'd be damned if she gave him further cause to consider it.

"Storm's coming," murmured the third member of her team from beside her. Torin wasn't talking about the weather, Mira knew. Like a lion taking stock of new surroundings, the big vampire tipped his burnished blond head up toward the cloudless night sky and drew in a deep breath. A pair of braids woven with tiny glass seed beads framed razor-sharp cheekbones and finely chiseled features, an unconventional, exotic look for someone as expertly lethal as Torin, one that hinted at his sojourner past. The glittering plaits swayed against the rest of his thick, shoulder-length mane as he exhaled and swiveled his intense gaze toward Mira. "Bad night to be down here. Something dark in the air."

She felt it too, even without Torin's unique ability to detect and interpret shifts in energy forces around him.

The storm he sensed was living inside her.

It had a name: Kellan.

The syllables of his name rolled through her mind like thunder. Still raw, even after all this time. Since his death, the storm of emotion left in his wake grew more turbulent inside Mira, particularly around this time of the year. Whether in grief or denial, she clung to Kellan's memory with a furious hold. Unhealthy to be sure, but hope could be a cruel, tenacious thing.

There was still a part of her that prayed it was all a bad dream. Eventually she'd wake from it. One day, she'd look up and see the young Breed male swaggering in from a mission, whole and healthy. One day, she'd hear his deep voice at her ear, a wicked challenge while they sparred in the training room, a rough growl of barely restrained need when their bouts of mock combat sent them down together in a tangle of limbs on the mats.

She'd feel the formidable strength of his warrior's body again, big and solid and unbreakable. She'd gaze into his broody hazel eyes, touch the crown of tousled waves that gleamed as copper brown as an old penny and felt as soft as silk in her fingers. She'd smell the leather-and-spice scent of him, feel the kick of his pulse, see the sparks of amber heat fill his irises and the sharp white glint of his emerging fangs, when the desire he held in check so rigidly betrayed itself to her despite his best efforts to contain it.

One day, she would open her eyes and find Kellan Archer sleeping naked beside her again in her bed, as he had been the night he was killed in combat by human rebels.

Hope, she thought caustically. *Such a heartless bitch.*

Angry at herself for the weakness of her thoughts, she picked up the pace and glanced at the intersection ahead, where half a dozen human couples had stumbled out of a trendy hotel bar and now stood awaiting a traffic signal. Across the street from them, one of the city's ubiquitous Faceboards took the liberty of scanning the group's retinas before launching into an obnoxious ad, custom-tailored for the interests of its captive audience trapped at the crosswalk, waiting for the light to change.

Mira groaned when the digitally rendered 3D image of business tycoon Reginald Crowe, one of the wealthiest men on the planet, addressed the couples by name and proceeded to hawk discounted stays at his collection of luxury resorts. Crowe's face was everywhere this year, in press releases and interview programs, on entertainment blogs and news sites . . . anywhere there was a webcam or a broadcast crew willing to hear him talk about his newly unveiled technology grant—the biggest science award of its kind. It probably irritated him to no end that neither that story nor the announcement that Crowe was helping to champion the upcoming Global Nations Council summit enjoyed the same depth of coverage as the ones concerning the billionaire's recent divorce from Mrs. Crowe the sixth.

"Come on," she said, stepping off the curb to avoid the wait at the light.

She led her team across the street, heading up the block toward Asylum, a local watering hole that in recent years had become an unofficial neutral ground for its mix of vampire and human clientele. Another squad from the Order was meeting them tonight. Mira hadn't been much in the mood to socialize—least of all in this city, on this night—but the teams deserved to celebrate. They'd worked hard together for the past five months on a joint mission—black ops stuff, the kind of covert, specialized assignments that had become the Order's stock-in-trade over the past two decades.

Thanks to the combined effort of Mira's squad and the one she spotted at a back table as she entered Asylum, the GNC had one less international militant group to contend with. It was a victory that couldn't have come at a better time: Just a week from now, government leaders, dignitaries, and VIPs from all over the world, representing Breed and humankind alike, were scheduled to gather in Washington, D.C., in a much-publicized show of peace and solidarity. All of the Order elders would be in attendance, including Mira's adoptive parents, Nikolai and Renata.

Back home in Montreal, the mated pair were still waiting for her to confirm whether she'd be going with them too. Although neither had said anything, she knew their invitation was given in the hope that she might expand her social circle, maybe meet someone she might consider bonding with someday. It was also their well-meaning but none-too-subtle attempt to take her off the battlefield, even for a little while.

She must have been scowling when she arrived at the table with her team, because as she sat down, the captain of the other squad narrowed a concerned look on her.

"You all right?" Nathan's voice was level and unreadable beneath the thump of music and the din of noise rising up from Asylum's bar and dance floor. His greenish blue eyes were steady and unblinking beneath the military-short cut of his jet-black hair. "I wasn't sure you'd be up for this."

Not sure she'd be able to handle being back in Boston. Especially on the anniversary of Kellan's death.

She caught his meaning, even though he didn't specifically say the words. He knew her too well, had been one of her dearest friends for almost as long as Kellan had. Longer, now that Kellan had been gone eight years. Nathan had been there that night too. He'd been right next to Mira, holding her back from the flames and falling debris when the riverfront warehouse exploded into the dark sky. And he'd been standing at her infirmary bedside days later, when she woke up and learned there'd been no trace left of Kellan or the human rebel scum he'd pursued inside the booby-trapped building.

Mira cleared her throat, still tasting ash and smoke all these years later. "No, it's fine. I'm good." He didn't believe her, not at all. She looked away from his probing stare and took in the rest of the warriors gathered around the table. "In case I didn't say it already, nice work, all of you. We kicked some serious ass out there together."

Torin and Webb nodded in agreement, while Bal shot a crooked grin at the three members of Nathan's crew. "Captain's right. Damn good working with you ladies. After all, every skilled surgeon needs someone to mop up the spilled blood and guts or hand him the right tool when he calls for it."

"I got a tool for you right here," quipped Elijah, Nathan's second in command, a brown-haired Breed warrior with cowboy rugged looks, a quicksilver smile, and a slow Texas drawl. "And if you want to talk surgical precision, we've got you beat in spades. My man Jax over here? Poetry in motion. Two of those rebel bastards had the bad judgment to open fire on us, but Jax took them both out with a single toss of his hira-shuriken." Eli made a low whistling sound as he drew his finger across his neck and that of Rafe, his teammate seated next to him. "Thing of fucking beauty, Jax."

Jax gave a mild bow of his dark head at the praise. Half Asian and 100 percent lethal, the big, ebony-haired vampire was renowned for his deadly grace, and for his skill with the razor-edged throwing stars he handcrafted and carried with him wherever he went. Mira knew without checking that Jax likely had half a dozen of his hira-shuriken on his person now.

She carried her own pair of custom blades too, daggers she'd had since she first learned how to use one properly. They were always within her reach, even though it was illegal to discharge weapons of any kind in civilian sectors of the city. Only uniformed officials with the Joint Urban Security Taskforce Initiative Squad, a government-directed police detail comprised of hand-picked Breed and human officers, were licensed to carry unconcealed arms or use deadly force in nonmilitary situations.

Reflecting back on the success of their completed mission, Mira nodded to Nathan's other squad member, blond, blue-eyed Xander Raphael. "Good job providing the cover we needed to breach the rebel's compound," she told him. "You've got serious skills, kid."

"Thanks." Though hardly a child, Mira had known Rafe since he was an infant. Of the group seated around the table now, he was the newest recruit, fresh out of training ten months ago. Mira was almost a decade older than he, but the young Breed warrior was capable and wise well beyond his years. He was also the son of an Order elder, Dante, and his mate, Tess. Like all Breed offspring, Rafe had been gifted with his mother's unique extrasensory talent. Tess's ability to heal with her touch was a conflict for her son, who had also been born with his father's innate courage and virtually unmatched fighting skills.

Rafe's other gift from his mother was his fair hair and eye color. On Tess, the honeyed waves and aquamarine gaze was stunning, infinitely feminine. On Rafe, six foot six and wrapped in lean, hard muscle, the combination turned every female head in his vicinity.

One such female, a twenty-something brunette who'd been watching their table from the bar with a gaggle of her friends, was doing everything she could to catch Rafe's eye. He'd noticed. And there was no doubt he knew what the pretty girl would be offering him too; Mira saw that spark of male arrogance lift the corner of the warrior's mouth in the moment before he and a few other males at the table swiveled their heads to greet her.

"Hey," the young woman said, eyes on Rafe for the longest. She'd made her choice, no question.

"Hey, yourself," Eli answered for the rest of the table. "What's your name, beautiful?"

"I'm Britney." A smiling glance at him and the other males, then back to stay on Rafe. "My friends have been daring me to come over here and talk to you."

Rafe smiled. "That right?" His voice was smooth and unrushed, that of a male totally at home with his effect on the opposite sex. Or another species, in this case.

"I told them I wasn't afraid," Rafe's admirer went on. "I told them I was curious what it was like—" She gave a quick toss of her head, flustered but flirtatious. "I mean, I was curious what *you* were like . . ."

Fang-girls, Mira thought with an amused roll of her eyes. Despite the ongoing civil unrest between human and Breed, there was never a short-age of women—and a large number of men—looking to donate their fresh red cells in exchange for the sensual high of a vampire's bite.

Balthazar chuckled. "Very brave of you to come over all by yourself, Whitney."

"It's Britney." She giggled, nervous but determined. "Anyway, they said I should do this, so . . . here I am." Licking her lips as she inched closer to Rafe, she pushed her long brown hair back over her shoulder. The adjustment bared the delicate white column of her neck, and Mira felt the air go sharp with the instinctual reactions of more than one Breed male at the table.

"No reason for your friends to be shy." Torin's voice was a smoky, dark invitation that made even Mira's dormant senses prickle with aware-ness. He drew in a breath through parted lips that didn't quite hide the pearly white points of his fangs. "Call them over and let's see if they're as daring as you are, Britney."

When the girl excitedly motioned for the others to join her, Mira got up from the table. Fresh off a mission and deserving some kind of re-ward, the warriors had a right to accept the indecent proposal being extended to them here. But that didn't mean she wanted to watch.

"Feeding time ends at midnight, boys. That's ten minutes from now, in case any of you were worried about breaking curfew laws."

Nathan stood now too, the only one of the vampires seemingly unfazed by the approach of several warm, pretty females willing to play blood Hosts to them tonight. "What are you doing?"

"Getting out of the way. I'll be back in a few."

He frowned. "I should go with you—"

"No, stay." She held up a hand, gestured with a nod toward the arriving women. "God knows these fools can't be trusted without adult supervision."

The taunt got the anticipated rise out of Eli, Bal, and the others, but Nathan's gaze remained solemn. When his broad mouth went flat in disapproval, she reached out and cupped his jaw in her palm. She felt him tense at the contact and suddenly wished she could take back the tender gesture. Nathan may have spent more than half of his thirty-three years of life with the Order, but the scars of his dark childhood might never be buried. Touch and tenderness always put the former assassin on edge, made him twitch like no amount of bloodshed and battle ever did.

"Have some fun, Nathan. You earned it too, you know." Mira started walking away from the table. "Ten minutes," she called over her shoulder. "Somebody be nice and have a drink waiting for me when I get back."

She was fine until she reached the exit. Then the weight she'd been holding off all night settled on her chest and brought hot tears like needles in the backs of her eyes.

"Shit. Kellan . . ." She let his name escape her lips on a rasped breath as she leaned against the brick exterior wall several yards away from Asylum's crowded entrance. God, she hated how much it hurt to think of him. Hated that she hadn't been able to find her way free of the hold his memory still had on her. No, his death had killed something in her too. It had broken her somewhere deep inside, in a place no one but he had reached, before or since.

Mira hung her head, not bothering to sweep aside the loose blond tendrils that had escaped her braid and now swung into her face like a veil. She cursed under her breath, struggled to pull herself together. Her fingers were trembling as she wiped the moisture from her cheeks. She blew out a frustrated sigh. "Damn it. Get a grip, warrior."

The angry self-rebuke worked well enough for her to lift her head and square her shoulders. But it was the high-pitched, human chortle from within the nearby throng that really snapped her out of her sulk. Mira would know that barnyard hoot anywhere. Just the sound of it made her veins go hot with contempt.

She spied the young man's head—his ridiculous red mohawk—bobbing along in a group of petty thieves and troublemakers now walking past the crowd that waited to get into Asylum. That upright comb of bright scarlet hair, along with his distinctive laugh, had helped earn the delinquent his street name of Rooster.

Son of a bitch.

She hadn't seen the bastard in years. Her blood boiled to spot him now. A known rebel sympathizer, strutting around with his repeat-offender friends when he should be rotting in a prison somewhere. Better yet, dead from choking on the business end of her blades.

When the top of his red mohawk turned the corner up the block with his four pals, Mira hissed a curse. Not her concern what Rooster was up to. Not her damn jurisdiction, even if it turned out he was up to his usual no good.

Still . . .

Impulse propelled her into motion, even against her better judgment. Rooster was an occasional supplier to human militant groups and rebel factions. And that occasional alliance made him Mira's permanent enemy. She fell in behind him and his friends at a covert distance, her lug-soled boots silent as they devoured the pavement in stealth pursuit.

The men shuffled up the block and entered an alleyway door of another place, one that had long ago been a popular dance club in the North End. The former neo-Gothic church was far from holy now, and far less reputable than it had been even a decade ago. Graffiti and old shelling scars from the wars all but obscured the fading "La Notte" sign painted on the side of the old redbrick building. No longer pulsing with silky trance and synth music, the current proprietor favored hardcore industrial bands with screaming vocals in the street-level club.

All the better to drown out the raucous shouting and bloodthirsty cheers of the customers taking part in the establishment's underground arena.

It was to that part of the club that Rooster and his pals now descended. Mira followed. The stench of smoke and spilled liquor hung like fog in the air. The crowd was thick at the bottom of the steep stair-well, thicker still in the space between the entrance and the large, caged-in, steel-reinforced fighting arena at the center of the room.

Inside the cage, two huge Breed males circled each other in bloody combat. Outside, gathered around the perimeter and standing a dozen rows deep, the crowd of human spectators cheered and hollered, bets placed on their favorite. This match had been going on for some time, based on the amount of blood in the ring and the fevered pitch of the crowd outside of it. Mira had seen the outlawed games before and hardly flinched at the sight of the two powerful vampires wearing only gladiator-style leather shorts and U-shape steel torcs around their necks. Titanium spikes rode the knuckles of their fingerless leather gloves, making each blow a savage shredding of flesh and muscle.

Rooster and his friends paused to watch one of the fighters take a hard strike to the sternum. His hooting laughter shot up through the crowd as the combatant crashed backward into the bars. The downed vampire was already in bad shape, pitted against an undefeated fighter who never failed to bring in the big crowds and heavy purses. Now, spit-ting blood, heaving under the force of this last blow, the losing male scrabbled to reach the mercy button inside the cage. Rooster and the rest of the spectators hissed and booed as the call for mercy temporarily halted the match and delivered a punishing jolt of electricity to the wounded combatant's dark-haired opponent. Unfazed, the immense Breed fighter took the hit as if it were no more than a bee sting, fangs bared in a cold smile that promised yet another win for his record.

The cage thundered with violence as the fight resumed, but Mira ig-nored the spectacle of the arena. Her sights were locked on her target. Her own need to punish boiled like acid in her veins as she stalked Rooster through the throng.

She thought of Kellan's final moments as she watched the rebel sym-pathizer cackle and hoot, he and the other humans cheering each ter-rible strike, frothing for more Breed bloodshed.

She didn't know at what point she'd drawn her blades from their sheaths at her back. She felt the chill of custom-tooled metal in her hands, her fingertips light on the scrollwork of the daggers' hilts. Felt her instincts itching to let the blades fly as Rooster shot a sudden glance in her direction.

He saw her, realized she was coming for him. Something flashed in his eyes as they met hers. Panic, certainly. But Mira saw guilt in that worried gaze too. In fact, his oh-shit look seemed to say that she was the last person he expected or wanted to see. He shrank back behind one of his hoodlum pals, as if that fiery shock of upright hair wouldn't give him away.

Mira felt a snarl curl up from the back of her throat. Son of a bitch was going to bolt. And sure enough, he did.

"Damn it!" She shouldered her way through the thick crowd, trying not to lose sight of her quarry as she maneuvered for a clear shot at him with her blades.

Someone saw her drawn weapons and a scream of warning went up. People scrambled out of her way—just long enough that she saw her chance at nailing Rooster. She took it without a hint of hesitation. Her twin blades flew. They arrowed on an unerring path that hit her moving target and skewered him to the far wall, one dagger buried to the hilt in each of the human's thin biceps.

He howled, no longer amused now that he was on the receiving end of a little pain. Mira shoved a few gawking stragglers aside as she closed in on him, venom hot in her veins. She'd already broken one law here tonight; looking at the rebel ally just beyond arm's reach from her, she was tempted to add aggravated homicide to the tab.

A strong hand came down on her shoulder.

"Don't do it, Mira." Nathan. He and the rest of the warriors stood behind her now, disapproval on each hard face.

She realized suddenly how hushed the club had gone. The illegal contest in the cage was over, the spectators now watching the new one Mira had started. The human proprietor of the place and some of his Breed fighters moved in from other areas of the club, their mere presence threatening added trouble if things got any further out of hand.

Shit. Mira knew she'd stepped in it this time, but her blood was still on a hard boil and all she could think about was settling the score for Kellan. One less rebel bastard tonight was a good place to start.

"Let it go," Nathan said, his voice soldier-cool and emotionless, the way she'd heard him speak a thousand times before, even under heavy combat fire. "This is not the way you were trained. You know that."

She did. She knew it, and yet she still threw off Nathan's grip and took a hard lunge toward Rooster, who yowled like a banshee, writhing where he was pinned to the wall. Nathan blocked her. He moved faster than she could track him, placing himself between her and the human.

"Get out of my way, Nathan. You know who this scum hangs with—rebel pigs. Way I see it, that makes him one of them."

"Somebody help me!" Rooster howled. "Somebody call the cops! I'm innocent!"

Mira shook her head, meeting her teammate's disapproving gaze. "He's lying. He knows something, Nathan. I can see it in him. I can feel it. He knows who's responsible for Kellan's death. Damn it, I want someone to pay for what happened to him!"

Nathan's curse was an airless growl. "For fuck's sake, Mira." His eyes were intense but tender. Holding her with a pity that she'd never seen before and hated to acknowledge now. "The only one you're making pay for what happened to Kellan is yourself."

The truth in his words hit her like a slap. She absorbed the blow in a stunned kind of silence, watching as the rest of her squad and Nathan's moved in around the two of them.

"Probably not a good idea to linger down here," Webb remarked to Mira and Nathan when neither had relaxed from their unspoken stand-off. "If we don't clean this up quick, things could turn ugly."

Bal swore low under his breath. "Too late for that."

Pouring into the underground club from the street outside came twenty black-clad officers from Joint Urban Security. The JUSTIS detail stormed in, heavily armed, dressed in full riot gear. Mira could only watch—and blame no one but herself—as the law enforcers surrounded them, their automatic weapons trained on her and her teammates.

2

LUCAN THORNE COULD THINK OF A HUNDRED OTHER THINGS he'd rather be doing at a little after 1:00 A.M. than sitting idle at his desk in the Order's global headquarters in Washington, D.C., pushing papers and sifting through video mail. Not the least of those preferred other things being the craving to seek out his Breedmate, Gabrielle, and feel her warm, soft curves beneath him in their bed.

No, that was a craving he hadn't been able to shake in all the time she'd been his. A short twenty-plus years with his woman, and she owned him like nothing else had in more than nine centuries of living.

His body eagerly agreed, responding to just the thought of his beautiful mate. Lucan groaned low in his throat and shifted to adjust the sudden tightness in his groin. His pen scraped across the paper as he signed off on what seemed an endless pile of classified Global Nations Council documents and agreements, most pertaining to the world peace summit taking place in the city in less than a week's time.

The pre-summit meetings with other GNC heads—an equal mix of human and Breed world leaders—had been anything but peaceful. But at least the saber-rattling and firefighting had been kept behind closed doors. To their credit, the Council members seemed to understand that letting their personal agendas, political egos, and private mistrust of one another leak out to a wary public would serve no one well. The summit had become as much about putting a shiny, friendly face on human–Breed relations as it was about negotiating true accord between the heads of state who ultimately would be responsible for enforcing that peaceful future for the generations to come.

Lucan could only hope it didn't all crumble down around him before it even began.

He scrawled his signature onto a GNC security briefing and added it to the stack of assorted other approvals he'd already reviewed and cleared for implementation. As he reached for the remaining sheaf of reports, his tablet chimed with an incoming, top-clearance message. He tapped the receive button on-screen and paused to enter the password required to play the v-mail. It was from one of the GNC's senior officials, an elderly human statesman named Charles Benson. The man was also among the more moderate-minded on the Council, an ally Lucan felt would be sorely needed as talks to forge stronger relations between man and Breed continued long after the pomp and flash of the overhyped peace summit had faded into the grit and mundanity of daily reality.

Lucan set down his pen and watched, guessing that the message must be important for Benson to have contacted him privately and under high-security clearance, besides.

"My apologies for disturbing you with this request at home, Chairman Thorne." The wrinkled face appeared anxious in the recorded video message, thin lips pressing into a flatter line as the old man cleared his throat. "I have a favor to ask of you, if I may. Of the Order, that is. It's of a personal nature, you see."

Lucan scowled at the monitor as the hemming went on. "It's about my nephew. Perhaps you're aware that Jeremy is to receive a very important award from Reginald Crowe's foundation on the eve of the summit gathering."

Lucan's scowl deepened with mounting suspicion. He knew who Benson's genius nephew was. Knew that Jeremy Ackmeyer's work was respected around the world and that the human was regarded as one of the most gifted minds of all time—a recognition that had recently earned the young scientist a sizable cash prize to be presented personally by one of the world's wealthiest men. "I'm afraid Jeremy is somewhat . . . eccentric," Benson's message went on. "My sister's boy. From the day the child was born, I warned her not to coddle him." A dismissive wave of a thin, bony hand before the councilman finally got to his point. "I'm embarrassed to say that Jeremy has refused to appear at the summit gala. He's a fearful boy, an irrational shut-in, if I'm to be perfectly frank with you. He refuses to travel for fear of dying from one cause or another. I suppose I was hoping I might convince you to provide some means of escort for him to Washington—"

"You've got to be fucking kidding me." Lucan cut the message off with a stab of his finger on the end button and a low, muttered curse.

Since when had the Order become a personal chauffeur and security detail for hermit eggheads?

Politically ill-advised or not, he glared at the tablet, ready to tell Councilman Benson that his paranoid nephew would have to make other arrangements. But as his finger hovered over the record button on the screen, the sound of rising voices outside drew his attention toward the tall, curtained windows of his private study.

Protesters.

Lucan stalked to the window and drew open the long drapes. Apparently the graveyard shift had reported for duty. He counted fifteen human men and women—Christ, even a sign-carrying, shouting little girl—standing on the other side of the towering iron gates at the street. The signs bore the same tired vitriol that had been hurled at the Breed for two decades now: *Go Back Where You Came From! Earth Is for Man, Not Monsters! You Can't Make Peace with Predators!*

Since the announcement of the summit, picketers and chanting protests representing both human and Breed dissent were hardly uncommon outside the GNC building near the Capitol or at the Order's heavily secured D.C. headquarters. Tonight, with a headache from hours spent poring over Council rulings and the now-throbbing ache of his molars as he ground his teeth in outrage over the ridiculous request from someone he'd been counting on for political support down the line, the thought of a mob of hate-spewing rabble-rousers annoyed Lucan more than usual.

At least it was only picket signs and shouting, not the all-out street combat and acts of terror that had occurred on both sides in the months and years following the Breed's discovery by mankind. War had been inevitable then, even though Lucan had hoped to avoid it. There'd been too much blood spilled, too much fear and suspicion. While the Breed had lived alongside man in secret for thousands of years, all it took to undo centuries of care and discretion was the unspeakable act of one

Breed male two decades ago, who, in his villainous lust for power, had freed scores of incarcerated, blood-addicted vampires, loosing them onto an unsuspecting human population.

It had fallen to the Order to help clean up the carnage and stop the Rogues who were cutting a bloody, horrific swath across the entire globe. But Lucan and his warriors couldn't act swiftly enough to curb the violence that broke out in the wake of the attacks. Whole cities were razed, buildings tumbled, governments dissolved by anarchy and rebel uprisings. The Breed's civilian communities suffered daytime raids that left the Darkhavens in shambles, families slaughtered or exposed to the killing rays of the sun.

Then, when it seemed the fighting between man and Breed couldn't possibly get worse, a massive chemical weapon was deployed in the Russian interior, rendering hundreds of thousands of acres of wilderness an uninhabitable wasteland. It was a catastrophic move, one that neither humans nor Breed had admitted responsibility for to this day.

It could have been worse. To think what might have been, if the weapon of that size and power had been unleashed on a major city instead.

Still, the impact of the damage had been felt around the world. And it had prompted Lucan to send the Order in swiftly and in full force to destroy all of the nuclear silos and chemical weapons facilities in every corner of the globe.

Although it had been the right thing to do—the only sane thing to do—there were individuals of both races who held Lucan in contempt for the heavy-handed tactic. Some feared he would not hesitate to appoint himself sole judge and jury for the world once more, if the strife between man and Breed were to escalate.

Goddamn right he would.

Lucan only hoped it was a decision he'd never have to make.

A knock sounded on his study door, a welcome intrusion on the grim path of his thoughts.

"Enter," he called, more growl than invitation. Letting the drape fall back into place, he turned away from the window.

He'd been expecting Gideon, the Breed warrior who had long been the technical genius of the Order's complicated operations center and compound. Gideon was currently on task to provide Lucan with security updates on the summit meeting facility, so that Order assets could be assigned to cover the multiday event.

But it wasn't Gideon at the door.

"Darion."

"Am I interrupting your work, Father?"

"Not at all." He gestured for Darion to join him inside.

Just the sight of his boy—the tall, muscular nineteen-year-old man bearing a dark chestnut shade of his mother's auburn hair and her same soulful brown eyes—made the weight of Lucan's current burdens fall away. It was the other traits Darion bore—Lucan's angular facial structure and strong jaw, coupled with an inflexible iron will inherited from both parents—that usually put father and son at odds. Apart from Gabrielle's coloring and her extrasensory ability, both passed down to her son, for Lucan, being around Dare was like looking in a mirror.

Darion was too much like his father in many ways, a recognition that unsettled Lucan more than he cared to admit. But where Lucan had struggled with his natural tendency to lead others, Dare had no such qualms. Too bold, more often than not. Fearless in anything he attempted. These were qualities that made Lucan's blood run cold with a father's fear when he pictured his son eventually dressed for combat as a warrior of the Order and charging out to battle.

If Lucan had his way, that moment he'd been dreading would never come.

Darion strode into the study, casual in dark jeans and a black shirt with rolled-up sleeves, unbuttoned at the collar. "More protesters tonight," he remarked, lifting his squared chin in the direction of the windows, where the din of voices outside was rising. "Seems like the numbers are increasing the closer we get to the date of the summit."

Lucan grunted, gave a curt nod. "For all their bleating, it's only background noise to bigger problems, unfortunately."

"I take it today's meetings did not go well?"

"No better or worse than any other these past few weeks." Lucan indicated a chair on the other side of his desk, then walked around to take his own seat as Darion sat down. "More and more, this summit is becoming a mockery. How can we expect to bridge the gap of mistrust between the races when the GNC's own Council members can't agree on the most basic principles?"

"That bad?" Darion asked, his deep voice as grim as Lucan's thoughts.

"Yes," Lucan said. "And then some. The politicians are using the summit as their personal campaign rallies. Corporations are seeing gold, turning the whole event into a media and advertising sponsorship circus. And let's not forget moneyed clowns like Reginald Crowe who're gilding every stage and pavilion with huge donations in exchange for seeing their names in lights around the world." Lucan muttered a ripe curse. "This summit should have been held sacrosanct from any exploitation. Instead, it's become a goddamned joke. Too much palm-greasing and favor-currying on both sides. Too many people—human and Breed alike—looking to cash in or use the summit as a platform on which to build their personal empires."

"So shut it down," Dare replied, dark brows flat over his serious gaze. He leaned forward, resting his strong forearms on his spread thighs. "Yank the plug on the whole bloody thing. Then set a new course, a better one, that you control. Let the other GNC members get in line behind you or get out of the way."

Lucan smiled with wry amusement, hearing a younger version of himself in Dare's decisive, black-or-white approach. "Tempting, Dare. I'll be honest with you on that. But it's hardly been twenty years since the last time I brought my fist down on human–Breed relations. To do it again now, in the middle of a high-visibility celebration of our so-called peace and optimistic plans for the future?" He shook his head, considering the idea for what hadn't been the first time. He was a warrior, and had been for most of his long life. He was accustomed to the feel of a weapon in his hand, the blood of his fallen enemies pooling at his feet. He was a hard man, not well suited to the diplomacy his new role required of him, let alone gifted with an iota of tolerance for reckless fools or oily opportunists. "Disrupting the summit would undo all the good strides we've made so far—few though they may be. Worse, there are those on both sides who would be all too eager to call it an act of treason by the leader of the Order. War, even."

Lucan felt too confined suddenly, and rose to pace behind his desk. "I tell you, Darion. More and more, I fear that true peace between mankind and Breed is sitting on a keg of gunpowder. All it will take is one spark to blow all hope for our shared future sky-high."

Darion listened, still and contemplative, while Lucan wore a track in the floor across from him. When he spoke, his deep voice was grave. "If someone were to light that spark, be they rebels or other malcontents, what better place to incite a war than at a peace summit? We need to be prepared for that, be ready to act on even the smallest threat."

Lucan's answering curse hissed through his teeth and emerging fangs. He'd thought the same thing, of course. Gideon and he had been taking every precaution to ensure the summit was nailed down and secure on every conceivable level. If he had to personally pat down every dignitary who entered the event, by God, he would do it.

He glanced at Darion, reflecting on how easily he slipped into confiding in his only son as his equal. He respected Dare as a man. Marveled at his keen intellect and the strength of his convictions. Darion, the squalling, helpless infant who had somehow become a man, seemingly overnight to someone like Lucan, whose life spanned nearly a thousand years.

Lucan had hoped that Dare might one day take a seat beside him on the GNC, despite the exemplary skill that the young male had demonstrated during his training in weapons and combat. That hope died a little as he met his son's intense gaze. The gaze of a warrior, though his father was loath to admit it. As a parent, he wanted to keep his son close. Keep him safe.

"I can help," Darion said. "You know I want to help. You know I'm ready."

Lucan dropped back into his chair and reached for the pile of documents still awaiting his approval. "Don't wish for war, boy. You're too young to remember the hell of that word."

"I was six when the wars were at their worst. I heard enough. I learned enough in my studies at the Order's compound and at university. I've listened to you talk about battles and fighting for most of my life. I understand what war means, and I understand what it takes to be a warrior."

Lucan's pulse spiked, more from concern than anger. He aggressively scrawled his name on one of the GNC agreements, then grabbed for another set of documents. "Reading and talking about war doesn't make you a warrior. It doesn't prepare you to witness or be part of the things people do to one another under the banners of war. As your father, I hope you never know those things."

Darion's temper was a palpable thing, a force of power rolling from across the desk. "You still see me as a child in need of your protection."

Lucan set his pen down. "That's not true," he replied, sober now. Regretful that his conversations with Darion always seemed to end up in this same place. At this same cold impasse.

His son's jaw was clenched tight, a tendon ticking in his cheek. He scoffed, holding Lucan's stare, unblinking. "I trained under Tegan from the time I was twelve years old, because he is—in your own words—one of the best warriors you've ever known. Why send me to learn from the best, if you never intended to give me a place within the Order?"

Lucan couldn't tell him that he'd sent him to Tegan because of all the warriors ever to serve the Order, it was under Tegan's hard, merciless training that Dare stood the best chance of breaking. But Darion hadn't broken. No, far from it. He'd excelled. Smashed all expectations.

"You have your place here."

Dare grunted. "Advising on tactical stratagems and mapping out ops I'll never be part of in the field." He leaned back now, a negligent sprawl, with his long legs outstretched and one muscled, *dermaglyph*-covered arm draped along the back of the chair. His frustration was evident in the pulsing color that had begun to seep into the flourishes and arcs of his Breed skin markings. "Just once, I'd like to put my training to a true test, on a true mission, not mocked up in a computer program or scribbled on the walls of the war room. I could do more, if you'd only give me the chance."

"Your role with the Order is no less important than any other." Lucan picked up his pen again and calmly began to sign his name to the rest of the documents littering his desk. "I don't imagine you came here at this hour to reopen our same old argument. If you did, it will have to wait."

"No. That's not why I'm here." Darion took out his comm unit and touched the screen of the slim device. "I wanted to ask you about something I ran across in the headquarters' private archives today."

Lucan looked up at the mention of the chamber in the D.C. compound that housed a large and ever-growing history of the Breed and its otherworldly origins. A history the Order had been collecting for the past two decades through the sole efforts of an extraordinary woman. "You've been reading Jenna's journals?"

Dare's smile was dry. "I have a lot of free time. Not like I'm spending it all on Facebook."

Lucan chuckled, glad their conversation wouldn't end in a heated stalemate after all. "Tell me what you've found."

No sooner had he said it when Gideon arrived in the open doorway of Lucan's study. The Breed male's spiky blond hair was more disheveled than usual, raked up in all directions as though Gideon had just repeatedly run his hands through it, as he often did when faced with a problem he couldn't solve in three seconds flat. Or when he found himself appointed the bearer of disturbing news.

The look in Gideon's blue eyes as he peered over the tops of wireless silver shades told Lucan that nothing good was coming his way right now.

"Trouble with the security schematics?" he guessed, rising to face the other warrior as Gideon entered the room.

"Trouble in Boston a short while ago." Gideon gave Darion a slight nod in acknowledgment, then looked to Lucan for permission to speak of Order business in front of the younger male.

Lucan inclined his chin, a scowl furrowing deep in his brow. "Tell me what happened."

Lucan listened as Gideon gave a rundown of the incident at the club that had landed two of the Order's most decorated teams in JUSTIS custody. "She discharged deadly weapons to attack an unarmed civilian. Unprovoked. In a public establishment.

"Not that Mira needs me to make excuses for her," Gideon interjected, "but apparently the human she chased into the place has ties to rebel groups in the area."

"No, she doesn't need anyone's excuses," Lucan replied, his blood rolling toward a boil. "And you know as well as I do that she's got a hard-on for anything with a whiff of rebel involvement. That doesn't give her license to break half a dozen laws and defy my command."

Neither Gideon nor Dare said anything in the quiet that fell over the room while Lucan considered the female captain's fate. "Where is she now?"

"There have been no charges pressed, so both teams were released shortly after JUSTIS officers cleared out La Notte. They're all cooling their heels with Chase at the Boston Op Center."

Lucan grunted. "She's lucky this shit went down where it did. La Notte's proprietor probably forked over a good chunk of payola to JUSTIS so they'd forget the whole thing. As for the human Mira tried to shish-kebob, who knows why he let her slide. Doesn't matter."

Gideon nodded. "What do you want me to do?"

"Tell Chase I want Mira's team sent back to Montreal immediately. She stays behind. I want her on video call. Right. Fucking. Now."

3

MIRA LET A CURSE FLY ALONG WITH HER BLADE AS SHE CONTIN-
ued a vigorous solo session in the training room of the Boston Operations Center. It was late—or, rather, early. Barely three in the morning,
and she probably should have been in bed sleeping off a bad night that
had only gotten worse with a well-deserved reprimand delivered personally by Lucan Thorne.

Instead, on her dismissal from the video-conferenced rebuke and the
news that she was being pulled from active duty effective immediately,
Mira had headed straight for the indoor target range. For the past hour,
she'd been pushing herself hard, driving her body toward exhaustion in
an effort to purge the tight coil of anger and frustration that was still
knotted up within her.

Her training had taught her better discipline than what she'd demonstrated a few hours ago in the city, and apart from the disapproval of the
Order's founder and commander, she hated that she'd let emotion rule
her. All the more so when her actions had put a very public stain on
both her team and Nathan's, as well as the Order in general—at a time,
Lucan had reminded her, when the Breed and mankind needed nothing
to derail their hard-won progress toward peace.

He was right, of course. No matter how deep her ache over the loss
of Kellan, nor her contempt for those she held responsible, her duty to
the Order had to come first. As a warrior, she should be above such
weakness. She had to be stronger than that, damn it. But she'd failed.

And now she would have to pay the price.

Remorse and self-directed anger put a hard edge to her stride as she stalked back into ready position on the range. Tucking loose strands of her blond hair back into her long braid, then wiping at the moisture that beaded her brow and added to the sting of unshed tears in her eyes, Mira prepared herself for another punishing round of training. With ruthless focus, she drew the remaining dagger from the pair of sheaths strapped to the thighs of her black fatigues, then completed a rapid series of strike and counterstrike moves against an imaginary opponent. She was breathing hard, sweat trickling down her temples and between her breasts as she drove herself through another round of mock combat, then still another.

She kept going, until she was panting from exertion, muscles screaming, her white tank damp and clinging to her skin. Then, with a final thrust of power, she pivoted into a battle crouch and loosed her weapon from her nimble fingers. The blade shot forward in an arrow-straight path, nothing but a flash of gleaming metal in the instant before it struck home in the target at the far end of the range.

"Flawless execution." From behind her, Nathan's voice caught her by surprise. "Your blade work is impressive, as always."

Mira hadn't even heard him come into the room, a fact she attributed to both her deep concentration on what she was doing and her friend's unnerving furtiveness. Not that Nathan's lethal silence came as any shock. Being Breed, he could move faster than any outside his kind could see, let alone match. But Nathan's stealth went deeper than that.

He had been bred and raised in a madman's laboratory, created for the sole purpose of dealing death, until he was recovered by his birth mother and taken in by the Order when he was just a teen. Mira had known Nathan from the time she was a child, had long ago come to hold him as dear and trusted as her own family. Still, she hid her face from him now, brushing the sweat and hot tears from her cheeks while keeping her back to him.

"Don't look at me, Nathan." Not because of her tears but for another, bigger reason. She gestured to the lens case that held her custom-made contacts. "My eyes. They're bare. I thought I would be alone in here, so I left my Sight unshielded while I trained."

Like all Breedmates and the Breed offspring they bore, Mira had an extrasensory gift unique to her. More powerful than many, hers was the ability to show someone a glimpse of their destiny in the reflection of her clear, mirrorlike irises. Often those glimpses were unwelcome, even horrifying. She couldn't control what people saw, nor was she privy to the details of the vision herself. And the cost for using her gift was an incremental degeneration of her eyesight.

As a girl, she'd worn a short veil over her face to protect her vision and mute her Sight. After her parents, Nikolai and Renata, had brought her with them to live under the protection of the Order, Mira had been given special contacts like the ones she wore to this day.

The air behind her stirred subtly with Nathan's movement, then the smooth plastic lens case was pressed into her palm. "Why didn't you let me stand with you when Lucan called tonight? You didn't have to face him alone. I would have vouched for you, shouldered some of the blame for what happened."

"I would never ask you to do that nor allow you to," she said, dismissing the idea outright as she put the violet-colored contacts into her eyes. The last thing she would've wanted was for Nathan or any member of their two squads to be undeservedly penalized for her actions. The only one she'd like to see hurting was the rebel sympathizer she let slip through her fingers earlier tonight. "Has there been any word about Rooster? I suppose the JUSTIS detail has released him back into the wild by now."

When she swiveled around to look at Nathan, he gave a vague shake of his head. "He'd committed no crime, has no outstanding warrants. There was no cause to hold him, so he was free to go."

"Damn it," she muttered, ignoring the Breed warrior's assessing look. "Who knows how long it will take before the bastard resurfaces again."

Without waiting for his reply, she strode away from Nathan, down the length of the target range to retrieve her blades. When she returned, he was watching her in his cool, detached way, studying her as he might a tactical plan or a puzzle in need of solving. "I hear it didn't go well for you with Lucan."

She lifted her shoulder in acknowledgment. "He was right to be upset with me. I acted out of line, and that's unacceptable. I should have been more careful. If I wanted to take care of that human rubbish, I should've done it out of the public eye. Next time, I'll know to be more discreet."

"Next time." Nathan swore low under his breath. "You've been relieved of duty until further notice, Mira. There can be no next time, or you can expect to find yourself pulled from the ranks permanently. That's not what anyone wants. I know that's not what you want."

"No," she said. "What I want is vengeance."

"And so you charge into every battle with a head full of fury, guns blazing, knives flying, and damn the consequences." At another time, she might have taken it as a compliment to her bravery, but the indictment in her friend's expression was impossible to deny. He was silent for a long moment, studying her. "A warrior driven by such selfish means is not a warrior fit to lead others into battle. Maybe unfit to serve at all."

Lucan had told her much the same thing earlier tonight. That she had earned the disapproval of the Order's founder and commander was bad enough. Disappointing Nathan and the other warriors who served alongside her was much harder to bear. "I'm sorry," she said, meaning it wholeheartedly. "I wish I could forget him, Nathan, but I can't."

"You still love him."

Not a question, and she couldn't begin to deny it. Nathan, along with most of the Order and their mates, had long ago recognized the bond that had formed between Kellan and her over the years. What had begun for her as a childhood crush on a sullen, damaged boy had blazed into something much deeper as she matured into a young woman and watched Kellan become a courageous soldier, a good man of unshakable honor.

Mira had loved Kellan from the time she was eight years old. Growing up, he'd been her best friend, her favorite sparring partner when she'd entered training to become a warrior. He'd been her first kiss at fifteen. Her first taste of desire, when sparring and laughter turned to heated glances and caresses that left her virgin body trembling and hungry for more.

Kellan had been the only one for her. How many times had she imagined their life together? How often had she dreamed of their future, of sharing an eternity with him as his blood-bonded mate?

But he'd always held something of himself back from her. She'd never understood why. And then they'd shared one incredible night together—a night when she'd had all of him, at last—only to lose him forever a few short hours later in the blast that took his life.

"I can't forget him, Nathan. And I can't forgive the ones who tore him out of our lives. How do you do it? After all, Kellan was your friend too."

"The best I'll ever have." Nathan and Kellan had been as close as brothers. Maybe closer, having walked into combat together countless times as members of the same Order squad. They'd faced death together unflinchingly, dealt it without mercy when duty called for it. And they'd done it as friends, family, brothers-in-arms. Mira could see the pain of that loss in Nathan's greenish blue eyes, even though his handsome face held its stoic, soldier's expression. "I miss him too, Mira. I hate like hell that he's gone. But he *is* gone. He's dead. Throwing away your future won't bring him back."

God, if it would? For a brief, sharply desperate moment, she wondered what she would be willing to sacrifice to have Kellan alive again. Nearly a decade without him, and she still ached to see him, to touch him. Pathetic, how deeply she longed for that. Some stubborn piece of her still clung to the hope that this was just some awful, cosmic mistake that had to be corrected soon and then everything would be as it should be once again.

Right. Pathetic.

"When do you return to Montreal?" Nathan asked, a welcome break from her dark thoughts, drawing her back to reality. Which wasn't much brighter at the moment.

"I don't go back. Not for a while, that is." She slanted him a rueful glance. "I've been summoned to D.C. for an in-person Council review with Lucan and the other Order commanders. Where, I'm all but sure, I'll be asked to step down from my post as captain. Webb's standing in as my replacement. Lucan's decision. He's already sent the team back to base without me."

Idly, she traced her thumb over the scrollwork of one of her hand-tooled daggers—a gift from Nikolai and Renata, who were the closest thing to parents that she'd ever known. The blades were fashioned similarly to the ones Renata wielded so beautifully, but this pair had been designed especially for Mira, presented to her on the day she was promoted to captain.

The hilts of her two daggers were carved on each side, etched by the same artisan, bearing the same words that graced Renata's four: Courage. Sacrifice. Honor. Faith.

She'd never felt more unworthy of holding them.

Nathan eyed her in grave silence, and even though he spared her from his opinion on the matter, she could tell that he understood as well as she did that her position with the Order was tenuous at best. She'd been exiled to a kind of no-man's-land, not fully yanked from her footing but cut adrift just the same.

"Has a date been set for your Council review?"

She nodded. "Four days from now, just before the GNC peace summit begins. But my demotion starts immediately." Adding to the sting of her censure, she had also been relegated to a special assignment that was anything but special. "I've been drafted into nanny detail for one of the summit's award recipients. Some egghead recluse named Ackroyd or Ackerman."

"Ackmeyer," Nathan corrected. "Jeremy Ackmeyer. The human is a science wunderkind, Mira. Eccentric, but brilliant. Ackmeyer holds patents on everything from textiles and plant genomes to solar energy."

She acknowledged with a mild shrug. "That's the guy. Genius or not, apparently he spooks at everything, including his own shadow. He's also related to one of the GNC's directors. Lucan said the Order had been asked to provide personal escort for Ackmeyer from his home in the Berkshires down to the summit, make sure he arrived in time to accept his much-hyped award from Crowe Enterprises."

She could hardly keep from rolling her eyes at the thought of being part of Reginald Crowe's circus sideshow, even if her role was being forced on her. Although Lucan hadn't framed the assignment as punishment, Mira knew it was his way of ensuring she had her hands full—of tasking her with something menial that would keep her out of trouble and off the streets—until such time as he was able to deal with her personally and decide her fate within the Order.

Nathan considered for a long moment. "It could be worse. You can't have fallen too far out of Lucan's regard if he's still willing to keep you in play with a solo mission."

She exhaled a humorless laugh. "This is hardly a mission; we both know that. And the only reason I'm solo on it is because Ackmeyer insists on daytime travel only. That automatically rules out ninety-nine point nine percent of the Order's membership, unless they want to risk ashing themselves along the way."

Ackmeyer had other requirements for his escort to the summit as

EDGE *of* DAWN | 35

well, phobias about mass transit and airborne diseases that restricted him to traveling by car—brand new, of course, the interior vacuumed extensively and scrubbed from top to bottom with disinfectant. He demanded no more than four hours of drive time per day, yet he refused to stay in public lodging. Which meant by the time they reached Washington, an eleven-hour drive would take more than sixty, all of it spent together in the close confines of the car.

No wonder Lucan had assigned Ackmeyer's safety to her. Any one of the warriors she knew would likely strangle the oddball human before they reached the southern Massachusetts state line. She hoped like hell she wouldn't be tempted herself. If she stood even a slim chance of salvaging her position within the Order, delivering a throttled guest of honor wouldn't be the best approach.

In some private, dangerous corner of her heart, she knew that if Lucan bounced her from the Order, she would continue to fight. She would still want justice, vengeance against the rebels who had upended her world when they took Kellan from it. She didn't know how far she would go to right that wrong, but it terrified her a little to consider it. Her hatred ran too hot, had scarred her too deeply.

Her blades felt cold, tooled hilts biting into her palms. She flipped the daggers around in her fingers and slid them home into their sheaths on her thighs. "Anyway, I leave in a few hours, then it's on to meet my fate in D.C.," she told Nathan. "I should head to bed, try to get some sleep before I go."

"Mira," he said as she started to walk away from him. She didn't want to talk anymore. Didn't want to think about what waited for her at the end of her journey in just four days' time, nor where she might go from there. "Mira, stop."

She paused, swiveled around to meet her dear friend's sober gaze.

"Be careful," he said, eyes holding her in an unblinking stare that seemed to penetrate right to the core of her. "The line you're walking is thin enough. Do this right. You're too good to give up now. Don't give Lucan any more reason to cut you loose."

"There's nothing to worry about." She forced a mild scowl and lightly shook her head, deliberate in her misunderstanding. "I'm on babysitting detail, not a mission. Nothing's going to go wrong."

4

THAT SAME MORNING, ADHERING TO THE METICULOUS INSTRUC-
tions she'd received from Jeremy Ackmeyer himself, Mira arrived at his
home in rural western Massachusetts at precisely 9:00 A.M. The house
was large but minimalist in the extreme. No perimeter fence, no elabo-
rate gate or layer of guards to shield the reclusive genius. Just an expres-
sionless single-story block of white concrete, angled rooftop solar panels
and steel-louver shaded windows, sitting on a broad knoll in the middle
of a naked five-acre parcel of ruthlessly trimmed lawn.

Even without a gate or guards, to Mira, the house seemed more a
prison than a place someone would call home—even an odd duck like
Ackmeyer.

The germophobe scientist didn't want her coming inside the house
and potentially contaminating anything but had stipulated he'd meet
her in the garage below and proceed directly into the car to depart. She
dutifully rolled up the long driveway to the underground parking garage
as she'd been instructed and braked at the electronic access panel in
front of the closed door of the bay on the right.

Mira slid the driver's-side window down, thankful for the incoming
gust of fresh morning air. The sedan's interior still held a strong disinfectant scent, lingering from the top-to-bottom sterilization Ackmeyer
had insisted upon before he'd agree to set foot in the vehicle. Fomites,
he'd explained, as if the word struck cold terror into him. What would
he do if she decided to lick the side of his face as soon as she got close to
him? Probably collapse in a fit of apoplectic shock. It would certainly

make the drive pass a little quicker if her cargo spent the duration of it in a dead faint.

Smiling at the idea, Mira drew in and savored a couple of long breaths of the crisp country air. That small taste of freedom would have to last her for the next five days of torment. Pressing the arrival button on the garage access panel, she leaned forward and recited the temporary entrance password Ackmeyer had given her when she spoke with him earlier that morning to arrange his pickup. *"Annus Mirabilis."*

Had Ackmeyer chosen the Latin password for its obvious play on her name, or for some other reason? She'd almost asked him when he gave it to her but decided to wait, figuring she'd have plenty of time to ask him on the drive. God knew she'd need some decent conversation starters for the many hours they were about to spend together on the road to D.C.

The garage door wasn't moving.

Mira put her head out the window and tried the password again.

Nothing.

"Oh, come on," she muttered, scowling at the unresponsive bay door. For all his obsessive-compulsive tendencies, he hadn't noticed that his home security system was out of service?

She gave it another shot, and when the garage door still didn't budge, she squinted through the windshield at the house above. Ackmeyer had specifically instructed her to wait for him in the garage, forbidding her or anyone else from entering his house under any circumstances. He didn't say she couldn't walk up onto the yard to tell him she'd arrived.

Mira got out of the car and hoofed it up the knoll and around to the front of the house. "Mr. Ackmeyer?" she called, walking up to one of the shaded windows to try to peer inside through the steel slats. "Jeremy, are you in there?"

Her nape tingled with a warrior's instinct that something wasn't right here. Then again, when she'd spoken with Ackmeyer a few hours ago to arrange the trip, he hadn't exactly sounded eager to make the journey in the first place. He didn't conduct his work for awards or accolades, he'd insisted, something Mira respected him for in spite of his personal quirks. He was being forced to attend the gala in D.C., out of obligation to his socially and politically motivated family and due to pressure from Reginald Crowe himself.

Not her place to care about any of that, though. She had a duty to fulfill here, and that meant delivering Jeremy Ackmeyer to the summit celebration safe and sound, as expected.

But something wasn't right here.

Not right at all.

The thing that struck her most was the quiet of the place. Total, unnatural quiet.

And then, a crash.

It sounded from somewhere inside the house.

Was the place being robbed in broad daylight?

Mira felt her blade in her hand before she even realized she'd drawn it from its hidden sheath at her back. Her battle senses clashed with the need to know that Ackmeyer was all right inside. "Jeremy? If you're in there, you need to let me see you."

A loud, heavy thump answered. Then a thundering rush of boots on a stairwell. How many, she couldn't be sure. There were hushed voices, followed by a pained and muffled shout, cut off too abruptly for Mira's peace of mind.

Holy shit.

She flexed her fingers around the hilt of her dagger as she crept along the perimeter of the house, gauging the situation to determine her best course of action as one person against an unknown number inside.

Mira was good with her knives and hand-to-hand combat, but now she wished like hell she had ignored Ackmeyer's stated abhorrence of weapons and violence of any kind. She'd kept her daggers concealed on her person, but to avoid upsetting him, she'd hidden her gun in the glove compartment of the car. Damn it. She sped back down the knoll and yanked open the passenger-side door of the idling vehicle.

No sooner had she torn the big 9-mm out of its holster and thrown the safety than the left bay of the garage lifted and an unmarked black delivery van barreled out and past her like a bullet.

The van narrowly missed her, tires screaming on the pavement, smoke curling up in its wake as it roared up the drive. Mira rolled into a crouch and opened fire on the retreating vehicle.

She shot out one of its rear tires, continuing to blast rounds at the van as it swerved crazily, slowed by the damage. She fired until she had exhausted the magazine, then dived into the open passenger door of her car and leapt across the seats to the driver's side. Shifting hard into reverse, she stomped on the gas and swung around into a forward-facing spin.

Eyes on the limping van ahead of her, she slammed the car into drive and ground the pedal to the floor. Rather than ram it from behind and risk disabling her own vehicle, Mira roared up alongside the van and used her car to corral her quarry, steering it away from the paved driveway and onto the rough yard where it would be more difficult for the blown tire to roll. Given little choice, the van began to slow. It struggled on the uneven terrain, angling off to the right with Mira riding its side perpendicularly, holding fast to her course.

She waited to be met with a hail of gunfire from the van's occupants, but the driver, a young female with long black hair, and the hard-eyed blond man riding shotgun seemed more interested in evading Mira than shooting her dead. But the man was agitated, flailing his hands across the seat and shouting orders at the driver. She kept her cool, maneuvering as though she thought she might steer out of Mira's trap eventually, but her partner had no such patience. He lunged for the wheel, crawling over the driver and shoving her aside to take the seat himself.

He swerved crazily, then jerked hard to the left to scrape the side of the van into Mira's sedan. She dug deeper, foot to the floor on the gas, arms shaking with the effort to hold the wheel steady against the opposing force of the van. When the driver suddenly hit his brakes, Mira realized her mistake. Too late to stop her forward momentum, she ended up in front of the van.

Not even a second later, he rammed her from behind.

The hit was off center, smashing the rear right side of her car. Her body flew sideways with the impact, slamming her shoulder and head into the driver's-side door and window. Light exploded inside her skull. She smelled blood, felt warm, wet heat spread over her scalp and down the left side of her face.

Her vision was fading, filling fast with a thick black fog as the sedan lurched into a vicious spin. Everything slowed . . . then stopped.

Voices coming closer now.

She didn't know how many. Couldn't reconcile where they'd come from, until she lifted her head and glimpsed the black van. All of her senses were blanketed in a heavy gauze, sight and sound a confusion of input that her brain struggled to process. She tried to move, but her limbs refused the weak command.

"Come on, Brady. We don't have time for this." A man's voice, clipped and anxious on his approach. "We gotta roll now!"

"You heard Bowman's orders on this job." The reply was female. "No casualties, Vince. Secure the target and get out. That was the plan."

"And we've got Ackmeyer, so mission accomplished. Now let's get the fuck outta here."

"I'm not going anywhere until I make sure she's okay." A long-legged gait rushed toward Mira's slump in the car. The driver's-side door groaned open. "Jesus. Oh, shit . . . go get Doc. I need him out here on the double."

"She dying?"

"You better pray like hell she's not." A terse answer. "Go get Doc, right now."

Through the thick fog swamping Mira's senses, she felt the air stir as the man crept closer. Heard his sudden indrawn breath as he leaned over his comrade to get a better look. "Holy hell. This bitch is one of the Ord—"

"I know who she is," snapped the woman. "Go back to the van and get Doc. And have Chaz get busy switching out that wasted tire. I'm calling the base. Someone's got to tell the boss we just fucked this thing up bigtime."

She didn't seem to notice the tiny flex of Mira's fingers. Didn't realize that the twitch of muscle response bumped Mira's hand against the hilt of the dagger lying on the floor next to the front seat where she sat slouched.

Mira focused on the cold metal hilt of her blade as the man ran off to carry out his instructions, and the woman turned away to contact the one who led them.

"They should be here by now." Bowman's voice was more snarl than words as he stalked through his stronghold nearly three hours after the call came in from the botched field op.

The petite young woman in charge of communications for the rebel base camp located south of Boston hurried to keep pace with him in the bunker's gloomy corridors. She hooked a lock of her short indigo-dyed hair behind an ear bearing a dozen tiny metal loops. "I've been trying to reach them for a situation update, but so far no response."

"When's the last time you tried, Nina?"

"Five minutes ago."

Bowman's answering curse echoed off the dank, block-granite walls. He rubbed a hand over his jaw and the trim goatee that darkened his chin. "Try them again. Do it now."

"Yes, sir." She already had her comm device activated, speaking the command that would connect her to the team en route. It took only seconds before she gave him a grave shake of her head, big brown eyes serious with concern. "Still nothing."

"Son of a bitch." Something was wrong. Something worse than the obvious complication that took place at Ackmeyer's house a few hours ago.

Bowman wasn't about to sit around with his dick in hand, wondering and waiting. He'd hated the taste of that inactivity from the moment he gave the okay on this job. Now it burned like acid in the back of his throat.

Combat boots striking hollowly on the concrete floor of the abandoned military fort, he rounded a corner to head deeper into the bunker, toward a hand-hewn tunnel leading underground to the gun battery that served as the rebel base's small fleet garage.

"I'm sure they'll be here any minute," Nina said, jogging to stay alongside him. "I'm sure they've got everything under control now."

Bowman grunted, kept walking. If only it were that simple to just sit back and wait it out, knowing how badly things had gone off the rails out there.

"What are you going to do? You can't mean to go after them . . ."

He didn't answer, didn't slow down.

Damn it, he never should have put this job into play. He'd had a bad feeling about it to start with, but after waiting months for the opportunity to make his move on Ackmeyer, he hadn't been willing to risk losing that chance simply because it was a daytime grab to be conducted under less-than-perfect conditions.

Less than perfect seemed the understatement of the century as he stormed down the long corridor with Nina racing behind him, making another frantic attempt to reach Brady, Doc, and the others.

How long had they been developing their plan to get close to Ackmeyer? Nearly a quarter of a year of meticulous espionage, of putting out the right feelers to the right people, of waiting for the perfect moment to strike. It might have taken months more to get the necessary pieces in place. Too long, and hesitation could prove catastrophic, if

Ackmeyer was permitted to continue his work. All the worse, should he decide to profit from the formidable fruits of his labor.

That was the argument that persuaded Bowman to green-light the mission this morning, despite its numerous risks. Last-minute intel had arrived from one of the rebels' Boston contacts. Ackmeyer would be making a rare public appearance in a few days, as part of the peace summit gala. And as the celebrated guest of none other than Reginald Crowe.

There could be no more waiting, no more guessing. Ackmeyer could not be permitted to arrive on that stage.

The consensus among Bowman and his rebel crew had been immediate, and the plot to grab the reclusive scientist was put into motion. He'd trusted in the team sent to carry it out. They were capable and skilled, proven in the field time and again. He'd been counting on them and never doubted they'd succeed, with or without him leading the charge.

They would have succeeded, he was certain, if not for an unexpected obstacle.

After taking great care to avoid such a problem, he had now stepped into direct conflict with the Order. He only hoped his crew—hell, the rest of the world in general—didn't end up paying for his mistake.

Bowman picked up his pace as he neared the mouth of the tunnel leading to the nearby battery. No sooner had he reached the yawning maw when he heard a distant commotion of voices spilling toward him through the darkness.

"Is that them?" Nina asked, worry creasing her forehead.

A woman's scream tore loose in that next second. Then a man's sharp, angry shout.

Bowman spared Nina only a fleeting glance before taking off like a bullet onto the lightless path ahead. Chaos was erupting—more shouting and commotion. A metallic clatter, punctuated by the sudden olfactory punch of spilled blood.

He emerged from the tunnel just in time to see Doc on the floor near the van with a fresh stab wound from the dagger lodged in his abdomen. Vince slumped next to a bound and unconscious Jeremy Ackmeyer in the open side-panel door of the vehicle. The rebel's left arm was wrapped in a makeshift tourniquet from what appeared to be an injury that had been tended to en route. He had bruises on his face, clothing shredded in several places. Meanwhile, Brady and Chaz tried unsuccessfully to subdue the hooded, partially restrained female who fought like a demon.

No, Bowman mentally corrected in the second he watched her, she fought like a warrior.

The warrior he knew her to be.

In that fraction of time, between the moment he was simply the leader of these renegade soldiers and the one that held him motionless in awe and respect for a woman he had betrayed so long ago, Bowman didn't think to look in Vince's direction.

Not until it was too late.

Face twisted with rage, Vince launched himself into the fray. He had something in his hand—one of Doc's pressure injectors. He hit her with it, tearing off her black hood and shoving the dosing gun up against her neck. He pulled the trigger and she went down like a rock, limbs crumbling uselessly beneath her.

Bowman's roar shook the entire fortress.

One minute he was standing at the open mouth of the tunnel, the next he was holding Vince suspended by the throat, his fingers all but crushing the man's larynx as he bore down on him in total, murderous fury.

"What have you done!" he snarled.

Eyes wide, nearly popping out of his skull, Vince sputtered and squeaked, tried to form words. "S-something had . . . had to do . . . something. Attacked us in the van . . . might've killed Doc just now . . ."

Bowman pressed harder, the heat of his anger bathing Vince's face in a rising amber glow. The blood spilled would have been enough to set him off, but it was pure rage that put the sharp ache in his gums. He peeled his lips back from his teeth as his fangs erupted into deadly points.

Vince's eyes went wider, fear filling his entire expression. Bowman could feel the sharp tang of that fear in the rapid pound of the human's heartbeat against his fingertips. He could hear it in Vince's thoughts, taste it through the touch that allowed Bowman to burrow into the human's mind and divine the truth of his intentions.

The sheer panic that had provoked Vince to attack the woman deepened to dick-withering fright as he stared up at Bowman and struggled to pull air into his lungs. "P-please . . ." Vince gasped. "Don't . . . don't kill me."

"She's okay." Brady's voice carried across the room now, level and cautious. "It was a tranq gun, that's all. Once she wakes up, she's going to be fine."

Bowman kept his eyes trained on Vince. "You don't touch her. Never again. If you do, you die. We clear?"

The rebel soldier gave a weak nod. "Please . . . let me go . . ."

Bowman dropped him, left him where he fell. He swung around and sank into a crouch beside the female warrior who lay on the floor nearby. She wasn't completely out yet. Her eyes rolled behind her lids, opening in drowsy intervals as she fought against the sedative Vince had pumped into her veins. She murmured incoherently, her voice so quiet, going weaker with every second.

He noticed dried blood in her blond hair, crusted at her left temple where a small red birthmark rode along her hairline. The sight of that tiny teardrop and crescent moon, coupled with the lily-sweet scent of her spilled blood, tightened the knot of regret that had settled like a rock in his gut from the moment of his team's call from the field.

That she'd been harmed during this operation—injured even before the tranq gun that was leaving a dark bruise on the delicate skin of her neck—made his veins turn cold with self-directed fury.

The urge to touch her was nearly overwhelming.

He wanted to offer her comfort, hold her close, assure her that she was safe.

But he couldn't do those things.

He didn't have that right.

Not anymore.

He was no longer that man. To this band of human rebels, he was, and had been for the past eight years, simply Bowman. He was their leader, who also happened to have been born Breed, not *Homo sapiens* like the rest of them.

But the injured and bleeding young woman lying before him now had known him from a much different time, in a different place. When he'd been a different person, born with a name none of his rebel followers would recognize.

"Kellan . . . ?"

Her voice was hardly a whisper, barely audible, even to him. He felt her hand brush his, feather-light, questioning. Against his own will, he glanced down into her face. Her eyes were not even half open, heavy-lidded and unfocused. She drifted off in that next moment, her fingers falling away limply, head lolling to the side in a heavy, drug-induced slumber.

He briefly closed his eyes, expelling the past and reaching for the only thing he had left.

"Show's over, people. Now look alive. We still have work to do."

5

SHE HADN'T EXPECTED TO WAKE UP.

Hell, she hadn't really expected to be alive. Not after fighting with her captors in transit, sticking the one named Vince with her dagger soon after they'd shoved her into the van at Jeremy Ackmeyer's house. They might have killed her then. And she couldn't have blamed them if they'd finished her off during the struggle she'd put up once they'd arrived at this place either.

This . . . wherever she was.

She tried to open her eyes where she lay now but saw only darkness. The pressure on her face told her she was blindfolded. Handcuffs bit into her wrists, which were fastened somewhere above her head. She gave them a tug and heard the shackles grate on what she guessed was a metal headboard. Her ankles were restrained too, fixed to the bottom of the bed.

Her mouth felt as dry as if it had been packed with cotton, but at least they hadn't gagged her. Then again, what good would it do her to start screaming? She didn't have to see the walls of her prison to know that they were made of thick, impenetrable material. Stone, she was guessing, from the dank, stale odor of the place, more than likely without a single window in the room.

She smelled the faint brine of the ocean in the damp air. Heard the low roar of waves rolling onto the shore from not far off in the distance. Beyond that, only silence.

No, raising her voice in this place would only alert her captors.

Mira shifted on the thin mattress and winced at the dull ache that flared in the side of her neck. She remembered getting punched there with something sharp. Something that took out her legs and sent her mind reeling. Tranqs, it was obvious to her now.

But it didn't take much to recall the sudden, overwhelming sense of floating, falling . . .

Dying, she had thought.

She'd even seen the face of an angel in those final few moments of fading consciousness. Kellan's face, handsome and haunted, his soulful hazel eyes holding her in a gaze that seemed mournful, somehow heart-broken.

God, they must have given her some powerful shit.

It took more than a little effort to shake off the soft pang of longing in her chest that always followed in the wake of Kellan's memory. Instead, Mira rallied herself around her present reality—which, at the moment, wasn't looking too promising.

She tested her shackles again, to no avail. Next, she shifted her head around on the pillow, trying to use friction to slide the blindfold away from her eyes. It moved up only a fraction on the right side, not enough for her to see anything.

And she'd apparently made enough noise already, because now she heard the heavy jangle of a key turning in a lock. From somewhere beyond the foot of the bed, a heavy panel door creaked open.

"You're awake." The woman with the long black hair. Brady, they called her. Mira recognized her voice and the long-legged gait as footsteps approached the bed. "How do you feel?"

"Like I'm going to vomit," Mira replied, her own voice raw from disuse. "But then, being near rebel scum tends to have that effect on me." She cleared her arid throat. "That's what you are, right? Rebels. Lowlife cowards who plot and skulk around in the shadows like a den of rats, making messes for other people to clean up. Taking the lives of people worth any hundred of your kind."

The woman said nothing in response to all that venom. There was a soft rustle of movement beside the bed near Mira's head, then the liquid sound of something being poured into a glass. "Drink this," she told Mira. "It's water. The sedative you were given will have dehydrated you."

Mira turned her head when the cool glass came close to her lips. "I don't want anything you give me. Tell me what you've done to Jeremy Ackmeyer."

A soft sigh. "You don't need to worry about him. He's not your concern."

"I'll decide what's my concern or not." Mira tried to rise, but there was nowhere to go with the restraints digging into her wrists. She dropped back down on a hissed curse. "Where is he? What do you want from him?"

The water glass came up to Mira's mouth again. "We're going to release you tonight, unharmed," the female rebel said, ignoring her questions.

"Release me?" Mira scoffed, refusing the drink a second time now. "And you think I believe that? I've seen all of your faces. I may not know exactly where you brought me, but I know we're not far out of Boston. Somewhere very close to the bay—so close, I can hear the water. I can taste it in the air. Some kind of bunker would be my guess. Something very old. It won't take long to figure out where this hideout is, and then I'll come back for all of you."

"We've considered that." No worry in that calm reply. "Precautions will be taken, of course."

Precautions, Mira pondered silently. Were they taking Ackmeyer to another location? Or did this imply the rebels would be moving their base of operations tonight, scattering somewhere like the vermin they were?

No way they'd ever outrun her, let alone the Order, no matter how far or wide they fled. And if they thought hooding her for the ride back to this base earlier and keeping her blindfolded now would protect their identities or the location of their lair, they would be sorely mistaken. Short of lobotomizing her, which would definitely negate the "unharmed" part of their promise, Mira didn't see how these humans figured they could turn her loose and expect to get away with it.

"You know who I am," Mira said, not a question.

"Yes," the woman replied quietly. "I know who you are."

"Then you have to know that I will find you and the rest of your criminal friends, and I won't be alone when I do." Mira wished she could see the rebel's face and gauge the fear that must surely be there. No one took on the Order without a good deal of trepidation or stupidity, and this woman didn't strike Mira as anything close to an idiot. "You need to tell your pals that if any of you think I'm leaving this place without Ackmeyer, you've got another thing coming."

"It's not up to me to decide," she said. "Now, please. Take some water."

The glass came back toward Mira's mouth. This time, instead of drinking or turning away, she lunged forward and bit the fleshy base of the rebel's thumb.

The woman shrieked and leapt back, dropping the glass to the floor. It shattered beside the bed, as loud as a crash of cymbals in the quiet of the thick-walled cell.

Mira used the opportunity to fight her restraints again. She bucked and struggled on the bed, managing only to shift the blindfold down from one of her eyes as the open doorway filled with the immense male form of another rebel, responding to the commotion.

This guy was big and menacing, radiating a dangerous heat that made even Mira's breath catch in her throat. She could see only a sliver of him over the top edge of her skewed blindfold. Broad shoulders. Dark, copper-shot brown hair.

As tall and muscular and powerful as any one of the Order's warriors.

A sense of unease—of bone-deep alarm—arrowed through her on that thought.

She levered herself up on the bed for a better look, watching as he went to the female rebel's side and wrapped a protective arm around her.

"Candice, are you all right?" Not Brady as the other men had called her, but a feminine name, spoken with genuine concern, true affection in the deep, low-toned voice. His head was down, most of his face obscured by the wild fall of his shoulder-length hair. "What the hell happened?"

"Nothing, I'm okay. I'm sorry, Bowman. I should've had better control of the situation."

Quiet words, an absolving stroke of the man's large hand over the ebony hair of his comrade. Mira's breath was sawing out of her lungs as she watched the private exchange, all of her senses focused on the deep murmur of the rebel leader's voice.

Something about him—no, in fact, *everything* about him—began to stir something cold and rusted inside her.

The tendons in her neck pulled tight as she strained to see his face. Angling her head to hear more of that silky, dark voice. His presence drew everything in her to full attention. Her skin went tight and hot and confining. Her pulse pounded like the wings of a caged bird, trapped inside her chest.

Her instincts knew this man. Her heart knew, even if the illogic of it left her mind struggling to catch up with the rest of her.

Curiosity twisted into desperation as the man began to move. Letting his arm fall away from the other woman, he pivoted toward the bed, moving too smoothly, emanating too much raw power for a human.

Because he wasn't human.

All the air left Mira's lungs as he approached the bed where she lay.

"Impossible," she whispered. "No . . . this can't be real."

But it was real—*he* was real.

Not an angel. Not a ghost, either, but flesh and blood. Alive.

The impossible answer to so many of her hopes and prayers.

"Kellan," she whispered.

Her shock was so profound in that moment, they could have uncuffed her and she would've had no strength to lift her head, let alone prove any kind of threat. And even as she strove to make sense of what she was seeing, a part of her heart was going cold with an awful realization.

If it was he, what was Kellan doing here after all the time he'd been missing? How could he possibly know these people? What did any of them mean to him?

"It is you?" she asked, needing to hear him confirm what her mind still refused to fully believe.

Without answering, without meeting her searching eyes, he glanced down at her. Drew away the blindfold from her face and gently removed it from around her head. All the while, deliberately avoiding her gaze.

"Candice," he murmured. "Bring me the contact lenses."

Of course, Mira thought. Kellan would know about her gift. Kellan knew everything about her. He had been her best friend for most of her life. The only person who truly had known and understood her.

The dark-haired woman handed him a small dish filled with clear liquid, then quietly exited the room. He fished out one of the pair of purple lenses suspended within. Mira could hardly breathe as he took her face in his hands and carefully put the lenses into her eyes.

Once they were in place, her powerful ability muted, he finally lifted his hazel gaze. Oh, God . . . there was no denying that it was he. Under the thick mane of copper-infused hair, his greenish brown eyes were deep set and intense. His cheeks seemed leaner now, razor-cut and strong, his square jaw framed by the trim lines of the goatee that gave his handsome face a darkly mysterious edge. But within that rakish beard, his mouth was grim, unreadable.

He gave her no words of comfort. No explanation for how she'd come to find him here, living among killers, thieves, and traitors. The very enemies he'd been fighting against when he'd been one of the Order.

Mira stared into his eyes in agonizing confusion. One part of her was elated and relieved to the very core of her being to see Kellan living and breathing, so undeniably real and alive. Another part of her was in abject misery, realizing that his death had been a mistake—or worse, a lie. And now, the bigger betrayal, to see him standing among these people, treating them as friends—as family—while she had been left to mourn him alone.

"You died," she finally managed to croak. "I was there. Eight years ago, almost to the day, Kellan. I watched you run into that warehouse. I saw it explode. I still have shrapnel scars from the debris that fell out of the sky that night. I can still taste the smoke and ash from the fire."

He stared at her in a terrible silence.

"There was nothing left of the building," she went on. "Nothing left of you, Kellan. Or so you've let me believe, all this time. I cried for you. I still do."

His eyes remained on Mira, but he spoke no words. No plea for her forgiveness. No insistence that it had all been some unavoidable mistake.

She might have been tempted to believe him. The way her heart was cracking open in her chest, she might have been willing to accept any crumb of explanation he gave her. But he offered her nothing.

His silence was killing her. "Don't you have anything to say to me?"

He swallowed. Glanced down. "I'm sorry, Mira."

When his eyes returned to hers, they were somber. Sincere, for all she knew of him now. But they were unflinchingly remote.

"You're sorry." Her shattered heart turned to cinders under the cool simplicity of his response. "Sorry for what part?"

"All of it," he replied. "And for what I still need to do."

With that, he rose. Moved away from the bed. Away from her.

"Candice," he called toward the open door. She appeared in an instant, waiting for his command. "Make sure Vince gassed up the beast like I told him to." Kellan paused, pivoting a brief, sidelong glance in Mira's direction. "I'll be heading out at nightfall to take care of the complications from his fuck-up today."

So, that's what she was to him now. Nothing.

A complication.

An unpleasant wrinkle in his plans.

And now she thought back to something Candice had said earlier, after Mira had told her they'd be as good as crazy to release her tonight and assume she wouldn't come after them later.

Precautions would be taken.

Mira hadn't imagined then that the rebels had one of the Breed on their side. Now she understood. And while she didn't think Kellan would stoop to killing her, he had other ways of ensuring she never found him again.

The truth of his betrayal sank in with a pain she could scarcely bear. It hardened something inside her, devouring the love she'd carried for him for so long, spitting out the grief.

As she looked at Kellan now, at the man he had become—a man who had just now declared himself her enemy—Mira's anger and hurt turned the ashes of her heart into tiny diamonds of contempt.

Because as badly as she wanted to reject the idea, Kellan Archer no longer existed.

And the man who stood in his place was not only allied with these rebel bastards, he was leading them.

6

WITH LUCAN AND GIDEON SEQUESTERED IN CLOSED-DOOR meetings most of the day, Darion Thorne had spent the past few hours sparring in the training facility of the Order's D.C. headquarters. The rigorous exercise felt good, but it was a temporary distraction. It hadn't quelled the restless energy that lived inside him. It never did.

He was a warrior—he knew that with a certainty in his soul. How could his father not see that he was wasting a valuable asset by keeping Dare tethered to the command center when he belonged in the field? How long could Dare stand to have his hands tied before he threw off those chains and led the charge—with or without his father's approval?

It was that question that dogged him as he sat hunched over a thick volume in the Order's archive library. His hair was still damp from the shower, training garb switched for a dark T-shirt and jeans. His blades and throwing stars now replaced by a pen, which he tapped in idle rhythm on the long wooden table that stretched the center of the expansive, book-lined chamber.

Even though his body yearned for action, his mind thirsted for knowledge. And the history contained in this room alone was enough to keep him busy for decades.

Not surprising, since it had taken a full twenty years to collect it. The library represented millennia's worth of information, everything from the otherworldly origins of the Breed and their alien forebears, their language and customs, their lineage here on Earth, to their often-violent past as powerful, savage beings perched at the top of the food chain. The wealth of insight was nothing short of staggering.

And Jenna Tucker-Darrow, the woman responsible for the archive, was adding more volumes all the time.

"If you spend any more hours in here, I may start worrying about my job security."

Dare swung his head up at the sound of Jenna's voice. She was smiling as she entered the room, wearing a little black dress and strappy high heels. Her brown hair was shorn close to her scalp, showing off her lean cheekbones and big hazel eyes. She was dressed for a date, no doubt with her warrior mate, Brock, but she carried what looked to be a newly completed journal in her hand.

"I don't think you ever have to worry about job security," Dare told her. "No one can do what you do."

She winked at him. "I am cyborg, hear me roar."

Strolling over to a bookcase far across the room, she slipped the journal onto one of the shelves, carefully selecting its placement. It was hard not to stare at the female, and not only because she was beautiful and Dare was a man with two eyes in his head. Jenna was stunning for an altogether unique reason as well.

Her simple black dress plunged low in the back, baring her pale, slender neck and spine, both of which were covered in a graceful tangle of *dermaglyphs*. Unusual, particularly given that Jenna was neither Breed nor Breedmate.

She'd been fully human once, but all of that changed twenty years ago, when the last of the alien fathers of the Breed transplanted a biotech chip from his own body into Jenna's. The Ancient likely had his reasons for leaving behind a piece of himself before he was killed by the Order. For Jenna, that bit of alien DNA and technology had meant numerous astonishing physical and psychic changes, coupled with memories of a long, often-disturbing past that did not belong to her.

It was those memories that now filled the countless volumes of handscribed journals lining the built-in bookcases of the archive chamber.

"I hadn't heard you and Brock had arrived from Atlanta," Dare said.

Jenna ran her fingers across the spines of several journals on the shelf, pausing to rearrange one that apparently had been misfiled. "We got in before dawn this morning. I wanted to come early, do some work in here before the summit later this week. Dante and Tess are coming in to-night. Tegan and Elise too. Everyone else should be arriving over the next couple of nights, from what I understand."

Dare nodded. Lucan had informed him of the gathering of all the Order elders and their mates from their various districts of command around the world. It would be good to see them all again. The warriors and their mates were as close as kin to him, but Dare couldn't help re-senting the fact that the summons to publicly assemble was anything more than a command performance instigated by the GNC members. A means for them to show the world that the Order endorsed the peace summit wholeheartedly and would abide by the GNC's terms without question. The politics of it all disgusted him.

Jenna regarded him over her shoulder. "Will you be at the gala recep-tion too, Darion?"

He grunted. "Me, in a monkey suit? Not likely. I can think of a hun-dred things I'd rather do than stand around kissing the rings of those posturing GNC blowhards. That goes double for kissing their useless asses."

Jenna's brows arched upward. "You're a lot like your father, you know that?"

"I'm nothing like him," Dare insisted. "He's too willing to let the humans have the reins. He's too careful with their fragile egos, when the world would be a better place—a safer place for mankind and our own—with the Order firmly in charge."

"And if you ask the humans, they would argue the opposite. Sooner or later, it would be war." Jenna strode over to him and took a seat on the edge of the table. "Things were different before First Dawn, simpler. The Breed kept their own counsel, lived in the shadows. Now that we're out to the humans, we have more freedoms. We have more power now that we don't have to hide our existence, but there are trade-offs. And the line we must walk to maintain peace is even thinner. Lucan's actions impact the entire Breed nation now. He doesn't take that responsibility lightly."

"He doesn't trust anyone to help him shoulder that burden either." Dare glanced away from Jenna's sage expression and gave a curt shake of his head. "He doesn't give anyone the credit that they could be useful, maybe even as capable as him, if he gave them half a chance to prove it."

When he looked back up at her, Jenna held him with a knowing smile. "Still fighting that same battle with him, are you? He'll come around one day, Darion."

He scoffed. "Have you met my father? He doesn't bend."

"Neither does his son, from what I've seen." Still smiling, she leaned over to see what he was reading in the open journal. "Ah, that's one of the oldest volumes. I was working on that one before First Dawn."

The frustrations of politics and parental misgivings fell away as Dare returned his attention to the journal he'd been studying for the past couple of weeks. "Do you know what this numerical sequence might be?"

Jenna peered at the handwritten page and gave a mild shrug. "The things I record don't always make sense. Sometimes there are symbols or numbers—like this one—that don't mean anything to me, but because I see them or hear them through the Ancient's memories, I make sure to write them down."

Dare nodded, but it wasn't the answer he was hoping for. "This isn't the only occurrence of this same sequence in the journals."

"Really?" Jenna's eyes brightened with interest.

"The same one appears in two other volumes that I've found so far," Dare told her. "I'm betting I'll eventually find it in more of them too."

"Well, what are we waiting for? Let's see if you're right." Jenna slid off the table and started heading for one of the nearby bookcases. She kicked off her delicate sandals and raised up on her toes to reach for a high shelf. "We should start on the older volumes first, then work our way forward in time."

Dare felt the air shift in the second before Brock's deep voice rolled into the room. "I might've known I'd find you in here." The immense warrior gave a nod of greeting to Darion, but his dark-brown eyes were on his mate alone. "It's damn near impossible to drag this woman away from her work. You know, a lesser man might get a complex."

Brock was dressed in a charcoal-gray suit and deep wine-colored shirt, left unbuttoned at the neck where the arcing tails of his *dermaglyphs* rode on his dark skin. Dare had seldom seen the hardass Breed warrior out of his combat gear, and as much as he wanted to chuckle at the sight of him all spit-shined and civilized, it was obvious from Brock's loving gaze on Jenna that the GQ getup was all for her.

Her answering smile as she pivoted around to face him said she knew it too. "Work? Who needs work?" She picked up her sandals and went into his waiting arms. "I've suddenly got an irresistible urge to play hooky."

Brock grinned, shooting Darion a brief, sly look. "I like the sound of that. Maybe we should skip the dinner date routine and go straight to the hooky part."

Jenna laughed. "What, and waste this killer dress?"

"Believe me," Brock growled, low under his breath, "it's far from wasted."

Dare chuckled as Brock swept Jenna into a hungered, uninhibited kiss. He wondered if he'd ever know that kind of passion. The kind strong enough to make him want to take a mate of his own. A forever kind of thing, not the casual, sweaty encounters he used to burn off restless energy and sate his need for blood.

"Let's get out of here," Brock murmured, nuzzling his mate's neck. "Dinner out is optional."

"Wait a second." She ducked out of his embrace and jogged to one of the bookcases to pull a slim journal from the far corner of the shelf. She came back, held the aged, leather-bound volume out to Dare.

"What's this?" he asked, taking it from her.

"My very first journal. I wrote it in the weeks after I arrived at the Order's old compound in Boston."

Darion smoothed his hand over the faded brown cover, then carefully opened the book. The spine cracked softly, pages brittle as he turned them, looking at Jenna's bold script that filled the journal.

"If you really want to study the Breed and learn your own history, you need to start at the beginning." She smiled at him, her once-human eyes holding him in a gaze that was as wise as the most sage elder of his race. "You might also gain a better understanding of your father from this book."

Darion held her stare, then glanced down at the journal he held so carefully in his warrior's hands.

When he looked up again, Jenna and Brock were gone.

Darion opened to the first page and began to read.

Kellan drove to the back of a closed community park in Brookline and cut the headlights on the old Wrangler. Mira hadn't said a thing the entire trip north from the rebel base in New Bedford, aside from the choice words she had for him when he'd placed her in the vehicle wearing a blindfold and handcuffs. True, after he finished with her tonight, she wouldn't remember anything about where she'd been or how he and his crew operated, but Kellan wasn't taking any chances.

"I'm sorry, but it was necessary," he said, reaching over to remove the restraints from her hands. "We can't risk any more problems than what we already have."

As soon as he freed her, Mira tugged down the blindfold and slanted him a measuring look. "Are you going to kill Jeremy Ackmeyer?"

"If I wanted him dead, don't you think he would be already?"

"Maybe he is." Her eyes narrowed on him before she turned her head to look out toward the vacant parklands. "How do I know anything you say is the truth?"

Kellan cursed under his breath. "He is alive, Mira. He'll stay alive, so long as he agrees to my terms."

"What terms?"

He felt her eyes on him again, but this time he was the one who stared at the sea of dark nothing ahead of him through the glass. "Ackmeyer has something I want. Something of extreme value that I can't allow anyone else to get their hands on."

"So, this is about money?" She practically spat the words. "Is that what you've become—a common thief, like your friends back at your bunker?"

"I am not a thief, Mira. Common or otherwise."

"No," she replied. "From the way they fawn and lick your boots, I'd say you're practically their king. Congratulations, by the way. You must be incredibly proud of yourself, seeing how far you've come in these past eight years."

It burned, the acid in her tone. He turned a level glance on her, not wanting to let on how deeply it would wound him if she truly hated him. What would be the point in letting her know that now? "You shouldn't make assumptions about things you don't understand."

"Then enlighten me . . . Bowman, is it?" She shook her head, her pretty mouth twisted in a humorless smile. "Kellan Archer dies a much-mourned hero, and in his place rises Bowman, leader of the rebel resistance. Traitor to everything he once believed in."

"I'm not proud of the way I handled things." And he hated like hell to think how close she was coming to the heart of his reasons for wanting everyone he cared for to believe he was dead and gone. "I never planned to be in this place, Mira. You just have to trust that I had my reasons. I did what I had to."

"Trust?" She barked a sharp laugh. "Oh, that's rich, coming from you. Especially now, when you're sitting here, about to give me a good old-fashioned mind scrub. That's why you brought me here tonight, isn't it?"

He killed the engine and the ancient Jeep rumbled to a stop. "Come on," he said. "Let's get some fresh air."

She didn't budge. "Aren't you worried I'll make a break for it?"

He smiled despite the gravity of the moment. "You never go down easy, do you?"

"Never."

"You may be tough, Mira, but you're not Breed," he reminded her. "You can't outrun me."

"And you made sure I couldn't fight you either. Don't think I haven't noticed your thieving colleagues kept my daggers."

"You'll get the blades back after this is over. I'll see to that."

"Even the one I dropped during the ambush by your rebel underlings?"

Kellan scowled, caught off guard.

"Oh, didn't you know?" she asked, visibly pleased by his surprise. "They must not have noticed, and left it behind. My comm unit too. It's in the glove compartment of the car I was driving."

"Fuck," Kellan growled through gritted teeth.

"*Homo sapiens.*" Mira sighed with no little drama. "So careless sometimes. I'm sure Lucan's going to be curious why my comm signal hasn't moved in the past, what . . . twelve hours?" She gave him a cold, satisfied smile. "It makes you wonder, doesn't it? What else might your crew have overlooked that will come back to bite you in the ass later?"

Kellan considered the possibility, reluctant to admit she had a point. But she underestimated Candice, Doc, and Chaz. Even Vince had plenty of pros to make up for the frequent cons of his hair-trigger temper and tendency toward excessive force. The team had phoned in the problem of Mira's disabled vehicle, and so Nina had tapped a contact in that area to toss the plates and hack the VIN before towing the heap to a scrap yard. Mira's comm unit was very likely nothing but crushed circuitry and dust by now.

"Let's take a walk, Mira." Before she could argue or throw another verbal volley at him, Kellan got out of the car and rounded the hood to her door in less than a second. The speed was deliberate. He figured it couldn't hurt to remind her what she'd be up against if she thought he was playing games. He opened her door and instructed her to get out.

She obeyed, much to his surprise, and he walked her into the peaceful darkness of the empty park.

"I would've expected you to scrub and dump me in the city, not out here."

"I wanted to be alone with you," he said as they strolled alongside each other in the crisp, moonlit grass. "I didn't want to do this in a parking lot somewhere, or be rushed by crowds around us."

"Romantic," she mocked. "I hope there aren't any rapists or rebels hiding out between here and Boston proper when I make the walk back to the city."

Kellan ignored the jab. "I'll watch over you once we're done here, make sure you get back to the Order's headquarters safely."

She blew out a sharp exhalation. "Don't do me any favors. I'm a big girl, all grown up, in case you haven't noticed."

Oh, he'd noticed. The first time had been when Mira was about fifteen. Scrappy and stubborn as always, but that year the reed-thin tomboy with her mop of pale-blond hair had emerged seemingly overnight as a powerful young woman with curves in all the right places and legs that went on forever. He wasn't the only male in the Order's training program that summer who lined up to spar with stunning Mira.

But for some reason that still eluded his understanding to this day, she only had eyes for him. Her best friend, she'd dubbed him, from the time she was an annoying eight-year-old, refusing to give up on the sullen teenager who'd come under the Order's protection after the slaying of his entire family, save his grandfather, Lazaro Archer.

Mira was still stunning, even with the passing of eight years since he'd last been this close to her. He could see traces of that time under her eyes and around the full curve of her mouth. She hadn't taken another Breed male as her mate. If she had, their blood bond would have enhanced her beauty. It would halt her aging, keep her youth intact.

There was a time that Kellan imagined he might be the male to stand at Mira's side. He'd wanted that, right up until the morning of the last day he spent with her. Then everything changed. What he wanted became impossible, and later that night, he had simply ceased to exist.

And now, here she was, walking beside him in the dark.

Hating him, as she had every right to.

Still, the urge to touch her was nearly too much for him to resist. But Kellan knew if he touched her now, he would only want more. Things he had no claim on. Things that were now and forever out of his reach.

How had he managed to keep his distance all these years? Not very well, he reminded himself. He hadn't really ever been that far from her. He'd lost count of how many times he'd watched her in secret, both in Boston and Montreal, curious to know how she was faring. Proud to see her accomplishments. Dismayed when her fierce independence—that unyielding stubborn streak—landed her in trouble.

His plan upon waking up and realizing he hadn't been blown to pieces along with the warehouse had been to get as far away from Mira and the Order as he could. It would've been better for everyone if he had. All the more so, given where he stood now. But the simple fact was, he hadn't been able to leave. She had a hold on him that he hadn't been able to break.

He'd told himself he would be careful, that there was no harm in staying close to where she was so long as he ensured their paths never crossed. But if he'd had any honor in him, he would have fled as far as possible, as soon as he'd been given the chance.

Mira's pace slowed beside him, then stopped as she pivoted to face him. "What happened to you inside that warehouse, Kellan?"

He grunted, gave a vague shake of his head. "Does it matter now?"

"It matters to me. I want to know." Her lips pressed together and she gave him an arch look. "Come on. You're going to scrub my memory anyway, so it's not like I'll remember anything you say or do here tonight. If you've got a conscience anymore, this is your perfect chance to clear it—when you know I will only hate you for a few more minutes before you take even that truth away from me."

It was an accusation, one that scathed him more than he wanted to admit. "I have to do this, Mira. It'll be better for everyone this way."

"Definitely better for you, at any rate." Bitter, angry words. She was hurting deeply, understandably so. But it was the sudden downward tilt of her head—the move that wasn't quite fast enough to hide the moist glint of her eyes—that undid him the most.

"You're right," he murmured. "I do owe you that."

"You owe me the truth," she insisted tightly, her pale eyes bright now, nearly dry when she looked up at him again.

She wouldn't allow herself to break in front of him. He could see that in her diamond-sharp gaze. She wouldn't give him that soft part of her. After tonight, never again.

When she spoke, her voice was schooled and level, a soldier recounting facts after battle. "I've seen your death a thousand times in my mind since that night. You were ahead of Nathan and me and the rest of our team, all of us on foot by then, fanned out and patrolling the riverfront after reports of rebel movement down at the industrial park. You radioed that you were in pursuit of several suspects, gave us your location and where you were heading. Nathan and I were closest to the area by then, so we joined up and proceeded in your direction to provide backup. We arrived just in time to see you disappear into the warehouse. Not even two seconds later, the explosion went off."

Kellan nodded, recalling the night as clearly as she did. But this was the point where their two accounts differed. "The rebel led me to that building. I didn't realize why until I was inside and smelled the taggant of live explosives somewhere nearby. It was a trap, Mira. I knew you and Nathan were right behind me. I couldn't risk that you'd be anywhere near the place when it blew."

"But you were," she said, her blond brows knit as she tried to put the pieces together in her mind. "You were inside the warehouse when it exploded."

"I was," he said. "But only long enough to spoil the trap. I flashed to where the C-4 and detonator had been planted. It was wired to the walls, no chance of ripping it out and disposing of it, certainly not without setting the whole thing off. So I killed it. Shot the whole thing up."

Mira gaped at him. "You detonated it while you were still inside? You would've had less than seconds to escape the blast once the charges blew."

He nodded again. "I didn't even know if I would make it out in one piece. But if it meant preventing you and anyone else from my team from getting hurt in the blast, it was worth the risk. As it happened, the bomb went off just as I was clearing the back door of the place. I remember feeling the percussion throw me airborne. I could smell the smoke and my own burned flesh. I felt my broken bones shatter even more as I hit the cold surface of the Mystic and sank into the murky water. After that, I suppose I lost consciousness. The next thing I knew, someone was pulling my bloody, broken body ashore."

Mira swallowed, utterly silent through his explanation. "Someone saved you?"

"Candice did." He saw her nearly imperceptible flinch at his mention of the human woman's name. "Candice hauled me out of a certain drowning and took me to her friend, Javier, a former Army sergeant who helped sew me up and heal my wounds. He's one of the best field medics I've ever known."

"Doc," she said, her sharp mind easily making the connection. "They had to know who—and what—you were. Why would rebels spare your life?"

"They weren't rebels then. Except for Vince, none of my crew was involved in any outlaw activity at the time. That came later." He cleared his throat and pushed on with the rest of what he had to say. "Anyway, it took two months before I was whole again. By then, you and everyone else I had known before assumed I was dead."

"So, you just let us continue to believe that?" Her expression was incredulous, her voice clipped and climbing toward outrage. "Why would you do that? How could you let everyone carry that pain when you knew it was a lie?"

Kellan shook his head, knowing that he would feel the same way in her place. Hating to see the anguish in her face when it was he who'd put it there. "My reason back then was more important than even my own life." He looked around at where he was, who he'd become as of this moment, and let out a harsh curse. "Everything's different. It doesn't matter anymore."

"You're saying you did this—you left me and everyone else who ever cared about you—all for nothing?"

"I don't expect you to understand," he told her, as gently as he could. "I'm not going to make you try to understand. Certainly not now, when it's too late for that anyway."

Her eyes held him in a stare that shredded him, so full of confusion and anger and hurt. "You have every right to hate me now, Mira. But that was never what I wanted."

"What about love?" she shot back at him. "You never wanted that from me either, did you?"

He swore under his breath. God, he'd been honored, humbled, by how openly Mira had always given herself to him. She'd loved him when he was at his weakest, angry and withdrawn, a self-pitying idiot who would've been happy to wallow in his misery forever. But she'd seen something in him worth saving. She'd pulled him into her light, pushed him until he was able to walk on his own, challenged him to be more. To be a better man than he ever would've without Mira as a part of his life.

Her love had been a precious gift. One he didn't deserve then and couldn't accept now.

When she started to turn away from him, he did what he'd promised himself he wouldn't. He reached for her, gently took her furious and wounded, beautiful face in his hands. "This isn't what I wanted, Mouse."

"No. Goddamn you, *no*." She wrenched away from him, pissed off and seething. Her finger came up in his face. "You don't call me that. My family called me that a long time ago. You're not family."

"No," he admitted quietly. Not anymore, not even close.

"You're not a friend either. Not after what you've done," she charged, breathing heavily with every clipped word. "After what you're doing to me now, I can't believe that you were ever truly my friend. Was it all a fucking joke to you, Kellan? Was I just a joke in your mind?"

"You were never a joke, Mira." He fisted his hands at his sides to keep from taking her in them once again. "I think you know better than that."

"Do I? How many times did you try to push me away when we were growing up?" She gave a brittle laugh. "I should've let you push. I should've walked away from you and never looked back, any one of the times you gave me the chance. God, I wish I'd never met you!"

"I know." He couldn't blame her, after all. "If I could take it all away for you right now, I would."

Unfortunately for both of them, a Breed mind scrub wasn't effective on long-term memory. He could erase today, but anything older was outside the bounds of his powers.

"You know this won't be the end of it," Mira pointed out. "Scrub my memory if it will make you feel better, but you know as well as I do that you're on the wrong side of this war."

"I'm trying to prevent a war, Mira."

"Bullshit!" She gave him a hard shove, hands flat against his chest. "What you've done might spark a war."

Kellan seized her by the wrists, trying not to notice the heat of her skin, the frantic beat of her pulse, ticking against his fingertips. He should have released his grasp on her, he knew that. But now that he had her, now that the staccato tempo of her heartbeat was echoing through him—a rhythm that stirred his own blood and sent it coursing through him at a more rapid pace—there was no letting Mira go.

She looked up at him, her purple eyes intense. "What do you think will happen if word gets out that an important human scientist was abducted while under the Order's protection? By a former member of our own ranks."

"No one will know that I was once a warrior," he insisted. "No one but my team back at the camp is even aware that I—that the man they know as Bowman—is Breed. They've kept my secret all this time. They won't betray my trust."

She scoffed. "How nice for you, to have that kind of confidence in the people you care about."

Kellan's answering curse was low and coarse and furious. Before he could stop himself, he hauled Mira up against him and slashed his mouth across hers in an unforgiving kiss.

At first, she resisted. Her lips were tense beneath his, sealed tight against his assault. The fine muscles in her wrists were taut as cables, delicate, skilled hands fisted where he held them between their pressed bodies. She was still angry with him, still rigid with loathing for everything he'd done to her, everything he'd admitted after so many years of deception.

But Kellan couldn't release her. And as he deepened his kiss, teasing his tongue along the stubborn seam of her lush mouth, some of the fight finally leached out of her. She parted her lips on a strangled moan, and he pushed inside, drawing her body closer to his, drowning in the taste of her after such a long time without.

His blood was on fire, scorching his veins. His fangs had erupted from his gums, filling his mouth as desire for this female sent heat and hunger into lower parts of his anatomy.

He told himself the kiss meant nothing. That in a few minutes she would remember none of it anyway. As for him, he was doomed. Because, holy Christ, this moment was going to stay with him for the rest of his days.

Doomed, to be sure.

Because in that moment, Kellan understood that scrubbing Mira was only going to postpone greater problems now that Ackmeyer was in his custody. What she'd said earlier tonight was the truth: If human law enforcement didn't catch up to him soon enough, the Order certainly would.

He should have known.

It wasn't like he hadn't seen it coming a long time ago.

Kellan broke away from her kiss with a savage, inhuman growl. When he spoke, his voice was gravel in his throat, rough from wanting and the sharp-edged reality of just how badly he'd screwed both their lives. "Come with me."

Mira rubbed her damp, reddened lips. Her eyes looked equally bruised, impossibly large, regarding him with a mix of longing and regret. "Time to be rid of me already again, is it?"

"Change of plans," he snarled. He took a firmer hold on her hand and led her back to the Jeep. "You won't be going anywhere after all."

7

AN HOUR LATER, MIRA'S LIPS WERE STILL TINGLING AND ALIVE from Kellan's uninvited kiss. Her blood was still thrumming in her veins, hot from anger and something equally heated that she refused to acknowledge. She tried to rub away the lingering memory of his mouth on hers as Kellan drove her south of Boston, through the city of New Bedford, continuing toward a flat, lightless promontory that jutted into the Atlantic on three sides.

"I know this place," she murmured as the Jeep rolled over the cracked, untended asphalt.

The road led to the entrance of what had once been a park in the days before First Dawn and the wars that followed. Long before that, during another war, the broad expanse of overgrown land and the squatty, elongated D-shape structure at the far end of it had served as a human military facility. Mira peered at the battered, bullet-scarred sign that had once welcomed visitors to historic Fort Taber.

Now the site was weed choked, dense with thickets and bramble. Up ahead, the concrete-block building was a forbidding stronghold, all but obscured by dark foliage and tangled vines. Kellan drove up on it and circled around the side, killing the headlights as they approached the yawning black maw of the fortress's entrance. He rolled into the darkness. Small lights came on deep inside, illuminating what appeared to be the interior of an old, unused gun battery. Up ahead was the black van that had been used to abduct Jeremy Ackmeyer and her.

"Not much of a fleet garage," Mira remarked, turning a sardonic look on Kellan.

"We don't have the Order's deep pockets." He came to a stop near the van and threw the Jeep's brake. "We have to scrape and work for what we have—meager as it is."

He said it not with accusation or complaint, merely fact. But there was the barest note of humility in his voice, and it left her to wonder if he was embarrassed in some way, if he had felt compelled to make excuses to her for the way he and his followers lived.

Kellan swung out of the vehicle and walked around to instruct her to do the same. Given little choice, Mira followed him into the gloom of the place. "Maybe it would be easier for you to find patrons if you did nobler work."

He scoffed, wheeling around on her. "You think we couldn't find people willing to fund our missions if we wanted to? We don't answer to anyone. We see things that shouldn't be going on, and we stop them. We don't dance on command or worry about stepping on delicate political toes. Not even the Order can say that anymore."

"Missions?" Mira tossed back at him. "The Order doesn't go around abducting civilians or disrupting diplomatic assemblies. The Order doesn't sabotage peace talks or appoint themselves the world's judge and jury whenever it suits them."

"Maybe they should." Kellan's eyes blazed with embers of outrage in the dim light of the bunker. "We do what needs to be done, because it *must* be done."

He started to stalk ahead, away from the parked vehicles and into a wide-mouthed tunnel.

"So self-righteous," she called after him. "I hope you're willing to die for your convictions."

He pivoted now and stormed back to her, his expression dark, thoughtful, even as his irises radiated with amber fire. "Yeah, I guess I am willing to die for what I believe in. Don't tell me you wouldn't be too."

She stood there, unable to argue. He knew her too well to believe any denial she tried to fling at him. Nor did he give her the chance. His fingers clamped down around her wrist and he hauled her after him, through the black tunnel and up a gradual incline, into another bunker. She recognized this one as the rebel base's living quarters.

EDGE *of* DAWN | 69

Kellan's crew was in the sparsely furnished, cavernous main room of the place. Candice was cleaning firearms with the man called Vince and the other one they'd called Chaz. Doc was seated at a weathered metal table, eating from a tin that looked to be old MRE military rations. Straddling a backward-facing chair beside him was a blueberry-haired waif with multiple facial and ear piercings. Her fingers were flying over the touchpad of a tablet computer, not skipping even the smallest beat, when she and the rest of the rebels turned their heads to gape at Kellan and his obviously unexpected companion.

Candice was the first to find her voice. "Um . . . everything okay, boss?"

He gave a curt nod, his hand still fastened tightly around Mira's wrist. "I'm altering course a bit. There's nothing to be gained from re-leasing one of our captives right now. So, I've decided she stays."

Vince scowled. "You think that's wise, considering who she is and all? We keep one of their own, it could make us a target of the Order."

Kellan's reply was swift and without inflection. "We're already a tar-get of the Order. As soon as word reaches them—which is only a matter of time, hours at most—we become enemies of Lucan Thorne and his warriors."

Vince considered, raking thick fingers through his shaggy dishwater blond hair. Then he nodded as if suddenly understanding, an unfriendly smile tugging at the corner of his mouth. "In other words, you think we may need some leverage with the Order. Some kind of bargaining chip if things go south with Ackmeyer?"

Kellan growled, pinning his man with a lethal, amber-bright glare. "This female—this warrior," he said, addressing Vince and the others together, "is mine alone to deal with. She stays under my watch and under my handling only. Understood?"

An immediate and unanimous chorus of murmured agreement an-swered him, but Kellan was already moving on with Mira in tow. He led her away from his rebel crew and into his private quarters. Mira didn't have to ask if the modest chamber belonged to Kellan; she could smell his scent all around her, the dark, spicy warmth that had long ago been branded into all of her senses.

He closed the door behind them and finally released his hold on her. "If you cooperate with me, Mira, I will not feel it necessary to restrain you."

"I'm touched," she said, glowering at him as she watched him pull a blanket off the lone bed and toss it to the floor.

"But if you make a move to escape," he went on, not missing a beat, "or if you attempt to interfere with my mission goals in any way, I will put you in a cell until this is over."

She studied him as he spoke so stiffly, watched his robotic movements and the way his eyes never lit on her for more than the most fleeting instant. He hated being a party to this, maybe as much as she did. But only he held the power to end it.

"It's not too late to stop this now, Kellan. Obviously your friends are on edge about this crime they've committed, afraid of what the Order will do. They should be afraid. Treason charges are a capital offense, carrying a capital penalty. You have to know that."

Kellan didn't answer, but she watched a tendon tick furiously in his rigid jaw.

"You can release Ackmeyer to my custody before it goes any further." She took a deep breath, still trying to process how it was possible that she could be standing in front of Kellan Archer, pleading with him to turn himself in as a rebel mastermind, before he died a second time. "Release Jeremy Ackmeyer and me tonight, Kellan, and I will tell Lucan and the GNC that you were remorseful. That you and your followers treated us well."

He swung an arch look at her, one dark brow quirked in bleak humor. "Not much of a bargain from where I'm standing."

Mira gave a slow shake of her head. The ache in her breast was sharp at the thought of Kellan facing charges, but what he'd done—even so far—could not be excused without some kind of recompense. "Lucan will be fair, you know that. As fair as he can be."

Kellan grunted. "And if Ackmeyer should die?"

Panic arrowed through her. "You said you didn't kill him. That you wouldn't—"

"If he agrees to my terms," Kellan reminded her. "But if he doesn't . . ."

Mira's throat constricted at the mercenary tone of his voice. "If you don't get what you want from him, you'll have no qualms about killing him in cold blood."

"To save thousands, maybe millions of other lives?" Kellan nodded. "I've killed for less than that under the banner of war. So have you."

"But this isn't war, not yet." Mira stormed toward him, finding it all but impossible to resist pounding her fists against his broad chest. She steeled herself against the urge to strike at him, if only because she knew that touching him—even in anger—would only tempt her toward something more. Something she could not afford to feel for him, not now. Not ever again. "It doesn't have to be war, Kellan. Not if you stop this, right here and now. It's not too late—"

His snarled curse abruptly cut her off. "It *is* too late. It was too late months ago, when this all began."

He cursed again, more savagely this time, and stormed over to a trunk at the foot of the bed. He dropped down on his haunches, yanked the lock off in his hand, and threw open the lid. "You'll need a change of clothes at some point." He tossed a folded T-shirt at her, followed by a pair of his well-worn sweats. "If you need anything else that I don't have, Candice will get it for you."

"When what began?" Mira asked, inching toward him. "You said this all began months ago. What happened?"

He rose, standing face-to-face with her now. "How much do you know about Jeremy Ackmeyer?"

Mira shook her head. "Beyond his basic résumé? Not much." She gave an abbreviated list of his scientific achievements and accolades as best she could recall. Kellan didn't flinch or react, apparently hearing nothing that surprised him. "And obviously you're well aware that he's been tapped to receive a big cash award from Reginald Crowe at the summit gala in a few days."

She watched his lack of reaction and realized something now. "This isn't about political dissent or disrupting the peace summit, is it? You said Ackmeyer has something you want . . ."

Kellan held her searching gaze, his eyes no longer bright with amber fury but banked and cooling, the level hazel that always seemed to bore straight through to the core of her being. "Three months ago in New York City, a Darkhaven male was gunned down in the street by human thugs. An innocent Breed civilian, killed without warning or cause, by men who drove away in a government vehicle."

Mira thought back, frowning, skeptical. "There have been no such killings, certainly not that recent. It would've made headlines. Hell, it would still be in the news."

"No body. No witnesses," Kellan replied. "Or so they thought."

"What do you mean?"

"A woman saw the whole thing. She watched it from her apartment window over the alley where the murder occurred." Kellan's expression was grim. "There was no body because it was ashed on the spot, Mira. The rounds these human bastards shot him with were made of super-concentrated UV light, converted to liquid form. They were bullets made for the express purpose of killing vampires."

Mira considered for a moment, then gave an incredulous laugh. "Come on, Kellan. You can do better than this. Government assassins using liquid UV rounds? That kind of technology is pure science fiction. It doesn't exist."

"Doesn't it?"

"No," she insisted. "For one thing, it breaches the ban on potentially catastrophic armaments. It would never get past the GNC for approval. For another, the Order would personally never permit that kind of weaponry to be developed. They would destroy it before they'd let something as potentially devastating as UV bullets come into existence."

He shrugged, unconvinced. "And yet it has been, obviously."

"Then prove it."

He said nothing, merely dug into the pocket of his dark jeans and withdrew a spent bullet casing. "The woman recovered this from the ashes of the dead vampire. He was her lover. She said he didn't have any enemies, was just walking home before sunrise when the humans accosted him, started provoking him with anti-Breed slurs, then shot him dead like an animal. Worse than that."

Mira swallowed past the anger in her throat as she looked at the unmarked, spent round and pictured the horror of what the woman who loved that Darkhaven male must have felt, seeing him killed before her eyes.

"She didn't know who to trust or where to go," Kellan said. "So she came to us."

"Who is she?"

"You saw her in the other room a few minutes ago—Nina. She's a friend of Candice's, now one of my team."

Mira shook her head, trying to absorb everything she was hearing. "Are you trying to tell me that Jeremy Ackmeyer is responsible for this somehow?"

Kellan took the bullet casing from her and slipped it back into his pocket. "It's his technology. It took all this time, but we finally traced the tech back to Ackmeyer. We'd been planning to raid his lab, but the place is a fortress—even more so than his home. But then word arrived that Ackmeyer would be on the move. He was expecting a security escort at his house."

"Me," Mira said, feeling like a pawn.

"We had to act quickly," Kellan explained. "I didn't know Ackmeyer was expecting an escort detail from the Order. It was a daytime op, and with roughly ninety-nine percent of the Order's warriors being strictly night patrol—"

"Who gave you the intel?"

Kellan stared at her. "We have our sources around the city."

"Rooster," she guessed, then barked out a humorless laugh when he didn't deny it.

"The guy is garbage," Kellan admitted, "but he serves his purpose."

"Did you know he was the reason I was assigned to escort duty with Ackmeyer?" She pursed her lips, gave a vague shake of her head. "It was punishment from Lucan, for skewering the little redheaded bastard down in the cage arena at La Notte. I should've aimed for his heart."

Kellan arched a brow. "You really hate him."

"I hate every rebel," she said sharply. "I hate them for what they took from me."

Kellan met and held her simmering stare. When he finally spoke, his voice was sober, deep with regret but not apology. "And now you count me in that number too."

"I never wanted us to be enemies, Kellan. You've done that, not me. You're making certain of it right now, and only you can change that fact."

She watched him, waited for him to tell her it was all a terrible mistake and he would fix it. That he loved her, still, and somehow, together, they would find a way through this dark trap that was closing in on them with sharp, lethal teeth.

But he didn't say any of those things.

"I'll ask you to remember what I said about trying to escape or attempting to interfere with my operation. I don't want this to be any harder on you than it already is, Mira."

She steeled herself to the remorse in his voice, focusing instead on the fact that nothing she'd said had convinced him to change his mind. He was lost to her, as much now as he had been eight years ago.

"Spare me your pity, *Bowman*. I don't need it. I don't need anything from you."

He looked at her for a long moment, then conceded with a vague nod and left her alone in his room while he stepped out and summoned his rebel troops for a strategy meeting.

It was after midnight and no one had heard from Mira. Word out of D.C. was Lucan was pissed over her neglect to check in from her assignment, but when Nathan heard she was out of contact all day, he'd a cold suspicion that something was terribly wrong. Which was why he had assembled his team that same night and headed to rural western Massachusetts, where Jeremy Ackmeyer lived.

What they'd found at the reclusive scientist's home was a whole lot of bad news and trouble.

The moonlit lawn was scarred with deep tire gouges and shattered headlight glass. Burned rubber had left the paved driveway streaked with black. Half a dozen spent casings littered the ground from what Nathan could only guess was Mira's Order-issued 9-mm.

No sign of her or her vehicle.

No sign of Jeremy Ackmeyer.

"Nothing's tossed inside, but we do have signs of a struggle," Elijah drawled. His face was grave in the darkness as he and Jax rounded the front of the house and approached Nathan near the open garage bay. "Whoever they were, these guys knew exactly what they came for, and they wasted no time getting the hell out once they had it."

"And now they have Mira." Nathan's voice betrayed none of the fury that seethed inside him at the thought of one of the Order's own having fallen into apparent enemy hands. That it was Mira, a female as close to him as any family could be, made his blood run cold and quick in veins.

"Hey, Captain," Rafe called to him grimly from across the side lawn, where the worst of the skirmish seemed to have taken place. "You'd better have a look at this."

Nathan walked over, his nostrils filling with the chemical stench of leaked fuel and vehicle fluids. Another scent drifted on the warm night air too—faint and fading, the lily-sweet perfume of Mira's blood.

Small droplets stained the grass and torn-up ground. Nathan hunkered down on the fouled lawn, brushed his fingers over the drying splatters of the Breedmate warrior's blood at his feet. Mira had been injured, but he would bet all he was that she hadn't gone down without a fight.

"She must've dropped this in the scuffle," Rafe said, holding a slender, hammered-metal object out to Nathan.

He didn't have to look to know what it was.

One of Mira's treasured blades.

Nathan took the hand-tooled dagger from Rafe's grasp. The carved hilt was rough against his fingertips. He turned it over in his palm, reading the words that graced each side of the intricately crafted weapon: *Faith. Courage.*

He knew Mira had no shortage of the latter. As for the other, he was certainly no fair judge of that. Nathan operated on logic and strength, skills he'd mastered as a child being reared in a madman's assassin ranks. Faith was as elusive to him as magic. In his worldview, it simply did not exist.

But he knew hope. And through his cool logic, he knew a colder fury. He felt it build inside him as he slid Mira's beloved dagger into his weapons belt.

She would survive; he knew that. She would fight the bastards who took her today—whoever they were, whatever their reasons—and her courage would keep her alive, long enough for the Order to reach her.

And when they did, Nathan would see to it that whoever took her suffered.

Before he made them pay for this day with their miserable lives.

8

KELLAN PACED THE MAIN CHAMBER OF THE REBEL BUNKER, FEEL-
ing a twitch in his bones that told him dawn was rising outside the thick
concrete walls. His crew dispersed hours ago, gone about their daily
duties of replenishing the camp's food stores, refueling vehicles, tending
to weaponry and general maintenance of the base's solar power panels
and grounds.

Morning for their Breed commander usually meant a couple of hours
of undisturbed shut-eye, but Kellan would get no sleep today. Not with
Mira stowed away in his quarters.

His blood was still running hot from his confrontation with her . . .
to say nothing of the kiss that had been unplanned but unstoppable. A
kiss his libido was all too eager to repeat. And Kellan knew that if he let
himself get that close to her again—if he let himself touch her, even in
some small way—it would be only a matter of time before he found a
way to get her naked beneath him.

Bad, bad idea.

But damn, did the thought of it make everything male inside him
stand at full attention.

He hadn't returned to his room all night. No, he'd conveniently
called rank and sent Candice in his place. She'd looked in on Mira a few
times during the evening, made sure she had water and something to
eat, took her to the bunker latrine the humans shared so she could use
the toilet and shower. Candice had reported back that Mira seemed
cooperative enough, but her eyes never stopped taking stock of her sur-

roundings, studying every corner of the place as Candice led her through the fortress at gunpoint.

God, it killed him to have to treat Mira like this, to drag her into the crossfire of a battle he'd never wanted to fight. One he dreaded he might not survive in the end, let alone win. And now the woman who'd once mattered to him more than anything was sitting behind the locked door of his chamber, hating him. Wishing him dead for good this time.

As far as fucked-up scenarios went, he couldn't imagine how things could possibly get any worse.

There was a weak part of him that wanted nothing more than to go to her now and ask her forgiveness. Try to make her understand that this was not what he wanted. It was, in fact, the very thing he'd wanted to avoid. All these years, all this time, of distancing himself from everyone who'd ever cared about him, everyone he'd ever loved.

But he hadn't gone far enough.

He couldn't outrun fate, and now here it was, striking him hard across the face.

Kellan swore viciously under his breath and stalked out of the main room of the rebel bunker. He resisted the temptation to seek Mira out, instead turning his boots in the direction of the holding cell deep in the bowels of the old fortress.

Since he was stoked up and aggressive, he couldn't think of a better time to pay a visit to the individual who truly deserved some of his menace. Jeremy Ackmeyer sat in the dank darkness of a ten-by-ten-foot cube of windowless concrete block. A heavy iron grate was secured with a key lock, the cell's bars rusted from age but impenetrable. Not that Ackmeyer seemed intent to try them.

Thin and wiry, a gangly young man dressed in sagging jeans and a dated plaid button-down shirt, Jeremy Ackmeyer stood motionless in the center of his prison. Long, mousy-brown hair drooped onto his forehead and over his thick glasses. Ackmeyer's head was slumped low, slender arms wrapped around himself, hands tucked in close. He glanced up warily but said nothing as Kellan approached the bars.

The tray of food Candice had brought him hours ago lay untouched on the cell's concrete bench. Of course, calling the tin-canned MRE slop food was probably a stretch. Not that Kellan or his kind had any experience with human dietary preferences.

"What's the matter, Ackmeyer? Rebel menu choices not to your liking?" Kellan's low voice echoed off the walls of the place, dark with animosity. "Maybe your tastes are a little too rich for such common fare."

The human's eyes blinked once behind the distorting lenses of his glasses. He swallowed hard, larynx bobbing. "I'm not hungry. I'd like to get out of this cell. It reeks of mildew and there is black mold growing in the corner."

Kellan smirked. "I'll fire the housekeeper immediately."

"It's terribly unhealthy. Toxic, in fact," Ackmeyer went on, seeming more frightened than arrogant. He shifted on his feet, his movements awkward, anxious. Less the diabolical scientist than a nervous, confused child. "It's airborne poison. Do you realize the spores reproduce exponentially by the millions? Deadly dangerous spores that you and I are breathing into our lungs right this very second. So, please . . . if you would, unlock this cell and let me out."

Kellan stared, incredulous that the man seemed more terrified of microscopic bacteria than the other, more obvious threat facing him now. If it was an act, the guy was a first-rate player. "You're not going anywhere until I say so. Which means you'll have to either hold your breath or learn to make quick peace with your neuroses."

Ackmeyer shrank back at Kellan's clipped tone. He fidgeted with the hem of his untucked shirt, his thin brows pulled into a frown. "What about the woman?"

"What about her?" Kellan growled.

"She was at my house when everything happened. I heard her calling to me just before I was knocked unconscious." He glanced up, brown eyes soft with worried regard. "Is she . . . okay?"

"She is none of your concern." Kellan approached closer to the iron grate, peering at Ackmeyer through the bars. He barked a laugh, caustic and rough in the quiet of the bunker. "You'd like me to think you care about another person, wouldn't you? If you're looking for mercy, you won't get any from me."

Ackmeyer blinked rapidly, gave a vague shake of his head. "You are free to feel however you wish. Since the attack occurred at my home, I assume this has to do with me, not the woman."

"A brilliant observation," Kellan snarled. "Care to venture a guess as to why you now find yourself sitting in front of me in a locked, mold-riddled cell inside this rebel bunker?"

Ackmeyer slowly met his gaze, but a tremble shook his scrawny body. "I suspect you plan to either ransom me or kill me."

"I'm not looking to get rich off the blood of another man," Kellan replied coolly. "Are you?"

"No." Ackmeyer's answer was instant, filled with conviction. "No, I would never do that. Life is precious—"

Kellan's coarse scoff cut his words short. "So long as that life doesn't belong to one of the Breed, right?"

He knew his eyes were on fire. The amber heat of his contempt for this human's destructive genius was bleeding into his vision, turning his world red as he glared through the thick metal cage—the meager barrier that separated Kellan from lashing out at the scientist with fists and fangs.

Ackmeyer saw that threat full and real now. He backed farther into the cell, realizing if only just in that moment exactly what he was dealing with here. "I-I don't know what you're talking about, I swear!"

"No?" Kellan's voice was a gravel-filled snarl. "I have evidence to prove otherwise."

The human shook his head frantically. "You're mistaken! I'm a man of science. I respect all life as the natural miracle it is."

Kellan gave a dark chuckle. "Even an abomination like me, like my kind?"

"Y-yes," Ackmeyer sputtered, then suddenly realized what he'd said. "I mean no! That's not what I was trying to say, I—I just mean to say that there is something very wrong here. Whatever offense you think I've committed against you, I swear I'm innocent. There's been some kind of mistake. A terrible mistake . . ."

As much as he wanted to dismiss the human's protests as the desperate denials of a cold, profiteering killer, something unsettling began to unfurl within Kellan's gut. Something that put him on the edge of a deeply disturbing realization.

That something was an earnestness that made him peer at Jeremy Ackmeyer a bit closer, searching for some trace of the lie he was certain had to be there.

With a flick of his mind's power, Kellan released the lock on the barred door of the cell and mentally pushed the metal grate open. Ackmeyer cowered, scuttling back toward the far wall until his rail-thin spine was up against the mold-streaked concrete blocks. Kellan strode inside the dank cell, crowding the human. Moving forward until he loomed over him.

"You want to know why you're here?" He stared down at Ackmeyer, seeing the young man's face take on a hot amber glow in the blaze of Kellan's irises. "It's because of the Breed-killing ultraviolet technology you created."

Ackmeyer shook his head, his voice evidently gone mute with fear now.

"You're here because that UV tech was used to ash a Darkhaven civilian on the street a few months ago. Liquid sunlight, just the kind of equalizer your species would kill to have." Kellan kept talking, ignoring the tears that sprang into the human's widened eyes. "Are you going to stand there and deny that you had any part in this?"

"I don't know what you're talking about. Have I discovered a means of harnessing UV light and converting it to liquid? Yes. It's one of several prototypes I've been working on under my Morningstar project. But none of my data or models has been released to the public. And they're all light-bringing technologies, not weapons. The project's chief purpose is to benefit the planet, to revolutionize energy consumption—"

"They used to say the same thing about nuclear power." Kellan growled. "I don't have time for bullshit. Who'd you sell the tech to?"

"No one!" Ackmeyer dissolved into a shaking, hiccupping lump on the floor of the cell. "It's not even out of testing yet. And besides, I've never sold any of my work for profit. I've certainly never created anything with the purpose of inflicting harm on someone. If anyone claims they have it—if someone has used my work, as you say—they must've stolen it. You have to believe me! You have to trust me when I tell you that I've done nothing wrong!"

No, he didn't have to believe him. Nor did he have to trust.

Kellan had a much more reliable tool at his disposal than ordinary intuition.

He reached out and palmed Ackmeyer's trembling skull.

The jolt of understanding came swiftly, irrefutably.

Kellan's Breed talent stripped through the human's intentions, drilling straight to the core of truth hidden deep within Jeremy Ackmeyer's soul. All Kellan found was honesty, the purest of motivations. The absence of any guilt whatsoever.

Holy hell.

Kellan drew his hand back as if burned. The realization sank in like bitter acid, corrosive and impossible to scrape off now that it had touched him.

Jeremy Ackmeyer had been telling him the truth. He had no idea his work had been used as a weapon for assassination against the Breed.

Kellan had ordered the kidnapping of an honest, innocent man.

"Anything more I should know about the situation?" Lucan Thorne's grim face filled the flat-screen monitor on the wall of the Boston Command Center.

He hadn't been pleased to hear Nathan's report from the field, but where the Gen One leader of the Order had every right to swear and bellow over the simple escort mission gone so terribly wrong, he clearly struggled to accept the fact that one of the Order's own had gone missing from an assignment. That it was Mira, a female raised by the Order from the time she was a child, made the gravity of the loss all the more difficult to deal with objectively, not only for Lucan, but for Nathan and the other pair of Order members gathered with him in the private conference room that morning.

Sterling Chase, the Breed warrior who'd helmed the Boston operation for the past two decades, sat soberly in the room beside his mate, Tavia, his big hand resting over her slender fingers on the table. Tavia accepted the tender gesture, despite that she was no delicate Darkhaven lady, sheltered from the realities of the world.

Born in the same laboratory, of the same alien DNA that had spawned Nathan and a small army of assassins bred and raised just like him, Tavia was an awe-inspiring rarity among the race: a genetically crafted, Gen One female, and a daywalker besides. Where Nathan would perish after minutes of exposure to UV light, his half sister Tavia and her offspring—a set of fraternal twins named Aric and Carys—could sunbathe all day in the tropics without breaking a sweat.

"If anything's happened to Mira," Tavia murmured, her leaf-green eyes sparking with flecks of amber, "if she's harmed in any way—"

"We'll find her," Nathan assured them all. "I won't rest until she and the human scientist are located."

On the monitor, Lucan nodded his dark head. "I know we can count on you. That's why I'm giving this whole thing to you as a solo assignment. It's crucial that we keep this problem out of the public eye. I want a lid clamped down tight on this, and I want the bastards dealt with cleanly and permanently. Your training makes you ideal for this kind of surgical precision job, Nathan."

He inclined his head in acknowledgment. "I will do whatever it takes."

"I know." Lucan's gray gaze bore into him through the video screen. "You have my permission to remove any and all obstacles in order to meet your mission objectives. If there's fallout afterward, I'll take sole responsibility for the op."

Nathan held the Gen One's grave stare. "It will not be necessary."

"Nikolai and Renata will need to be informed about this," Chase said, his thumb stroking idly over the back of Tavia's hand. "There'll be nothing to keep them from joining the search."

"Nothing, except the fact that Renata is pregnant and due very soon," Tavia pointed out. "But Chase is right. They need to know, Lucan. Mira's their daughter."

The Order's founder pressed his lips together in a flat line but acceded with a sober nod. "It's not the kind of news any parent should hear," he remarked woodenly, the lines of his face seeming more pronounced as he considered the advice. "Gabrielle and I will make the call to them together, as soon as we finish here." To Nathan he said, "This is a kill op. I don't want any of these rebel bastards left standing to rise again after the dust settles. Agreed?"

Nathan accepted with a downward tip of his chin. "Yes, sir."

A few minutes later, the call was ended and Nathan left the conference room to find his team waiting outside the door. Rafe, Eli, and Jax were joined by Aric Chase, who rose as soon as Nathan came out. "What happened in there? Has Lucan assigned a team to go after these sick fucks and bring Mira back?"

The twenty-year-old son of Sterling and Tavia, Aric had trained under his father's direction alongside his best friend, Rafe. But where Rafe had finished months earlier, Aric had not yet been inducted as a full-fledged member of the Order. In a few weeks, he would get his chance, leaving the East Coast for Seattle, to be assigned as a newly minted warrior on one of Dante's teams in that district.

Nathan did not respond to the recruit's rookie question, and the rest of his team knew better than to prod for answers about a private conference with Lucan Thorne. The other Breed males followed Nathan as he set off toward the corridor that would take him to the command center's training facility.

"Damn, I wish Lucan had tasked me with escorting Ackmeyer to that summit gathering," Aric said, falling in with the rest of them. "I would've made sure those *Homo sapiens* sons of bitches OD'd on lead and steel. Let them take on a Breed in the daytime and watch the rebel cowards piss themselves a river of please-god-save-us."

Even Nathan had to admit the idea held some amusement. He felt grim humor tug at his mouth as the banter between his fellow warriors continued, each of them ratcheting up the fear factor on the pain and terror they'd like to deliver on the bastards who'd taken Mira.

As they cuffed one another and slung good-natured insults, Nathan held himself apart from the pack with a remoteness that came as naturally to him as breathing. He had let a friend—a brother-in-arms—into his life once, and the loss when Kellan died had been as visceral as a limb torn from his body. These other warriors were his team, his comrades, but he'd learned better than to let himself care for them beyond their role as soldiers under his command.

And now Mira was gone too.

If she didn't come home whole and unharmed, he wasn't sure how he would handle it.

No, he mentally corrected.

He'd been trained the first thirteen years of his life to shut out all emotion, to steel himself to caring for anything but his master's commands. If things went badly for Mira, he would draw on the harsh lessons of his upbringing to get him through.

But first he would kill her captors. Every last one of them.

His mind was already preparing for the covert mission he would begin as soon as the sun set. So much so that it took him a moment to realize there had been a shift in the air temperature up ahead in the corridor. The source of that change appeared a moment later, in the form of Carys Chase, ducking out of a room off the long hallway. The crisp scent of morning rushed in behind her, clinging to her caramel-brown hair and the form-fitting black blouse and leg-hugging skinny jeans that disappeared into the tops of spiked ankle boots.

"Carys?" Aric stopped in his tracks in the corridor, gaping at his twin sister. "What the hell are you doing?"

Nathan and his team had paused now too, all of them staring at the beautiful young Breed female as she sauntered toward them, attempting nonchalance. Slender brows arched slyly over sparkling blue eyes fringed in long black lashes. "What does it look like I'm doing, big brother?"

Aric's scowl deepened. "It looks like you just dragged yourself in through a back window of the estate after staying out all night doing god knows what."

She laughed. "Good lord, Aric, you sound just like Father. Besides, since when did having fun with friends become a crime?"

"It's not safe out there, Car. Not for a woman alone, without someone to protect her."

Nathan shot a quelling look at Aric Chase, a subtle warning not to divulge the details of what had happened to Mira and the human scientist, nor the Order's suspicion that rebels were to blame for their disappearance. Aric caught the silencing glance and had the good sense to cool his jets.

"I told you, I wasn't alone," Carys insisted. "Jordana Gates and I met some other friends in the North End. It was perfectly safe."

Aric's jaw went tight in response, but he kept his argument to himself. "I just worry about you, that's all. I don't want to see you get hurt."

She gave him a warm smile. "I know that. And while I may be female, big brother, I'm also Breed, as strong as any of you males. Just because I'm not combat-trained like you, don't think I'm incapable of taking care of myself." Studying her brother's disapproving expression, Carys caught her bottom lip between her teeth and looked up at him from beneath her long black lashes. "You're not going to tell Mother and Father about this, are you?"

"I should," Aric said. "I'm sure Father would be very interested to talk to Jordana's parents too. I doubt the venerable Gates clan of Beacon Hill would be happy to hear their Breedmate daughter was traipsing all over the city, staying out until dawn."

"But you won't tell," she said, smooth and coaxing, yet Nathan was certain he'd detected a note of worry creeping into Carys's bright blue eyes at the mention of her Darkhaven friend. Carys moved closer to her brother and rested her palms on his chest. "You won't tell on me, Aric. And in return, I won't tell Mother and Father about the trio of dancers you and Rafe shared at a Chinatown sim-lounge last weekend."

"How did you hear about that?" Aric practically choked the words out, but Raphael merely grinned, a slow curve of his mouth that showed absolutely zero repentance. "Who the hell do you hang out with that you would hear about something like that?"

"You have your little secrets," Carys chided with a smile and an arch look, "and I have mine. Let's agree to keep it that way, shall we?"

She rose up and gave her brother a peck on the cheek, then she was on her way, tossing a wave at Nathan and the others as she pivoted on her tall heels and strode up the corridor.

While his warrior brethren resumed their trek for the training facility, Nathan felt his instincts prickle with a vague but undeniable suspicion. He turned a curious look behind him at Carys. The retreating female glanced his way, a quick, cautious glimpse over her shoulder, before she picked up her pace and disappeared around a curve in the long hallway.

9

MIRA WOKE UP FROM AN EXHAUSTED SLEEP, THE WARM, SPICY scent of Kellan all around her. At first she thought it belonged to her dreams—dark, seductive dreams, where he was not her enemy but the lover she'd yearned to touch again, the only man she'd ever wanted.

But it wasn't a dream that filled her senses now. It was reality. Kellan's cold and empty bed, she all alone in his locked quarters in the rebel base he commanded.

Mira sat up, pushed her tangled hair out of her eyes. The room was quiet. He hadn't returned since he'd left her there the night before. The blanket he'd put down for himself on the floor was right where he'd dropped it, the makeshift sleeping area undisturbed.

Where was he? Since he hadn't come back to his own quarters, where had he chosen to spend the night?

Maybe with one of the pretty human women under his command. Candice, with her easy smile and nurturing, competent hands. Or the indigo-haired sprite, Nina, with her sad eyes and pixie-cute face. A pang of jealous suspicion shot through Mira, uninvited and bitter with an acid bite.

She didn't need to wonder who Kellan wanted to spend his nights with. He wasn't hers to worry about. He wouldn't be ever again.

And maybe he never truly was, if leaving her behind had come so easily to him.

Her heart wanted to deny that, but her head was still struggling to make sense of the fact that Kellan had been alive all this time—living just outside Boston in this new, lawless life he'd created for himself as someone else entirely. He'd never tried to reach her. Never cared enough to end her grief and tell her that he was safe—even if that gesture would come with the sting of learning who he'd become. He had simply walked away and never looked back.

The hurt in her chest cracked open wider, but she refused to let it break her.

And she shouldn't give a damn who Kellan—or, rather, Bowman— decided to share a bed with, so long as it wasn't her.

Mira swung her bare legs over the edge of the mattress and poured herself a glass of water from the tumbler Candice had left on the bedside table. Her contact lenses sat in a small dish of saline solution, also courtesy of the pretty, raven-haired woman. Mira put them in, then downed her glass of water, grateful for both kindnesses Kellan's rebel comrade had provided her.

Mira rubbed a damp chill from her arms as she put her feet on the cold floor. She was wearing just her panties and the extra-large T-shirt Kellan had given her out of the chest at the foot of the bed. Her bra and his borrowed sweatpants were folded over a weathered wooden chair. She was about to get up and grab them when the tumbler on the locked door clicked open.

Kellan walked in, no warning or excuse.

His gaze shot to her in his bed. For a moment, she couldn't tell if it was surprise or regret in his hazel eyes. But there was something dark in them too, something troubled and grim. He stepped inside the room and closed the door behind him.

When he spoke, his voice was coarse like gravel. "You look well rested."

Mira scrambled out of his bed, all too aware of her state of undress and too conscious of the fact that Kellan was noticing it too. "You look like hell," she told him, keeping the sarcasm ripe in her tone as she edged away from the rumpled mattress. "I hate to think you had to find another bed to sleep in, with your private quarters turned into my prison cell."

He grunted as he prowled farther into the room. "Who says I slept?"

Mira watched him, wishing it wasn't so easy to picture him warming another woman's bed. For all her mental reassurances that she shouldn't care what he did—or with whom—seeing him unrested and tense with menacing energy made anger spike in her veins. "Where have you been, Kellan?"

He barked out a caustic laugh. "Masterminding rebel business." He pinned her with a dark look, showing the gleaming tips of his fangs. "That's what I do, remember?"

Mira stared at him, taken aback by the barely restrained anger in his voice. His face was taut with aggression, the lean angles of his cheeks and goateed jaw even sharper now. Kellan was mad. Furiously mad.

She watched him stalk over to the clothing chest on the floor like he was marching to war. He stripped off his wrinkled black T-shirt with savage force, threw open the lid of the trunk. His *dermaglyphs* were livid with color. The swirling arcs and flourishes of the Breed skin markings that covered his chest and biceps churned and pulsed with stormy shades of red and black and midnight blue. Mira swallowed. "Something's happened, hasn't it? Something bad."

He exhaled sharply. "You could say that."

His gaze met hers, and now his irises were bright with amber sparks, skewering her where she stood. Mira could feel his fury rolling off him, could see it in his hot glare, as if he couldn't stand the sight of her today.

"Aren't you going to tell me what's wrong?" she asked, refusing to be cowed. "You can talk to me, Kellan—"

"Talk to you?" he snarled. "I don't want to talk. I need to think. This is my problem. You're not a part of it."

"I am a part of it, whether you like it or not," she reminded him. "Whether either one of us likes it or not, you've made me a part of this."

He slammed the chest lid down so hard, it echoed like a cannon shot. He came up out of his crouch in an instant—less than that—and was standing right in front of her before she could take her next breath. Less than a hand's width separated them; she was close enough to feel the heat radiating from his every pore.

The *glyphs* that had been pulsing with the furious hues of Kellan's anger and frustration a few moments ago now deepened. There was still rage in them, but Mira watched the colors morph toward need and something darker as Kellan crowded her with the massive bulk of his body. His fangs seemed enormous, as sharp as daggers behind the menacing curl of his lip.

"You want me to tell you how badly I fucked up, going after Jeremy Ackmeyer?" Kellan's eyes blazed as hot as coals as he spoke, his pupils reduced to thin slivers of black in the middle of so much amber fire. He went on, his words vicious with self-directed fury. "You want to hear how I've grabbed an innocent, decent man—a man who wouldn't harm a fly, much less another person?"

Mira tried to process what he was telling her, but hearing his torment, she could hardly breathe. Dark emotion played across his face, turning his handsome features stark and fierce.

A low snarl curled up from the back of his throat. "You want me to explain how my orders will mean a certain death sentence for Candice and Doc and the rest of my crew if I don't figure a way to straighten this shit out?"

Mira's heart was pounding in her ears. She wanted to touch him, comfort him somehow, but she held herself in check, focusing instead on the truth of what he'd just said. "Jeremy Ackmeyer is innocent?" She searched Kellan's face, braving the enraged heat of his glare. "I thought you traced the UV tech back to his lab."

Kellan answered with a growl. "The tech is his. Ackmeyer didn't release it to anyone, not for money or otherwise. Someone stole the technology from him."

"He told you this?"

Kellan nodded. "And I read the truth of it when I touched him. He's innocent, Mira."

"You have to let him go," Mira murmured. Now she did reach out to Kellan, turning his face toward her when he tried to dodge her gaze. His jaw was rigid in her palm, a tendon ticking hard against her fingertips. "You have to release him. Take him straight to the Order and tell Lucan what you've discovered about the UV tech and the killing of Nina's lover."

He looked at her for a long moment, then exhaled a curse, shook his head.

"We can do it together, Kellan." Mira searched his blazing eyes, determined to convince him. "We'll go tonight, as soon as the sun sets. We'll fix it, Kellan."

His answering scoff was brittle as he flinched away from her touch. "I can no more do that now than I could before I realized Ackmeyer was innocent."

"Yes, you can. This changes everything—"

Kellan's eyes blazed even brighter. "It changes nothing. I'm still guilty of kidnapping and conspiracy. The GNC won't care what my reasons were for taking a human civilian hostage. Do you really think the Order will, especially when they learn where I've been all these years, what I've been doing?"

"Then we'll make them understand," Mira said, not even sure herself how they might accomplish that, but damn it, she was determined to try. All she needed was Kellan to agree. "We'll go to Lucan together and explain everything. There has to be a way. Once they see Jeremy Ackmeyer is free and unharmed, they'll be willing to listen, Kellan."

He stared at her for a long moment, considering, she hoped. But the look on his face was hard, unyieldingly so. "You're right about one thing, Mira. I have to release him. I'll release both of you. But not until my crew has a chance to dismantle our base and find shelter somewhere else. I need to know they'll be safe too, after all of this is over."

He stepped away from her, about to turn around and leave. Mira took hold of his arm. "What about you? Where does all of this leave you?"

She didn't like the flinty look in his glowing eyes. "Don't worry about me. This time I'll do what I couldn't before."

"What do you mean?"

He touched her face, so gently it threatened to break her heart all over again. "I'll put as much distance as possible between us. This time, I promise, I'll make sure our paths can never cross again."

The vow struck her like a physical blow. Now she was the one seething with fury—instant, blood-boiling fury. "You selfish son of a bitch! Don't you dare pretend you're doing this for me."

"It's the truth," he stated flatly. "I don't want to hurt you, Mouse. I never wanted that."

Unable to contain the hurt and anger that was raging in her, Mira slapped him, hard across the face. "I want nothing more than to hurt you now," she seethed. She pounded her fists against his strong, naked chest, wishing she had a blade in her grasp. "I want you to hurt like this too, damn you. I would make you bleed if I could!"

Kellan calmly caught her punishing hands, tucking them into a tender hold between their bodies. If he had grabbed her with force, she would have railed against him with all she was worth. She wanted that excuse. She wanted to curse and strike and hate him for this moment and all the others that had brought her so much heartache because of him.

But Kellan's touch was gentle. His face was sober, eyes full of heat and regret as he bent his head down and kissed the white knuckles on both of her clenched fists.

Mira's body heaved with impotent fury. She wanted to scream at him, but all that slipped past her lips was a choked little moan. She couldn't move, could hardly pull air into her raw lungs, as Kellan's gaze bored into hers. His grasp loosened, and he reached out to smooth his fingers along the side of her face, tracing past the tiny teardrop-and-crescent-moon birthmark that rode at her left temple.

His breath left him on a whispered curse as he put his mouth to her forehead and pressed a kiss there, his trim beard gently abrading her brow. Another kiss to her Breedmate mark . . . then still another, this one landing softly, sweetly on her parted lips.

She wanted to tell him no, but everything female within her responded to his kiss with melting, undeniable welcome. His lips brushed over hers, warm and wet, making her thirst for something more. She darted her tongue out to meet his and felt his strong body go tense against her. He broke away only for a moment, just looking at her, his breath hot against her cheek with his growled curse.

His big hands trembled as he brought them up to cradle her face in his palms. So gentle. So heartbreakingly reverent. His thumb caressed the line of her jaw, then drifted down along the side of her neck, pausing over the pulse point that throbbed like a drumbeat with every careful stroke of his touch. Wordlessly, he bent forward and kissed her again.

She couldn't stop him from claiming her mouth, any more than she could stop the wild jolt of pleasure that traveled through her like liquid fire. Kellan seemed equally moved, equally helpless to keep from touching her, kissing her, desiring her as much as she craved him. His skin felt hot to her touch, his *dermaglyphs* pulsing in reaction to his body's needs. His arousal was swift and obvious, a ridge of unyielding granite pressing with demand against her abdomen. She reveled in the feel of him, so hard and wanting, so powerfully alive.

No matter what he said, he wanted her. There could be no mistaking that now. Not even the circumstances that held them apart—the untenable situation that put them on opposite sides of the law—could erase the desire they once knew. The desire that hadn't banked in all the years Kellan had been gone, no matter how badly they both might wish it had.

And he was hungered in another way too.

She felt that hunger swelling as his mouth left hers on a snarl and drifted along her jawline, then down the sensitive column of her neck. His fangs grazed her skin, sharp and deadly, a bite she craved more than her next breath. The vein beneath her earlobe went electric with each teasing abrasion of his fangs against her throat.

Desire swamped her, pulling her head to the side as his sharp kiss roamed the length of her neck. As reckless as it was to wish for it, she wanted to feel that delicious scrape linger at her carotid. She wanted to feel her tender flesh yield for him—only him—something she'd craved from him for as long as she could remember.

Something he'd resisted with an iron will that seemed unbreakable, even now.

"No," he growled, a savage, raw sound. His eyes were searingly hot, pupils razor-thin, otherworldly. He was shaking, his beautiful chest and arms livid with the colors of twining thirst and desire. And yet his hands remained on her, strong fingers trembling as they continued to caress her. "Jesus Christ, Mira . . ."

She knew he felt the same powerful pull that she did. She knew he desired her, craved her body and her blood. She knew he wanted to sink his fangs into her with the same fevered need that she felt to be the Breedmate beneath his binding bite.

God help her, she would give him that right now, right here, and to hell with everything else. Kellan would be hers, again and forever. They would figure the rest out somehow, together, bound by blood.

"Please," she whispered, not caring a damn for how weak and vulnerable she sounded. All that mattered was Kellan's hands on her, his breath warm and moist on her throat, fangs pressing deliciously against her willing flesh.

"No," he snarled, more forcefully this time. His fingers dug into her arms as he set her away from him with a gruff shake of his head. "I won't, Mira. I can't. Don't let me make a bad situation worse."

He didn't wait for her to reply. No, he didn't even give her that chance. He dropped his hands from her and backed away. Then, with a further, vicious curse, he wheeled around and stalked out of the room.

What the fuck was he thinking?

Kellan stalked out of his quarters, every nerve ending on fire and snapping at the bit for a taste of Mira. His pulse hammered hard, echoing in his ears and temples, throbbing in his chest and groin. Everything male in him was lit up with need. Everything preternatural, other-worldly and wild, was roaring with the urge to take what he so badly wanted.

Mira.

In his bed, naked and hot beneath him. He wanted to feel her wet heat swallowing him whole. Wanted to pleasure her until she screamed his name, not in anger or distress, but urgent, desperate release.

And yes, he wanted to pierce her vein and draw her lily-sweet blood into his body until nothing else mattered.

Until she was bound to him as his eternal mate, where no laws, no lies, no damnable fate could keep them apart ever again.

Holy hell.

The urge to make that a reality—right here, right now—nearly set his boots on a reverse course, back to his chamber. It took all the self-control he had to keep himself moving on his forward path. His footsteps echoed sharply on the earthen floor of the bunker's corridor. His transformed eyes threw a bright amber glow against the dingy concrete walls. His head rang with the fevered pound of his pulse, each beat a reminder of the thirst that raked him.

A thirst he knew only one woman would ever truly sate.

Unfortunately, he was Breed, and regardless of what—or whom—his heart craved, his body had needs that could not be ignored. He couldn't recall precisely the last time he'd fed. Too long by far, based on the savage state he was in now.

Kellan stalked up the dark hallway of the old fort, snarling and ripe with aggression. If it were nightfall outside, he'd break for the city and run until exhaustion purged the worst of his dual fevers. Hunting for a blood Host was easy in the thickly settled neighborhoods of Boston and its surrounding boroughs. No trick at all to find a willing and able human vein, even under the strict feeding laws and curfews imposed since First Dawn.

But it was morning beyond the thick cement walls of his rebel lair.

And he knew damn well the wait until sunset would be a torment he couldn't withstand. Not so long as Mira was under the same roof.

Not so long as everything savage and inhuman within him was hammering with the demand to seek her out again. To take her.

To keep her as his own, regardless of the hell they would both be forced to pay in the end.

He let a growl roll through his teeth and fangs as he headed for the main area of the bunker. Up ahead, he heard the soft drip of water in the shower room, the shuffle of bare feet on a wet concrete floor.

Kellan glanced inside as he reached the open entryway. Candice was seated on a stone bench in the dressing area, combing out her wet black hair. Her skin was damp under her white V-neck T-shirt, the ink of her many tattoos bleeding through the thin fabric. She glanced over her shoulder at him as he paused in the doorway.

Hazel-green eyes met his amber gaze and went wide for a second. She saw his hunger. She understood. She always had. With a mild nod, she set down her comb and made room for him beside her on the bench.

Kellan hesitated, knowing this wasn't what he wanted, not really.

Candice knew that too. He saw the understanding in her gentle eyes as she watched him hesitate at the threshold of the room. She knew what he wanted, and from whom, and yet she still gave him a compassionate smile.

She held her hand out to him, as she had so many times before.

Kellan exhaled a ragged breath.

Then he stepped inside.

10

FOR LONG MOMENTS AFTER KELLAN LEFT, MIRA DIDN'T SO MUCH as move.

Confusion rooted her bare feet to the floor. Hurt made it hard to breathe for the ache in her breast. And all the while, her pulse was still thrumming, her body still warm and vibrating with futile, foolish desire.

Don't let me make a bad situation worse.

Kellan's rejection stung, more than she wanted to acknowledge.

So, that's all she was to him now—a bad situation that was likely to turn worse?

She didn't want to believe that. His eyes had told a different story, full of amber heat and raging need. So did his body, hard with desire, *dermaglyphs* lit up like fireworks, his powerful hands trembling when he'd set her away from him and told her it couldn't be.

It was his words that left no room for error.

He didn't want her.

It should have been enough, him telling her he would not have her. He could not let himself feel anything for her, despite the fact that their kiss had lost none of its fire in the time they'd been apart. Or that they still went up in flames for each other with the slightest touch. Still craved each other with a passion that defied even Kellan's iron will.

It should have been enough. It should have relieved her, giving her the chance to put him into an emotional compartment where he belonged: as her enemy. It should have provided some much-needed clarity about her duty as a warrior and her mission to ensure Jeremy Ackmeyer's safety versus her impossible wish to see Kellan somehow brought back into the fold with the Order.

Total fantasy, that.

And yet there was a part of her that refused to let him go, even now. *Especially* now.

It outraged her that he could just walk away from her and assume she'd accept it. Still pushing her away, the same way he'd done as that sullen, broken thirteen-year-old boy who'd arrived at the Order's compound so full of pain and grief over the loss of his parents and kin. She hadn't stood for that then, at age eight, and she sure as hell wasn't about to stand for it now.

Mira glared at the closed door he'd stormed out of a few moments ago.

She thought about how hastily he'd gone—so hastily, she hadn't heard the lock tumble into place behind him. She crossed the floor and tried the latch. It was open.

Holy shit.

A number of choices presented themselves to her in rapid succession. One, she could simply stay put like he expected her to and fume until he decided what to do with her next. Which totally wasn't happening.

Two, she could consider his rejection a gift to her mission objectives and attempt an immediate escape with Jeremy Ackmeyer. A risk, considering she and her human package would have to get past Kellan and all of his well-armed rebel crew.

Or three, she could go after Kellan right now and make him face her. Force him to tell her that he cares nothing about her anymore, or if he does, then make him explain to her why he won't try to fix things so they could try to renew what they once had together.

No contest. She was taking Door Number Three.

Mira had years of practice pulling Kellan out from behind the walls he'd constructed around himself. She wasn't about to give up now.

She quickly tossed on his sweatpants under the oversized T-shirt she'd slept in, then slipped out the door and into the hallway outside.

The bunker was very still, little sign of early morning activity at this end of the stronghold. Mira headed in the direction she recalled would lead her to the base's main room, where she assumed she might find

Kellan. Worst case, if she ran into one of his crew instead, they would no doubt immediately summon their leader to her.

But the place was so quiet, Mira wasn't even sure anyone was around.

Until she heard it . . . a soft sound, coming from up ahead, in one of the chambers off the corridor. The showers, where Candice had taken her to clean up last night.

The sound coming from inside that room now was muffled, wet. Intimate.

Something went tight in Mira's stomach as her feet continued a silent trek up the hallway.

There was a low murmur of voices—a female, then a male. Mira's heart gave a heavy thud, like a clump of lead lodging in her rib cage. She knew that deep, low rumble. She knew the cadence of the softly spoken words. Private words. Caring words.

Ah, God.

Dread unlike any she'd known—not since the night she watched a warehouse go up in flames with Kellan inside it—seized her as she crept forward, agonizing, slow steps that eventually brought her to the open doorway.

Candice was inside, seated on a flat bench outside the showers. Her long black hair was damp and glossy against her thin white T-shirt, her head tipped back, eyes closed in a reverent kind of bliss.

And suckling at her wrist was Kellan. He crouched beside her, his dark head bent low over the human female's arm, his sharp white fangs sunk into the tattooed flames that rode from Candice's wrist to her forearm. With her free hand, Candice gently caressed his bare back with an easy familiarity that cut Mira straight to the bone.

No, she corrected, finding it impossible to catch her breath.

This cut straight to her broken heart.

Horrified, all the fight drained out of her in an instant. Mira backed away silently, grateful she'd been unnoticed.

Maybe this was why Kellan didn't want her help bringing him back to the Order. Maybe this was the reason he seemed determined to stay with the human rebels who saved his life eight years ago.

Maybe this was why he apparently found it so easy to turn his back on Mira and what they once had. Because he'd found someone else. Pretty, compassionate Candice.

Now Mira's idea to escape and take Jeremy Ackmeyer with her sounded like the better one by far. The way her chest ached, as though it might crack open any second, she couldn't wait to get out of this place. She had to get as far away as possible, before the pain had a chance to dissolve her where she stood.

She pivoted around—and came face-to-face with Vince.

"Well, well. What have we here?" His mouth went flat along with his gaze. "The boss know one of his chickens has flown its coop?"

Mira winced at the deliberately loud warning in the rebel's voice. Movement in the shower room now. Urgent scrambling. A combination of combat boots and bare feet on the concrete floor.

"Get out of my way." Mira shoved Vince with all she had. The human stumbled backward on his heels, obviously caught off guard by her strength.

She ran past him, heading up the corridor.

Kellan was behind her now. Mira could feel his presence in the corridor but, against her own will, stole a glance back at him. He was wiping Candice's blood from his lips. His eyes were bright amber, fiery orbs devouring pupils reduced to thinnest slits in their centers. His fangs were huge, and his *dermaglyphs* pulsed, still saturated with vivid color even after his feeding.

The sight of him like that—fresh from drinking of another female—crushed her.

Mira wheeled back around and bolted, for where specifically, she had no idea. Just away from Kellan and everything she'd just witnessed.

"Everyone, stay put," he barked, voice rough and otherworldly. "Mira!"

She ignored him, tearing up the corridor, desperate to be gone from him.

Out of nowhere, she felt a rush of cool air brush past her. Then Kellan stood in front of her, blocking her path. "Mira, stop."

She shook her head. Her voice had dried up, leaving only a raw sob in her throat. She choked on it, tried to feint past Kellan. He grabbed hold of her shoulders.

"Let go!" she cried hoarsely. "I want to go. I have to get out of here right now!"

"I can't let you do that." Calm words, allowing no argument.

She didn't care. "Try to stop me," she hissed, and managed to wrench herself free.

She spun around to head in the opposite way now. Vince and Candice waited at that end of the corridor, both of them gaping, observing the whole disastrous scene in quiet judgment. Mira had never felt more the fool.

Kellan ordered them to go. "This is private business. I don't need an audience."

They cleared out quickly, but Mira didn't feel any better once she was alone with Kellan. She took a few hurried steps and he was there in front of her again, forcing her to face him. "We can do this all day, Mouse. Calm down, be reasonable for a minute."

She choked on a hard laugh. "Be reasonable? Fuck you. How's that for calm and reasonable?"

Once more she spun away from him and lunged into a bolt with all she had. He moved so fast this time, she didn't see him or feel him—not until she was swept off her feet and scooped into Kellan's powerful arms.

"Let go of me!" She fought his hold, but he was strong—warm and solid and unyielding, a tangible reminder of the fact that he was something more than man, something deadly, dark, and formidable.

He ignored her struggles and carried her back to his quarters. Kicked the door closed behind him with a heavy bang. He set her down but gave her no chance to get away from him. Before she could take her next breath, Kellan had her spine pressed against the closed door, hemming her in with the bulk of his body, muscled arms caging her on either side.

She glared up at him, trying to ignore the hot spike of awareness that arrowed through her at the near press of their bodies. Her breasts ached to feel him against her, nipples going hard despite the rolling boil of her fury.

Kellan exhaled gruffly, amber eyes searing into her. "Damn it, Mira. I told you not to leave this room."

"Afraid of what I might see?" She lifted her chin, jealousy still burning like acid in the back of her throat. "Guess you should've been more careful, Bowman. You're the one who left the door unlocked."

His stare didn't leave her, not even for an instant. But behind her, she heard the metallic clack of the tumbler sliding into place, turned by the force of his mind alone. "It's locked now."

He bared his teeth and fangs as he said it, his voice a dark growl that should not have made her heart race like it did. Her veins shouldn't have been humming, pulse gone wild and electric, as he held her there, trapped in an unbearable place between anger and hurt, awareness and need.

She didn't want to crave him—not now. Not when she was fuming, still fighting off bitter tears that threatened to spill at having seen his mouth on another woman. A human woman who could feed him, nourish him, give him something Kellan had never taken from Mira.

"Why didn't you tell me?" The words, a broken whisper, slipped off her tongue before she could call them back. "Why couldn't you just say there was someone else?"

Fiery eyes flared brighter. "Because it wouldn't be the truth."

"I saw you, Kellan—just now, with Candice. I saw your fangs in her wrist. Her blood was on your lips—"

"Yes," he admitted, unblinking, unflinching. "I fed from Candice out of necessity. I've fed from her many times, because I am Breed and I cannot live without blood. I feed from her because I can trust her and because she demands nothing from me."

Mira huffed out a harsh breath. "How convenient for you."

She meant it to sound sharp and uncaring, but there was no hiding the fact that she was wounded. She hated the rawness inside her, hated that he might hear it now, would certainly see it in her moist eyes. She shuttered herself with a downward glance, but Kellan wouldn't permit it.

Merciless, he lifted her face, then made the ache even worse by smoothing away the trail of one fat tear with a brush of his thumb across her cheek.

"Look at me, Mira. Tell me if you think there's anything more to what you saw back there than what I'm telling you it was." His voice was level yet intense. "Look at my eyes. They're still glowing. They're still inflamed with hunger, even though I drank my fill of Candice's blood. Look at my *glyphs*, Mira. Do you see satiation in them, or are they still livid and churning with hunger and with the dark colors of a different, deeper need when I'm standing here in front of you?"

Mira didn't want to look at him, but he gave her no choice. And as she obeyed his demands to see him—really see him, as a formidable man and a dangerous, preternatural creature both—she realized that everything he was saying now was the truth. While the edge of his blood thirst had been curbed, he was far from satisfied.

Kellan pressed into her, letting her feel the full, hard length of his body. He bent his head down next to hers, his voice a low growl against the sensitive shell of her ear. "Do I feel like a man who's taken what he wants from someone other than the one woman he craves above all others?"

Mira's breath caught in her throat, leaking out of her in a small moan. She felt his rigid arousal, felt his desire for her radiating out of him in palpable heat.

Kellan muttered a dark curse. "For eight years I've wished I could find someone to make me forget you. But there's been no one, Mira." His lips closed around her earlobe, suckling it gently between his teeth and fangs. His warm breath rasped against her ear, reaching down into her, making her pulse race and her thighs tremble. "There's been no one since you, Mira."

He took her face in his hands and kissed her. Not the gentle nip and brush of his mouth just a moment ago, but a fierce claiming. Possessive and hot, his kiss invaded her without patience or mercy. It was a demand, raw and unbridled.

And Mira gave in to it with abandon.

She couldn't deny him, nor the passion that shot through her body in molten waves as he dragged her deeper into his kiss, pulling her body against his hard planes and rigid edges.

Like a dam breaking, Mira's meager resistance flooded out of her, along with the last small bit of her fight. She wrapped her arms around him and opened herself to his plundering kiss. Inside, she was melting. Blood ran hot, pooling in her core. Limbs went weak and unsteady, turning to gel beneath her.

She wanted him. God, how she wanted him.

Wanted this moment to last forever.

"Kellan," she murmured, arching into the heat of him.

She gasped a second later, when his strong hands skimmed around to the front of her and slipped beneath the loose cotton of her T-shirt. His fingers were rough against her bare skin, more callused and hardened, battle-worn. But his touch was light, raising a shiver on her as his palms skated up her ribs, toward the naked swells of her breasts. He cupped them in his hands, squeezed them, rubbed his thumbs over the nipples that were tight as pebbles under his caress.

Mira buried her face in the curve of his strong shoulder, relishing the feel of his hands all over her bare skin. She touched him too, running her fingers along the muscled bulk that flanked either side of his spine, retracing every inch of him, remembering his body as though they'd never been apart. "Oh, God . . . Kellan. I've missed this so much. I've missed you . . . *us*."

His reply was a low growl that vibrated all the way to her marrow. Without words, without asking for permission, he wheeled her around in front of him and guided her toward the bed, kissing her every step of the way.

She couldn't have resisted if she tried. Everything female in her was willing and wanton and wet, so ready to welcome him back to her.

He pushed her down onto the mattress and followed her, covering her with his body. His tongue delved deep into her mouth, thrusting and withdrawing, telling her exactly where they were heading. Mira opened to him, meeting his tongue with hers, taking when he retreated, submitting when he came back for more.

She clung to him, arched for him, yearned to have him buried deep inside her.

He knew what she needed from him, even now. He knew just how to touch her, just how to kiss her. He knew everything, still, after all this time.

Mira speared her fingers into his thick chestnut hair as he took her mouth in a hotter, more demanding kiss that left her gasping and drugged beneath him. She didn't know how he managed to strip off her sweats and panties, didn't much care. Because suddenly Kellan was moving down the length of her body, pushing up the hem of her T-shirt and kissing a warm, wet trail along the flat plane of her belly. She moaned, bowing up off the bed as he kneaded her breasts, then took one peachy nipple into his mouth. He kissed the other one too, giving it a teasing graze of his teeth.

"You taste the same," he murmured against her skin. "Still sweet and tender."

She couldn't reply, could only twist her fingers in the sheet and suck in her breath as his mouth began a downward trek, leaving a trail of fire everywhere his lips touched her skin. He paused at her hip bone, licked its delicate ridge. "Sweeter here."

Oh, God.

She lifted her head and watched as he drifted lower still. He glanced up at her as he moved into the apex of her thighs, his irises swamped with amber, swallowing the thin vertical lines of his pupils. That otherworldly, predatory gaze stayed locked on her, the tips of his fangs stretching longer, sharper as his broad mouth spread into a carnal smile. Then he parted her legs and sank down between them.

He kissed the triangle of light curls at the mound of her sex. Mira held her breath, pulse racing, veins filled with liquid fire. Another kiss, this one lingering much longer, the tip of his tongue cleaving into the sensitive folds. He licked her slowly, suckling her, drawing the tender bud against the wet heat of his tongue. His approving growl vibrated against her quivering sex as he went deeper. "So sweet and juicy. This is what I thirst for. You, Mira."

He went down on her again. The air shuddered out of her lungs on a ragged sigh, sensation shooting through her like tiny lightning bolts, the coming of a storm. He played with her, teasing her clit, tonguing her, making the petals of her body weep for him.

"I need you," she gasped, rising up to reach for him, fingers digging into the hard bulk of his shoulders. "Please, Kellan. I don't want to wait. I'm afraid to wait another second . . ."

Afraid the moment would somehow shatter and reality would toss them both back where they'd been just a few minutes ago: Enemies, not lovers. Strangers, not friends.

Back to a man and woman with a distant, shared past, an uneasy present, and a dubious, uncertain future.

Mira couldn't let go of him, not now. "Come up here. I need to feel you against me again. I want you inside me."

Whatever he said was lost in a deep, rumbling growl. He moved back up on the bed, shucking his pants along the way. Mira drank in the sight of him, naked and lean and beautiful. So strong and powerful.

So alive.

How long had she dreamed of this moment—being with Kellan again, having him back from the dead?

It made her greedy for him now. Desperate to hold him close, as close as their bodies possibly could be.

Kellan covered her, every inch of him pulsing with warmth and masculinity. He kissed her again, deep and long and possessive. His thighs were wedged between hers, his arousal heavy and hard, the thick shaft nestled upright in the moist cleft of her sex.

Not close enough.

Mira shifted her hips, seating him for his first thrust. She sucked on his tongue, and his cock gave a little kick in response. Kellan moaned into her mouth, a raw sound of need. He broke their kiss with a curse and stared down at her, propped up on his fists.

"I want to go slow with you, but . . ." His voice trailed off, and he shook his head, giving a slight press of his pelvis. The head of his penis nudged into her, testing. "Ah, Christ . . . you feel too good."

Mira's heart was banging in her chest like a caged bird, every nerve ending quivering with an urgent need. "I don't want to go slow. There's been too much time standing between us. No more, Kellan. Not right now."

He nodded, eyes rooted on her as he gave another experimental thrust. "You're so tight. Just like the first time we were together."

She'd been a virgin that first time—the only time—she and Kellan made love. He had been too. Although their desire had been mutual, undeniable for years before that night, they'd never taken it so far. She'd been too young at first, then, later, when she was a woman, Kellan had thrown himself into his duty with the Order, taking on missions that sent him away for weeks, sometimes months at a time. But he always came back to her, and when he did, it never took long for them to end up in a tangle of arms and legs and questing mouths.

They'd learned to pleasure each other in other ways before that moment eight years ago until, finally, need had proven greater than any amount of denial or restraint. Mira had given herself to Kellan and he to her.

It had been magical. Miraculous. Until a few hours later, when a rebel's bomb took all of that away.

She gazed up at Kellan, poised above her in the soft quiet of his bed. Her heart was still broken from everything that had happened that night and in the time since. But this moment was real. It was now. It was theirs.

She smiled at the feel of his nakedness all over her, moaned in pleasured pain as the head of his cock stretched her impossibly tight around him. He was so careful with her. Too careful. She reached up, stroked his handsome face. "There's been no other for me either, Kellan. Not in all this time."

A flash of bewilderment raced across his features. "No one?"

She shook her head. "Only you."

"Ah, God." He closed his eyes for a moment, and when he opened them again, they were blazing with a newer, fiercer light. He wasn't happy. Not at all. "Ah, Christ, Mouse. Damn you for that. Damn both of us for not having the sense to let go."

With a growl through gritted teeth and fangs, he pushed inside her on a swift, deep thrust. Mira cried out as he filled her, biting her lip as the sharp, initial sting of his invasion gave way to a glorious completion.

Oh, fuck.

He felt so good.

She felt so good, holding him buried within her.

She knew this dance with him, every instinct within her responding like it had been only yesterday that she'd last kissed him like this— naked and breathless, skin on skin, melting with pleasure and hungry for more. Their first time together had been branded into her senses, a memory she'd carried all this time. It had been all she'd had left of him, and she'd clung to it as she would her own soul.

And now she had Kellan with her again. Inside her.

His name was a ragged whisper on her lips as he increased his tempo, each long push going deeper, stoking the fire that was already roaring inside her. His mouth covered hers as the first broken cry of her climax curled up from the back of her throat.

He showed her no quarter, but then, she hadn't wanted any. Not like this. Not when her need for him was still so raw and unsated.

But her orgasm was building swiftly. It raced up on her with his every stroke and retreat, every kiss and caress carrying her higher, closer to the edge. Kellan drove into her with relentless purpose, pushing her mercilessly toward the cliff.

"Oh, God," she gasped as the first hot waves crashed into her. "*Kellan.*"

Mira held on to him and tumbled headlong into the pleasure of the moment.

The pleasure of this reunion, no matter how fleeting her heart feared it might be.

11

ONLY ONCE IN HIS LIFE HAD KELLAN FELT THE TIGHT, WET BLISS of Mira's body sheathing him. Only once had he known the sweet clench of her womb around his cock, the tiny undulations of her climax milking him, wringing him out. He'd remembered that one time with vivid clarity—or so he'd thought, until the sight of Mira coming for him now, clinging to him and gasping his name in heated frenzy, made everything he thought he knew seem pale and dry as dust.

Christ, she was beautiful.

Her blond hair was a wild tangle on his pillow, her porcelain-perfect skin gone pink with the rush of blood to her cheeks and across the lovely mounds of her pert breasts. Her eyes were heavy-lidded, dark lashes at half-mast. She sucked in a sigh through parted lips that were bruised a dark red from his kiss, her rosebud mouth trembling with each rising pant of her breath. She clutched at him as another deep shudder racked her.

Transfixed, triumphant, Kellan watched her orgasm sweep over her. It gripped him in its hot fist as she trembled with the force of her release. His cock twitched, leapt, ready to explode, his own climax building to the point of torture.

But it was a delicious agony. A pain so good, he wanted to keep it going forever. Mira began to shatter again, her small body going tense beneath him, her breath racing, pulse thudding hard against him everywhere they touched. He coaxed her higher, rolling into her with deep, penetrating strokes, fanning the flames of her pleasure.

"Don't stop," she whispered brokenly. "Oh, God, Kellan . . . please . . . don't ever stop."

He growled in agreement, male pride swelling inside him like a tidal wave.

She was his.

Again.

Still.

Always . . .

It was that last thought, the lie of it, that stuck him like a barb. Always wasn't theirs anymore. No matter how much he wanted it to be true.

And it had been unfair of him to take this from Mira—her pleasure, her surrender, her undeserved fidelity and affection—knowing that it wouldn't last. It *couldn't* last, not with the grim future that awaited him.

But it was hard to feel the dread of that fact right now. Hard to feel anything but pure masculine satisfaction as he held her sweat-sheened, naked beauty against him and reveled in the pleasure she was taking from him.

He kissed her as the last of her orgasm ebbed, caressed her pretty face as her bliss-drugged gaze lifted up to meet his amber eyes. When he spoke, it was with a gravelly depth that sounded more animal than man, even to his own ears. "I knew we'd end up like this, naked together in my bed."

He wasn't proud of it. But he sure as hell couldn't muster much regret.

Part of the reason he'd held out so long with her in the first place, before his life took the detour he was currently on, was that he knew giving in to his desire for Mira—consummating it—would only make him crave her that much more. Loving her like this only made him want to taste her. To bind her to him. Things he had no right to want anymore.

Years ago he'd resisted his temptation for her with a rigid will he could hardly fathom now. What a fool he'd been to hold her at a distance, to push her away. Now all he wanted was to keep her close. He couldn't keep her close enough.

He gave a slow thrust of his hips, groaning at the delicious, wet friction of their bodies. He caressed her face, brushed a damp lock of hair from her forehead. "I knew when the call came in from my crew at

Ackmeyer's place, and I made the decision to bring you here . . . I knew if I saw you again, I would not be able to resist touching you, kissing you." He pressed his lips to her brow, tracing his thumb over the outline of the Breedmate mark that rode at the hairline of her left temple. "And I knew that if I let that happen, if I touched you, kissed you, there'd be no stopping me from eventually getting inside you again too."

Mira's fingers were twined in his hair, cupping the back of his skull. "I don't want you to stop." She pulled him down for a fevered kiss that made his whole body go taut and electric. She moved beneath him, rocking into him with ungentle demand. Her kiss ended with a nip of her teeth on his lower lip. Her breath was hot against his mouth, hungry. "Don't stop, Kellan."

Ah, Christ.

He couldn't have stopped now if his life depended on it.

He took her mouth in a hard claiming, at the same time driving his cock deep and slow, filling her with all of him, seating his thick shaft to the hilt. Her gasp spurred him on, her soft mewls making his arousal knot ever tighter, each thrust a possessive, hungered thing.

He swept his hand down the length of one smooth thigh, bending her at the knee and bringing her leg up onto his shoulder. He rolled his pelvis against her in another deep push, his tempo rising, racing to match the fierce beat of his pulse.

"I can't get deep enough inside you," he snarled against her mouth. "I want all of you."

"Yes," she whispered, holding on to him as he drove harder, lost to everything but the feel of her sheath wrapped around him like a glove, her delicate muscles clenching him with sweet ripples of pressure.

He touched her cheek, wanting to see her face in the moment he exploded inside her. It was roaring up on him quickly, a coil of heat at the base of his spine.

Mira turned her head within the cradle of his palm and pressed a kiss there. The tip of her pink tongue darted out, moist and hot against his skin. He pumped harder, about to lose all control. And then she turned her head and took his thumb into her mouth. She sucked him deep, the pad of her tongue cushioning him, cleaving to him, just as her tight channel clutched and suckled the rigid length of his cock.

Kellan thrust with frenzied abandon, the knot of pain and pleasure building, ratcheting up with each heavy throb of his pulse. Mira didn't let go of his thumb. She swirled her tongue around him, her eyes locked on his as he slid in and out of her mouth, shuddering deep in his bones at the feel of her blunt little incisors grazing his skin. Then she closed her teeth, clamping onto him in a bite that triggered every sensory switch in his body.

Kellan roared as his orgasm erupted.

He couldn't hold back, feeling the wild rush of his seed shooting through him, filling her. He came hard and fast and frenzied. The force of his release staggered him, left him shaking as he spilled himself deep inside Mira's hot, wet sheath.

As he came, he knew a sudden sense of relief that regardless of how wrong it was to be taking his pleasure with her, at least he wouldn't be planting a child in Mira. No, that would take more than the pure, reckless impulse that put him between her thighs today. It would also take the fertile time of a crescent moon phase and the simultaneous exchange of blood between a male of his kind and a woman bearing the Breedmate birthmark.

Thoughts of blood and bonding were dangerous things. Especially now, when Kellan's fevered gaze was already drawn to the artery ticking like a caged butterfly in the side of Mira's delicate throat. Beneath the intoxicating scent of Mira's skin, dewy with clean sweat and the musky perfume of sex, Kellan's Breed senses caught the faint lily sweetness of her blood.

His hunger to drink from her—to pierce his fangs into the smooth white column of her neck and bind her to him as his mate for life—returned with the force of a gale storm, almost too much to bear.

"Shit," he muttered, closing his eyes and turning his head away from the temptation.

Mira's gentle hands brought him back, her palms framing his face. But her eyes held a note of sadness. Confusion in her softly murmured words. "You never wanted to take that last step with me. You never wanted to bond with me."

"Do you really believe that?" He searched her gaze, hoping that behind the purple lenses that shielded her eyes' true color—lenses that muted her seer's gift—Mira knew she was the only one he'd ever imagined would stand at his side as his blood-bonded mate.

But even that hope was a cruelty on his part, because whether he wanted her for his own or not, fate, apparently, had other ideas.

Kellan had seen it for himself, on another morning like this, when he'd held Mira naked in his arms, their bodies intimately joined, pleasured and exhausted, just as they were now.

He leaned down and placed a tender kiss on each of her eyelids, apology or absolution, he wasn't quite sure. "It would've been you, Mira. If I could believe we have some kind of future together—any kind of future that won't end with me hurting you deeply—then it *would* be you. But I can't give in to something irrevocable, something that would be eternal and binding, when I know there's no good to come from it."

The sadness and confusion that had been in her gaze a moment ago turned a little flinty now. She blew out a scoff, her mouth twisting into a look he'd seen often enough when they were growing up together. "Part of me wants to call you a first-class asshole for saying that while you're still inside me. But that wouldn't be fair, would it? Because I wanted to fuck you as much as you evidently wanted it too. Not that any good will come of this either."

Kellan winced. "This wasn't just a fuck, for crissake."

"What was it, then?"

He gave a shake of his head, his mind filled with a thousand adjectives that wouldn't even come close to describing what he was feeling, lying there with Mira, growing hard within her all over again.

He gave a slow thrust of his hips, moaned when she met him with an arch of her spine that took him even deeper. "God, I wish you didn't feel so good. I wish you didn't feel so right. I'm not ready to leave you yet." He lowered his head and kissed her, a long, passionate joining of their mouths. When he finally broke away from her lips, his breath was sawing out of his lungs, rasping through his elongated fangs. "Ah, fuck . . . this was a mistake. Now that I have you under me, I'm not sure how I'm going to let you out of my bed."

Mira braced her hands on his bare chest and pushed him onto his back. She went with him, keeping him nestled inside her as she came up astride him. "Now you're under me, and maybe I'll have something to say about whether or not we get out of this bed."

She rolled her pelvis, seating him as deep as he could go. Then she began to ride him slowly, drawing out each stroke to agonizing lengths. She closed her eyes as she moved atop him, her lithe warrior's body arching and flexing with a dancer's grace as she held him inside her, rocked him toward a swiftly building climax. Her small breasts bobbed as she found her tempo, and it was all Kellan could do not to come in a rush as he watched his thick cock disappear into her cleft with each bouncing stride.

God, she was sexy. The hottest thing he'd ever known. Tough and stubborn and courageous, tenacious in everything she'd ever taken on in life, including him.

No male—Breed or human alike—could ever hope for a better woman to call his mate. And for one crazy moment, Kellan let himself imagine that she was, in fact, his. That everything was different, and he didn't have to let her go.

That he hadn't looked into her naked eyes eight years ago and glimpsed a future that would tear them apart. One that would brand him a traitor to everyone he'd ever loved.

The vision came back to him in ruthless detail.

Kellan arrested by Lucan and the Order, accused of conspiracy and murder, high treason. All of the charges indefensible. All of his crimes carrying capital punishments.

And Mira, standing before Lucan and the Global Nations Council in a cavernous meeting chamber, begging them for mercy.

Dissolving in grief a moment later, when the judgment was handed down.

Death.

Kellan didn't realize he'd gone still beneath her until Mira's hands stroked his face. "Are you all right? Where did you go just now?"

He shook his head, tried to purge the vision and the heavy regret that had become lodged in the pit of his stomach. "I'm right here," he said, reaching up to caress the worry from the downward twist of her mouth. "I'm good. Right now, everything is good."

She smiled, turning a kiss into his palm. She started moving on top of him again, sighing as she found her rhythm once more and rode him with beautiful abandon.

When she was moaning with arousal, arcing above him in the throes of another orgasm, Kellan tumbled her down beneath him and took her pleasure higher. He wanted to give her nothing but joy in that moment, enough to last.

Enough to last them both.

12

MIRA WOKE UP SOMETIME LATER THAT MORNING, NESTLED INTO the crook of Kellan's strong arm. His warmth surrounded her, a cocoon of peace and contentment she hadn't known for a very long time.

Not since the morning eight years before, when she'd awakened in a similar pose, in a similar state of blissful exhaustion.

That day had ended in a nightmare of fire and ash and tears. Today she felt renewed. Hopeful. She felt happy, and that scared her more than anything. Especially when her happiness had come in the arms of Kellan Archer. Not the teenage boy she'd adored as a child. Not even the young Breed warrior who'd trained alongside her with the Order and had become her dearest, most trusted friend and confidant.

No, her happiness had been delivered by the leader of an outlaw band of rebels, who'd not only abducted an innocent civilian but defied Lucan Thorne and the entire Order by disrupting an operation and taking one of its members hostage.

A hostage who had very willingly tumbled into bed to sleep with the enemy.

Among other things.

Wicked, wonderful things.

Mira couldn't resist kissing the bulky biceps that caged her against Kellan's big body. She tongued the arcing lines of the *glyphs* on his arm, delighting in the flood of dark color left in the wake of her teasing kiss.

He stirred. With a low moan, he flexed his arm and tucked her farther into his embrace. His chest was a wall of solid heat against her nipples, his ridged abdomen like sun-warmed granite against her belly. And lower still, his arousal was quite obviously apparent, nudging into her hip, stiff and hot. Much too tempting for her roaming hands.

Mira carefully traced her fingers along the smoothness of his chest and abs, past his navel, to the bristly thatch of crisp hair and the jutting girth of his sex. She stroked him once, marveling at the softness that encased so much rigid steel. And the fat plum that crowned his shaft, already weeping with a bead of moisture as she ran her fingertips over the head of his penis.

She flicked her gaze up to see if she'd woken him.

Ember-bright eyes stared back at her, blazing with wide-awake desire.

"Pleasant dreams?" she asked him, attempting innocence.

He wasn't buying it. His dark goatee stretched wickedly around his mouth, lips peeled back in a smile that was purely carnal. "Who needs dreams when reality is fondling me so sweetly?"

He rolled her beneath him, moving with a speed that startled her, even though she was well aware of the power and agility that was always at his command. Mira spread her thighs to accommodate him, ready for him again. Her heart knocking like a hammer in her breast.

Kellan bent to take her earlobe between his lips and teeth, murmuring blush-worthy plans for all the ways he intended to enjoy her in those next moments.

Mira's pulse was clamoring so urgently, her body so ripe for his taking, it took her a second to realize he'd gone suddenly still and tense above her. He lifted his head, stock-still now.

"What the fuck—"

Someone was in the corridor outside, banging on the door. The rapping came again, fast and hard. Panicked.

"Bowman! Are you in there?" A female voice, pitched high with worry. Not Candice, but the other woman of the rebel base. "Bowman, come quick!"

"It's Nina," Kellan murmured, already rolling off Mira and throwing on his pants. He sent her a sober look. Mira scrambled out of the bed and hurried into his T-shirt and sweatpants. He glanced to make sure she was clothed, then flipped the lock with his mind and opened the door on Nina's ashen face.

"Oh, my God," the human woman gasped. "It's Vince. He—oh, my God!"

"What's going on?" Kellan demanded. "Where is he?"

"I don't know!" Nina shook her head, indigo hair tossing, sending the dozens of tiny metal loops swinging in her pierced earlobes. She was sobbing now. "Vince is gone. He took the van. He's got Ackmeyer with him."

Although Mira tried to stay in the background, she couldn't bite back her gasp of alarm. Even Kellan seemed to take the news with no small amount of shock. He went still for an instant, silent. Then seemed to shake it off like the leader he now was.

"Where?" His voice was a roll of thunder, dark and lethal, fully Breed. He stepped out into the corridor. "Where did he take him?"

"I don't know," Nina cried. "But Chaz and Candice tried to stop him. Oh, God . . . he killed Chaz. He's dead, Bowman. Vince slit his throat—"

"Jesus Christ," Kellan muttered. His shoulders slumped a bit, but when he spoke, his voice was level with cold command. "When did this happen? How long has the bastard been gone?"

Nina shook her head. "I don't know. A little while ago, not long. He killed Chaz, then he stole the van and took off."

Mira closed her eyes, absorbing the weight of all she was hearing. Jeremy Ackmeyer in the hands of a cold-blooded killer. Kellan betrayed by one of his own. A death among the ranks of his comrades.

"And Candice," Nina went on. She sucked in a hitching breath, then dissolved into more tears. "Vince stabbed her too. Doc's trying to take care of her, but she's bleeding really bad. He says the blade nicked an artery in her thigh. He can't get it to stop."

Kellan's answering curse was quiet but savage. He swung a look over his shoulder at Mira, somewhere between misery and apology. Mira's own guilt gnawed at her with sharp teeth. All of this violence and betrayal had happened while she and Kellan were making love.

Her body was still humming from the pleasure of Kellan's touch, but her chest was heavy with the knowledge that one life had been cut short today, another stolen away with Vince's escape. If anything happened to Candice now, Mira could see in Kellan's tormented eyes that he would never forgive himself.

She gave him a faint nod, understanding that whatever they'd shared in the privacy of his bed for the past few hours was over now. He wasn't hers in this moment; he belonged to them. To his comrades. His friends.

"They need you," Mira said quietly, meant for his ears alone. "Go to them."

Kellan took off like a shot, Nina trailing after him at a run.

Kellan didn't have to guess where Doc was treating Candice. The olfactory blast of spilled fresh red cells led him like a beacon to the cell where Ackmeyer had been held.

Jesus Christ.

Blood was everywhere. Pooling almost black under the crumpled slump of Chaz's unmoving body inside the opened cage. Splattered on the cement block walls. Smeared in a chaotic path by Vince's boots and Jeremy Ackmeyer's stumbling feet as he'd obviously been dragged away. And then there was Candice.

Lying supine inside the cell, arms splayed out at her sides, she was covered in blood from the front of her T-shirt down, with still more of it seeping out beneath her. Her legs were bare; Doc had apparently removed her jeans so he could work on the nasty puncture in her right thigh. His brown eyes sober, he glanced Kellan's way only briefly before returning all of his focus to treating Candice's wound.

Kellan's skin went tight, fangs filling his mouth. His vision had gone instantly red—not only in physical reaction to the presence of so much fresh-flowing blood but in deadly rage for the betrayal by one of his own. A betrayal that had resulted in the slaying of one friend and the grave injury of another.

All of this havoc and loss wreaked while Kellan had been distracted by the pleasure of having Mira in his bed.

He'd failed his crew in the worst possible way. Failed Jeremy Ackmeyer too, whom Kellan should have freed immediately upon learning of his innocence several hours ago. None of this would have happened if Kellan had kept his head on straight as the leader these people expected him to. They had entrusted their lives to him, trusted him to protect them.

Instead, he'd allowed himself to get caught up in a romantic entanglement with Mira that could only end in disaster. So, yeah, he'd failed her today as well, and it was too late to call back any of his mistakes.

"Goddamn it," he snarled, self-directed anger making his voice sound raw and violent, even to his own ears.

More than anything, he wanted to tear out of the bunker and hunt Vince down—daylight or not. He wanted the bastard to suffer for this, wanted to make him bleed. But it was Kellan's crew that was bleeding and suffering now—one of them bled out on the floor in front of him, another possibly heading that way too.

The sight of Candice injured so severely jolted Kellan back to his duty as the commander of this base and its people. He ignored the coppery gut-punch of Candice's bleeding wound as he walked to her side and went down on his haunches next to her.

Her breath raced between slack, pale lips. Her eyes were wide and unblinking, fixed on the ceiling as Doc bent her leg at the knee, elevating the wound, before fastening his belt around her thigh as a tourniquet.

Kellan grabbed her discarded jeans and rolled them into a makeshift pillow. As he lifted her head off the floor and rested it back onto the softer fabric, her glassy gaze slid to him. "Vince . . . I tried to stop him, but he—"

"I know. Don't worry about him. You just hang in there, you got it?" Her eyelids drooped with her weak nod. Kellan clamped his teeth and fangs together as he smoothed his fingers over her clammy brow. "How we doing, Doc?"

"Be a helluva lot better once I get the blood flow stanched," Doc replied, hands slick with red, face grim as he tightened the belt on Candice's thigh.

Kellan shot a glance over his shoulder to Nina, who hovered nervously in the doorway. "Clean towels, lots of them. Cloths too. Bring whatever you can find."

"On it." She took off at once.

Candice's teeth started to chatter. Her eyes were glazed, alternating between rolling back in her head and sliding over to focus on him. "I'm s-scared, Bowman. Don't want to die."

"You're going to be all right," he assured her. "Doc's treated worse. You remember the shit condition I was in when you dragged me in to meet him that first time?"

"Yeah." Her voice was thready, small. "I remember."

Kellan nodded, swept a lock of damp black hair from where it was plastered to her cheek. Her skin was cold, alarmingly so. "Doc didn't let me die that night; neither did you. He and I aren't about to let you die now either. So, you hang in, Brady, that's a fucking order."

"Okay," she said, giving him a faint smile as her eyes drifted closed. A shudder went through her whole body, prolonged, bone-deep. She trembled, blue-lipped and shivering, despite the summertime humidity of the bunker. "Freezing in here," she murmured. "I'm so cold."

Before Kellan could respond or turn to find something to provide her some warmth, a blanket appeared from somewhere behind him.

Mira.

He looked up to find her standing at his back, holding a blanket she'd brought from his bed. She moved around him to cover Candice's torso, gently tucking it under her chin and shoulders to keep in as much heat as possible.

When she was done, she stepped back, her hand coming to rest tenderly on Kellan's shoulder. He reached up to meet her touch, clasping her fingers in a grateful squeeze. His guilt and self-recrimination was still acid in his gut, but the sight of Mira standing near him, the feel of her touch on him in silent support and understanding, was a balm he couldn't deny. He saw Doc's gaze flick to the unspoken exchange, saw the question in the rebel's eyes as Kellan's hand lingered on Mira's, possessive and intimate.

"Tell us what you need us to do, Doc."

"Keep her awake," the medic said, going back to work on the wound. "Shock will make her want to sleep, but we can't let her do that. She needs to stay conscious right now."

Kellan nodded. "Open your eyes, Candice. I need you to look at me, stay focused," he prompted, letting go of Mira's hand to give Candice's shoulder a rousing shake. "I need you to tell me what happened in here with Vince. Can you do that?"

"Yes," she murmured. Her eyelids lifted, though she seemed to struggle with the effort. "Came in here to pick up Ackmeyer's meal tray. Chaz came with me . . . gonna take Ackmeyer for a bathroom break."

Kellan grunted in acknowledgment, his eye drifting to the upended tray of half-eaten food that lay scattered on the floor nearby. When Candice shuddered again, struggling to suck air into her lungs, Kellan reached down and stroked his palm over the top of her head. "You're doing great. Take your time, but you stay with me. You stay awake, Brady."

"O-okay. I'm okay." She looked up at him and took a few deeper breaths. "Ackmeyer asked if we were letting him go . . . started going on about how he was innocent . . . never meant to hurt anyone with his inventions."

All the things Kellan heard from the scientist himself. Things Kellan's touch had vouched for as truth.

"He said someone must've stolen his work," Candice went on. "Said he wanted to help us find out who it was and see them punished . . . he said if what happened was true—that his work had been used for harm, for murder—he would personally make sure the technology was destroyed, no matter what it was worth."

Kellan's jaw tightened at the thought of how wrong he'd been in going after Jeremy Ackmeyer. He'd assumed the worst, and he dreaded that the fallout from that bad call was far from over.

Candice weathered another full-body shudder as Nina came in with an armful of towels and handed them off to Doc. Mira pitched in without being asked, she and Nina helping Doc wrap Candice's wound as she continued with her account. "We didn't realize Vince was in the room . . . not until he asked how much Ackmeyer thought someone might pay for his technology."

"Son of a bitch," Kellan muttered, needing no further explanation to understand what Vince would be up to next. "What did Ackmeyer tell him? How much did he say the UV tech was worth?"

"He didn't," Candice replied. "He told Vince it didn't matter . . . said it wasn't for sale, and he wouldn't allow anyone to profit from it now."

"Which obviously didn't sit well with Vince," Kellan snarled, his every fiber still seething with predatory rage and the need to make his traitorous comrade pay.

Mira met his gaze from where she crouched near Doc and Nina, working like a member of the team, not the unwilling captive she'd been just the night before. He didn't want to think of her as one of his crew. Didn't want to think of her in any of the ways he was now. He tore his gaze away from her and put it back on his wounded colleague. "Keep your eyes open, Candice. Tell me the rest now."

"Everything happened so fast," she said, her voice a thready whisper. "Vince had a dark look on his face . . . Next thing I knew, there was a knife in his hand. He lunged at Chaz . . . stabbed him hard in the chest. Then he grabbed Ackmeyer . . . had the knife under his chin . . . said he was going to start doing things his way."

Kellan's growl rumbled in the quiet cell. His vision burned a deeper shade of amber, fury roiling through him with each word he was hearing.

"I tried to stop him, Bowman." Candice's eyes lifted to him now and stayed there, glassy and lethargic, but fixed on him as though searching for forgiveness. Kellan swore, low and coarse under his breath. "Even after he stabbed me, I tried to stop him from taking Ackmeyer, from getting away," she said weakly. "I tried . . ."

"It's all right." Kellan cupped the side of her skull in his palm. "You did everything you could, I know that. I'm the one who should've been there to deal with Vince." His glance strayed to Chaz's body and the three grave faces that were all staring at him in the blood-soaked cell of the rebel bunker. "Bastard's a dead man. He's going to know that now."

Kellan rose to his feet and stalked out of the room without further explanation.

He wasn't surprised to hear Mira right behind him as soon as he took his first step in the corridor outside, but he was far from pleased. "What are you doing?" she demanded at his back, running to keep up with his furious gait. "Kellan, where are you going?"

The sound of his name on her lips—his true name—put a dangerous edge in his answering growl as he wheeled around to face her. He grabbed her upper arms and steered her back against the nearest wall. "One of my men is dead back there. Another of my crew could bleed out in a few minutes, if Doc doesn't work some kind of magic on her leg. And a captive under my watch has been taken by one of my own—right under my fucking nose—likely to be sold to the highest bidder or killed before sundown tonight. You think I'm going to sit back and let this go unmet?"

"It's the middle of the day. You can't go anywhere—"

"Let me deal with that," he snapped, knowingly harsh as he let her loose and pivoted to leave her behind him in the hallway.

But Mira had never been one to give in that easily. No, not her. She marched right after him, bare feet padding in determined strides at his back. It took her only moments before she was in front of him, blocking his path with her body. A body that looked entirely too damn good in his T-shirt and overlong sweatpants, rolled up at her ankles.

"Don't be an idiot," she said, eyes flashing behind the purple tint of her contact lenses. "You'll die out there right now."

"I've got a good half hour before I need to worry about exposure," he pointed out. "I can be in the city in less than ten minutes on foot."

"Then what?" she countered hotly. "Twenty minutes to turn Boston upside down looking for Vince and Ackmeyer before you're toast? It's suicidal and you know it."

He scoffed, even though she was right. "You got a better idea?"

"Yeah. I'll go after them. If I don't find Vince myself, I'll work my way through every rebel piece of shit in the city until someone rats him out."

Kellan barked out a caustic laugh. "Forget it. This is my mess to clean up, not yours. You're not a part of it, Mira. And I'll walk into the sun itself before I put you in the middle of this shit."

If he'd had any kind of honor, he would have done that eight years ago, ensuring that he'd never have the chance to hurt her the way her vision showed him he would. But he hadn't been able to cut himself off from Mira, not totally. He'd stayed close, closer than was wise. He should have put continents between them, anything to make certain their paths would never cross again.

But he hadn't done any of those things.

Even now, it was nearly impossible to keep from reaching out to touch her. He crossed his arms over his chest when the temptation to smooth her outraged scowl proved almost too much to resist.

"You bastard." Mira drew in a breath, then pushed it out on a sharp exhalation. "God, you are still the most infuriatingly pigheaded male I've ever known. You're going to stand there and tell me I'm not a part of this—that you would rather kill yourself than let me into your world—when you just had your cock inside me? You said a lot of sweet things to me, things I was almost fool enough to believe—"

Kellan cursed. "I meant everything I said. Every word, Mira. But that was before."

She gaped, stricken and breathing hard. "Before what?"

"Before everything that went down in that cell back there," Kellan replied. "Before what happened with Vince just now reminded me that this is never going to work. It *can't* work."

He uncrossed his arms and ran a hand over his scalp, trying to figure a way off the path that fate seemed determined to place him on. But there wasn't one. Vince defecting with Jeremy Ackmeyer in tow had all but made sure of that fact.

"Whatever happens now, whatever Vince ends up doing with Ackmeyer, I want you out of it. To anyone outside this bunker, you're still my captive, an unwilling participant in anything I've done. I intend to keep it that way. I won't have you jeopardizing your future, thinking you can help me. You can't, because I'm not going to allow it."

Her slender blond brows lowered even farther over her flashing eyes. "That's not your decision to make. I don't need your permission to care about you, Kellan. You don't get to decide what's important to me."

God help him, but it didn't take much to remember the stubborn little girl who'd told him pretty much the same thing in word and deed time and again when he'd been a withdrawn, stupid teen who didn't know how to accept her friendship, let alone her love. By sheer force of will, she'd made him participate in life when grief and anger over his family's annihilation had all but crippled him inside. As a girl, Mira had held his hand and led him out of a dark place. As a woman, she'd held his heart, despite his efforts to protect himself from caring for someone he could never bear to lose.

Now he only hoped he'd find the strength to push Mira away, when all he wanted was to pull her close and never let her go.

He kept his voice quiet, the words as gentle as he could make them. "This time I do get to decide. Bad enough I couldn't stay away from you, even though I knew damn well where this would take us in the end." He lowered his head and held her searching gaze, needing her to hear him now. She needed to understand. "When I go down, I'll be damned if I take you down with me."

Mira had gone utterly still in front of him. She didn't blink, barely drew breath. "What do you mean, you knew where this would take us in the end?"

Kellan stared into her eyes, those muted mirrors that had cursed him on what had so briefly been a perfect morning eight years ago. Now they looked up at him imploringly, searching for a truth he hoped she'd never need to hear.

"Tell me," she said, a slight tremor in her soft voice. Her anger was gone now, replaced with a gravity—a tangible dread—that caught his heart in a stranglehold. "What did you mean by that, Kellan?" She spoke hardly above a whisper, hardly breathing, for all he could discern. "Tell me what you know, damn it."

He reached for her, but she flinched away from him. Gave a slow shake of her head, her eyes never leaving his. "Tell me."

"That morning," he said, the words coming out of him dry and rusty. "The morning before the warehouse explosion . . ."

"We made love," she murmured.

"Yes."

"We made love for hours, earlier that night too," she said, filling in the blanks when his voice seemed to desert him. "For the first time."

He nodded. "The first time for both of us. It was the best night of my life, Mira. Until a few hours ago when I was with you again, that night eight years ago and the morning I woke up next to you were the best moments I've ever known. I never got the chance to tell you that. I should've said the words then, but I didn't know."

She swallowed, her delicate throat visibly clenching. "You didn't know what?"

"That it was all going to end that night. I didn't know I'd be leaving you so soon. I thought I would have time to explain." He shrugged lamely, shaking his head. "I thought . . . I prayed we'd be able to sort it all out, find a way—somehow—to make it right."

"I don't know what you're saying, Kellan." She scowled even deeper now, and despite her denial that she understood, he could see in her eyes that realization was settling in hard the longer she looked at him. "What happened that morning? Did I do something wrong? Did I say something, or—"

"No. God, no. You didn't do anything wrong." He cupped her jaw in his hand and smoothed the pad of his thumb over her trembling mouth. "You were perfect. You were everything I could've wanted. More than I ever deserved."

"But you left me," she said quietly. "Why, Kellan? The truth this time. Something happened the morning we were together. Something bad enough to make you think I'd be happier believing you were dead in that explosion."

"Ah, Mouse," he murmured, letting his hand travel up from where it caressed her lips, to the Breedmate mark riding at her temple. He stroked the tiny teardrop-and-crescent-moon birthmark, then leaned forward and pressed a kiss to each of her eyelids. When he drew back from her, there were tears welling in her eyes. "You see? You would be happier if I'd died that night. And I would rather have left you mourning someone you loved than one day pleading for my life as the traitor I was destined to become."

Her hands came up to his chest, pushed him away. "What are you saying?"

"I saw it, Mira. In your eyes, that morning when we woke up together, naked in your bed. Your eyes were naked too. The lenses that mute your visions—"

She sucked in her breath. "No."

"I looked into your eyes, only for a second—"

"No." The denial was short and sharp. She gave a shake of her head, then another, more vehement this time. "No, I don't believe it. I would've known. I would've felt my eyesight weaken afterward. Using my ability always takes a bit of my sight along with it—"

"I know that," he said gently. "And that's the only reason I looked away as quickly as I did. I didn't want you to pay for my inadvertent lack of care. But there was a part of me that could've gotten lost in your naked gaze forever."

"No!" She gaped at him incredulously, aghast. "You wouldn't have done that. You know better than to look at my eyes when they're unprotected. *Everyone* knows better than that!"

"I wasn't thinking about your visions or what I might see in your eyes, Mouse. I rolled over that morning to kiss the beautiful woman who'd invited me into her bed and given me more pleasure than I knew was possible. You gave me the sweetest kiss I ever tasted, and then you smiled at me and opened your eyes."

"Oh, God. No, Kellan. Why did you look?" She moaned, a miserable sound that cut him to the marrow. When she turned her head away from him, Kellan brought her back to face him.

"Your eyes are extraordinary, Mira. They're bright as diamonds. Clear and flawless, like crystal pools. In that one fleeting moment that I looked into your gaze, I felt like I was seeing you—all of you—for the first time. And I'd never witnessed anything so beautiful." He caressed her face, wiped away the tear that rolled down her cheek. "That was worth the price. Worth any price fate may make me pay down the line."

"What did you see, Kellan?"

He had little choice but to tell her. "I saw myself, being led before Lucan and the GNC. There were charges against me—capital charges. Conspiracy, murder, treason. They judged me guilty on all counts. And so they sentenced me." He wanted to deliver the words gently, but there was no easy way to tell her what needed to be said. "The sentence was death, Mira. And I saw you there with me, begging for them to spare me. I don't want to think about the pain I saw in you, the grief that all of this will cause you when I'm put to death for my crimes."

She didn't speak. Just stared at him in silent torment, tears streaming down her face.

Kellan tried to smooth them away, but he couldn't keep up. He swore softly, hating that he'd caused her this hurt now and hoping he wouldn't bring her any more.

"I told you I thought you'd be happier believing I was dead eight years ago," he said. "But I had a selfish reason too. I would rather keep the memory of your sweet smile that morning in bed after we made love the first time than see the way you're looking at me now."

Behind them in the corridor, subtle movement sounded. Nina awkwardly cleared her throat. "Bowman? Doc needs to move Candice so he can cauterize her wound and stitch her up. He asked me to come find you—"

"Be right there," Kellan replied, his eyes locked on Mira, even as he drew away from her.

When he finally pivoted to return to his rebel comrades, he hoped Mira would take this chance to leave him and never look back.

He wouldn't blame her if she did.

13

RECLINING ON HIS ELBOWS ATOP THE BROAD PLANKS OF A PICNIC table in one of suburban Boston's conservation area parks, Vince tipped his head back on his shoulders and let the midday summer sun bathe his face in heat. Overhead, a crow sailed against the blinding blue of the sky.

That's me, Vince thought, grinning smugly up at the clouds. *Free bird.* Soon to be a *filthy rich* free bird.

He didn't know precisely whom he was meeting at this rendezvous Rooster had set up for him. Didn't much care either. All he knew was that making the call to the red-haired snitch after fleeing the base with Ackmeyer was about to net him serious pay dirt.

Rooster had immediately put out feelers with a few folks he knew, who in turn put out feelers to folks they knew, and then *bam!* Less than an hour later, they had a live one on the hook, ready to plunk down God-only-knew how much in exchange for the scientist and access to his Breed-smoking UV technology.

If Bowman had been smart—as smart as Vince—he would've thought of cashing in on Ackmeyer himself. But nope. He'd been too preoccupied with sniffing around the bitch from the Order to recognize the true opportunity he had with Ackmeyer. Then again, Bowman and Vince never had seen eye to eye on how things should be done.

Bowman's missions were always based on high-principled bullshit, like evening scores and righting wrongs. There wasn't a lot of cash to be made leaking intel on dirty politicians or exposing corporate grifters, but that never seemed to stop Bowman. And he had no qualms about derailing the ops of other rebel groups if he deemed their goals or methods too extreme.

As far as Vince was concerned, Bowman and his lofty morals could both get fucked. He preferred to operate based on profit and deal making.

Especially when those two objectives sent all the benefits directly into his hands, as they were about to do any minute now.

It was hard not to fantasize about what he was going to do and buy with the nut he stood to collect. Couple million, easy. Hell, maybe he should set his starting price at a cool five and see where it took him.

Gonna get himself a sweet ride, first of all. A swank place of his own too. Maybe he'd set up his own base of operations, recruit a fresh crew of his own and really shake shit up. Unfortunately, he'd have to open shop somewhere far from Boston, because no doubt about it, after the move Vince pulled today, Bowman was going to be coming after him hard.

Vince couldn't lie to himself; the thought of being on the receiving end of a pissed-off vampire's fury was more than a little disturbing. Didn't help that he'd seen Bowman in action enough to understand that there would be major hell to pay. The Breed male had skills that went beyond supernatural genetics. He was lethal even without the advantage of his otherworldly DNA, easily as badass deadly as any warrior of the Order. And for the first time since he'd known the vampire commander of the rebel base in New Bedford, that realization gave Vince serious pause.

Vince had always assumed Bowman's identity as a member of the Breed was his biggest secret, but now he wondered if there wasn't something else the vampire had been hiding . . .

Not that it mattered.

If Vince had his way, he was going to be big enough that he and his crew could go after Bowman themselves. Hell, maybe he'd use some of today's windfall to take out a hit on the Breed son of a bitch. How poetic would it be to see Bowman ashed with some of Ackmeyer's UV rounds?

Yeah, that was definitely going on the immediate agenda. Vince's first act, and a prime way to announce he's the new man in charge.

As he closed his eyes and ruminated on the pending birth of his rebel empire, the low rumble of an approaching, unmistakably expensive vehicle drew his chin back down to his chest. Vince raised his arm to visor his eyes, squinting as the sleek black sedan eased to a stop and a man in a dark suit and shades climbed out of the passenger-side door. With the micro-size comm unit clinging to his ear and his buzz-cut salt-and-pepper hair, the guy had a distinct government vibe about him, but the pricey wheels screamed private enterprise. Extremely lucrative private enterprise.

Imagining what he might look like prowling around town in a ride like that, Vince mentally upped his price tag on Ackmeyer.

The guy in the impeccable suit strode from the empty parking lot across the grass toward the picnic table. "Mr. Sunshine?"

Vince smiled, amused by the fitting alias he chose for this transaction. "That's me. And you are?"

"Why don't you come have a seat in the car? We can talk more comfortably inside."

It wasn't an answer. Hell, it wasn't even friendly. Sounded more like a command than the kind of respect Vince felt he was due. He didn't appreciate the superior attitude, and he wasn't stupid enough to get into a vehicle with someone he didn't know from Adam. No matter how much money was on the line.

"I'm enjoying the nice weather," he said, dropping his arm to his side and wishing he'd thought to bring sunglasses with him to this meeting too. Instead, he was forced to squint through the harsh daylight. He tried to work it in his favor, sneering in the hopes of looking more badass. "Listen, I'm a busy man. I got several interested parties for what I'm offering here today, so let's get down to business."

"Of course," replied the suit. "Where is the package?"

Vince chuckled. "Somewhere safe."

He also wasn't stupid enough to have Ackmeyer on-site until a firm deal was in hand. Vince had his hostage stowed and secured in the van, which was parked about a mile down the road, in another part of the conservation area. Once he had cash in hand, Vince would turn over his goods, but not a second before.

The guy in the suit didn't seem to understand the concept. "Until I can assure my employer that you will deliver what you promise, we have nothing to negotiate."

"Your employer?" Vince echoed, not a little put out to hear this. "I thought I'd be speaking to the man in charge, not some lackey."

"Do you intend to produce the package or not?" asked the suit, unfazed but unyielding.

"Hell no, I don't!" Vince vaulted off the picnic table, agitation vibrating through him. "You're wasting my time, man. I got four—no, five!—other potentials I could be talking to right now, every one of them ready, willing, and able to pony up serious cash." A bluff, but anger was making him cocky. He started pacing a tight track in front of the sharp-dressed gofer. "I'm in a situation where I want to get this done pronto, so tell you what. I'm willing to make a quick deal with you—or, rather, your employer. Ten million cash. Right here and now, no games, or I fucking walk."

The guy didn't say a word. Vince wasn't even sure he was listening. He watched as the guy lifted his hand to the comm device in his ear. "Status," he murmured, more of an order than an inquiry. A second later he grunted, said, "Excellent," then lowered his hand and continued to stare past Vince as if he were invisible.

"Well?" Vince demanded, impatient as hell and quickly getting beyond pissed at the lack of respect. "What's it gonna be? Make me wait another second for your answer, and my price doub—"

A sudden engine roar and screech of tires in the parking lot cut Vince off mid-threat. Not the throaty purr of another sweet sedan but the rusty bellow and knock of a vehicle he knew well. The same vehicle he'd stashed in what he assumed to be a safe place in another part of the park.

The van that contained Jeremy Ackmeyer, Vince's future fortune.

Some other goon in a dark suit was seated behind the wheel. The guy standing in front of Vince in the grass gave the driver a brief nod.

"What the fuck!" Vince shouted. "What the fuck is this?"

How the hell had this gone so wrong, so fast?

He didn't have time to guess. When he swung his head back around to look at the guy in the suit next to him, the nose of a black 9-mm pistol was leveled dead center on his face.

Now the suit finally managed to show some interest. He cracked a thin smile. "Get in the car, asshole."

Vince was shoved into motion, the gun ensuring he kept moving.

As he staggered toward the waiting sedan, he had a sinking feeling this was the closest he would ever get to feeling a few hundred grand worth of metal and leather and high-end performance machinery wrapped around his stupid, sorry ass.

* * *

Mira dumped an armful of wet, blood-soaked towels into a sink of cold, soapy water in the bunker's shower room and watched as the suds turned scarlet.

She should have left when she had the chance.

She should have just run away after hearing what Kellan told her. Back to the Order. Back to her teammates in Montreal. Back home to Niko and Renata.

Anywhere but here.

If what Kellan said was true, that fate would take him from her again—for good, this time—then she would do well to take whatever measures she could to spare herself that kind of hurt. She'd barely survived losing him the first time. How would she be able to bear that kind of pain again?

But she hadn't been able to make her feet take the path that would have led her out the door of Kellan's rebel base.

She couldn't make herself walk away from him, not when she could see that she still meant something to him. He still cared. Some hopeful part of her wanted to believe that he still loved her, even if he refused to admit that to himself or to her.

So, Mira hadn't run.

She'd stayed, taking it upon herself to mop up the blood from Vince's attack, while Kellan, Doc, and Nina were elsewhere in the bunker, ostensibly seeing to rebel business and looking after Chaz's remains once Candice had been stabilized.

Mira plunged her hands into the bloodied water and started washing the towels and rinsing them out. She tried to separate herself from the reality of the task—the knowledge that the blood staining her hands and clothes, running in a scarlet river down the opened drain of the sink, represented a life taken today, and another one narrowly spared. She tried to tell herself that this place, these people who lived and had now died here, were not hers to worry about.

But she was worried.

Worried about Candice, about Doc and Nina, all of whom had lost an old friend and made a new enemy today. She was worried about Jeremy Ackmeyer too, because as frightened as she'd been for him in Kellan's keeping, it was nothing compared to the dread she felt knowing Vince had him now and was obviously willing to kill anyone who stood in his way.

And she was worried about Kellan, of course.

Stricken to her marrow with fear over the vision he'd seen in her eyes on the terrible morning she'd mistakenly believed had been so perfect.

Mira hung her head, running another basin of cold water for the next round of washing.

For what wasn't the first time, she wished she'd been born without her gift. Her cursed ability, which brought anguish to nearly everyone who had the misfortune of glimpsing her unprotected gaze. She'd never known if her eyes would tell her own future too. She'd never had the courage to test it.

Now she wondered if she should try.

Would she see the same thing Kellan did?

Mira submerged a couple more blood-drenched towels into the water and watched as the crystalline liquid turned deep, murky red.

If she stared long enough into her own naked-eyed reflection, could she deplete her gift's power for good? She was tempted to find out, never mind that her eyesight died a little every time she exercised her seer's vision. She didn't care about that. Better she blind herself than risk delivering any more pain to someone else with her terrible ability.

She found her face in the dark water that filled the sink. Pale, weary lavender eyes stared back at her. The pain she felt was stamped all over her, worry bracketing her mouth and bruising the delicate skin beneath her lower lashes.

She heard a strangled moan and didn't realize it was coming from her own throat until the haggard young woman in the bloodred reflection opened her mouth on a sob.

The stained water rippled with her ragged exhalation, shattering her image into a hundred wavering pieces.

It took a few minutes to collect herself, time Mira used to finish the washing. She hung the wet towels on racks that contained other articles of laundered clothing. Another scrub of her hands still didn't remove the stains that rode under her fingernails and deep in her cuticles. For that, she'd need a good soak and plenty of soap.

Later, she promised herself, drying her hands and then stepping outside to the bunker's main corridor. Once she was there, she realized she didn't really know where to go.

She couldn't bring herself to go to Kellan's quarters to sit and wait for him. And she knew it wasn't her place to intrude on discussions or activities taking place between him and his diminished crew. Mira started walking, and soon found herself stepping past Candice's room.

She glanced in only briefly, but it was enough to notice that the young woman was awake, lying in her bed on her back. Her injured leg was bent at the knee and elevated with a mound of pillows and folded blankets, most of which had at some point toppled off to the side. She was trying to reach for them, struggling helplessly.

Mira blew out a sigh and took a reluctant step inside. "Here, let me help you with that."

"Thanks." Candice settled back in a slump, watching as Mira straightened the mess and carefully placed the restored mound under Candice's leg.

Mira glanced up. "How's that?"

"Better." She was still as pale as the sheets that covered her, little color in her lips, which curved into a small smile. "Will you bring me a sip of water, please?"

"Sure." Mira grabbed the cup and straw from the rickety nightstand beside the bed and held the drink while Candice sucked weakly. "How are you feeling?"

"Good." She nodded for Mira to set the cup down. "Doc says I'm going to make it. No walking for a week or so, and I'll have to take things slow for a while."

"But you're alive," Mira pointed out, and she felt genuinely glad about it.

"Yeah. Doc's the best. He's a good man." Candice was looking past Mira now, her jet-black eyebrows knitting into a small frown. "Where's everyone else?"

"They're around," Mira said. "There were things that needed to be done. Things for Chaz . . ."

She said it gently, not wanting to upset Candice. But the woman's hazel eyes went a darker shade of green as tears welled up in them. "Have they already buried him?"

"Not yet. I heard them talking about taking care of that later tonight. They want to do right by him. I heard them say his life deserves a worthy acknowledgment."

"Bowman," Candice said, smiling again, bigger than before. "That sounds like something he would say."

Mira stared, neither acknowledging nor denying it. But it had been he who'd said the words. It had been he who'd carried Chaz's lifeless body out of the cell and into a private chamber somewhere deep in the bunker. It had been he who'd informed the others that he wanted to perform a burial worthy of the warrior who'd served with honor and had fallen too soon.

Candice's eyes were locked on Mira in soft understanding. "Bowman's a good man too. I have a feeling you know that better than any of us."

Mira started to shake her head, but the denial wouldn't come. Instead she murmured, "It was a long time ago."

Candice's expression softened even more. "I don't need to know what he was called then, but I know it wasn't Bowman. I knew that from the minute he gave me the lie, when he finally woke up after two months of watching over him, unsure if he'd ever open his eyes, let alone speak. I didn't need to know his real name then either, or what he'd done that put him in the middle of a war zone."

Mira couldn't speak. Could only look at Candice and listen, reliving the private hell of the night she'd lost Kellan and his new life began.

"I figured he'd tell me his name one day, but he never did. Eventually I stopped looking for those answers." Candice brought her hand out from under the coverlet and laid it over the top of Mira's. "It didn't take long before I learned all I needed to know about the Breed male named Bowman who chose to live among humans instead of his own kind. I saw for myself that he was honorable. Not long after he was recovered, he learned there was a rebel faction looking to sell a group of young women into prostitution. The deal had already been struck with some bad men from overseas, but on the night the rebels were to make the trade, Bowman stepped in to derail the exchange and free those girls single-handed."

Mira was hardly surprised to hear it, having seen Kellan in action when they were part of the same unit for the Order. He was a fierce warrior, afraid of nothing when it came to combat and protecting those who couldn't do for themselves. Apparently those qualities had followed him into this other part of his life too, in spite of the fact he now straddled a threadbare moral line.

Candice went on. "I saw from the start that he was courageous and just. But he was also scarred somewhere deep inside. He was alone and kept himself isolated by choice. I knew he belonged to someone else. I just didn't know who, until I saw the way he looked at you when we brought you back with us to the base that day."

"You saved his life," Mira finally managed to croak out of her dry throat, swamped by gratitude for this woman she hardly knew. "I thought he was dead, but you found him. You took care of him. You and Doc didn't know him at all, but you didn't let him die . . ."

Candice frowned slightly, gave a mild shrug. "He needed help. We gave it. That's all."

"You did all that, even though he was Breed."

"If you saw someone bleeding and broken in the street, would you stop to see if he was different from you before you lifted him up?"

Mira fell silent as Candice's words sank in. And then she knew a profound shame, because she realized that, not very long ago, she might have been the one to turn her back. Her hatred and mistrust of humans, rebels in particular, was so blind and deep, she likely wouldn't have even broken her stride if it had been one of them in need of her help.

It was ugly, what she'd allowed herself to become.

For so long, she'd held people like Candice and Doc and Nina in contempt, lumped together with lowlifes like Vince and Rooster—villains all of them, to be squashed under her boot or skewered by her blades.

And now . . . ?

She withdrew her hand from beneath Candice's loose grasp, feeling undeserving of the kindness she was being shown. She felt regret for the loss these people had suffered today. And she felt fear for what their future might hold, if what Kellan saw in her eyes eventually came to pass.

The coldness that thought brought with it settled in Mira's chest like ice. She needed to find some distance from the dread that was pressing down on her when she considered the price all of them might pay if her vision proved true.

Mira summoned what she hoped was a reassuring smile. "You should rest now. I'll let Doc know how you're doing."

At Candice's nod, Mira backed away from her bedside and pivoted toward the door. She paused there, gratitude rising inside her, swamping even the darker tide of emotion that was doing its best to pull her under.

She looked back at the human female who'd done the impossible eight years ago, bringing Kellan back from the dead and delivering the miracle Mira had hoped for so desperately. "Thank you for saving him."

Candice smiled. "My part was easy. Now it's your turn."

14

HIS CLOTHES WERE STICKING TO HIM IN THE HUMIDITY OF THE bunker, his hands and forearms splattered with caked, dried blood. Even the faint, stale copper tang of the dead red cells had Kellan's head pounding and his muscles twitching with aggression as he stalked through the main corridor of the fortress.

He wanted to kill, not only because the predator in him was provoked by the scent of so much spilled blood today but because people he cared about—good people—had met with undeserved harm.

Because of him.

Because they'd trusted him as their leader, and he'd let them down.

He hadn't gone after Vince that morning like he'd intended. He still seethed with the urge to tear down all of Boston to find the bastard, but his crew had needed him here more. And the rational part of his brain reminded him that Mira was right: A full-scale pursuit in broad daylight would've been suicidal. He'd be dead soon enough, according to her vision. And he couldn't help thinking that the fact he hadn't run out into the sun today only fortified that he was still on a direct collision course with the fate he'd glimpsed in Mira's eyes.

Kellan's boots thudded hollowly in the corridor as he strode toward his quarters to change his clothes and clean up. The marked silence of the bunker around him was striking. He didn't like it. Didn't like knowing that he'd brought this trouble down on the base.

Despite living on the outermost fringes of the law, Kellan and his small band of rebels had never had violence cross their threshold to attack from within. They'd never lost one of their own before, not even in the field. They'd been lucky, keeping a low profile, running tight operations, and living off the grid. Avoiding the kind of unwanted attention and notoriety on which other rebel factions seemed to thrive. Now that they had suffered this blow, their shock and grief was running deep.

Kellan was no stranger to the feeling.

All of this bloodshed brought him back to his past, when he was a sheltered Darkhaven youth and evil had robbed him of his family. In a single night, a madman's violence had destroyed the Archers' primary estate in Boston, stripping Kellan of everyone he loved but his grandfather, Lazaro. Fortunately for the two of them, the Order had stepped in to offer its shelter and protection. They'd brought Kellan and Lazaro into the fold as the Order's own, a kindness Kellan could never hope to repay.

Especially not now.

And Mira . . .

She'd been there for him from the moment he first arrived on the Order's doorstep. A pint-size pain in his ass who wouldn't let any of his bullshit slide, not even then. He'd been so terrified of caring for someone after losing so many people he loved, he had refused to let anyone in back then.

And although he'd been a stupid boy, hardly able to recognize the bone-deep fear at the root of his sullenness and pain, Mira had been far wiser, even as a child. She'd seen right through him. She'd stubbornly taken him under her tiny wing as her friend and had refused to let go, not even when he pushed.

No, whenever he'd pushed, she'd dug in her heels and stood steadfast for him—just as she'd done today, taking it upon herself to pitch in like one of his crew, to show them true concern and support, in spite of how he'd left things with her.

He wanted to be furious with her for that, the way the caustic, aloof teenage boy she'd known so well would respond to such an act of defiant generosity of spirit. But the man he'd since become couldn't muster any anger. What he felt instead was a squeezing in his chest, an all-too-pleasant sense of gratitude and pride that she was his.

Should have been his, he corrected himself harshly.

And, as her damnable vision assured him, could not be his for long.

His answering curse was rough and self-directed as he rounded a turn in the corridor and stalked past the closed door of the bunker's shower room.

The water was running on the other side.

It wasn't Doc or Nina, seeing how just a few minutes ago Kellan had left the two of them with Chaz's body at the opposite end of the fortress. And Candice wasn't going anywhere for days. She was resting quietly in bed when he'd checked on her on his way here.

Keep walking.

That's what he should do. And yet he paused outside the door and turned the latch.

Mira stood naked under the spray of the shower, her head tipped back, water sluicing over her pale-blond hair and down her creamy skin.

Kellan's breath left him in a rush. Instead of quietly closing the door and moving on, he opened it wider and stepped inside the steam-filled room. He pulled the door closed behind him.

At the resulting soft *click*, Mira covered herself with her hands and arms and looked his way. There was uncertainty in her lavender eyes. Lips parted but unspeaking.

Kellan stood there, taking in the sight of her. "You stayed," he murmured.

She swallowed, water dripping off her chin, spiking her long lashes. "I stayed."

He nodded, but he could feel a scowl furrowing deep into his brow. "I just looked in on Candice. She told me that you'd been in to see her, said the two of you talked . . . about me?"

"Yes," Mira said softly, still hiding herself from him, not quite ready to drop her guard, not that he could blame her.

"You didn't tell her my name," he remarked. "You didn't tell her about my past with the Order." Head lowered, eyes rooted on her, he took a step forward. Then another. "You kept my secrets. All of them."

"Of course," she replied.

"You protected me," he acknowledged. Now he was standing directly in front of her, right at the edge of the open shower. "You did that for me, even though I gave you no reason to."

She gave him a faint nod, arms still crossed over herself like a shield. "Yes."

Her inhaled breath turned into a little squeak as he walked into the water with her, clothing, boots, and all. He stood before her, getting drenched head to toe and not giving a damn about it. "You could've made a clean break today. Goddamn, I wish you had."

"I—" she began, but he cut her off with a hissed curse.

"You could've been gone from all of this. Instead you helped clean up a mess that belonged to me, then you had the tenderness of heart to look in on one of my injured crew." He shook his head and gently took her hands in his, pulled them away from her naked body. He dropped a kiss to each of her clenched fists. "After everything I told you out there today, you stayed."

She stared at him, her lips parted slightly, breasts rising and falling with each rapid breath she drew into her lungs. Kellan was still holding her hands. Slowly he lowered them to her sides, away from the beauty of her nude body. "After everything I've done," he whispered harshly, "not only today, or eight years ago, when I left, letting you believe I was dead, but since the first day we met, Mouse. Ever since then, since the very beginning, you've stayed with me. You've always had my back."

"I always will," she replied. Her voice was quiet, but her eyes were resolute. "When you love someone, that's what you do."

Kellan went still. He could hardly move, could hardly command his lungs to pull in breath. "Don't say that, Mira. That's the worst thing you can say to me right now."

"Why?" She gazed up at him under the spray of the shower, her skin bathed in warm light from the heat of his eyes as their hazel color flashed with sparks of amber. "Why shouldn't I tell you how I feel about you?"

He searched for his voice but found only an otherworldly growl. "Because when you say that, it makes me want to hold on tighter to you when I should be letting you go. And I need to let you go . . . before things get any worse."

"Then let go, Kellan."

Her words took him aback. It was a command, spoken without edge, without the slightest waver. He stared at her beautiful face, at the courageous, unflinching eyes and impish nose with its smattering of light freckles. At the stubborn mouth that had never given him an ounce of pity, not even when it came to pleasure. A mouth that was pressed into a flat line now, waiting for his response.

"If you don't love me," she said, "if you truly want me gone . . . then let go."

He didn't. His fingers stayed clamped around her hands, going tighter, despite every sane and logical cell in his body telling him—no, demanding him—to release her now and walk away.

"Fucking hell, Mouse," he hissed, low and lethal. Then, without a second's warning, he brought his head down to hers and took her mouth.

The kiss was hard and deep and possessive. He couldn't give it to her any other way, not in that moment.

And she took him for all he was worth. He sent his tongue past her lips, groaning with animal need when she sucked at him, her mouth opening to him on a broken sigh.

His veins were on fire, shooting lava through his limbs, into his head and heart, into his groin. He laced his fingers through hers and guided her around with his body, until he was crowding her back against the wet wall of the shower. Her nipples were beads he could feel through the soaked fabric of his T-shirt. Her curves were soft and lush, melting perfectly against his hard planes and ridges.

Kellan lifted his arms, taking hers with them on an upward slide along the wall, until he held her hands high above her head. He pinned her there, caught in his grasp and bound by the weight of his body leaning into her. Still kissing her, devouring her mouth, he ground his stiff erection against her abdomen. She felt so good, his pelvis jerked on its own, his cock giving a hard leap behind the tight confinement of his jeans.

He dropped his head to her neck and kissed her there, making her moan and shudder beneath his lips. "Fuck, Mira," he growled against her delicate, water-sluiced throat. "Fuck."

He rocked into her, his clothing soaked, head delirious with the warm, wet scent of her naked skin and the sweet, honeyed fragrance of her arousal. His fangs throbbed, filling his mouth.

A taste of her sweetness.

He needed it now.

Her blood called to him, but it was another nectar that drew him away from her neck on a ragged snarl. Only then did he let loose her hands, sinking down in front of her, kissing his way past her breasts and ribs, then lower, along the muscular softness of her belly.

She made an impatient noise in the back of her throat as he took his time getting where he was heading, mouth and tongue and lips sampling every inch of tender skin they ran across. With one hand on her breast, he smoothed the other along her side, raising gooseflesh in his wake and making her tremble with tiny, sigh-laced spasms.

As he kissed her body, his roaming hand slid down the length of her thigh, then came around to the inside and began a lazy upward path along her tender flesh. A nudge of his fingers opened her thighs to him. He smiled against her stomach at her eager response, then delved the tip of his tongue into her navel while he trailed his knuckles over the silky petals at her core.

He parted her with his fingertips and slid them into her hot cleft. She quivered in his hand, breath catching and shaky as he stroked his thumb over the tight little pearl nestled at the top of her slit. Kellan's fangs surged even longer in his mouth, desire knifing through him.

He was down on his knees before her now, head lowering between her legs as the warm spray of the shower pelted him from above. On a deep growl, he turned his face toward the inside of her thigh and suckled the tender skin there. She moaned and gasped, her climax already building and he hadn't even put his mouth where he wanted it to be.

Kellan lifted her leg onto his shoulder, kissing her some more, taking wicked enjoyment in the fact that she was so ready for him, so eager and responsive. For *him*, he thought greedily. She'd said it herself that morning in his bed. There had been no one but him, not in all this time. Not ever.

A tide of possessiveness swamped him. Unbidden. Undeserved.

Yet undeniable, especially when Mira was melting for him so sweetly.

He swiveled his head back to admire the flushed pink temptation of her sex. A brief kiss made her shiver. His lips and fangs teasing the juicy petals made her suck in a sharp breath, sent her hands into his hair, holding him steady as he cleaved her flesh with his tongue and brought the intoxicating taste of her into his mouth.

"Oh, my God," she rasped brokenly. "I'm going to come."

"Not yet," he murmured. Then he reached around to grasp her firm little ass in both hands and hauled her to his hungry mouth.

He buried his face in her, drinking her in, drowning in her. In that next instant, she shattered against his mouth, hips bucking, spasms rippling through her in pretty waves. He lapped her up, thirsty for more.

As her climax began to ebb, she swung her leg down off his shoulder and grabbed at him. Her fingers were demanding, twisting in his soaked T-shirt, trying to yank it off him. "Inside me," she panted. "Now, Kellan."

He rose without argument. Pulled off his shirt and tossed it to the shower floor in a wet heap, then kicked off his boots while Mira worked on the buttons of his drenched jeans. She fumbled more than once and he took over. No sooner had he opened the last button, Mira pushed his pants down over his hips, freeing his engorged cock into her wet, waiting hands.

She stroked him a few times, and God help him, it was all he could bear.

Gathering her up in his arms, he lifted her thighs around his waist and drove home in one deep thrust. Both of them grunted with the force of their joining, both of them shuddering as he seated himself to the root, filling her, stretching her like a silken glove around his girth. He pumped his pelvis a few times, but he was too far gone to take it easy.

He fell into an urgent rhythm, holding fast to Mira, watching her face as the crest of another climax rose up on her. She clutched at him, heels digging into his ass, fingernails scoring his shoulders. His own orgasm was coiling at the base of his spine, heat shooting through his veins.

Mira gripped him more fiercely, her pleasured sighs turning into rapid pants as the first tremors of her release coursed along the length of Kellan's shaft. He plunged deeper, harder, pushing her toward it. Holding back his own need until he felt her start to splinter around him. She let out a throaty cry as she came, her breath blowing like a furnace against his ear.

Kellan kept his fevered eyes on her, drinking in every nuance of her release. She was so beautiful. So damn sexy. So hot and wet and greedy, her tiny muscles milking him as he thrust at a frenzied tempo, his cock pistoning in and out of her slick sheath.

His orgasm rolled up on him like a freight train, fierce and uncontainable.

He came on a roar, hips bucking wildly, unable to stop even after the last of his seed had poured out of him. Spent but far from sated, he dropped his head to the curve of her shoulder and simply rocked into her, savoring the feel of her body pressed to his, the hot, wet haven of her sex holding him inside.

"You stayed," he murmured, mouth moving over the side of her neck, where her pulse throbbed in time with his.

Her softly whispered answer sifted into his hair where her lips rested against the top of his head. "You didn't let go."

15

THEY MADE LOVE AGAIN, SLOWLY, THEN TOOK TURNS WASHING each other under the warm spray of the shower.

A few minutes later, Mira was in Kellan's quarters, getting dressed with him in a comfortable silence. She could almost imagine that they were a couple in truth, sharing this space as bonded mates. Sharing the bed as lovers, which shouldn't have been as tempting to her, considering the number of times he'd just made her come.

Mira watched Kellan move as he put on fresh clothes, a black T-shirt that clung to his muscled chest and shoulders, short sleeves tight around his *glyph*-adorned biceps. His long, firm thighs disappeared into dark jeans that hugged his fine ass and rode at just the right level on his sharply cut hips.

He was gorgeous, and a few minutes ago she had tasted every divine inch of him. She allowed herself to savor that memory for a moment, standing near the foot of the bed in just her bra and panties.

It was so easy to feel normal around him. To feel whole. She wasn't ready to give that up. She'd never be ready for that, no matter what her damned vision had shown him.

Kellan shot her an appraising glance over his shoulder as he buttoned the fly of his jeans. "Good as you look like that, you'd better put something on before I jump you again." He lifted his chin, indicating his clothing trunk at her feet. "You'll find more shirts in there. Take your pick."

The black jeans she'd had on the day she and Jeremy Ackmeyer were brought to the rebel base were still in decent shape, a bit worse for wear, but doable. Her shirt had been toast, ripped up in the scuffle and ruined with blood and grime. Mira hunkered down on folded legs in front of Kellan's clothing locker and sifted through the dozen or so Ts and jerseys stacked neatly inside.

Her hand bumped against something cold and metallic, tucked between a few of the articles. She pulled it out to see what it was. A hand mirror, elegant and feminine, the back of it fashioned of polished silver, inlaid with delicate black onyx cut into the shape of a gracefully arched bow bearing a nocked arrow—the Archer family emblem.

"It belonged to my grandmother," Kellan said when Mira looked up at him in question.

"It's stunning." She ran her fingertip over the careful craftsmanship, admiring each flawless line. "How did you get this?"

When he disappeared years earlier, he'd taken nothing with him but the clothes on his back the night of the patrol that had gone so wrong.

Kellan strode over and gently took the mirror from her grasp. He turned it over in his hands, his mouth curving into a distant smile. "A couple years ago, I ran reconnaissance on a militia group I planned to shut down. They were dealing drugs and small arms out of Maine, north of Augusta. Realized when my intel gathering was over, I was only a few miles from my grandfather, Lazaro's, old place up there."

"The temporary compound the Order moved into after our headquarters in Boston was compromised." Mira recalled it well, even though she'd been just a girl at the time she and Kellan and the rest of the warriors and their mates had lived there.

After First Dawn, it was decided by Lucan and the other elders that the Order needed to spread its resources around the United States and Europe, to better combat uprisings and violence that occurred in the wake of the Breed's outing to mankind. Lazaro Archer, Kellan's grandfather, was now the leader of the Order's command center in Italy.

Mira thought about the many good times—and the handful of bad—that had taken place in that hidden Darkhaven compound nestled in the deep woods of northern Maine. Her first snowball fight, pitted against Kellan and Nathan. Her first Christmas tree, shared with Renata and Nikolai and the rest of her new family, all of the warriors and their mates. The presentation ceremony for Xander Raphael, Dante and

Tess's son, who'd been born just days before the Order's emergency relocation from Boston.

So many memories, and she could see that Kellan was reliving them
too.

"The place was vacant, or I never would've risked going near it," he
said. "But there were a few things left behind. Furnishings, some clothing . . . and this." He touched the bow-and-arrow emblem with reverent
fingers. "It was in my grandfather's quarters, on top of a dressing table
he'd made for my grandmother out of the surrounding pines. The mirror was charred and blackened with soot and ash. I realized then and
there that he must've gone back to our Boston Darkhaven after it had
been razed. He must've crawled through the rubble to retrieve this,
even though he'd vowed he would never go back to the scene of her
death. Back to the house that took her and my parents—all of my kin,
his kin—down in flames."

"Kellan," Mira whispered, her heart squeezing in her breast.

"I had no right to take it, but once it was in my hand, I couldn't leave
it behind." He carefully replaced the mirror into the chest, setting it
gingerly on top of the soft contents. "I have something else that I have
no right keeping either."

He strode over to his bureau and opened the top drawer. Took out
her treasured dagger and walked it back to her. She took it from his
outstretched hand with a small, grateful smile.

She read the word that was carved onto each side of the precious
blade. "Honor. Sacrifice." The other one, the other half of the pair,
which she'd lost the day she was brought back into Kellan's life, bore
another set of tenets she strove to live by: Faith. Courage. "It feels
strange, just the one," she murmured. "Unbalanced. Not as strong without its mate. I never thought they'd be separated."

Kellan's eyes were tender on her, his expression sober, regretful. He
clearly understood that she could as easily be speaking about the two of
them. "I never wanted to take anything away from you, Mouse. Least of
all your happiness. I didn't want to cost you anything, including the
blade that I promised you'd have again, before everything went so
wrong. Just another way I've let you down."

He reached out, gently lifted her to her feet. He stroked her face, his
touch so careful and kind, she nearly choked on the sob building in her

throat. "If I could go back in time, I'd change so much," he said. "I would do whatever it took to make sure you'd never be caught up in this with me in the first place."

"No," she replied, pulling herself together and giving a firm shake of her head. "No. I wouldn't trade a minute of what we just shared. Would you?"

He didn't speak for a long moment, just caressed her cheeks and brushed his thumb over her lips, before settling his warm hand along the nape of her neck.

"Would you really take it all back?" she asked, terrified of his answer.

His smile was slow as his eyes crackled with banked but still burning heat. "I'm still holding on to you, aren't I?"

He kissed her, and Mira couldn't curb the dread that rose in her when she thought of losing him again. She didn't want to let the awfulness of her vision ruin this moment, but it was there just the same, refusing to give her any peace. She drew back from Kellan's sweet kiss and tipped her head down, closing her eyes as he rested his forehead against hers, still holding her close.

"Kellan," she said, then pulled away, looking up into his amber-flecked hazel eyes. "Tell me again about the vision you saw. About the charges leveled against you."

His handsome face sobered, jaw going a bit tighter as he clamped his molars together. "They were capital charges, Mouse. Just like I told you."

"Yes, but what were they, specifically?"

"Conspiracy," he said evenly. "Treason. Kidnap and murder."

Her pulse skidded on the last one. "Murder. How many people have you killed, Kellan?"

"Too many to recall," he replied, no apology in his voice. "You know about all of them. You were there with me for far too many, when the streets were red with spilled lives."

"No," she said. "That was wartime, not murder. How many unsanctioned kills, Kellan? How many times since you became Bowman have you taken someone's life?"

He stared, considering. He stared for a very long time, then gave a resolute shake of his head. "There is no way of telling how far into the future the vision is destined to occur. We only know that it will, because your visions never fail, Mira. They haven't, in all this time." He paced away from her, raking a hand through his dark copper hair. "Besides, that doesn't negate any of the other charges that I am guilty of: kidnapping Ackmeyer, the relative of a high-ranking GNC government diplomat, and, in so doing, conspiring to disrupt a peace summit. By doing both of those things, I've knowingly led myself and my crew into an act of treason."

"But not murder," Mira stressed. Now that she had a shred of hope in her grasp, she wasn't about to let it slip through her fingers. "You aren't guilty of the last charge. That's something in your control now, from this moment forward. And if the vision is wrong about one of the charges, it can be wrong about any of them. Maybe we can change the course of this, Kellan. Together."

He came back to her, standing right in front of her but saying nothing. His eyes bore into hers, his face gone utterly still except for the sudden tick of a tendon in his jaw. She could sense the wheels turning in his mind. She could feel his pulse throbbing hotly, vibrating the air in the scant inch that separated their bodies.

He swore, vicious and raw, under his breath. Not a sound of anger but one of relief.

Of hope.

His hands shot out and he pulled her to him, kissed her hard on the mouth. Then he let go and spun away to grab for his comm unit on the bureau next to his bed. He checked the time, swung a fierce look on her. "It'll be sundown in thirty minutes." He grabbed a dry pair of boots from nearby and stomped into them. "I'm heading into Boston. I need to find Vince and bring Ackmeyer out of this alive."

"I'm going with you," Mira announced, already wearing one of his T-shirts and yanking on her black jeans. She reached for her combat boots, but Kellan stopped her with his hand coming down firmly on her wrist.

"You stay put," he said. "I'm not putting you in harm's way. Besides, I can cover more ground faster on foot."

She got right up in his face, just like when they were kids. "Either I go with you, or I go alone, Archer."

That tendon that had been ticking in his jaw before now started to pound. His eyes were blazing, searing her with their sharp flashes of amber. She didn't cower. She glared up into those dangerous eyes and held them steady. It was a look he had to recognize, one he had to understand meant she was not about to back down.

"Goddamn it," he growled. "We leave in five."

He stormed out of the room ahead of her. Mira tucked her dagger into the sheath on her belt and went after him.

The knock on the door of the ground-level apartment of the rat-infested triple-decker in Boston's Charlestown neighborhood came roughly seven minutes after sundown. Prompt, considering Rooster had been summoned there only five minutes ago by his friend's urgent, unexplained phone call.

Nathan casually eyed the dead heroin-dealing pimp who lay sprawled where he'd fallen, windpipe crushed five and a half minutes ago, after the human had the bad sense to think the vampire in his living room could be gotten rid of with the help of the revolver stowed under a sofa cushion. The butt of the unused Smith & Wesson was still wedged between the tattered, plaid-covered foam and a fleece throw that didn't quite mask the stains and cigarette burns riddling the filthy upholstery.

Nathan assumed the weapon was loaded, not that he cared. He'd been trained as a boy to kill a hundred different ways with his bare hands. And he'd never taken a hit in all this time. His record was flawless. His mercy nonexistent.

Rooster's rap on the door came again, two staccato beats. "Yo, Billy! You gonna open this damn door or—"

His words dried up in his throat in that next instant, as Nathan had the door open, Rooster yanked inside, and the dead bolts thrown home in the time it would have taken the human to utter another syllable.

"What the fuck!" he hollered, falling back onto the sofa where Nathan dropped him. His bloodshot eyes were wide under the ridiculous plume of his scarlet mohawk as he scrambled to right himself, trying to get his bearings inside the gloomy apartment. His confused, searching gaze finally lit on Nathan, standing in the shadows in front of him. "Oh, shit . . . no fucking way! Billy, what the fuck you doin' with the Order, man?"

Nathan stared down at him. "I need to talk to you, Rooster. Tried your place first, but you weren't home."

"Talk to me? I got no business with you, man. Got no business with the fuckin' Order!" Rooster's eyes went a bit wider, the whites rolling around in his skull as he glanced around him, no doubt looking for some support from his friend. Support he wasn't going to get. He realized that a moment later, when his panicked gaze landed on the motionless limbs and sightless stare of the corpse lying just a few feet away. "Holy shit! That Billy right there? Naw, I don't fuckin' believe this shit! I just talked to him, like five minutes ago."

Nathan shrugged. "Billy made the call to you because I asked him to. Then Billy got stupid and now he's dead."

"Oh, God!" Rooster howled, burying his head in his hands. "Shit, man . . . this is messed up! What the hell do you want from me?"

"Information, to start," Nathan said.

He'd done some discreet digging during the daylight hours between Lucan handing him this solo task and the wait till sundown, when he could finally hit the streets and start taking care of business. Word came back that most of the local lowlifes hadn't known the first thing about a civilian abduction, so whoever was responsible was keeping the intel close to their vest. But the common denominator when it came to rebel factions and related activity around Boston was the red-combed loser spluttering and twitching on the sofa in front of Nathan.

"Ain't got no information," Rooster whined. "You got the wrong guy, man."

Nathan narrowed his look on the human informant. "I know you're not going to sit there and deny you have business dealings of potential interest to me. I'm not talking about drug-dealing flesh-peddlers like this asshole Billy over here, but other associates of yours. Ones who might know something about a situation that went down a couple days ago over in the Berkshires."

Rooster's upper lip twitched. "What kind of situation?"

"Kidnapping," Nathan replied. "Someone very important. Potentially very high profile."

A sharp inhalation as the snitch fidgeted, crossing and uncrossing his arms. He was clued in now. He had information. He would talk. Just a matter of time, but unluckily for Rooster, Nathan's mission meant he was short on that commodity.

"This kidnapping also netted another hostage," he told the man. "One of particular interest to the Order and to me personally as well."

Rooster let out his breath in a gust of sour air. "I don't know anything about her, I swear."

"You just told me you do." Nathan's lethal instincts prickled to full attention, but he remained as outwardly calm as his years of unforgiving training as a born-and-bred killer had made him.

He took hold of Rooster's biceps, sure that the injuries Mira had inflicted with her blades at La Notte a few nights ago still pained the human. He squeezed, ignoring Rooster's sharp cry of anguish. "Take a look at your friend. You remember how I said Billy got stupid before he got dead?" That red mohawk wobbled with its owner's jerky nod. "Don't be stupid, Rooster. Tell me where they took Mira and Jeremy Ackmeyer."

When he didn't hear an answer through the groan of agony coming out of Rooster's mouth, Nathan increased the pressure.

"I don't know," the human howled. "I don't fuckin' know! Last I knew Ackmeyer was with Vince, man. You should be lookin' for him, not me!"

"Vince who?" Nathan demanded.

"I don't know the dude's last name, just know he runs with Bowman and his crew. Or did until today."

"Bowman," Nathan repeated, the first he'd heard of that name among rebel circles. "Where can I find Bowman?"

"Don't know. Never met him." Rooster's face was screwed up in a grimace when Nathan didn't relent for an instant on his wounded arms. "All's I know is, he heads up a small operation somewhere outside Boston."

Nathan noted the new intel but returned his focus to the rest of Rooster's statement. "And this other individual—Vince. He's got Ackmeyer now? Vince decide to run solo or something?"

Rooster nodded. "He was lookin' to make a ransom when he contacted me this morning. Never heard the dude so fired up and cocky. Said Ackmeyer was some kind of genius. Said he invented some kind of UV technology shit that was worth a fortune to the right buyer."

Although Nathan had a cursory awareness of Jeremy Ackmeyer's public résumé and his contributions to the science and technology arenas, word of an invention of the type Rooster just mentioned came as a surprise. A very disturbing one.

He said nothing in reaction to this news, his mind playing out a host of possibilities that might come out of a scientific breakthrough involving ultraviolet light. None of them good where the Breed was concerned. And he could only imagine the kind of interest the availability of such technology might attract.

"What else do you know about Vince's plans to ransom Ackmeyer? Did he mention who he was looking at as potential buyers?" Nathan peered at the twitchy informant with assessing eyes. "Let me guess. That's why Vince got in touch with you—to put him in front of someone who might want the deal he had to offer."

Rooster swallowed, still wincing at the pain Nathan was inflicting. "He promised me a cut of his take, so I made some calls. I don't know who took the bait. All's I did was put the word out."

Nathan felt justified in killing Rooster for that offense alone, but he still had Mira to think about. "What about the female? Was Vince looking to turn some kind of profit on her head too?"

"Like I said, man, I don't know nothin' about her. Only what Vince said when I saw him today."

"And what was that?" Nathan all but snarled.

"He said Bowman seems to be having a real good time with her." This Rooster announced with remarkably reckless amusement. He chuckled, even through the pain he was enduring. "Don't ask me to feel sorry for the bitch. After what she did to me the other night, far's I'm concerned, she can suck my dick too."

Nathan's fury stunned him, it roared up so violently inside him. It seethed through his veins, although it was clear from Rooster's continued blathering, the human didn't sense the sudden shift in the air from dangerously tense to lethal still.

He went on, his stupidity far greater than Billy's ill-intended move to defend himself against certain death. "I hope she's gettin' it real good. I hope she got it from Vince and all the rest of Bowman's crew too. Teach that uppity bitch a lesson, put her in her fuckin' place."

Nathan's control snapped, just like that, but outwardly he didn't so much as blink.

He released Rooster's arms and grabbed his head between both palms. Then gave a twist, severing the human's spinal column in one swift twitch of his hands.

He let the body drop, and Rooster's head with its bright red comb of hair flopped at a grotesque angle in the dead man's lap.

Then Nathan turned and calmly walked out of the dump and into the night to continue his mission.

16

THEY HAD BEEN IN THE CITY FOR MORE THAN AN HOUR, BUT SO far, Rooster was as good as a ghost. He wasn't at his apartment. Hadn't been seen all day, according to the lowlifes he tended to hang with, dealing drugs or fencing electronics down in West Roxbury. No one had seen or heard from him since he'd run with them the night before.

As for Kellan, although he knew he'd recognize Rooster's signature hairstyle on the spot, he'd never had direct contact with him, always filtering messages and intel by way of Vince. Now he regretted that lack of connection. Finding the bastard would have been much easier if he'd been able to call Rooster and personally threaten his sorry life if he didn't cooperate in locating Vince. Not a good way to avoid the murder charge he had no intention of inviting.

But while Kellan's frustration level was steadily climbing toward lethal fury, Mira wasn't deterred by the lack of success thus far. She charged forth with her usual stubborn-headed determination, dragging him along to Boston's old North End, to the club and cage-fighting arena where she'd last seen Rooster a few nights ago.

"Since we're down here anyway," she said as the neo-Gothic silhouette of the converted church rose up into the night sky ahead of them. "It's early, so if he's not inside the club somewhere, our next best bet is a crackhead who calls himself Billy the Kid. He and Rooster did a stretch together in Bridgewater for possession a while back. From what I've heard, they're still tight."

Kellan grunted, impressed with her as usual, and finding it far too easy to fall back into the rhythm of seasoned patrol partners. He had to remind himself that this was not an op shared by fellow warriors. He was not a member of the Order, and Mira was risking her life just being with him—not because of the danger of what they were undertaking here but because of who he was, of who he'd become over these past eight years.

Fortunately, he'd been careful to keep a very low profile. His name, Bowman, might be uttered in dark rooms and back alleys from time to time, but he could practically count on one hand how many people had ever seen his face. Most of those people were back at the base in New Bedford. And now one of that number was dead.

Heavy bass throbbed, grinding guitar chords screaming, as Mira strode for the vestibule door of La Notte's main entrance and pulled it open. Kellan walked in alongside her, surveying the place with a judicious eye. Although the club was crowded for the early evening hour, most of the clientele gathered in front of the head-banging, five-man group looked like kids out of the suburbs and assorted tourist types. Primarily human, although Kellan noted a trio of Darkhaven youths skulking in the far corner, eyes trained on a clutch of big-haired, scantily clad young women who had a table full of empty glasses and seemed more than ready to keep the party going.

"The cage matches don't start until close to midnight," Mira told him, leaning in close to avoid having to shout over the din of music and chatter in the room. "This is just the warm-up."

Her breath beside his ear went through him like a lick of flame, unbidden but hard as hell to ignore. He narrowly resisted putting his hands on her, his head suddenly full of images of her naked in his bed, in the shower. But then Mira put her hand on his forearm, and her fingers bit in as she tugged him into the crowd. "Come on. Rooster's not here. Let's move."

"What's wrong?" he asked, pivoting his head on a scowl to scan the area behind the bar, where she'd been looking just before she grabbed him away. His gaze lit on a pair of males—one of them unmistakably Breed, with long blond hair pulled back in a braided leather tie, accentuating cheekbones that would have looked more in place on a female, if not for the killer coldness of his pale-blue eyes. He stood with massive arms crossed over his chest, listening to the other male who faced him, his back to Mira and Kellan.

"That's Syn," she said, nodding toward the Breed giant. "He's one of the newer fighters. That human he's talking to?" Her chin lifted, gesturing at the equally tall but less bulky man who was dressed in head-to-toe black leather that sported gleaming buckles and bristling spikes. His silver-white hair was shorn in a smooth wedge that rode his skull like a halo. Not that there was anything remotely angelic about him. "That's Cassian, the owner of this place. We shouldn't let either of them see us in here."

Neither one of the men looked happy. Nor did they break the focus of their intense conversation as Mira led Kellan to a shadowed back stairwell. They descended the flight of steps into what appeared to be the bowels of the old church. At the bottom, they emerged into a basementlike walkway illuminated by sparsely placed dim bulbs, aged brick walls tunneling ahead of them and foot-worn stone at their feet.

"This was once used as a crypt," Mira informed him. "Now the fighters' private dressing rooms are down here, along with the arena."

Kellan had never been near one of the illegal cage-fighting clubs, and he wasn't enthused to realize how familiar Mira had become with them. A surge of protectiveness rose up in him as he watched her hips sway with each quiet stride of her combat boots on the stone floor. He didn't want her in the vicinity of dangerous males, let alone dangerous Breed males who made their names and fortunes by tearing one another to shreds for the amusement of violence-thirsty humans willing to pay to watch the spectacle.

"Hey." He snagged Mira's hand and drew her to a halt. Pulled her closer to him than was necessary, if only to feel her heat radiating toward him in the dank coolness of the corridor. "Where the hell are we going?"

"To see Rune."

Now Kellan bristled. He knew that name, knew it belonged to a denizen of Boston's underground, someone feared even by the city's most dangerous criminal circuit. More specifically, Rune was a brutal Breed fighter reputed to have never lost a match. It was a well-known fact that some of his opponents had forfeited their lives to him in the cage.

"Fuck no. You're not going anywhere near that guy." It was a command, spurred by pure masculine possessiveness, and Kellan couldn't bite it back. No more than he could keep his hands from going even tighter where he now held on to Mira.

The answering curve of her lips seemed equal parts pleased and annoyed. "I'm a big girl, Kellan. I can handle myself. We need intel, and Rune might have some." She came up on her toes and planted a quick kiss on his lips. "But I kind of like seeing you all growly and protective."

She didn't give him a chance to argue, which he damn well would have. Pivoting away, she resumed her trek down the corridor and paused in front of a battered, unmarked door. She dropped her fist on it a couple of times, the hard raps echoing like gunfire in the narrow passageway.

"Fuck off." A terse, snarled reply.

Mira knocked again, glancing to Kellan as he took his place beside her, battle instincts at the ready.

"Holy bleeding Christ." The voice was deep, all gravel. A more menacing snarl from the other side of the door, before heavy footsteps approached at an impatient gait. The old door squealed on its hinges as it was forcefully yanked open. Then roughly six-and-a-half-feet, three-hundred-plus pounds of bare-chested, pissed-off vampire stood in front of them. "What part of 'fuck off' do you not fucking comprehend?"

"I need information, Rune. It's important," Mira replied, speaking over the low growl that had crept up Kellan's throat. His response was automatic, an alpha reaction to the potential threat this other deadly male presented to the Breedmate standing in front of them.

My Breedmate, Kellan's every instinct declared.

He faced off against the dark-haired fighter, chin lowered, eyes fixed on him in silent warning.

But Rune didn't appear to be in the mind to test him. His midnight blue eyes slid only briefly from Mira to Kellan, and when he spoke, his tone was gruff, uninterested. "Not in the business of providing information or anything else to anyone. Least of all the Order." He eased off, started to close the door.

Mira's palm went flat against the scarred wood panel before Kellan could pull her back. "If you can help me," she ventured, unfazed by the fighter's curt dismissal, "I promise I'll see that you're compensated."

Sparks leapt into the darkness of his narrowed gaze, and the gravel of the fighter's voice took on sharp edges. The tangle of *dermaglyphs* on his chest, which had been infused with dark color when he first appeared in the doorway, now churned with menace. "Do I strike you as the kind of man who can be bought—at any price?"

"The lady is asking for your help," Kellan interjected, subtly stepping in to put himself between the partially open door and Mira, now standing behind his shoulder. "You going to give it to her or not?"

"Lady," Rune mused, uttering the word like he wanted to chuckle. "I've seen the way she wields those daggers of hers. She may be female, but she's no lady. Who the fuck are you?"

Kellan felt his own eyes light with flecks of rising amber, his pupils thinning to catlike slits as his temper spiked. "Someone prepared to carve your larynx out of your throat if you lift one finger against her."

Rune stared. "I believe you would. Or try, at least." The words were a challenge thrown, but then the big vampire's fierce expression relaxed a fraction. "I don't hurt females. Not even the ones armed with blades and too much attitude for their own damn good. Not even the ones who come down to my lair, interrupt my off time before I have to go pound some asshole into a bloody pulp in the ring, then stand in front of my face and insult my integrity by implying my assistance might come with a price tag."

"I apologize for that, Rune," Mira said from behind the shield of Kellan's body. "Please, let us inside so we don't have to talk around your door."

Rune didn't budge, but behind him in his quarters, Kellan caught the sudden, swift movement of another person in the room. Draped in nothing but a black satin bedsheet and a veil of honeyed brown hair that obscured her face as she ducked out of sight.

Now Kellan understood the other male's irritation at being disturbed. Rune's sparking eyes leveled on him as if to dare him to mention the presence of the naked young woman who'd since disappeared into a back room of the fighter's private chamber.

"I'm not the one interested in talking, so spit out what you have to say, then leave. Got things to do, and I don't appreciate wasting time."

Mira exhaled a short curse. "We're looking for Rooster. It's important that we find him, and I mean yesterday."

Rune's mouth went flat. "Still got a hard-on for that piece of shit, eh?"

"Have you seen him?" she pressed.

Rune gave a vague shake of his head. "Not since a few nights ago, when you nearly took the bastard's arms off with those wicked blades of yours. In front of a full house down in the arena, I might add."

Kellan didn't say anything in the wake of that disturbing news flash, but he did pivot a questioning look on Mira. No doubt she caught his displeasure at such a reckless move, but she merely glanced into his stern gaze, devoid of excuse or remorse.

Rune shrugged. "Anyway, haven't seen him since. I heard JUSTIS let him go that same night and sent you back to your boss with your tail between your legs. Heard you might've got bounced from duty with the Order on account of it. Fact, I figured you were back in Montreal by now, licking your wounds."

Kellan realized then that Jeremy Ackmeyer's kidnapping and Mira's unintended sweep into the fray were not yet common knowledge in the city. Not even a shady individual like Rune was privy to the intel that rebels had grabbed a notable scientist who'd been under the protection of the Order.

Which made him guess that Lucan had likely clapped a lid on the situation, given instructions to his warriors to keep the information out of the public eye.

And that was not good news for Kellan or his crew.

Because if Lucan and the Order were keeping Ackmeyer and Mira's abduction quiet, that probably meant there was a black op in motion right now. Almost certainly a death squad with license to kill anyone standing in their way.

Kellan had been part of the Order long enough to know that Lucan Thorne didn't mess around, especially when a strike hit close to home. Taking Ackmeyer hostage and possibly disrupting the tentative peace at the GNC summit would be bad enough. Involving Mira was an offense Lucan would not forgive.

Nor would Nikolai and Renata, Mira's adoptive parents.

Or Nathan, who'd been a best friend and brother to both Kellan and Mira since the three of them were kids.

Not to mention the rest of the warriors and their mates, including Lazaro Archer, who would be ashamed of his grandson for having vanished like a coward, only to rise again nearly a decade later as a villain they'd all be within their rights to despise.

Fuck. Even the most positive endgame of this whole scenario didn't promise a great outcome, regardless of whether he and Mira were successful tonight in tracking down Vince and getting Ackmeyer to safety.

Mira apparently hadn't absorbed what Rune's disclosure had just revealed. She peered around Kellan, frowning at the other Breed male. "Who told you I'd gotten reprimanded by Lucan? Where'd you hear I might have gotten bounced off patrols?"

"Make a difference where?" Rune shrugged. "Most folks I see around here have no love for the Order. People talk. I could've heard it anywhere."

"Well, whatever you heard," she said, "here I am now. And I'm looking for your help in locating Rooster. I'm not screwing around, Rune. I need to talk to him. So, if you see him in here tonight, I need you to find a way to hold him for me until I come back. I wouldn't ask you if I knew of anyone else who might be able to help me."

He considered for a long moment. "I don't do favors for anyone. I sure as hell don't do them because I want to get paid."

"Then do it because it's important," Mira pressed. "And it *is* important, Rune. I won't lie to you, it's a matter of life and death."

"Whose life we talking about?"

Although she didn't so much as look Kellan's way, he felt her body tense beside him. "Does it make a difference who?" she replied, echoing the fighter's words back to him.

"Might," he said. "Might not."

"I need to talk to Rooster, the sooner the better," Mira told him. "And no one can know that I'm looking for him. No one."

Rune's hard stare bore into her, then slid to Kellan in what felt a lot like suspicion. "What about the Order?"

"No one," Mira stated firmly.

It took the menacing Breed fighter a long moment to respond. When he did, it was with a curt inclination of his head. Agreement, even though he started closing the door on them again, in earnest this time. "If that's all, I've got more important business to attend to."

The sharp turn of the lock punctuated his exit. Then Kellan and Mira were standing alone in the passageway once more.

"Let's get out of here," Kellan said, taking her by the hand to make their way back up the stairwell to the club at street level.

They had no sooner cleared the back stairwell and were on their way through the noisy crowd, heading for the door, when a low voice sounded from behind them. "Thought you got the message a few nights ago when you were in here causing trouble, warrior."

Kellan and Mira slowed to a halt, then together turned to face Cassian, La Notte's proprietor. His eyes were the color of peridot, shrewd and hawklike beneath his dark brows and snowy crown of short-cropped hair. No small man in stature or build, he stood with arms crossed over his leather-and-buckle-clad chest, his long legs braced in a commanding stance.

"In case there was any doubt, you're not welcome in my club." His mouth curved in a smile that bordered on profane. "Or are you in here slumming with your friend?"

He wasn't looking at Kellan when he said it, but Kellan's hackles rose at the sight of the guy. Tension seeped into his limbs, tightened his grasp on Mira's hand.

"We were just leaving," she replied.

"Who's this with you?" Cassian asked now. "New recruit?"

Kellan lowered his head as the man strolled toward them, moving with a rolling, pantherlike smoothness that belied that rough edges of the rest of his demeanor. Cassian's bright green eyes pinned Kellan in a hard stare. "I know you."

"Don't think so," Kellan growled, certain he'd never met the human. He would have recalled the arrogance and the none-too-subtle undercurrent of menace that vibrated around him.

That shock of silvery white hair seemed glacial under the swirling, colored lights from the stage behind them. A huge Faceboard monitor on the opposite wall flashed live coverage of a bloody human boxing match, no doubt meant to be an appetizer for the real fights set to take place later that night in the club's basement. The monitor's images illuminated Cassian's angular face in harsh relief and shadows. "Yes," he said, letting the word out slowly, almost a hiss. "It's been some years, but I have seen you somewhere once before."

Kellan dropped Mira's hand because his were suddenly fisting of their own accord at his sides. "And I said you're mistaken."

"Let's go." Mira took his arm in both her hands as though she were prepared to drag him away from the confrontation with La Notte's owner.

Cassian chuckled. "She likes you, wants to protect you. That's intriguing. Figured she might've gone the other way . . . not that I didn't find that thought intriguing too."

The man had the poor judgment to take a step toward Mira, and Kellan's hand shot out like a viper, blocking him. The chest that flattened against his palm was rock solid, unyielding. And where Cassian's gaze was ice, his body was hot like coals beneath the leather, radiating a power Kellan could hardly reconcile.

As he held the man in place, physically keeping him from getting close to Mira, Kellan's psychic gift roused awake inside him. It reached out through his touch on Cassian, searching for the truth of the human's intentions.

And came up blank.

Utterly unreadable.

How the fuck could that be?

Cassian held his gaze for a second longer than Kellan liked, then the man simply stepped aside and strode toward the bar, where a group of inebriated, pretty young women were having trouble staying upright on their spiked heels.

Kellan was still trying to process what he'd just experienced, and he was surprised Mira didn't have something to say about Cassian's sudden lack of interest in them and their business at his establishment.

But Mira wasn't looking at the man anymore.

She stared transfixed at the Faceboard monitor across the expanse of the place. Kellan followed her gaze. All the blood seemed to drain out of his head.

The monitor was no longer displaying the boxing match. On-screen now was a JUSTIS Department news alert, barely audible over the din of the crowd and the band still playing its set onstage. But the ticker scrolling across the huge monitor told Kellan all he needed to know.

Laboratory explosion in western Massachusetts today claims life of renowned scientist Jeremy Ackmeyer . . .

Second body recovered on-site, identified as Vincent DeSalvo, ex-convict with established ties to Boston area militant and rebel organizations . . .

Global Nations Council calling for thorough investigation
into what it's calling an act of conspiracy and premeditated
murder . . .

"Kellan," Mira murmured, her body unmoving, seeming frozen in place, even after he took her hand in his. "Oh, my God, Kellan . . . Jeremy Ackmeyer is dead."

17

THE GRIM MOOD AT THE ORDER'S D.C. HEADQUARTERS HAD NOT improved in the hours since word of Jeremy Ackmeyer's death at rebel hands had made headlines all over the world. As leader of the Order and the de facto public head of the Breed nation as a whole, Lucan Thorne's mood was darkest of all those gathered.

Now, at sometime past midnight, most of the Order's elder members based in the United States were present along with their mates, the group gathered in the drawing room of the mansion, situated just a few miles from the GNC headquarters at the National Mall. It was an odd juxtaposition: half a dozen long-lived, lethal Breed warriors more accustomed to combat gear and high-powered weapons, now seated in fancy, velvet-upholstered settees and delicate neoclassical armchairs.

Lucan wasn't a particular fan of the frou-frou furnishings, but it made his Breedmate happy, so he'd been obliged to go with it. Gabrielle had insisted they preserve the architectural authenticity of the place, which included a small fortune in eighteenth-century artwork and Asian porcelains gifted to the mansion's original owner, who'd served as a U.S. ambassador in the early 1900s.

She had, however, replaced a large, seventeenth-century English tapestry of Alexander the Great with another, far older one, which she said depicted a hero she much preferred to look at instead.

Lucan paced in front of that medieval-period artifact now, feeling the hand-rendered likeness of his own face judging him from within the woven threads of the tapestry that once hung in his quarters at the Order's Boston compound. Gabrielle, Gideon and his mate, Savannah, Brock, Jenna, and several others gathered in the drawing room in prolonged silence as Lucan practically wore a track in the Oriental rug beneath his boots.

Rio and his Breedmate, Dylan, were less than an hour arrived from the Order's base in Chicago. The Spanish warrior with the scarred face and normally easygoing demeanor was coiled forward where he sat, elbows resting on his knees, topaz eyes intense.

The other recent arrivals, Tegan and Elise, had come in from the base he commanded in New York City. The tawny-haired Gen One was one of the Order's original members from the time of its founding—and within the past twenty years had become one of Lucan's closest friends. Tegan and Elise had their own issues to contend with, namely, their twenty-year-old son, Micah, who was fresh out of warrior training and already embarking with his team on a black ops mission taking them to Budapest.

Elise was openly worried about letting her only surviving child out of her sight, but Micah was his father's son, and Lucan knew as well as anyone that holding on too tight would only risk making the break that much more permanent when it came. He saw that in his own son every day, a weight that settled on him even in the midst of the more immediate problems he faced tonight.

The remaining members still due at the D.C. headquarters included Hunter and Corinne, coming in from New Orleans in a few more hours. Scheduled to arrive tomorrow night were Dante and Tess, now in charge of the Order's base in Seattle, and Kade and Alex, overseeing the command center in Lake Tahoe. In light of the night's events in Boston, Chase and Tavia were staying put there until the eve of the summit gala, when they'd be coming in to attend.

Across the elegant space now, Nikolai's muttered curse was a hiss ripe with malice as his blond head swung away from his pregnant Breedmate and his glacial blue eyes hit Lucan. "Do we have any more intel about who these rebel bastards are and where they're hiding?"

"Only what you already know from Nathan's call tonight," Lucan replied gravely. "Unfortunately, his best lead so far was the information that one of the rebels had defected from his fold, taking Ackmeyer with him for ransom bait. We all know how that turned out."

Niko grunted. "And we have nothing on Mira. Not where she is or what they want with her. Or if she's already been . . ."

That the Siberian-born, battle-hardened warrior had been unable to finish the thought told Lucan just how deeply Niko's concern went. Renata's too. The tough-as-nails female who'd become a valued, highly effective member of the Order's combat missions these past two decades was slumped close to her mate, her jet-dark hair drooped into her face but not quite masking the lines of worry there. Renata's mercilessly lethal hands trembled a bit where they rested on the pronounced bump of her late-term pregnancy.

"We don't have anything more yet, but we will," Lucan told them. "We'll get her back safe and sound, I promise you."

He considered the kill op he'd sent Nathan on, its purpose to recover Mira and the human and shut down their captors with a minimum of noise or attention. Nathan's skill and suitability for the job would never be in question, but the laboratory explosion and the killing of Jeremy Ackmeyer had blown their mission objective to pieces.

And the fallout from that disastrous event was creating newer, bigger problems of its own.

In just the handful of hours since the news of the prominent human scientist's death broke, there had been a swift, and extremely vocal, public outcry for justice. An outcry made all the more troubling when reports suggested not only that rebels were involved but that the Order was partially at fault for his abduction and resulting murder.

Lucan was still pissed that Ackmeyer's uncle, GNC director Charles Benson, had immediately gone to investigators and the press with the fact that the Order had been enlisted—and had ultimately failed—to keep the civilian safe on what was supposed to have been a simple security escort to D.C. for the upcoming summit gala.

The already uneasy human population reacted with paranoia and suspicion, a few vitriolic prophets of doom warning that this failure only confirmed what they already feared: that the Breed, and the Order in particular, could not be trusted to value human life.

Peace, the worst of them were shouting to anyone who would listen, could never be had living alongside inhuman monsters.

The answering panic was widespread and quickly gaining ground. Riots in Boston had begun spreading to other cities. The small number of protesters that were commonplace in front of the Order's D.C. headquarters had swelled to dozens in just a matter of hours. And while the civilians' upset was trouble enough, militant groups around the world were now using the attack on Ackmeyer's lab by suspected rebels as a rallying cry to vandalize and loot, to lash out at governments they deemed too willing to capitulate to the might and will of the Order and the rest of the Breed.

The current situation was, in a word, chaos.

With Lucan and the Order now standing squarely in the middle of it.

"We need to shut this shit down," Lucan growled, anger spiking as the rumble of picketers outside the estate's gates droned on. "We should be back on watch at our district command centers, in case the response to tonight's news escalates from aggravating provocation to all-out anarchy."

"Then again," Gideon interjected, "it may be more important than ever for us to stand with the GNC, show the human public that their panic is without merit, and the Order is on their side. Show the world that we can be trusted as a partner in the effort toward peace between our races."

Lucan saw Gabrielle and a few others nod in agreement. He knew they were probably right, but at the moment it was difficult to rein in the part of him that was ancient and answered to no one. The leader who, for centuries now, was accustomed to making the rules and, when called for, enforcing them with unstoppable might.

And right now, the last thing he gave a damn about was making a group public appearance at the summit, just to demonstrate solidarity with the GNC, whose members were apparently all too willing to throw the Order under the bus, or with the humans, who may never see the Breed as anything more than bogeymen just waiting for the opportunity to rip out their throats.

Diplomacy had never been his strong suit, and tonight it chafed more than ever.

Lucan curbed his internal aggression and paused to address Gideon. "Any leads on the name Nathan supplied us—this rebel bastard, Bowman?"

"I got zip so far," Gideon replied. "Bowman's kept his nose clean, that's for sure. I've dug everywhere I can for the guy—criminal activity, arrest records . . . no hard data on him anywhere. He's like a ghost."

Renata lifted her head, jade green eyes snapping with fury. "Meanwhile, he's got my child. If he's harmed Mira in any way—if he's . . . touched her . . . I want to be the one to personally eviscerate him."

"Not if I get to the son of a bitch first, babe," Niko said, his tone gentle, but his gaze lit up with amber rage.

Rio spoke next. "I say we gear up and head to Boston—the two of us, my friend. We'll hunt down this Bowman and the vermin he runs with, and when we find him, we'll make them dine on bullets and steel."

Lucan felt the same cold need to personally be the one to cut off the head of the enemy who'd taken one of the Order's own kin. That Bowman had also orchestrated Ackmeyer's abduction and death, inciting riots and jeopardizing the summit at the same time, only made Lucan's blood chill all the more.

As he considered the justice he would exact from the elusive rebel leader, Lucan's comm unit buzzed in his pants pocket. *Who now?* he wondered irritably, then barked out a curse when he saw who was calling him.

"Jesus fucking Christ," he snarled. "Bad enough I've been fielding calls all night from Council members, JUSTIS officials, and press. Now I've got that blowhard Reginald Crowe looking for a piece of me?"

Like a dog marking territory, the arrogant tycoon had been busy making sure he seized every opportunity to stake his claim on the summit. Hosting the pricey gala apparently wasn't enough for Crowe. He had also recently announced the unveiling of a sculpture commemorating First Dawn and the peace summit, presenting it as a gift to be installed at GNC headquarters during the gathering. Given Crowe's inflated sense of self-worth, Lucan wouldn't be at all surprised if the piece was a life-size statue of the man himself.

Lucan ignored Crowe's call, putting the device on silent and shoving it back into his pocket on another ripe curse.

It wasn't even a moment later that Darion appeared in the open doorway of the drawing room. Lucan could tell just from a glimpse at the young warrior's serious expression that more shit was about to rain down on them.

"What is it, son?"

"Director Benson," Dare replied, his deep voice tight with barely restrained outrage. "He's just made a public statement. It's on all the news outlets right now. The GNC was offered—and has accepted—a private security detail from Crowe Enterprises for the summit gathering. According to Benson, Crowe's team will augment and oversee the Order's involvement, effective immediately."

A few of the Breedmates gasped, punctuating the other, more vivid responses from the rest of the warriors gathered in the room.

Lucan grunted. "We'll see about that." While he absorbed the bullshit development with an air of stone-cold fortitude, inside he was seething. And the brunt of his contempt settled on the unknown face of the rebel leader who'd incited this entire fiasco.

Lucan grabbed his comm unit and hit Nathan's number. "Head into base now and await further command. This kill op is gonna go full-scale mission, with as many teams on the ground as needed to find Bowman and bring Mira home. He and his rebels need to be shut down hard, preferably in full public view. And I mean they need to be shut down *permanently*."

Kellan sat alone on the cool, moonlit thatch of overgrown grass that covered the stone mound of the seaside bunker. He and Mira had been back at the rebel base for several hours, after news of Jeremy Ackmeyer's death broke and the reaction in the city began to turn ugly fast. He didn't want Mira anywhere near an upset, volatile public, but Kellan was also more than a bit concerned about the prospect of an Order death squad working its way closer to him with every second.

Sooner or later, regardless of how cautious he'd been all these years, someone was going to mention the name Bowman and point a finger in the direction of the New Bedford base camp. And when that moment came, Kellan intended to meet it alone, sparing Mira and his remaining crew—his friends—from becoming collateral damage.

The fact that Cassian from La Notte insisted he'd recognized him from somewhere only increased Kellan's sense of ill ease. Ignoring the fact that the club owner had betrayed nothing of himself to Kellan's Breed talent, Kellan got the clear sense that the man was dangerous. Perhaps all the more so because he'd proven unreadable.

Kellan hadn't had a lot of time to worry about what his encounter with Cassian might mean down the road. His more pressing concerns were Mira and the handful of people who were counting on him to protect them. To lead them, even though he had never felt less equipped to navigate a safe course through what was becoming a fast-rising tide of wreckage.

He'd delivered word of the laboratory explosion that killed both Vince and Ackmeyer, along with news of the resulting public uproar to his crew when he and Mira had arrived. Then Doc and Nina had helped Kellan bury their dead while Mira assisted Candice outside for the ceremony. Chaz's grave on the grounds of the old bunker carried the scent of freshly turned earth, mingling with the pungent brine of the damp ocean breeze that rolled in off the cove to where Kellan sat, keeping watch through the night.

From his post on the broad point where the retired fort and gun batteries stood, Kellan stared out at the distant city lights of Boston. The bunker that had been built as a military stronghold during the humans' Civil War, and had survived nearly two hundred years afterward, now felt vulnerable and exposed. The Order could strike at any moment in the dark. In the daylight hours, the base was an easy target for raids by trigger-happy JUSTIS officers.

Kellan didn't know what time it was at the moment—early morning, certainly. But still dark. And so he waited. He watched. Prepared himself for what he had to do to keep Mira and his crew safe.

"Hey." Her soft voice caught him unaware, her movement quiet as she climbed up the side of the mound to join him. "Everyone's sleeping. Were you ever coming back inside?"

"In a while." He extended his arm and she crawled in close beside him. Her body fit so comfortably, her blond head a pleasant weight against his chest, her hair sweet and silky from a recent shower. He wrapped his arm around her shoulders, closing his eyes to savor how good it felt simply to hold her under the stars. He pressed a kiss to the top of her head. "You were great tonight, helping with Candice's wound and the funeral ceremony for Chaz . . . such as it was."

"I only did what needed doing, and as for your friend's funeral, it was a beautiful good-bye you all gave him," she murmured. "Simple but pure. You honored him well, Kellan."

The phrase she used—one reserved for the solemnest occasions in Breed traditions—touched him in a way he couldn't express. Instead, he tipped her chin up on the edge of his hand and kissed her. Not the hungered kind of kiss that they'd been sharing each time they'd connected since her arrival back in his life a few days ago but a kiss shaped by tender caring and gratitude, by profound respect . . . and, yes, love.

He loved this woman.

His woman.

He'd loved her nearly all his life. That feeling had never faded, not in all the time he'd been away from her. And now that he was feeling the power of having Mira close again, having her a part of his world—his heart—he wasn't sure how he would ever find the strength to walk away from her.

But he would have to.

Sooner than he cared to admit.

He didn't want to break their kiss now either, but Mira gently drew back. Her lavender-tinted eyes were gentle but filled with a quiet determination as they lifted to meet his sober gaze.

"We'll find a way through this," she declared, voice steady, as if she were heading into battle. "What happened tonight to Jeremy Ackmeyer—"

"Changes everything, Mouse." He caressed her stubborn jaw, then exhaled deeply, giving a slow shake of his head. "No, that's not right. It changes nothing. An innocent man was killed tonight. Murdered, just as your vision predicted."

"Yes, but not by you, Kellan. You didn't kill him."

He scoffed, low under his breath. "Didn't I? Would he be dead if I hadn't abducted him? My command to take him set this whole thing in motion. My hands are as stained with his death as those of whoever blew up that lab with him and Vince inside."

"But you didn't do it." He could hear her resolve slipping toward desperation. "You're not guilty of murder, Kellan, and you need to let the Order know that. They need to know everything. And they need to know it all now, before things get any more dangerous."

He smoothed a tendril of pale blond hair that stirred in the morning wind. "You're right."

"I am?" She swallowed, going suddenly still in his embrace. "You mean . . . you agree? You'll go with me to explain all of this to Lucan?"

"I will go to him, Mira."

With a small cry, she threw herself at him, arms holding him tight, face buried in the center of his chest, where his heart now labored with a regretful tempo. "I know everything will work out for us, Kellan. This is the only way—"

"Mouse," he said softly, pulling her up so she could see his face. She needed to understand the decision he'd reached. "I'll go to Lucan and the rest of the Order. I will tell them what I've done and why I left without explanation eight years ago. I'll tell them everything. But I will do it on my own terms. And I will do it alone."

Her expression fell, then hardened with confusion and no small amount of anger. "I need to be with you when you meet them. They need to hear my side of the story."

"When I meet with the Order, it won't be with any expectation that I'll be pardoned in this, Mira. If I were Lucan, I wouldn't see how mercy could possibly be granted. I am the leader of a rebel group. I have broken the law, too many times to count. I have committed conspiracy. And as of right now, I am culpable in the killing of a civilian. A human civilian, Mira." He blew out a low curse. "What do you think will happen when JUSTIS and the GNC hear that? When word leaks out that I—that the rebel leader known as Bowman—am actually Breed, the riots we're seeing tonight will look like a joke, like kids' pranks. There's no way the Order can excuse me without undoing all the strides the Breed has made toward peace with mankind."

"No." Her head swiveled side to side, then more resolutely. "No, I need to be able to vouch for what you tell them. If nothing else works, then I need to be able to throw myself on their mercy and beg them to understand, plead with them to make an exception for you. For me. For us. Kellan, you have to promise me you'll give me that chance—"

"I can't promise you that, Mira. I can't promise to put you through any more hurt or distress than I already have." He took her face between his palms, tenderly smoothing his thumbs over her cheeks and her trembling mouth. "But I will promise you this: I love you. God, I always have. Did you even realize that? All those months and years of trying to push you away when we were young. I was terrified of how much I cared for you. I'd lost so many people I loved, I couldn't bear the idea that if I let myself love you, I might lose you one day too."

"You'll never lose me, Kellan." A soft sob caught in the back of her throat as she reached up to put her hands around his neck. Her pale purple eyes glittered in the moonlight, filled with welling tears. "I don't care what the vision showed you. I won't let you go. I'm yours. I always will be."

"Ah, Mouse." He eased his forehead down against hers, wishing he had her stalwart courage. "You honor me well. Too well."

"I love you," she whispered. "I'll never stop loving you."

She clung to him now, and he held her close. As close as he could gather her to him. And still, it wasn't close enough. It never could be, when it came to his feelings for this extraordinary female.

He didn't want to die. And the last thing he wanted was to leave Mira again—all the worse, to leave her behind once more in true grief and pain. He would do everything in his power to prevent the vision from coming true, but he knew too well the power Mira's gift of Sight possessed. He had seen it predict fate with unerring accuracy. It was a knowledge he couldn't deny now, no matter how much he wanted to believe they'd find a way past the death sentence Lucan was destined to hand down to him.

But they still had the here and now.

They had this moment.

He rose with her, taking her up to her feet with him on the grassy mound atop the bunker. On the easternmost horizon, a thin glow was forming, just the barest edge of dawn. The night had passed and they were still safe. Still together, for now.

And they had hours of daylight in which to deal with decisions neither of them wanted to make.

Until then, Kellan wanted only Mira.

"Come with me," he murmured into her silken hair. "Let me love you for a while."

She slipped her hand into his and they walked, together, back into the sleeping fortress.

Back into the haven of his bed.

18

MIRA'S DREAMS WERE VIVID, WRENCHING. NIGHTMARES FILLED with tears and anguish and loss.

Such unbearable loss.

Kellan . . .

She came awake on a start, her eyelids lifting in the dark silence of a room that smelled of damp stone, distant brine . . . *and him.*

Thank God, only nightmares.

Kellan was right there with her, both of them naked in his bed. His heart thudded leisurely beneath her cheek, his bare chest warm under her palm. He was there. He was safe.

He stirred beneath her, and Mira held herself very still, not wanting to disturb his sleep after the long vigil he'd kept atop the bunker.

Not to mention the hours of unrushed lovemaking, which must have worn him out as well. Though she wouldn't have imagined it then, when he brought her to shattering orgasm three times, his own release never far behind.

The thought of his passion, the pleasure they'd given each other just a short while ago, helped soothe the panicked beat of her heart. It calmed her to recall his words—his tender promise of love—as they'd embraced under the waning starlight in the moments before he'd brought her to his bed.

Kellan loved her. He didn't want to leave her; she knew that. But he would. As he'd told her so gently tonight, when he was ready to surrender to the Order, he would do it alone. He didn't want her there.

And thinking about him facing judgment—and her vision's prophesied outcome—by himself put an icy knot in the bottom of her stomach.

She had to work to tamp down her dread, willing herself not to go back to her nightmares of a few moments ago or to the unbearable thoughts of what Kellan had described seeing in her eyes. Although the urge to cling to him now as he slept verged on desperation, Mira was too wired to lie still. Her head was buzzing, her limbs restless, worry nagging at her like tiny fish nibbling at her sanity.

Carefully she extricated herself from Kellan's side and eased her way to the edge of the bed. He sighed and rolled over, his breathing settling into a deeper slumber. Mira rose, unsure what to do or where she could go to shake off the heavy weight of her anxiety. What she needed more than sleep or distraction was answers.

She needed to know what her future held with Kellan. More than anything, she needed some glimmer of hope that they could, somehow, overcome the trouble they were in and find a way to be together.

She shot a glance over her shoulder, toward the foot of the bed. Her eyes lit on the trunk that rested there on the floor. The trunk that held Kellan's grandmother's mirror.

No. It was dangerous even to consider it.

She didn't even know if it would work.

And yet she reached for her empty contact lens case on the night table beside the bed, then her feet were moving her silently across the floor, carrying her to the wooden locker. She crouched down in front of it. Silently lifted the lid.

The silver hand mirror lay facedown on top of a stack of Kellan's shirts. Mira picked it up, her fingertips brushing over the carved design of the Archer family emblem.

She had to try.

She had to know, even if it terrified her to do this, something she'd never attempted before. The worse terror was not knowing, fearing that what Kellan saw might actually be his fate.

If there was any chance that looking into her own unprotected gaze might give her even a slim hope of a future together with Kellan, she would risk anything. She would pay any price to know for certain if he was destined to live . . . or doomed to die.

Mira pivoted, putting her back to the trunk as she kneeled on the floor and removed her contact lenses to their case. The mirror in hand, she closed her eyes and took a steeling breath deep into her lungs.

She could do this.

She *had* to do this.

She brought the mirror up in front of her face, her eyelids still shuttering her talent. Her heart banged in her chest, so erratic and nervous, so loud in her ears, she half expected Kellan to wake from the sound of it. Her palms were damp, mouth dry as ash.

She had to try.

She had to know.

She lifted her lids and froze at the sight of her face staring back at her in the oval of polished glass. She looked so different without the purple lenses muting the crystalline intensity of her gaze. She hardly recognized herself like this—her features, of course, but lit with an icy fire that seemed ageless, not quite of this world.

Extraordinary, Kellan had said.

Startling, she thought. Unsettling. So unfamiliar, she couldn't . . .

The thought fell away as the clear pools of her irises began to ripple as she looked at them in the mirror, their surface wobbling as if a small pebble had been dropped into a serene lake.

Transfixed, astonished, she couldn't look away.

And then, within the fathomless, colorless depths, an image began to take shape. Several images, shadowed figures, a group seated at the front of a large, high-ceilinged room, a tall, raised bench in front of them, separating the group from the smaller figure that stood before them, awaiting their response.

Even before the images began to take clearer shape, Mira recognized the silhouette of the person standing before the court. She felt the person's trepidation, the bone-deep dread and uncertainty.

She knew, because that person was her.

In the vision, she tried not to tremble as she faced Lucan and the other members of the Global Nations Council seated in judgment on the bench, knowing that they held the power to either save her or destroy her with their decision. Their faces were impassive, without mercy.

She watched in anguished expectation as her vision-self pressed for leniency and got only stoic faces in reply. In the vision, she began to weep, her face dropping into her palms, shoulders shaking with the force of her sobs.

The pain of that image skewered Mira's heart in real time, made her lips tremble in echoed reaction. She wanted to look away now, before she saw any more. But then all heads in the gallery turned to look behind them as the accused entered the chamber to hear the sentencing.

Kellan.

Oh, God. It was just as he'd said.

He strode forward, broad shoulders squared, head lifted, but she could see resignation in his handsome face as he looked at her. Mira could nearly feel his stoic acceptance as she watched the scene unfold in her reflected gaze.

Her vision-self whirled back around to face the ones who held Kellan's fate in their hands. She pleaded with them. Tried to draw some of the blame to her instead. To no avail. They announced their edict just as Kellan had told her they would. For the capital crimes Kellan stood accused of . . . death.

As the vision continued, Mira knew her anguish could not possibly be worse.

But she was wrong.

Because then the terrible vision Kellan had prepared her for began to fade into a misty darkness. Another image began to take shape in her reflected gaze. Something dreadful. Something far, far worse than the prospect of Kellan's execution.

His lifeless body, pale and unmoving, laid out before her.

No . . .

No! Her mind screamed in anguish. Or maybe she'd actually screamed her horror out loud. All she knew was the incredulity, the bone-deep grief, that overcame her as her vision-self collapsed atop his dead body and began to wail.

It couldn't be true.

It could not possibly end like that for them.

She could never bear that level of pain.

She would rather die along with—

The mirror flew out of her hands and crashed into the nearby wall, raining shards of broken glass.

She jumped at the shock of what just happened, the abrupt startlement yanking her out of the vision's unbreakable hold.

Kellan loomed over her, seething so fiercely he shook with the depth of his feelings. Heat rolled off his body in palpable waves. His eyes were throwing sparks, his lips peeled back from his fangs.

"What the hell were you doing?" His voice was pure thunder, more furious than she'd ever heard him. "Mira, goddamn it. Tell me you didn't try to—ah, Jesus."

He looked away from her now, turning his head away from her naked eyes. Still shaken, still raw with the grief from the awful things she'd just witnessed, Mira scrambled to put her lenses in. By the time she had, Kellan had sunk down to his knees on the floor in front of her.

"Mouse, for fuck's sake. Why would you . . . What in God's name were you thinking?" He took her upper arms in a tight grasp, trembling. "Look at me, baby. I need to see you. I need to know you're okay."

She lifted her face to meet his blazing stare. His face blurred through the tears filling her eyes. "I'm . . . Oh, God, Kellan! You were right. The vision. The judgment. All of it."

"You saw," he murmured, and his grip went a bit slack then. "You used your vision on yourself. Mira . . . why?"

"I had to know. I didn't want to believe it. I couldn't make myself believe it . . . until now." Her voice caught, scraping in her throat. "I saw everything, just like you described it. And there was something more. Oh, God. Kellan, they sentenced you to death and then I saw you. You were—" She couldn't speak the word. On a sob, she fell against him, exhausted and hurting. "I can't bear to lose you. Not again. Not like that."

He gathered her close, wrapping his muscled arms around her. "I don't want to face that reality either. If I could keep you with me, hold you forever, I would."

She nodded against his warm chest, wishing desperately for the same thing. She needed to feel his arms around her. She needed to feel his heartbeat, his breathing, his body's strength and heat. She needed to feel for herself that he was with her, whole and hale. He was alive.

As she clung to him, her gaze drifted over the broken mirror and scattered, glittering splinters on the floor nearby. A new grief tore at her. "Your grandmother's mirror . . . Kellan, I'm sorry. It's ruined because of me."

"I don't give a damn about that," he whispered against the top of her head. "All I care about is you. You can't even be sure of the damage you've done to yourself tonight, Mouse. Do you realize that?"

"I had to know," she said, her outstretched hand drifting over one of the shiny pieces of glass. She plucked it from the floor and held it between her fingers, regretting that this one surviving memento from Kellan's past had been destroyed in his desire to protect her. "I wanted so badly to prove that you were wrong about what you saw. I just wanted some hope—even a little bit—that we would be together. But it was worse than I imagined. It was so much worse than anything I want to believe."

She didn't realize she was curling the razor-edged shard into her fist, until she felt its jagged edges biting into her palm.

But Kellan knew.

He'd gone still, his muscles immediately tense, his body taut like a cable. He drew away from her only slightly, enough that she could see his nostrils flare with his intake of breath. The embers that had been sparking in his eyes a moment ago had now turned into red-hot coals bisected with the thinning vertical slits of his pupils. He growled, a rumble that came up from his chest, vibrating into her bones. "Mira . . ."

He took her fist in his hand and pried it open, let the glass tumble out to the floor. Blood covered her palm, tiny rivulets trickling down her pale wrist. He stared at those dark crimson trails, and the curse he hissed through his fangs was raw, though not with anger.

He transformed even further, his face becoming starker, wilder. Otherworldly. She had seen him in his true natural form before, but never like this. This was Kellan Archer fully Breed, primal and thirsting, a formidable male predator with his sights set squarely on her.

He wanted what she would offer him now.

What had been his to claim all along.

"I belong to you, Kellan. There will never be another for me. Not even if I can't be with you. Not even if you're gone." She glanced down at her bleeding hand still caught in his grasp. The wound in her palm wasn't bad, but it didn't take much for a bond to be activated. One taste. That's all he needed to take, and he would be linked to her forever. "I need to be connected to you. In every possible way. Never mind what my vision says. It can't stop us tonight. It can't stop this."

He made a strangled sound in the back of his throat as his fevered gaze lifted to meet her eyes. His fingers didn't release her, remaining clamped around her wrist like a vise. His fangs elongated further, sharp points filling his mouth as he parted his lips on a groan. His *glyphs* pulsated, dark hues of thirst and desire churning all over his beautiful Breed skin.

Mira reached out with her free hand to stroke his face. "I offer you my blood freely, Kellan. If you'll have it now."

His blazing amber eyes slid back to her red-stained palm, his breath rasping through his teeth and fangs. He said her name, and it sounded like a tormented mixture of profanity and prayer as he drew her hand up to his mouth and licked the rivulet of blood that was running down toward her elbow.

Mira sighed as his tongue traveled back up her wrist, soft as velvet against her skin. He took his time, lapping up every bit that had spilled. Then he put his face in the heart of her palm, his trim goatee gently tickling, his lips hot and moist, his breath like steam against her sensitive flesh. He settled his mouth over her wound and drew his first true swallow.

She felt his body tense up, a jolt going through him as the bond to her took root. He moaned into her hand as he pulled in another taste of her. The vibration of his mouth, the wet heat of his tongue, the graze of his fangs against her palm—it combined into one of the most erotic sensations she'd ever known. Her body responded with a surge of pleasure and liquid fire.

Desire coiled deep within her, flowing out to every nerve ending as Kellan suckled from her palm. Her blood stirred to new life with each passing second, awakening to his kiss. She could feel it racing through her veins, eager to feed him. Arousal burned hot and fast within her, wet need pooling between her thighs. Twin points of radiant electric light bloomed inside her, one in her core, another at the spot where Kellan's mouth was fixed to her.

"God, Mira . . . you taste so fucking good," he murmured. "Your blood is so sweet, so powerful. Holy Christ, I can feel you in my muscles and bones, in my senses . . . so damn good."

She caressed him as he praised her, and between their naked bodies, his cock stood erect, stiff and heated, while she was melting. Craving to be filled by him.

"Yes," he said, his voice thick and hungered. "I can feel your need through the bond. I can feel your pulse, as if it's my own." His tongue swirled one last time into her palm, gently, sealing her wound. "I never realized how strong it would be . . . how complete. But I need to be inside you now."

Without another word, he gathered Mira up into his arms and placed her back on the bed. He prowled over her, strong arms braced on either side of her, his big body poised above her in the dark. And his eyes—she was bathed in their glow, mesmerized by the desire she saw smoldering in Kellan's otherworldly gaze.

She'd never seen him look so formidable, so incredibly powerful. He was magnificent in this state, fully transformed, nourished by the new bond that linked him to her for as long as they both drew breath. He was dark and fevered and gloriously aroused, and she quivered to feel all of his heated focus trained on her.

She was ready when he entered her, so ready. He drove in deep, the feel of him enormous, harder and hotter than ever as he moved inside her body. His mouth found hers and he covered her lips in a kiss that was demanding, fevered . . . thirsting.

Mira clung to him, wrapping her legs around him to bring him closer. She wanted to be fused together with him. Couldn't get close enough.

She cried out when Kellan's mouth left hers, then gasped as it drifted lower, settling just below her ear. "Take me," she whispered as his lips found purchase on her neck. "All of me, Kellan. Take me."

His answering snarl was feral-sounding and raw as his mouth clamped down more seriously against her throat. Desire spiked into her core as the tips of his fangs found their place at her carotid. Mira put her hand in his hair, fingers burrowing into the thick waves. She tightened her fist in demand, holding him in place. "Take me," she rasped. "I'm already yours."

"Yes," he answered, rough and wild and carnal. He made a sound of dark hunger in the back of his throat. "Mine," he said.

Then he pierced her.

Mira's gasp was pure elation as his fangs went deep, and his hips thrust hard and long between her open thighs.

He would be dying soon—in a few hours or days or weeks, he couldn't be sure—but Kellan had never felt more alive.

Pride swelled in him at the pleasured sound of Mira's cry as his fangs penetrated her delicate flesh and pierced the artery that pulsed so robust and lovely against his tongue. Possession rocked into him like a massive wave as her body clung to him, her sleek, wet channel enveloping him, milking his cock as the first tremors of her orgasm began to ripple through her.

Her mounting climax echoed in his own consciousness, in all of his senses. Such was the power of the blood bond that now joined him to her. He should hate himself for taking this step with her, knowing there was no future in it. But she felt too good, tasted like sweetest heaven. And he'd wanted this intimate, unbreakable connection to her for too long.

He was greedy for all she could give him now, primal in his claiming of her body and her blood. She belonged to him. Her whispered pledge spurred him on now, made his thrusts urgent, his bite locked onto her with animalistic fervor, drinking her in.

She was his.

In this moment, she was his forever.

So easy to think it. So tempting to believe that he could stretch this moment into an eternity with her, keep Mira at his side as his mate for as long as they both drew breath.

And it was nearly impossible to resist the need that rose in him now, a need that urged him to complete the blood bond, to seal their connection by opening his own vein and feeding Mira a taste of him in return.

He wanted it with a ferocity that staggered him.

She wanted it too. He felt her craving for him, raw and thirsting. He heard it in her breathless moan, as she clutched at him and arched beneath him, her head craned to the side on the pillow, granting him total access to her carotid.

She wanted more of him. More than he was willing to give. He couldn't let her drink now, not when her link to him would only increase her pain tenfold when they were parted by death.

"Please," she gasped. "Oh, God . . . Kellan . . ."

God help him, he nearly gave in to her plea when she came in that next instant, her fingernails scoring his shoulders, his name a throaty roar as her release crested and broke. He wanted to bleed for her.

More than anything in that moment, he wanted to bind her to him and give her the same depth of pleasure she was giving him now. But he reined in the impulse with narrowly held control and dubious honor. Pressing his mouth to her open vein, he sealed the punctures with his tongue and braced himself for the rolling tide of her climax. Every nuance of her emotions branded themselves on his senses. She came with the same unbridled intensity that she did most everything else in her life, her climax astonishing him with its force as the waves of her body's release flowed through his veins as if his own.

He couldn't slow the tempest building within him now too. With Mira's orgasm still crashing over him, Kellan came too, shouting with the ferocity of it as his seed blasted out of him, scalding and ferocious.

And Mira's sweet, welcoming body accepted all that he had to give.

He didn't know how long it took before the aftershocks finally began to recede. Could have been moments. Could have been hours.

All he knew was the warm cushion of her body beneath him on the bed, her limbs still tangled around his, her fingers playing in the hair at his nape while he rested his head next to her shoulder.

It was her quiet voice that brought him back to the here and now.

Back to the reality of what they still faced.

"I don't want you to go to the Order." He felt her worry in the dull throb of her pulse, in the tang of dread that filtered through their new bond, into him. "I've changed my mind, Kellan. About wanting you to plead your case, trying to convince the Order and the Council to pardon you. I don't want you to go anywhere near D.C. Neither one of us can ever go back there."

"Ah, Mouse." He kissed the bare curve of her shoulder, then came up on one elbow so he could meet her troubled gaze. "You don't mean that. You've never been one to run and hide. That was always more my territory, remember? And look where that's gotten us."

"I don't care," she murmured, a stubborn edge to her tone. "Let's just stay here, like this. For as long as we can, let's just be together and make this last. Whatever it takes."

He kissed her again, on the mouth this time, unrushed and tender. "I don't want this to end either. Not now or ever. But I don't want it if it means forcing you into a life of skulking in shadows and fearing what lies around every corner. I can't do that, Mira. And we can't stay here. It's not safe for any of us now. We all have to get out of here soon, go to another location. Somewhere out of the line of fire."

"Where?"

"Somewhere safe."

His dread about the Order closing in on him was still very real and disturbing. And the prospect of either a stealth death squad or, after last night's turn of events, a full-scale invasion was more than he was willing to risk. A sick guilt weighed down on him when he thought of Candice and Doc and Nina coming under heavy weapons fire amid the chaos of a raid. As for Mira, he knew his Breedmate well enough to realize that she would fight to her own death if she thought she could save him.

As he would for her.

And would, in a short time from now.

He hadn't been much of a leader to his crew of rebels, not that it had ever been his intent to lead them. He hadn't been anything close to a worthy mate to Mira either, and that he wanted more than anything.

But he still had time to do right by them all. He could put measures in place that would ensure a minimum risk of injury or bloodshed to his Breedmate and his friends. Only then would he be ready to do what he needed to do—confront the fate that waited for him at the other end of this increasingly inescapable path.

His plan took shape with resolute clarity as he took Mira's hand in his, stroking his fingers over the perfectly healed heart of her palm. "We'll leave as soon as possible this morning."

She frowned up at him. "In the daylight?"

"As soon as we can," he reiterated. Now that he knew what needed to be done, he wanted the plan in motion. "Nina has friends who can get us a vehicle, no questions asked. I'll ride in back, out of the sun's reach. One of my crew can do the driving. We can be there in a few hours."

Mira was staring at him, a question in her muted gaze. "You're taking me with you?"

"I want you safe," he said, lifting her chin to meet his kiss. "You're mine now, remember?"

"I'm yours." Her smile nearly broke his heart, it was so pure and trusting. She burrowed deep into the curve of his body, molding herself to him. "Don't let go, Kellan. Promise me you won't let go."

"I won't let go, Mouse." He wrapped his arms around her, pressing a kiss to her forehead as she snuggled tighter and her breathing slowed to a contented rhythm.

And in that moment, he was glad for the absence of her link into his emotions.

Because if she'd been bonded to him by blood, she would have understood no matter how much he wished he could keep that promise to her, before the next dawn, she would know it had been just a pretty lie.

19

BY NIGHTFALL, NO LESS THAN A DOZEN MEMBERS OF THE ORDER
had descended upon Boston.

Nathan led a unit comprised of his team of three and Mira's squad,
Bal, Torin, and Webb, who'd come in from Montreal to aid in her recov-
ery. While Nathan and his crew scoured the old North End for leads on
the rebels who held her, the other side of the city was getting a shake-
down by Nikolai, along with Tegan, Hunter, and Rio, diverted from the
D.C. headquarters and joined by Sterling Chase, director of the Boston
command center.

To a man, they'd all vowed that dawn would not come without Mira
being brought safely back into the fold of her family of the Order.

That pledge was cold water in Nathan's veins as he and Rafe Male-
branche split off from Eli and Jax and Mira's three teammates, taking
their search into establishments known to be friendly to rebels and their
ilk. The club La Notte was their first stop, given that Rooster was a
regular at the illegal arena there.

Nathan and Rafe walked in together, both warriors scanning the
crowd. Upward of a hundred people were partying inside, clad mostly
in black leather and heavy eyeliner, convulsing to the grinding pulse of
an industrial rock band screaming about pain and betrayal onstage.
Goth girls and punks, most of them human. All harmless clubbers. No
sign of the criminal element Nathan was currently searching for.

As he and Rafe sliced through the churning throng, Nathan noticed

La Notte's proprietor eyeing them with less than enthusiastic regard. Cassian broke away from a pair of attractive women easily a decade too young for him and strode toward Nathan. He was dressed like many of his patrons, in head-to-toe black leather and heavy lug-soled boots. Tonight his cropped hair was a crown of gelled spikes, his bright green eyes accentuated by dark brows, each pierced by a pair of tiny silver rings. A black stud was stuck through the tip of his tongue.

"Didn't realize my club was so popular with the Order," he drawled. "I don't know if I should be flattered or offended."

Nathan hardly paid Cassian any attention. "Check the arena," he told Rafe.

As the warrior turned to carry out the order, Nathan continued to prowl the club at street level. Cassian was right at his heels. "The fights don't start for hours, warrior."

"We didn't come to watch your blood sport."

"No," Cassian replied, "from the look of you, I'd guess you were here to start some of your own. Wouldn't have anything to do with the hotheaded female from your operation, would it?"

Nathan had his hand clamped around the other male's throat before Cassian could take his next breath. "What do you know about her?"

Some of the proprietor's henchmen, including the cage fighter called Syn and a couple of others, emerged from out of nowhere and started closing in. Still caught tight in Nathan's grasp, Cassian dismissed his thugs with a glance and a subtle twitch of his head.

"He won't kill me," Cassian said. "He would've finished it by now if that were his intent."

Nathan was tempted, but intel was more crucial. "What do you know about Mira?"

By this time, Rafe had come back from downstairs. Nathan noticed his brother-in-arms from the corner of his eye. Skilled and deadly, Rafe had a blade in one hand, his other ready to draw the 9-mm semiauto holstered on his weapons belt.

Nathan didn't let up the pressure on the human's throat. "I asked you a question. If you know where Mira is, you would be wise to tell me now."

Cassian smiled, unafraid. Amused, even. "So many surprises lately where that one is concerned."

"You know something," Nathan pressed, certain he'd found the lead he needed. "Do you know where Bowman is holding her?"

"Holding her?" Cassian's smile stretched wider. "My guess would be he's holding her quite close."

Nathan squeezed, taking uncharacteristically sadistic satisfaction in the man's answering sputter. As Cassian coughed and wheezed, his henchman and fighters advanced another few paces. Rafe moved with effortless speed, placing himself between Nathan and Cassian and the approaching guards.

"Tell me where to find Bowman," Nathan demanded coolly, "or I will kill you. Make no mistake. Your life is only worth the information you give me now. Where is Bowman keeping her?"

The club owner sucked in a restricted breath. "I can't tell you anything about the rebel leader or your MIA comrade. Pity you weren't here last night. You could've asked them yourself."

Nathan's blood went still in his veins. "What are you talking about?"

"They were here," Cassian said. "Both of them. Talking to Rune downstairs at his dressing room."

Son of a bitch.

Nathan slanted a stunned look at Rafe, who took off immediately for the back stairs. Nathan glared back at the man caught tight in his grasp. He let up only enough to permit Cassian to speak. "Was she all right? Did it look like he'd harmed her in any way?"

"Still had her sharp tongue and attitude intact, if that's what you mean."

"You spoke to her?" He didn't like the sense of confusion that roiled through him now. He was accustomed to cool logic, calm calculations. This revelation was the last thing he expected, and despite his keen mind, he struggled to make sense of all he was hearing. "What did she say to you? Did you speak to Bowman too?"

Rafe came up from the floor below, shaking his head. "No sign of Rune down there."

"No," Cassian said, his tone unfazed, conversational. "Rune took the night off."

"Where?" Nathan demanded.

Cassian chuckled, the black stud at the end of his tongue gleaming as he spoke. "Find the daywalker and I reckon you'll find Rune."

Although Nathan was taken aback, it was Rafe who spoke first. "What the fuck? You mean Aric Chase?"

"No," Cassian replied. "The other one. The female. Hot young thing that's been slumming around my club for the past few weeks. Find her, and I guarantee you, Rune won't be far."

They made the long drive to his grandfather's old Darkhaven in northern Maine earlier that afternoon.

Halfway there, Mira had come down with a vicious headache. She had assured Kellan she was fine, but he'd felt the blast of pain in her skull through their bond. He could feel it still, while she slept in the large master suite of the Darkhaven. Her discomfort was less now that she was sleeping, but the fact that she'd been hurting at all—especially after tapping into her Sight for how long, he could only guess—disturbed him more than he wanted to admit.

At least she'd found some peace once they arrived in Maine. Her exhaustion had taken her down more than two hours ago, and when Kellan had gone in to check a few minutes ago, she hadn't even stirred when he sat down next to her on the bed.

As for his crew, they'd quickly adapted to the relocation. After getting Candice settled and tending to her wound, Doc and Nina had gone to work sweeping out the whole place, dusting off the old furniture and appliances that hadn't been used in years, and restocking the pantry and weapons cache with supplies brought with them from the New Bedford bunker.

The Darkhaven was a huge step up from the primitive amenities of their previous base, with a kitchen full of top-grade appliances, a fully functioning refrigerator and range, room after room of comfortable furnishings, and nearly ten thousand square feet of living space. But their stay could only be temporary. Just a safe haven to hold them for a short while, until Kellan had the chance to confront the storm closing in on him from all sides.

On that score, he only hoped his instinct was good.

He prayed it was, or he had likely risked all their lives doing what he had today.

Standing at the French doors that overlooked the thick woods outside the big house, Kellan didn't even hear Nina approach from behind him until she quietly cleared her throat. He turned, frowning at the small white bottle she held out to him.

"Migraine meds," she said, giving the container a little shake. "I've only got a few left, but you can have them if you think they might help . . . your friend."

He nodded, took them from her outstretched hand, and slipped the bottle into his pocket. "Thank you."

The three of them Nina, Candice, and Doc—were all gathered in the great room with him. They'd been watching him pace for a while, and now he realized just how uncomfortable was the pall of silence that hung over the group. Part of that silence had to do with the events of the past twenty-four hours—the lab explosion that had made global head-lines and the resulting public unrest that followed; the somber good-bye they'd given Chaz; now this, the sudden flight to a place they'd never even known existed.

And part of his crew's unease had to do with the female warrior from the Order, who was quite obviously something more to him than just a captive being held against her will.

He looked at their faces now and saw their confusion, their wary uncertainty about who he truly was and what Mira meant to him.

It bothered him, those uneasy stares.

They didn't know him, not even after eight years of living side by side. They'd protected the secret of his Breed origins, but he'd given them nothing in return. They had offered him their trust and friend-ship, but he'd kept them out.

No more, he decided.

These three people—these humans, for crissake—had become his friends. They'd become his family, and it killed him that he was only seeing that just now. Now, when he would soon be forced to leave them behind.

"I haven't been fair to you," he said, giving a rueful shake of his head. "I've been lying to you all this time. You haven't even known my name. It's not Bowman. It's Kellan. My name is Kellan Archer."

Doc scowled, his black brows furrowing, brown eyes narrowing, suspicious. Nina cocked her indigo-haired head in question, her look of unease deepening. Only Candice met his gaze without perplexity or surprise. The sharp-witted, compassionate young woman had proba-bly figured most of it out for herself the other day, when she and Mira had spoken. The two of them had formed something of a kinship—what might have become a friendship, if circumstances had been different.

She gave him a mild nod, and he cleared his throat to continue.

"You've known from the beginning that I'm Breed. That's something I couldn't hope to hide from you. Candice and Doc, you knew it the night you pulled me from the Mystic and saved my life. Nina, you've known it for months. You've all known my secret and you kept it."

"We're your friends. That's what friends do for one another, Bow—" Doc's voice broke off abruptly, and he shook his head back and forth, blowing out a long sigh. "Friends watch your back. You've had ours too . . . Kellan?"

He nodded at the testing of his name. "I've still got your back, Javier. As long as I'm drawing breath, know that I'll watch all of your backs. And I want to lay it all out tonight, no more secrets. No more lies. I want you to know the truth—all of it. And part of my truth is sleeping in that room down the hall."

"You love her." Nina's expression had softened to one of understanding. Wistful and quiet, no doubt because of the love she'd known not so long ago. Known and lost, taken from her by whoever it was who'd absconded with Jeremy Ackmeyer's UV technology. "You've loved this woman for a long time, haven't you?"

Kellan nodded. "All my life. That's what it seems like. I've loved her since we were kids . . . when Mira and I both were raised by the Order."

No one said a word. Even Candice now looked at him in anticipation. "You are Order?"

"Was," he corrected. "A long time ago."

He told them about the destruction of his family's Darkhaven when he was thirteen years old, how he and his grandfather Lazaro Archer, the owner of the place they now occupied, were accepted into the Order's protection. He told them how he met an eight-year-old, pale-haired, stubborn little imp who'd refused to let him sulk over everything he'd lost, refusing to let him give up and forcing him to accept her as his friend. He told them how that same little imp had blossomed into an amazing woman and impressive warrior, how he and Mira had trained together with the Order, eventually becoming members of the same patrol team.

And then he told them how, after finally admitting to himself that he'd fallen in love with her, after at last giving in to the desire they shared for each other, his world came crashing down in an instant, when he glimpsed his future in her extraordinary eyes.

He told them about the warehouse explosion that should have killed him, but didn't. And how he'd been a coward, taking what he thought to be the easiest way out—running as far and as fast as he could from the vision he dreaded—and letting Mira and everyone else he cared about at the time believe he truly was dead.

"I thought I was being so careful, making sure our paths never crossed." He uttered a low curse. "And then the call came in from the field, after the grab on Ackmeyer didn't go off the way we'd planned. When I heard we snagged a member of the Order . . . a female warrior . . . I should've told you all then, I think I was still fooling myself that I could escape this. That I could evade the inevitable."

"Sounds like you're giving up, boss." Doc eyed him like the field surgeon he was, examining a mortal wound. "Sounds to me like you brought us here to say good-bye."

"I needed to do what I could to see that the three of you had the chance to come out of this unscathed," Kellan said, not yet ready to talk about farewells. "I want you to think about where you're heading with your lives, after all of this is over."

"What about you and Mira?" Candice asked gently.

He shook his head slowly, considering. "I need to know she's going to be safe too. She belongs with the Order; that's her family. They'll look after her. They'll help her through."

Candice watched him, her hazel-green eyes far too wise. "And you, Kellan? Where does all of this leave you?"

He grunted, wry with resignation. "Right back where I started."

At least he had honesty in this moment, with these people. At least he had a few precious days and nights with Mira, a gift that made any price he paid more than worth the cost.

He had her love.

She would always have his heart.

"I think she's finally awake," Nina said, a moment after Kellan heard a bump of movement coming from the bedroom down the hall.

He was already heading that way, jolted into action by a sudden burst of pain passed to him through the blood bond. His long strides ate up the distance. He opened the door and found the bed empty, covers pushed aside. "Mira?"

He saw her a second later, on the floor near the foot of the bed. Her hands were wrapped around her shin. As soon as Kellan opened the door, his nostrils flared with the inhaled punch of her lily-scented blood. "Jesus Christ. What happened?"

"N-nothing," she stammered. He saw now that she had a bleeding gash on her leg. "I must've been half asleep when I got out of bed. I banged my shin into the bed frame."

"I'll get you something for it." He dashed into the bathroom to wet a washcloth, then brought the cold compress back out to her. "Here, use this."

Her fingers trembled shakily as she took the cloth from him and put it on her wound. It wasn't anything serious, but the fact that she had stumbled—Mira, as sure-footed a female as he'd ever seen and a combat-proven warrior besides—made a cold knot form in his gut. "How are you feeling?"

"Fine," she replied quickly. Too quickly. And the blood bond told him another story. He registered fear and confusion running under the sting of her injury and the dull throb of her still-present headache. "Don't worry about me, Kellan. It's just a scratch."

He glanced at her face, at her eyes, which seemed to be looking past him, despite his effort to lock onto her gaze. Oh, Christ. He didn't want to acknowledge the thought that crept into his mind. He didn't want to consider the awful possibility.

"Mira . . ." He reached up to her face, up near her eyes.

Her gaze flicked a fraction but still didn't come to rest on him as he prayed it would. Her voice sounded so small. So heartbreakingly frightened. "What . . . what are you doing, Kellan?"

She didn't have any idea. He understood that without any doubt now. But he had to know, had to see the truth of it for himself.

"Hold still," he told her gently. "I'm not going to hurt you."

Carefully he removed one of her contacts.

"Kellan, don't—" She sucked in a sharp breath and tried to avert her face from him, but he gingerly brought her back and removed the second lens. "Kellan . . . I didn't want you to know. I thought maybe if I rested for a while, I would get better."

"Oh, Mouse." He could hardly speak. The words tasted like ash on his tongue. "Oh, Jesus, baby . . . *no.*"

Behind the lenses, her irises were no longer mirrorlike and clear.

They were milky white, opaque.

Her pupils stared straight ahead, minuscule pinpricks in the center of her sightless eyes.

20

NATHAN ALREADY HAD ARIC CHASE ON THE LINE BY THE TIME Rafe and he left La Notte. "Any idea where your sister is tonight?"

"Carys? Yeah, she's with Jordana Gates at her apartment in Back Bay."

Nathan glanced at Rafe, who nodded in acknowledgment. "I know the place. Commonwealth, a block off the Public Garden."

"What's she done now?" Aric asked, then, more soberly: "She's not in any kind of trouble, is she?"

"That remains to be seen," Nathan replied, knowing it was not the most reassuring thing to tell the young female's twin brother, but, then again, he didn't have a lot of practice when it came to diplomacy. "I'll update you once I've spoken to her."

He cut the connection without further discussion and slid the comm unit back into the pocket of his black fatigues. Then he and Rafe hung the corner and picked up the pace as they sped for the Back Bay. No sense taking their vehicle when their Breed genetics would carry them across the city in no time on foot. And if Rune truly was keeping illicit company with Carys Chase, Nathan wanted to be damn sure about it, before he tore the cage-fighting bastard to shreds with his bare hands.

In mere minutes, he and Rafe closed in on the white limestone Victorian mansion at the address Aric had indicated. They flew up the marble steps to the polished black double doors and stormed inside the foyer, combat boots thudding like the march of an encroaching army in the sophisticated quiet of the place.

A graying middle-age human male in a rent-a-cop's uniform stood up from behind a long mahogany reception desk as the pair of Breed warriors cut through the lobby. When the portly guard started to sputter a protest at them, Nathan silenced him with a dark look sliced his way and a flash of fang. Wisely, the human put his ass immediately back in his chair and got busy studying his fingernails.

Nathan sent a mental command at the elevator off the lobby and the absent car started descending for him. "Stay down here," he told Rafe as the doors slid open. "You see Carys or Rune try to make an escape while I'm upstairs, you keep them here. You call me."

Rafe gave a nod of his blond head, the young warrior's eyes grim with purpose while Nathan stepped into the elevator and psychically blew past the lock on the button for the penthouse.

A few seconds later, the lift's doors opened and he found himself staring at a locked, black wrought-iron grate. On the other side of that elegant blockade was the lavish interior of Jordana Gates's apartment. Soaring twelve-foot ceilings, gleaming white marble floor, soft golden lighting everywhere he looked, bathing a warm, inviting glow over walls painted in tranquil shades of cream and white and palest blue.

As he stood there, behind the wall of fused black iron, a light, feminine voice he guessed must belong to Carys's friend reached his ears before he had a chance to see her. "Seamus, don't tell me I left my umbrella in the lobby again."

An ethereal, tall and willowy blonde sailed around a massive marble pillar in the vestibule. Dressed in a tailored, knee-length ivory skirt and a silky blouse the color of polished pewter, which, he noted with more interest than he liked, was unbuttoned to an enticing spot between her breasts, she came to an abrupt stop on her delicate, high-heeled sandals. The tumble of thick, platinum waves cascading down to the backs of her thighs sifted around her as she froze in place and stared at him. She was . . . stunning.

"Oh," she said, just now realizing she wasn't talking to the guard from downstairs. Big, expressive eyes, in an electric shade of blue that seemed almost unreal it was so intense, met his unsmiling gaze from behind the black scrollwork of the grate.

"Carys Chase," Nathan announced firmly.

"Excuse me?" She frowned now, swallowed visibly. "No, I'm Jor—"

"I know who you are. I'm here for Carys Chase. I would speak with the female. Now."

Alarm bled into Jordana Gates's striking features. "Is . . . is anything wrong? Why would you think she's—"

Using the power of his mind, Nathan threw open the locked iron barrier. "I know she's here."

Jordana took a step backward as he entered uninvited. She shot an anxious look over her shoulder, raising her voice to a level that would, no doubt, be heard all the way to the back of the expansive residence. "She's not here, and I don't appreciate the Order barging into my home unannounced."

Nathan felt the corner of his mouth quirk, not so much in humor as in mild annoyance that this Darkhaven-raised socialite would imagine she could interfere with his purpose. He advanced another pace, but this time, instead of retreating, the Breedmate blocked his path.

"No," she said, planting her spiked heels firmly in front of him. "No. You can't just stomp through my private residence as if you own the place."

He cocked his head, perplexed and somewhat annoyed at her lack of fear and her continued resistance. "Carys Chase!" he roared, his voice rumbling high into the domed ceiling of the vestibule.

Jordana stepped in closer. "I said you're not welcome here. I want you to leave at once. I mean it."

His annoyance morphed into disbelief as she got right up in his face, totally uncowed by him. "I will not let you take one more step into my home, warrior."

Nathan couldn't bite back his chuckle. "Female, unless you've got an army of bodyguards camped out in your salon, just how do you intend to prevent me?"

He started to take a firm step forward, and so did she. But instead of pushing him or screaming for help, Jordana Gates did something even more surprising.

She kissed him.

Without any warning at all, her lips were on his, her fingers gripping his shoulders, her breasts mashed against his chest.

For a very long moment, Nathan stood frozen, utterly stupefied. The warmth of her mouth, the softness of her body, the way her lips were melting against his . . . all of it combined into a tempest of sensation he was ill-equipped to deal with, even under the best circumstances. Hand-to-hand combat and stealth executions, no problem. But this was a situation well beyond his skill set and training.

He wasn't a virgin—not even close. But the impersonal encounters he preferred to seek out never involved touching or embracing or kissing.

In that moment, Jordana Gates couldn't have shocked him more if she'd pulled his 9-mm out of its holster on his hip and shot him point blank in the chest.

So much so, he wasn't even aware they were no longer alone in the room, until he heard the low sound of a male clearing his throat somewhere nearby.

Abruptly, Nathan disengaged from Jordana's hold on him and put a healthy distance between them. Her oceanic blue eyes were wide, pupils enlarged, deepening the Caribbean azure of her gaze before the kiss to a stormy turquoise now. She brought her hand up to her mouth and backed off quickly, moving to the safety of her friend's side in the living room adjacent to the vestibule.

Beautiful, cultured Carys Chase stood there beside swarthy, dangerous Rune, her fingers linked through his. "Are you all right, Jordana?" she whispered. Then, to Nathan, with no gentleness in her voice at all: "Why did you come here? Why the hell did you just assault Jordana? Tell me what's going on!"

The other Breedmate shook her pale blond head, mute. Even Nathan had trouble summoning his voice for a second. He leveled a cold look on Rune. "That's what I've come here to find out: What the hell is going on?"

Rune held his stare, his dark eyes unflinching. "Just visiting friends on a rare night off from the job. I assume there's no law against that."

"Make no mistake, you and I will talk later about what you think you're doing with this female," Nathan replied. He slanted a hard look at Carys, adding "We'll talk too." To which her chin went up a notch, impertinent, unrepentant. "Right now, I'm here to talk about the friend you met last night at the club," he said to Rune.

The Breed fighter got a strange look on his face, but it lasted only a fraction of a second before he shuttered it with a mask of indifference. "Don't have any idea what you mean."

"That's not what Cassian just told me a few minutes ago when I was there," Nathan countered. "He said you had a visit from a rebel piece of shit called Bowman."

Now Rune chuckled, and from what Nathan could tell, his denial was genuine. "You've been misinformed, my man. I'm not gonna try to guess what game Cass is playing with you, but I don't hang with rebels. And I don't know anyone by that name."

"Really? Cassian told me Bowman was at La Notte last night with Mira." Rune's expression seemed to turn a bit stonier now. "Cassian says you spoke with them for a while in your dressing room."

"That's a lie," Carys interjected, her caramel-brown hair swinging as she gave a vehement shake of her head. "Rune didn't have anyone in his dressing room last night . . . except for me."

Nathan's curse drifted from between his flatly pressed lips. His dismay over that news flash was only slightly less than what it would be for Carys's parents or her twin brother. "Obviously, someone's lying to me right now," Nathan said. "And I'll warn you all just once that I do not have time for bullshit."

Rune stared at him, assessing. Almost suspicious. "Sounds like the Order's got some trouble on their hands."

"Did you or did you not see Bowman with Mira last night?" he asked the fighter. "If you know anything about what he's doing with her, I need to know. Her life could depend on it."

Carys clutched Rune's hand a bit tighter, Nathan noticed. But Rune gave nothing away in his face. "Sorry I can't help."

"Sorry." Nathan snarled the word. "I can make you sorry."

Maybe that's what the bastard needed. Nathan took a pace forward, and couldn't help noticing that Rune stayed put. Didn't matter, because in that next second, both women stepped in to put themselves between the two Breed males.

"Stop this right now," Carys cried. She spun toward Rune. "Both of you, stop this!"

Nathan couldn't take his eyes off Jordana but saw in his peripheral vision when Rune gently stroked Carys's cheek.

Nathan hated that he'd likely end up hurting her tender heart in the next few minutes, when he and her apparent more-than-unlikely boyfriend took their unfriendly discussion into a physical one.

As he considered doing just that, his comm unit buzzed in his pants pocket. He took it out, saw the caller was Eli, one of his teammates in Boston. Before Nathan could even ask for an update, Eli blurted out the news Nathan had been ready to kill tonight to have.

"We got a bead on Bowman."

"Where?" Nathan demanded, his impasse with Rune suddenly less important in light of this crucial intel.

"Tip turned up on a rumored rebel base down in New Bedford. Scumbag gun runner sold Vince a dozen semiautos last winter. Said he only dealt with Vince, never got a look at Bowman or anyone else, but the lead on the possible base seems solid. Not much, but it's something, right?"

"Agreed," Nathan said. "Where are you at?" Eli rattled off the team's location in the city. "Okay. Rafe and I will be there in less than five minutes. Touch base with everyone else on patrol tonight, let them know we're on it. We're moving in on New Bedford, no delay."

"Got it, Captain."

They cut the call and Nathan leveled one last look on the cage-fighting killer as he shoved his comm unit back into his pocket. "Anything happens to Mira because you wouldn't talk, I will make you sorry. That goes double, anything happens to this female."

Rune's dark eyes narrowed at the threat. "I would lay down my life for Carys."

Nathan scoffed, well aware of the Breed male's dubious background and his infamous mode of living. "She's worth ten of you, and you know it."

"Aye," Rune agreed, the first indicator of the accent he usually kept muted. His returning gaze was solemn but unapologetic. "That I do know, warrior."

With Jordana Gates staring at him as if he were the devil himself standing in the middle of her apartment and Carys holding tight to Rune's large, battle-scarred hand, Nathan wheeled around and exited the penthouse.

On the way back down to the lobby to get Rafe, Nathan had to concentrate on his training in order to bring his senses back to a state of cold purpose.

He strode out of the elevator on the ground floor, and beckoned his teammate over with a curt motion of his hand. He filled Rafe in on the new development, then the pair of warriors headed out, ready to deal a lot of pain and death to Bowman and his rebel followers.

And all the while, Nathan's mouth still burned from Jordana Gates's unexpected, disturbingly unforgettable kiss.

The darkness was complete, inky blackness.

The void around her cold, silent, as Kellan drew away from both her and the blindness that enveloped her. She didn't know what he saw in her eyes now, only knew that the hideousness of her unseeing gaze had pulled him away on a violent curse.

"Kellan, I didn't want you to know," she murmured, anguished by his withdrawal. "I didn't want you to see me like this—"

"Can you see nothing at all?" His voice was wooden, edged with a fury she knew would be written across his handsome face, could her eyes find him in the dark. When she slowly shook her head, his breath left him on a groan.

Behind her, although Kellan hadn't moved, she heard the lock on the door slam home like a gunshot. She jumped, her other senses going hyperalert in the absence of her sight.

When Kellan spoke again, his voice was airless, a tightly controlled whisper. "Damn you, Mira. Damn us both, for how badly we've fucked everything up."

"Kellan, I'm sorry—"

"Don't." He cut her off shortly, but then his hands were on her upper arms, and his grip trembled, his fingers holding her tenderly. Achingly so. "Jesus, don't apologize for anything now. Not to me. I don't deserve it. Look what I've done to you."

She wanted so badly to see his face. She needed to know if the emotion she heard in his voice right now was sadness for her or the pity it sounded like. She swallowed, so afraid she was losing him—not because of the fate that threatened to steal him away from her, but because she was no longer whole in his eyes. She was broken and had no one but herself to blame.

"I can't let you live like this," he murmured, breaking her heart even further. "I need to fix it, if I can. You need blood, Mira. The bond might be able to repair this."

How long had she waited to hear him say his blood was hers to take? How many years had she pictured them together as a blood-bonded, mated pair? Now she felt his offer like a slap to her face. It stung. It hurt her so deeply, she rocked back, stricken and numbed by the blow.

"I don't want you feeling sorry for me," she managed to croak. "Don't you dare give me your charity, Kellan."

"Charity?" he murmured thickly. One of his hands came up to caress her cheek. "God, no. What I'm feeling isn't pity. It's regret. And fear. And love, Mira. So much love for you." He blew out a raspy exhalation. "I never imagined things could go so wrong for us. There were so many times I wanted to ask you to accept me as your mate. I should have, but I was terrified of the pain I would feel if I ever lost you."

"You were the one who left," she reminded him. "I stayed. I would've stayed with you, even knowing how it might all end."

"I know," he replied, remorse thick in his deep voice. "And I owed you that choice. I see that now." He scoffed quietly. "I see a lot of things more clearly now, when it's too late to turn any of it back. But maybe not this," he said, his thumb brushing gently across her eyelid as he continued to caress her face. "I might be able to fix this for you. And I'm asking you to give me that chance, Mira."

Tender, beautiful words. She could feel his affection in the quiet hitch of his voice and in the careful way he stroked her skin. He cared. He loved her, she had no doubt now.

But he wasn't giving himself as her mate. He was giving her a chance to heal through his blood bond. He wanted her whole again, but would he be offering this gift if she were looking into his eyes in this moment, seeing him as the man she loved, the male her heart was bound to, with or without his blood to seal it?

Her own blood must have betrayed her to him, because no sooner had she thought it, Kellan's touch slid down along her chin, lifting her sightless gaze up to meet his eyes. "When I imagined sharing this part of me with you, Mira, it was a sacred thing. A thing done in passion, in pleasure, with a promise of eternity ahead of us. It was never like this," he said, his voice rough, so gentle. "It was never supposed to be done with you suffering and afraid and me helpless, desperate, ultimately damned to lose you. And never less suited to be the one you bound yourself to than I am in this moment."

"There's no one else I want, Kellan. There never has been." She reached out to him but struggled to find him, touching only air and darkness. Frustration boiled up in the back of her throat, erupting in a small, broken cry.

Then Kellan's hand found hers, took it into his strong grasp. "There," he said, pressing a kiss to the center of her palm. "I've got you, Mouse."

"Yes, you do," she replied, her love for him swelling inside her until she felt her heart might burst from it. "You won't let go, will you, Kellan? That's what you promised me. You won't let go."

His curse was a whispered oath. Then his mouth was on hers, claiming her in a possessive yet achingly sweet kiss. When he broke the contact a long moment later, she felt him moving his arm. She heard a soft, wet sound, smelled the spicy-dark scent of his blood.

"Open your mouth for me, baby," he whispered, placing his wrist against her parted lips.

Mira took him into her, the first sip of his blood like a lick of fire on her tongue. She swallowed, then drew another sip into her mouth. And another.

She hadn't been prepared.

How could she have ever been prepared to know the roar of heat and power that was Kellan's bond?

Mira drank him down in fevered, greedy gulps. As their blood bond completed, she could only hold on to him and give herself over to the rush of light and strength and something even more intense—something that defied all description—pouring into her every muscle, bone, and cell.

He was hers.

Kellan belonged to her in every way now, and if fate wanted to take him from her, Mira intended to give that cruel bitch one hell of a fight.

21

EMPTY.

No sign of Mira or Bowman or anyone else at the old military fort at the far end of New Bedford. The bunker and its collection of underground batteries, which crouched on an outcrop of overgrown, untended parkland banked on three sides by the Atlantic, appeared to have been vacated very recently. They'd missed the rebel bastards.

It was not the kind of report Nathan wanted to have to give Lucan. Hell, it was bad enough reporting it to Nikolai a few moments ago. He hadn't taken it well, erupting in murderous, black fury. Mira's father, in Boston with a small squad of his Order brethren, had been determined that Mira would be going home safe with them before dawn. Now that prospect was looking less and less feasible.

Nathan's team, along with Mira's three teammates, had just completed a full sweep of the purported rebel base and turned up nothing. Just abandoned furniture, tables and chairs, cots and beds, all still in place as it ostensibly had been when the base's occupants used it last. But Mira *had* been there; Nathan could almost feel her presence in his bones.

"Damn it!" The curse exploded out of him, a reaction too strong to contain. He didn't miss the turn of heads in his direction. The grave looks of his team and Mira's met him through the darkness as the warriors regrouped on the thick, weed-choked grass outside the bunker. Niko and his squad were heading there now too, to see the place for themselves and to strategize the rest of the night's patrol with Nathan and the other men.

"Cleared out fast, evidently," Balthazar remarked, the big vampire's typical humor absent tonight. "Like rats from a sinking ship."

Rafe nodded, grim. "Maybe someone warned them we were coming."

"If they did get a warning we were on to them," Eli put in, "that would mean they hauled ass outta here less than five minutes after our lead came in."

"Didn't take off in a panic," Torin said. He tipped his head back, long braids at his temples swinging against his sharp cheekbones as he read the energy in the air. "They had time to gather everything they needed. When they left—by the fade of it, my guess would be sometime late morning—they left on their own terms."

Jax twirled one of his hira-shuriken between nimble fingers, the metal winking with lethal precision under the moonlight. "Doesn't matter why or when they left. Only matters where."

"And that puts us right back at square one," said Webb, the warrior Lucan had put in charge of Mira's squad after the incident with Rooster not even a week ago. From the sober look on the Breed male's face, it was a mantle he accepted out of duty alone, not personal ambition. "Can't believe she hasn't kicked those rebels' asses single-handed by now and come strolling back to us like it was no big thing. Shit, the way Mira goes into combat?" Webb shook his head, contemplating. "Fucking Valkyrie, man. Doesn't matter she's not Breed; it would take an army of humans to knock her down and keep her there. And I, for one, refuse to believe she's not still breathing out there somewhere."

For what hadn't been the first time, Nathan's thoughts were going down a similar path. What had they done to Mira to keep her captive for so many days? Had she tried to fight back? And what of Bowman? How had he been able to bring her last night into La Notte, a public place, and she not find some way to break free of him?

A troubling scenario was beginning to take root in Nathan's mind.

He didn't like the taste of it. Didn't want to think that Mira might have gotten somehow unwillingly entangled with the rebels and their criminal acts. Or worse . . . could she possibly have allowed herself to be charmed by Bowman?

The last was almost laughable, it was so incomprehensible. There had only ever been one man for Mira, and he was eight years dead and gone. A handful of days in the company of human rebels—a class of individuals she openly despised—would not suddenly turn her away from the Order and her kin.

And yet . . .

It was that last disturbing possibility—the least logical of them all—that proved the hardest for Nathan to ignore.

There was something he wasn't seeing. Something he hadn't yet connected. Something he'd maybe glossed over and dismissed as unimportant amid the urgency of the bunker's search.

"Problem, Captain?"

He waved off the question without acknowledging who had asked it. His boots were already chewing up earth beneath him, his strides long and purposeful as he stalked back into the damp gloom of the rebel hideout.

He checked each room and corridor again, less rushed this time, sending his gaze over every rustic table, chair, and cot, into every corner and cranny of the place. And he found nothing.

Not until he stepped into the last room, the one situated at the far end of the concrete passageway.

Something crunched under his boot heel. A small piece of broken glass.

He paused, lifted his foot to pick up the sleek, silvery shard. Holding the tiny bit of shattered mirror between his thumb and forefinger, Nathan lifted his gaze and scanned every inch of the lightless room, his Breed eyes keen in the dark.

He cocked his head, narrowing in on an object lying in the center of the tumbled bedsheets. Even now he was tempted to dismiss it. Just a broken mirror, tossed in haste onto the unmade bed as the rebels raced to vacate the premises.

Except they hadn't left in haste.

Nathan had suspected as much earlier, when it was obvious they'd had time to take weapons and equipment, clothing and foodstuffs. Then Torin had confirmed it, reading the energy of the place left in the wake of the evacuation.

Bowman and his rebels had left with Mira on their own terms, not in a panic. They'd had time to sweep up all but one minuscule splinter of the glass that must have littered the floor, yet they hadn't bothered to remove the broken mirror along with it.

And now Nathan's Hunter instincts prickled with cold realization.

The mirror had been left behind, not tossed onto the bed and forgotten.

Placed there deliberately.

He walked over, picked it up. Stared at the intricately crafted design inlaid onto the polished silver back of the piece. The insignia was familiar at once, even though he hadn't seen it in a long time—not since the near annihilation of the family to whom the bow-and-arrow emblem belonged.

"Archer," Nathan murmured under his breath. Then a curse that was equal parts incredulity and outrage. "Bowman."

How could it be possible?

There was only one person he knew who might have this memento. One person who might possess the ability to be running under the radar of the Order, right under their damn noses.

But that person was dead.

Nathan had personally witnessed the explosion that killed the warrior who'd been like a brother to him. He'd seen the flames shoot into the night sky moments after Kellan Archer had gone inside—mere seconds before Nathan and Mira would have followed him into the warehouse to perish along with him.

But what Nathan hadn't seen, he realized now—what no one had ever sought to find in the ash and rubble left behind—was Kellan's presumed remains.

Son of a bitch.

Nathan's grip tightened around the delicate mirror bearing the Archer family emblem. He didn't like this sense of confusion that gnawed at him now, as he tried to logically sort the pieces of a disturbing puzzle he was just seeing for the first time. Could Kellan Archer be alive? All this time, deceiving everyone he knew, living in Boston like some kind of ghost? If so, how had he ended up in this place, with a new name and a band of human rebels under his command?

Betrayal wasn't something Nathan's lethal logic had trained him to combat. He'd never cared enough about something to experience any sense of unfairness when it was gone, but now the unfamiliar emotion roiled in his gut, bitter as acid.

And what about Mira?

As badly as he wanted to deny Kellan's deception, the prospect of Mira being pulled into the equation made the acid churning inside him turn cold. It made the assassin in him go still and calculating, preparing to sever all emotional ties in the execution of his mission.

Nathan considered the shattered mirror clutched tight in his fist. Either Kellan or Mira had left it, knowing—perhaps hoping—it would be discovered by someone who would recognize it. Someone from the Order. Maybe even Nathan himself.

If it had been Mira, perhaps it was a cry for help, some kind of clue to aid in her rescue. Except Nathan knew the Breedmate warrior too well to believe that. Her love for Kellan Archer had endured eight years of absence. If she were reunited with him now, after all that time mourning him, there would be no tearing her away from his side.

As for Kellan, Nathan knew him well too—or thought he did. Still, Nathan was certain the memento was intended to be found, not as a reckless taunt meant to incite the Order's full wrath.

No, Nathan understood now, it had been left behind as an invitation.

A clue meant to lead the right person directly to where Kellan would be found.

It was a token of surrender.

It wasn't so much a sound that woke Kellan but a sudden, quiet sense of expectation. He felt it in the air around him, in the moonlit darkness of the thick forest outside the Darkhaven bedroom's French doors. Silent, stealth, lethal.

They'd been found so soon.

Not that he was surprised.

No, he'd been prepared for this moment from the time he'd left the New Bedford base. Longer still, from the moment he'd found Mira gazing into her own reflection and understood in terrifying terms just how much his delay of the inevitable was costing her.

How much it had taken from her already.

He wanted it all to stop now. For her.

If he wasn't already too late.

Carefully extricating himself from Mira's arms as she slept naked beside him, Kellan slipped out of the bed. He pulled on his loose jeans and strode barefoot to the French doors. Opened them soundlessly and stepped outside to the cool summer night, scented by crisp northern air and dense pines.

A shadow peeled away from the inky blackness of the woods.

Nathan.

Garbed in black combat fatigues and a belted array of blades and firearms circling his hips, the former Breed assassin could have killed Kellan a dozen different ways by now. But he made no move to attack as he approached from out of the cover of the woods. Said nothing as he looked upon Kellan's face for the first time in eight years.

Kellan sent a quick glance in the direction of the surrounding forest.

"I came alone." Nathan's deep voice was quiet, barely a whisper in the stillness of their surroundings, and it held no trace of expression whatsoever. Flat and calm and unreadable. As was the look in his unblinking eyes. "No one knows where I am. I assume that's what you wanted."

Kellan gave a vague nod. "Hoped, yes."

"She's here with you?"

"Yes."

"She's been safe the whole time?"

Kellan could hardly confirm that, especially now, when he wasn't sure if she would ever be whole again. He'd fed her his blood more than an hour ago in the hopes their completed bond would restore her eyesight. She'd fallen asleep in his arms, trusting he would make her better, but it had felt to him like yet another promise he might fail to deliver to her.

"Mira's inside," he told Nathan, unwilling to lie to his old friend yet not quite ready to accept that Mira couldn't be healed. "She's sleeping, along with the three remaining members of my crew, who helped me bring her here."

Nathan grunted. "And you. Not dead, after all."

"I should've been," Kellan replied. "Someone helped me after the explosion that night, took care of me until I had healed. I never intended to disappear the way I did—"

Nathan cut him off, his voice cool, words clipped and efficient. "Explanations are unnecessary. At least as far as I'm concerned. I am not your judge and jury, just the Hunter come to retrieve a traitor."

Kellan lifted his chin, feeling the reply like a volley lobbed at him broadside. "I guess I deserve that, considering we're friends."

"My friend died eight years ago. I don't know Bowman."

"Yet you came alone after finding the clue that would lead to my arrest."

Nathan took a subtle step forward, his face grim. "Call it a kindness for the memory of my dead friend. And for the female who never stopped loving him. A female who deserves better than this, whose heart will be breaking all over again very soon, no doubt."

"Mira's the reason I led you here. She and my friends are inside this Darkhaven. I needed to know they would all be safe when this moment came. Making sure it happened here, like this, was the only way I knew how."

Nathan's eyes narrowed slightly under the ebony slashes of his brows. "How can you be certain of that?"

"Because you came alone," he replied. "And because despite your training, I know you are no killer of innocents. I'm the one you and the Order want. I mean to go with you peacefully. All I ask is that my crew goes free and Mira goes home safely, taking no blame for anything that happened to Jeremy Ackmeyer or for her time spent with me."

Nathan's cool stare pierced him even deeper now. "She doesn't know you're surrendering." Not a question; a cold, accurate statement of fact. "Why would you do this to her?"

"I've hurt her enough. I want this—all of it—over."

Nathan's brows lowered into a scowl. "You care for her, that's obvious enough, even to me. I know she cares for you. Why not run somewhere together? After all, you've lived a lie this long. Why throw yourself on the sword now?"

The irony of it made Kellan exhale a sharp breath through his nostrils. "Because I have no fucking choice."

Nathan cocked his head, studying him. "What is this—some eleventh-hour attack of conscience? Too late for that. If it's a sudden resurrection of your honor after such a long absence, I promise you, it's wasted. This thing has gone too far. It's gone too public now. There won't be any clemency for you—for Bowman. There can't be."

Kellan nodded. "I know that. This will only end one way for me. I've seen that for myself."

"You've *seen* it." Something cold and suspicious flickered in Nathan's steady gaze now. His voice, which had been carefully schooled and quiet, now notched a bit louder. "You mean Mira's shown something to you. A vision?" A curse, ripe and violent, erupted from between his old friend's lips. "You've used her ability, knowing what that costs her?"

"Jesus, no. I never would've done that," Kellan said. "Not intentionally—"

"Fuck you and your intentions," Nathan growled now. He stalked forward, dangerous in his outrage. "Did you use her? Did you use her gift for your own selfish gain?"

"Kellan . . . ?"

Ah, Christ.

Mira's worried voice sounded from behind him in the dark of the bedroom. He wasn't ready for her to walk into his conversation with Nathan yet. He wasn't ready for her to learn that he'd brought Nathan to them as a means of surrendering without bloodshed or casualties. Everything was happening too fast, a snowball picking up speed as it careened down the side of a mountain.

"It's okay," he told her, sending the reassurance over his shoulder as he heard her start to get up. "Mira, stay. I'll be right there and we can talk."

She kept moving, fabric rustling as she pulled a sheet from the bed and wrapped herself inside it. Her bare feet padded softly, carefully, on the wide pine floor as she made her way toward the open French doors. "Who are you talking to out there? Kellan, what's going on?"

And then a misstep. A halting, hitching movement that made Kellan's heart sink like a stone.

He pivoted and flashed to her side, catching her before she could fall. Her small cry of distress went through him, as sharp and unforgiving as an arrow. "Shh," he soothed her. "Shh, I've got you, Mira. It's okay now."

A low growl at Kellan's back made his neck prickle with warning. "Holy hell. It's even worse than I imagined."

"Nathan?" Mira asked, her pale, cloudy eyes searching in the darkness. "Kellan . . . what's Nathan doing here? Tell me what's happening. Kellan . . . ?"

"You goddamn bastard." The Hunter's voice was pure menace, all of it locked on Kellan. "You've fucking blinded her."

22

"NATHAN, NO!" ALTHOUGH MIRA COULDN'T SEE THE BREED WAR-rior move, she felt the crushing impact of his body as Nathan launched himself at Kellan. In her veins, she felt the echo of each punishing blow of the fists that came down onto Kellan's head and torso.

But the physical pain she experienced through her blood bond was nothing compared with the agony of knowing the two men she cared for so deeply—her two best friends, who'd been as close as brothers to each other at one time—were now engaged in a brutal fight because of her.

And *fight* was not the right term for what was taking place in front of her. Even though her vision was nothing but blackness and shadows, she could tell that Kellan wasn't even attempting to strike back at Nathan. He fended off the incoming fists, dodged when he could, but threw no punches of his own. He wouldn't fight his friend. Kellan had too much honor for that, despite what Nathan must think of him now.

"Nathan, stop!" Hindered by blindness and the sheet wrapped around her nakedness, Mira scrabbled in frustration, finally laying her hand on the massive form hunched over Kellan on the pine plank floor of the bedroom. She grabbed a fistful of his form-fitting combat shirt and yanked, trying to pull him away. "Nathan, it wasn't Kellan who blinded me. I did it myself. Damn it, listen to me. You have to stop this right now!"

The pummeling slowed, then halted as Nathan's bulk shifted be-neath her hold on him. She felt the heat of his gaze on her face and knew that his eyes had to be fully transformed—blazing hot with amber light and rage. His breath was sawing out of him, rough and heavy. Realizing just how furious he was—how deadly violent—Mira understood that Nathan could have killed Kellan then and there if he'd truly meant to. He could have killed him outside a few minutes ago, before she'd even known he was there.

"Let him up, Nathan. Kellan won't ask mercy of you, but I will." She searched for Nathan's face with her free hand, an inelegant movement that made him hiss a dark curse.

"Ah, fuck, Mira. Look what he's done to you."

"No," she said, shaking her head. "No, Kellan hasn't done anything. He tried to help me. He gave me his blood—"

"Jesus Christ." Nathan scoffed. His voice turned away from her then, and she knew he was looking at Kellan. "You wait all this time to come back into her life, only to ruin it by shackling her to you with the blood bond?"

"I love her," Kellan said. Mira heard him coming up off the floor, felt his warmth as he drew close to her. His hands came down light on her shoulders, comforting and strong. "I will always love her, no matter what fate has to say about it." His mouth pressed against her temple, tender and sweet. "I love you, Mira. More than anything else in this world or the next."

She knew that. Deep down, she knew he meant every word. But here he was, shattering her heart.

He was letting go.

"You promised me," she murmured, closing her eyes against the pain. "You said you wouldn't let me go."

"Ah, Mouse." Another kiss, this one landing gently on her eyelid. His voice was a rough whisper, low and intimate, thick with emotion. "Letting go of you is the last thing I ever want to do. If there was a way to turn this around, believe me, I would."

As Kellan soothed her with tender words of good-bye, elsewhere in the Darkhaven came the muffled sounds of infiltration and struggle. Deep, familiar voices commanding Kellan's crew to cooperate with their arrest and no one would get hurt.

Boots thundered heavily down the hallway toward the bedroom.

"You lied to me," Kellan said to Nathan. "You said you came alone."

Nathan grunted. "I wasn't about to leave anything to chance. As you told me outside, this meeting you instigated tonight was about ensuring

Mira's well-being. We had to make sure she'd come out of this safely too."

"Mira." Nikolai's low growl came toward her from the bedroom's now-open doorway.

"Daddy?"

She couldn't help herself from falling into his arms as he strode inside and pulled her into him for a tight embrace. She knew the instant he looked at her face—the instant he saw her clouded eyes. His snarl was fierce and animalistic, a lethal predator about to spring on the interloper who had wounded one of his young. "Son of a bitch. Fuck the arrest, I'll kill the bastard—"

Before Mira could say anything, Nathan stopped Nikolai with words alone. "She's bonded to him. Hurt Kellan, and you hurt her too."

"Is this true?" Niko asked her sternly. "Did you drink from him?"

"We're mated," she replied, clutching the sheet tightly around her under the cold blast of Niko's fury. "Our bond is complete."

The warrior's answering curse was vicious, rolling off the surrounding walls. "Get him out of my sight before I take his head where he stands."

Kellan didn't resist as movements indicated he was being taken into Order custody. Mira wished she could see his face. She needed to see him. Could not stand the idea that she might never look upon him again.

"Come on, baby," Nikolai said, wrapping her under the protective shelter of his arm. "Let's find some clothes for you and get you out of here. It's all over now. Let's get you home."

But it wasn't over.

Mira walked with him numbly, holding on to keep from stumbling as he slowly guided her out of the room.

For her, nothing was over yet. She walked in silence, having no voice to tell her father that once they arrived in D.C., the worst of her ordeal would be only beginning.

The Order's patrol teams arrived in D.C. from the old Darkhaven in Maine just before dawn, bringing with them Mira, Kellan Archer, and the three human rebels who had, incredibly, been serving under his command for the past several years.

Lucan had been brought up to speed on most of the situation some ten hours earlier, when Nathan called in the mission complete status from the field. Aside from the fact that the rebels were now in Order custody and Mira was recovered and on the way home, there hadn't been much good news to report. Lucan's head was still reeling from everything he'd heard, and after more than nine hundred years of living, it took a damn good lot to surprise him.

Still, the weight of the facts he'd been given hadn't quite set in for him until he stood in the mansion's foyer and watched as Niko ushered Mira inside. He was all but carrying the Breedmate, whose useless eyes were open but fixed on nothing as she shuffled slowly alongside her father, clinging to his arm for support and guidance across the smooth white marble floor.

The warriors' mates—all of the Order's women—converged on Mira en masse as soon as she entered the house. Lucan noted the rush of female concern and affection that poured onto the younger Breedmate as the women quickly escorted her away, all their focus centered on Mira's well-being. Lucan watched them go, knowing he would have his turn to visit with Mira later. When his head was cooler, and his blood was no longer seething with the need to do severe bodily harm to the bastard responsible for her abduction a few days ago and her current physical state.

The object of his fury entered the foyer now, shoved inside ungently by Tegan and Rio. Nathan and Rafe, along with the other two members of their team and Mira's squad of three, stalked in behind them.

"Chase and Hunter have the rebels outside," Nathan reported. "One of them is hobbled by a leg injury. It's had medical attention, but the wound is deep. She can't walk on the limb."

Lucan grunted. "Rafe," he said, glancing to Dante and Tess's son. "Help the woman inside. Have a look at her, see what can be done."

The blond warrior gifted with his mother's extraordinary healing touch gave a nod, then jogged off to carry out the order.

As for Kellan Archer, the eyes of a dozen-plus lethally skilled, pissed-off Breed warriors were fixed on him in barely restrained animosity as he was brought to a stop in the center of the glittering foyer. Damn, it was a shock to see him again, after believing him dead for going on a decade. Lucan had always liked the kid, but the outlaw standing before him now was making it hard for Lucan to resist adding some bruises of his own to the collection Kellan already sported.

And he wasn't alone in his outrage for what Kellan stood accused of. The rage of Lucan's brethren was a palpable thing, rolling off the group of vampires like a black wind.

"This way," Lucan said, before anyone was tempted to act on their impulses. His stern look set Kellan into motion and commanded the rest of the Order to hang back, letting the two of them proceed into Lucan's study alone.

Kellan walked to the center of the room and drew to a halt while Lucan closed the door behind them, then stalked back over to face the errant warrior one-on-one. Lucan could still see the courageous, forthright soldier in Kellan's steady hazel gaze and in the straight line of his spine and shoulders as he stood at grim attention before Lucan, ready to accept his wrath.

Prepared to face the truth that the path he'd chosen for himself had more than likely led to a literal grave end.

"Quite the clusterfuck of problems you bring into this house," Lucan remarked, bypassing unnecessary niceties and getting right to the point of this unexpected reunion. "Nathan briefed me on everything that's gone down these past several days. Bowman's one helluva busy guy. Kidnapping, obstruction, conspiracy, aiding a rebellion, and general defiance of the law. Let's not forget betrayal and usury. Apparently your strongest suits, judging from the condition you left Mira in out there. If you deserve to suffer for anything you've done, hurting that girl ranks right at the top as far as I'm concerned. Jesus Christ. And then to cap everything off, you bound her to you."

Kellan's stoic expression didn't crack until the mention of Mira's name. His deep voice was raw with a pain Lucan couldn't deny. "I wouldn't have given her my blood if I hadn't thought the bond might help repair the damage to her eyesight." Frowning, he gave a remorseful shake of his head. "It didn't work. I need to try again, Lucan. I need to give her some more. See if she gets better."

Lucan scoffed. "You've done enough, haven't you?"

"Then maybe Rafe or Tess—"

"Mira's where she belongs now," Lucan said, knowingly curt. He wasn't even close to sympathy over the obvious concern Kellan felt for the mate he'd claimed well beyond his rights. "The Order will see that Mira gets all the help we can provide. She's with family now. You have problems of your own to deal with."

Kellan held his gaze. "As long as Mira's safe, my problems mean nothing."

"Do you want to die, son?"

Kellan's response was immediate. "No." Then again, more vehemently. "Hell no. I want to live—with Mira beside me. I didn't realize how much I wanted that until I had her back in my arms again." He blew out a sharp curse. "But it doesn't matter what I want."

"Because of the vision," Lucan said. "Nathan informed me about that earlier too. You and I both know Mira's gift is a powerful thing. Unerring. But with or without that prophesied end hanging over your head, your involvement with rebels—for fuck's sake, your having led them as their commander—has all but tied my hands in this. Ackmeyer's death has been blamed on rebels, rebels under the direction of an outlaw called Bowman. It's given the public a cause to rail against, and they're doing it loudly. They're calling for blood—*your* blood. When word gets out that you're not only Breed but also a former warrior with the Order? The humans won't be satisfied until they have your head, son. I'll have little choice but to give it to them, or undermine all the strides we've made toward any kind of peace with mankind."

Kellan's steady gaze said he understood the impossible position. "If it comes down to that, I'll be ready to face whatever penalty is required."

Lucan raked a hand through his dark hair. "Shit, Kellan. This sure as fuck isn't how I imagined things would go with you when you first showed up at the Boston compound twenty years ago. Not how I imagined your life heading when you sailed through training with flying colors. Making the call to JUSTIS to come and pick you up tonight isn't going to be easy."

"I appreciate that," Kellan replied soberly. "Before you make that call, Lucan, if I could ask one thing for my crew? Their freedom, if you see fit to grant it to them. Don't turn them over to JUSTIS with me. I take total responsibility for my actions and those of the people under my command."

Lucan inclined his head at the request, feeling more than a little respect for the leader willing to bear the full brunt for those who followed him into battle.

"I want you to know," Kellan said, "I've done a lot of things I'm not proud of these past eight years. Worst of all, hurting Mira, and deceiving you and the Order—my family—about my death. I'm guilty of many things, Lucan, but murder isn't one of them. The night the lab was destroyed, Mira and I were in the city, looking for leads on Ackmeyer. We hoped to find something that would lead us to him, or to the member of my crew who defected that morning and took Ackmeyer to ransom."

Lucan scowled. "None of which excuses the fact that you abducted a high-profile civilian—Ackmeyer was practically a national treasure, for crissake. And then you grab a member of the Order besides? What the fuck were you thinking?"

"Taking Mira was never part of the plan. I didn't know she'd be there. We had last-minute intel that Ackmeyer would be on the move that day. We mobilized right away and closed in on him. Mira got swept into the net unintentionally. She was never part of it, and my mistake where she was concerned was not sending her back to the Order right away. But if you ask me to regret the time I had with her these past few days, I can't do that."

Lucan exhaled, studying the younger male. That he loved Mira was obvious. And Lucan couldn't help thinking back to his own mistakes and fuck-ups not so long ago, any one of which could have cost him the woman he cherished with all his heart, his Breedmate, Gabrielle. They'd been fortunate. Had the blessing of a shared life together and a son they adored, who made them both proud. Things Kellan and Mira would likely never know.

His heart heavier than he wanted to admit, Lucan cleared his throat and focused on the things that still needed answers. "Why target Ackmeyer? How had he managed to make enemies of you or your rebels?"

"Three months ago, a Breed civilian was shot dead in Boston. One of the women in my crew, Nina, witnessed the slaying. The Breed male was her lover. He'd left her apartment that night and was walking up the side street when a government vehicle rolled up. Two human men got out and killed him, unprovoked." Kellan stared at Lucan, his gaze intense, alive with an anger that simmered just below the surface of his outward calm. "Their guns held UV rounds. Liquid sunlight, neatly packaged into Breed-killing bullets. The vampire didn't stand a chance. He was ashed on the spot."

"Holy hell." Lucan rocked back on his heels, more grim than astonished. Mankind had always been ingenious, sometimes diabolically so, but the ramifications of ultraviolet technology being developed for arms and weaponry could be staggering. Given time and imagination, they could eventually wipe out the entire Breed race. "And you tracked the tech back to Ackmeyer?"

"Took some time and a lot of digging, but we managed to put it together. Ackmeyer had mentioned in a science journal interview last year that he was working on a pet project involving ultraviolet light. At the time, he'd said he thought it would be ideal for agricultural purposes."

"Until someone wagged a big paycheck in front of him, no doubt." Lucan raked his hand over his scalp, hissed another curse. "Is that what happened? Ackmeyer sold his tech to someone who thought it might be put to better use as a weapon against the Breed?"

"That's what I wanted to know," Kellan replied. "I meant to get answers, and if Ackmeyer didn't prove cooperative, I was prepared to persuade him to destroy the technology—by whatever means necessary. Problem was, Ackmeyer didn't know anything about his work being leaked outside his private lab. When I questioned him while he was in my custody, he said his project—something he was calling Morningstar— was still in testing stages, under lock and key. He swore up and down that he'd never allow his work to be used to harm anyone. I read the truth in him, Lucan. He was innocent. By the time I figured that out, the wheels were already in motion."

Lucan grunted. "You shouldn't have acted alone. You should've come to the Order with this."

"Come to you as Bowman?" Kellan asked, his expression grimly wry. "Or as the coward who'd turned his back on his brethren and his kin?"

Lucan knew he was right. His situation had been untenable either way. It still was. "Unfortunately, it may be too late to turn any of this back now."

Kellan nodded. "There are a lot of things I wish I'd done differently, starting with how I left eight years ago." He glanced down, exhaled a short breath as he shook his head. "Jeremy Ackmeyer is dead because of me, Lucan. Because ultimately I gave the command to abduct him. I accept that blame. But I'm telling you here and now, I didn't give the order to torch his lab or to harm him in any way."

"You're going to have a hard time convincing the public of that."

"I don't give a shit about the public and what they believe," Kellan said, a flicker of amber lighting in his eyes. "I need to know that you believe me. That I haven't lost your trust."

Lucan listened to the younger vampire—the once-sheltered, sullen

Darkhaven youth who had become a formidable, stalwart warrior under Lucan's tutelage, only to vanish without a trace before he'd reached his prime.

That warrior was still alive inside Kellan Archer. He was still prepared for the good fight, still held his honor intact, even though he'd lost his way for a while. What a waste it would be to see him slip away once more.

Lucan swore, low under his breath. "Of everything that's gone wrong here lately—and Jesus Christ, there's enough to choose from—I'm not sure what bothers me the most. The fact that you and Mira are blood-bonded under the worst circumstances, or that I have to be the one who tears you apart."

23

MIRA SAT ON THE EDGE OF A SOFT BED IN A ROOM THAT SMELLED of roses and lemon wax, surrounded by the love and support of the women of the Order.

She was home. Reunited with her parents, family, teammates, and friends—all the people who mattered in her life. And yet she'd never felt so adrift. So alone.

Because the one she needed most was the one farthest out of her reach now.

By his own choice.

Kellan had promised he wouldn't abandon her ever again, but he had. They might have stayed in the old Darkhaven in the Maine woods for weeks longer—a precious handful of months, if they were lucky. Instead, he'd willingly put an end to their time together.

She would have stayed with him as long as possible.

Instead, he'd let her go.

The warrior in her refused to accept this defeat. Blinded or not, she wanted to leap up and fight her way to wherever Kellan was being held. She wanted to demand he stand with her and take on his problems together. Take on the whole bloody world together, if they had to.

But it wasn't the Order or mankind or the world that stood between them.

It was fate.

Destiny had made a claim on Kellan's life eight years ago. Now it was coming to collect. And in her heart, she knew no amount of fighting, no amount of running, could ever be enough to win out over an enemy as powerful as that.

But that didn't make the prospect of what lay ahead any easier to accept.

Although she could see none of the Breedmates gathered in the room with her now, only shadows on shadows against a field of darkness, Mira heard their voices close to her. Heard more than one of the women quietly sniffling back tears after she had explained everything that happened during her all-too-brief reunion with Kellan.

"I'm glad it's gone," she murmured into the quiet room. "My sight. If losing my sight is the only way to mute my visions, then it will have been worth it."

"Don't say that, Mouse. You don't mean it." Renata sat beside her on the bed, holding Mira's hand in a comforting, protective grasp. The Breedmate who had rescued orphaned Mira when she was a little girl, taking her under her wing as her own child, was as skilled a warrior as any—the first female to fight alongside the Order as one of their own. Tough and deadly, impossible to break, Renata had hardly said a word in the time since Mira's arrival with Kellan and the others.

She was afraid. Mira felt it in the pregnant Breedmate's silence and the soft trembling of her fingers as she held Mira's hand.

Where Nikolai had been furious and vocal in his concern for Mira and his contempt for Kellan's part in all that had transpired, Renata's quiet, heartsick fear was even harder to take.

"Look at all the hurt I've caused," Mira said. "My vision is to blame for everything, Rennie. It was a curse that never brought anything good."

"No," Renata replied. "That's not true." Gentle fingers on Mira's chin turned her face toward the sound of her mother's voice. "You showed Niko that he and I were destined to be together, remember? And before that, your gift gave Hunter a glimpse of hope that not only saved your life as a result, but his as well. There's been good with the bad. Don't wish that all away too."

Mira didn't resist the tender, loving arms that drew her close. She rested her hand lightly on the swell of Renata's belly, smiling in reluctant joy when she felt the strong kick of a tiny foot against her palm. Her soon-to-arrive baby brother, already jealous of the attention he might be forced to share with her.

She wanted to see that child one day. She wanted to see Rennie and

Niko holding their newborn son, who would no doubt be every bit as adventurous and bold as his parents.

And she wanted to see Kellan again.

He wasn't in the mansion anymore; Renata had informed her that JUSTIS had taken Kellan into custody a short while ago, but Mira's blood bond told her in a more visceral way that he was no longer under the same roof with her. Being separated from him now was torment enough, but if her eyesight never returned—if she didn't get at least one last chance to be with him, to see his handsome face . . .

She didn't realize she was crying until a small, jagged sob tore out of her throat.

"Mira," said a gentle, nurturing voice from somewhere above her. Not Renata, but one of the other women of the Order. Dante's Breedmate, Tess. "I'd like to help you, if you'll let me?"

Mira had known Tess nearly all her life, had seen her talent for healing firsthand on more than one occasion when the Order had been headquartered in Boston. Trained as a veterinarian before she met Dante and bore their son, Rafe, Tess was still adept in traditional medicine and procedures. But it was her other healing ability Tess meant to employ now: her extrasensory gift for healing with the power of her touch— even the most grievous injuries and diseases.

"Close your eyes for me," Tess instructed as Mira sat up to let her assess the damage.

She did as she was told, feeling the other woman's thumbs come to rest lightly atop her closed eyelids. Tess's palms cupped her face, fingertips spread across her temples, creating slender bands of warmth. The heat from her touch fanned up and out, palpable energy running in tiny currents across the top of Mira's scalp.

And where Tess's thumbs hovered over her closed eyes, a stronger heat bloomed. A core of soft light began to flicker there, twin points of minuscule illumination that slowly ignited into a piercing bloodred glow. Mira flinched as the brightness blossomed behind her lids, glowing so intensely she thought her corneas might smolder.

"Am I hurting you?" Tess asked quietly. She drew her hands away, taking their power with them. "If it's uncomfortable, I can stop if you wish. We can try this another time—"

"No," Mira said. She shook her head vehemently. "No, please, keep going. Something was happening."

Tess resumed her work, and Mira weathered the unnerving heat and light that swamped her entire field of vision, filled her entire skull. She held on to Renata's hand like a lifeline, her other hand fisted in the silk coverlet on the bed.

The power of Tess's touch was lightning in her veins, in her bones and cells. Exploding behind her eyes. When she thought she couldn't take another second more, the intensity doubled. Then doubled again.

And then it was simply . . . gone.

Cool white calm settled over her, like a turbulent night storm giving way to placid daybreak.

Mira slumped forward, panting, wrung out. She felt the weight of each Breedmate's gaze as she struggled to catch her breath, slow her racing heart rate.

Tess lifted her chin on the edge of her hand. "Open your eyes."

Her lids felt like they'd been glued together, but as she carefully peeled them open, the yellow glow of a bedside table lamp seeped into her vision. Shadows took on crisper form, then cleared away altogether. She blinked up at Tess, astonished. She could see again!

She stared in total awe and gratitude, drinking in the sight of the lovely Breedmate's aquamarine eyes and halo of long, honey-blond curls. Tess nodded, holding her gaze as Mira struggled to absorb the fact that she was no longer blind.

"Oh, my God." Mira's voice was little more than a whisper, lost for words. She leapt up and pulled the healer into a tight hug. "Tess, thank you."

Dante's mate nodded, something wistful about her little smile as she stepped back to give Mira space to breathe.

And she needed it. Because all at once, she found herself caught in a round of joyous, relieved embraces from the other Breedmates in the room. Renata was first, her jade green eyes moist with tears as she hugged Mira fiercely. One by one, the rest of the women followed, showering Mira in so much love, her heart felt ready to burst.

She was so overcome, it took a moment for her to realize her eyes were bare. Not only did she risk undoing Tess's work, but her terrible talent was open to everyone in the room with her. "My lenses," she blurted, panic rising. She immediately sent her gaze downward to avoid making unintentional eye contact. "Does anyone have my lenses?"

"Here they are," Tess replied. She placed the case in Mira's hand, her voice quiet. "But I don't think you're going to need them anymore. At least, not to protect your eyesight."

"What do you mean?" Regardless of the reassurance, Mira put the contacts in before she glanced up to meet Tess's placid gaze. "Are you saying you healed me permanently?"

"I restored the sight you'd lost, but it's the blood bond that will make your gift thrive. It's been the same for all of us," Tess explained. "Kellan's blood couldn't reverse the damage, but the bond is strong inside you, enhancing your power." Tess smiled warmly. "I know you feel it."

She did feel it.

It hardly took any effort at all to recognize the steady hum of awareness that told her Kellan was alive, feeding her senses, connected to her through the powerful bond they now shared. She felt his strength living inside her, and hoped he could feel the same from her.

Tess gave Mira's hand a little squeeze and started to turn away.

"How do you know?" Mira murmured, just now realizing the impact of what the Breedmate had told her. "Tess, how can you be sure that I won't lose my sight if I use my ability now?"

And then she knew.

All of the elation Mira had felt a moment ago leaked back out of her. Her heart sank with immediate regret.

"Oh, God. Tess . . . just a few minutes ago. You were looking into my eyes."

She waved off the concern and that of the other women who had now shifted their focus onto the healer. Tess had seemed oddly quiet, reflective in the moments since Mira's sight had been restored. Now Mira understood why.

"Tess, I'm sorry." She'd be devastated if her vision had been reawakened only to wound the woman who'd helped her. "What did you see? Tell me it wasn't something awful."

"No," Tess replied, calm and kind. "Not awful at all."

"You would tell me?" Mira couldn't quell the worry that still fluttered in her breast. "Because if I hurt you just now—"

Tess shook her head slowly. Her mouth curved softly behind the fingers she brought to her lips. Her eyes kindled with a secret smile. She reached out and took Mira's hands in hers. "Your gift is extraordinary, Mira. Not a curse. It may not always be kind, but sometimes . . . sometimes it's beautiful." Tess hugged her then, warm and unhurried. Her mouth close to Mira's ear, she whispered, "Thank you for showing me the incredible family my son will have one day. I only wish my gift could bring you the same kind of miracle yours has just given me."

"Me too," Mira said, hugging Tess back.

Her flawless eyesight began to blur again . . . not with blindness, but with welling tears.

GNC director Charles Benson had to fight his way through a mob of shouting protesters camped outside the gate at his house when he returned home from the early morning press conference announcing the apprehension of the rebel leader responsible for Jeremy Ackmeyer's abduction earlier that week. Bowman's swift, covert capture by the Order had been welcome, timely news, particularly coming on the very day of the peace summit.

But it was the other revelation regarding the rebel's arrest—the discovery that not only was this villain Breed, not human, but that he was a former member of the Order besides—that had taken everyone aback, Benson included.

The public's outrage had only doubled upon that news. Outside Benson's home, the protesters' signs called the summit a mockery; some proclaimed it a deal struck with the devil himself. Other, more troubling posters were aimed directly at Benson, depicting him as a puppet dancing on the end of strings held by a caricature of Lucan Thorne, long fangs bared and slavering, catlike Breed eyes wild with mad glee.

As soon as the crowd spotted Benson arriving home, the volume and animosity of their taunts went from a healthy rumble to a skull-splitting din. Didn't they realize he was on their side? Didn't these people understand he'd been willing to sacrifice anything—too much, as it turned out—in order to ensure true peace for everyone who shared this planet with him?

Benson hurried out of his car, ducking his head to avoid the jeers as he hustled quickly across the cobblestone driveway, into the house. Once inside, he heaved a long sigh. Let his spine sag against the heavy oak front door.

The picketing was a new problem. Oh, he'd been aware of the Order's constant throng of chanting malcontents at their headquarters in the District, but to have the unrest and vitriol spread to other members of the GNC—to have it come to roost on his front stoop—was trouble he didn't need. Nor did he want that kind of negative spotlight aimed at him.

Not now. Not when he felt little pieces of his once-simple world beginning to crumble all around him.

As he collected himself, he heard his wife call to him from the kitchen, asking if she could make him a late breakfast.

"I can't right now, dear," he told her, trying to adopt a casual tone and still be heard over the ruckus outside. "I have a video conference to attend in a few minutes. I'll be in my office for a while. I don't wish to be disturbed."

His obedient wife of the past forty-six years wouldn't dream of interrupting his work. He loved that about Martha. Loved that she trusted him unquestioningly to manage all of the important things in their marriage and household, the same way she trusted him to be steadfastly moral in the business of his political office, devoting his life to ensuring the stability of the free world.

To Martha, even balding, gray, and wrinkled, he was a god. Not the puppet dangling at the end of someone else's strings.

Not the man whose conscience lately was a leaden weight becoming harder and harder to bear.

Benson crossed the gleaming foyer of his home and headed for his office down the hall. Instead of entering, he closed the tall double doors to make it appear he was sequestered inside, then ducked down the stairwell to the secret second office tucked behind a false wall in the wine cellar of the grand old house.

Inside this room was a private workstation, intended for a single purpose. He opened the computer and typed in the access code, waited with unblinking eyes as the security program scanned his retinas to confirm his identification. Once it had finished, he was connected via comm feed to a prearranged meeting with his colleagues. Not the GNC, but another, more recent, group of colleagues to whom Benson reported.

This group, totaling thirteen powerful men from both the human and Breed races—heads of state, business magnates, religious leaders—were stationed in all corners of the globe. Together they formed a secret cabal who called themselves Opus Nostrum.

Although he was openly known to them, Benson wasn't privy to their names, had never seen their faces. Anonymity was key, plausible deniability a must. Their goals were too important to risk. Their methods often too severe to reconcile.

As was the most recent decision, the one that prompted his emergency call to the brotherhood.

Benson sat back anxiously in his chair as a world map filled his monitor, then, one by one, the members of Opus Nostrum linked in from their various locations. Several reported in from North and South America. Others from Europe and Asia, even one from Africa. On-screen, each member was represented by a point on the map, their voices digitally masked.

Benson, however, was displayed to the thirteen men on video camera, his identity fully exposed. He knew this was intended to remind him of his vulnerability to the cabal, and it worked. They owned him now. After what he'd done for them in recent months, Opus Nostrum owned a piece of his soul.

One of the North American members was the first to speak when all thirteen positions had turned active on-screen. His computer-altered voice was pitched unnaturally low. "A most enjoyable press conference this morning, Director Benson. We are pleased to know the GNC has their villain in custody and the public will soon have the justice they crave. So much the better that the Order finds it's dragged into the fray by one of its own." A chuckle rumbled out of the computer's sound system. "We couldn't have laid a better snare for Lucan and his warriors if we'd planned Ackmeyer's abduction and killing ourselves."

Benson hoped his shaky smile didn't betray his unease. The other piece of public knowledge was the fact that Benson had enlisted the Order's protection for his nephew in the days leading up to the kidnapping. Benson had been worried about Jeremy's safety, fearful that something untoward might happen to the scientist—perpetrated by the faceless power brokers now waiting for his reply.

Benson cleared his throat. "I am . . . relieved that the brotherhood is pleased with how things have progressed. And I share Opus Nostrum's vision for a peaceful future for the world. That's why I gave you my nephew's ultraviolet technology."

"And you were handsomely rewarded for it," replied the one who always seemed to lead the others in these assemblies. "I trust you and the missus have been enjoying your prestigious new address these past several months."

Benson didn't answer. Fact was, he *had* been enjoying the stately residence in the District's most exclusive neighborhood. The keys to the mansion and a cleared deed, paid for in cash, had been delivered to his office by anonymous courier the morning after he'd turned over Jeremy's prototypes and data on the unreleased Morningstar project. Accepting the house in reward for stolen intelligence was one thing; living under a roof bought with the blood of innocent lives was another.

"You did the right thing, giving us the tech," said the detached, emotionless voice through the computer. "Tonight's event at the summit gala would not be possible without it."

"Yes, but . . ." Benson's voice went rusty, threatening to fail him altogether. In the silence, he could almost feel the weight of thirteen pairs of eyes trained on him, ruthlessly assessing him from within the secret, scattered lairs of the organization's far-reaching membership. "It's just that I thought . . . I never intended for Jeremy to be harmed, that's all."

"Is that why you contacted the Order to arrange for his private escort to the summit?"

Benson knew he blanched at the question, inevitable or not. "He was innocent, as innocent as a child about most things. I didn't want my involvement with Opus Nostrum to impact him in any way. I was afraid the brotherhood might have considered him some kind of liability. I was afraid something might happen to him—"

"So you thought it wise to betray our trust instead."

"No," Benson replied, shaking his head vigorously. "No, I didn't betray you. I wouldn't. I asked the Order to bring Jeremy safely to the peace summit, that's all."

And once arrived, once Opus Nostrum's mission for the summit had been unleashed and the world attempted to set itself to rights under a new paradigm of rule, Benson had planned to send his nephew deep into hiding, along with Martha and the rest of his family.

There was a long silence before the one in charge responded. "You sought to keep your nephew safe, yet it was your own actions that dictated his death. His abduction only made him a greater liability to the cause than he already was. Compound that risk when you factor in that it was a former member of the Order who held him. Why did these Breed-led rebels want him? What might he have told them?" The distorted voice had gone thin and low with menace. "These are troubling questions, Director Benson. Be thankful we were given a chance to correct part of your mistake. Your nephew's death is the only reason you and the rest of your family are being permitted to breathe right now. And the additional technologies we gathered from his laboratory before we razed it will further Opus Nostrum's goals for years to come."

Benson swallowed past the fear that sat like a cold stone in the back of his throat. These men would not be stopped. Nor was any one life worth more than an instant's notice if it stood in the way of their plans. He should've known that from the beginning, when they first approached him with their anonymous invitation to be part of a new, powerful vision for the future.

He should've known it three months ago, when men loyal to Opus Nostrum killed an unarmed, innocent Breed civilian in Boston, gunning him down in the street as a field test of Jeremy's ultraviolet technology adapted for use in weaponry.

"We are united in our purpose to usher in true, lasting peace," said the voice of Opus Nostrum. "Our goal is to bring about a new dawn, something that cannot be possible so long as the Order is in the picture. With them we run the risk that Lucan Thorne and his ever-expanding army of warriors can bring down their fist on anything Opus Nostrum puts into play. I'm sure none of us needs a reminder of how, just a decade ago after the accident in Russia, Lucan took it upon himself to eradicate all chemical and nuclear weapons facilities around the world."

"Accident," one of the brotherhood scoffed. "I wonder if we'll ever know who was responsible for turning that large swath of earth into Deadlands."

"Human or Breed, it doesn't matter," said the one in charge. "The lesson learned for us is that Lucan Thorne can never be permitted to exercise that kind of power again. How long do you imagine he'll be content to labor under the political yoke of the GNC? How long before he and his warriors decide diplomacy and negotiations have run their course? Is that a risk any of you here are willing to take with the future of our shared world?"

A round of supporting responses sounded from all thirteen members, and Benson gamely joined in, knowing that to disagree now would only put Martha and the rest of his loved ones in danger. The tentacles of his past actions held him trapped in this alliance now, and he had little choice but to play along.

After the group quieted once more, the first member spoke again.

"The Order must be eliminated. And what better way to demonstrate Opus Nostrum's might than to take them down in one fell swoop at the gala tonight, in full public view around the globe?"

Benson didn't bother to point out that the plan to kill Lucan and the rest of the Order would also mean the deaths of every Breed diplomat and civilian in attendance. The members of Opus Nostrum surely understood that fact, both the humans among the thirteen and those of them who were Breed.

No doubt they also realized that an annihilation like the one they had planned for the summit gathering could very well incite full-scale war between the vampire nation and mankind.

War that could last for decades. Or longer.

"No sacrifice is too great for the ultimate cause of a lasting peace," the leader of the conspirators reminded them. "A true peace that can only be had with the Order out of our way."

The group answered in unanimous agreement. Then someone began to chant the cabal's motto: *"Pax opus nostrum."*

One by one, each member joined in, until the phrase rumbled so loudly, Benson worried Martha might hear it through the walls of his secret hideaway in their ill-gotten abode. But he knew all eyes were on him, so he picked up the chant too, murmuring the Latin phrase that proclaimed "Peace is our work."

"Until tonight, my brethren," said the synthesized, inhuman voice Benson would hear in his nightmares for probably the rest of his days. "And a word of advice, Director. The eyes of Opus Nostrum are everywhere. Don't even think about betraying our trust again."

Benson nodded. He waited until the group signed off, then he closed his computer and exhaled, collapsing in a boneless heap onto the top of his desk. "What have I done?" he moaned into the crook of his elbow. "God, forgive me. What have I done?"

24

MIRA HAD JUST TURNED ON THE SHOWER WHEN A KNOCK sounded on her bedroom door at the Order's mansion. Still dressed in the clothes she'd arrived in a few hours before, she cut the tap in the bathroom and walked out to see who was there.

"Nathan."

A study in black, from his short ebony hair, to his fitted T-shirt, fatigues, and combat boots, he stood in the hallway, grim and unsmiling. "I heard Tess healed your sight. I'm glad you're well. How are you holding up?"

She lifted her shoulder in a faint shrug. "I'll be better once I see Kellan again."

Nathan didn't respond; instead he glanced down to the object he held in his hand. "I wanted to return this to you sooner, but with everything else going on . . ."

He handed her the blade she'd lost the day her whole life veered off the rails.

"You found my dagger."

He nodded. "The first night you were missing, Rafe, Eli, Jax, and I went looking for you. We found the blade in Ackmeyer's lawn. I kept it for you."

"Thank you." Mira turned the weapon over in her hands, grateful to finally have it again. Although her eyes took in the delicate hilt's intricate design and lettering, her mind raced back over everything that had occurred in the time since she'd lost the cherished blade. God, it all seemed like a hundred years ago. "Thank you for being a friend to me, Nathan . . . and to Kellan. I know things could've gone much worse for him last night."

He grunted. "I wanted to kill him for all he'd done. To you, to the Order, to everyone hurt by his deception."

Mira looked at her friend, the laboratory-bred assassin who was forever so unreadable and remote, always the most stoic warrior. She saw true hurt in him now. And he was angry too. His handsome face was schooled to stony neutrality, but Mira didn't miss the flicker of amber crackling in his greenish blue irises. "You're angry, but you don't hate him, do you, Nathan?"

He scowled, seeming to consider the question. "Last night, when I found the Archer insignia at the rebel bunker and suddenly realized the truth, yes, I did hate him. I never felt so strongly or so certain about anything before in my life. I was prepared to kill him, Mira. Until I saw him and realized I couldn't hate my friend. Not even after discovering he was my enemy." He exhaled a heavy breath. "I can't guess how you must feel. He's surely hurt you the deepest of all."

"He has," she admitted quietly. "But nowhere near as badly as it will hurt if I lose him all over again. I'm not going to let that happen, Nathan. If the GNC wants to take Kellan away from me, put him on trial to make some kind of political statement, they're not going to get him without a damned bloody fight."

Nathan's mouth pressed flat, his dark brows drawing together. He started to shake his head. "Mira, you can't expect—"

"I have to try," she insisted. "I'm not giving up on him. Fuck the GNC, and fuck fate too. I won't let go of him, even if that's what he wants. And I plan to tell Kellan the same thing when I go see him today, wherever JUSTIS is holding him."

"Mira," Nathan said, and something about his tone—so full of concern, so gentle—made her blood start to freeze in her veins. "Mira, there won't be time for any of that. Not now."

Her heart dropped, heavy as a stone. "What do you mean?"

She looked at him, realizing only now that his returning her dagger was only part of the reason he'd come to see her.

"Tell me what's going on, Nathan."

He glanced down, swore a low curse. "Since Kellan's former Order, Lucan got the GNC to agree to hearing the charges and handling the situation privately rather than turning Kellan over to the criminal courts for a full-blown trial."

"Okay," Mira said cautiously. "That's good, right?"

Nathan merely looked at her. "Because of the riots and public calls for justice, and because the peace summit opens tonight, the GNC feels it needs to demonstrate decisive action to avoid potential disruptions during the gala. It's agreed to the private hearing, but the GNC will be conducting it—and determining Kellan's sentence—at a special meeting. It's taking place at GNC headquarters today."

All her fears came rushing at her in a buffeting wave. She staggered back on her heels, feeling as if the air had been sucked out of her lungs. "They're going to decide Kellan's sentence . . . today? Can't Lucan delay it? There must be something more he can do."

"He's calling in every political favor he's got, Mira. He's been in touch with each member of the Council, trying to bargain with them for a promise of leniency."

"How many?" she asked, going numb with a dread that made her stomach roil. "How many have agreed so far?"

Nathan didn't speak for a long moment. "There are sixteen Council members, representing eight key nations, with one human and one Breed member each." Nathan cleared his throat. "He's got confirmed votes from a few, but there are still several more Council members left to persuade in order to have the majority. Lucan's making a lot of promises, Mira. He's putting his balls on the line for Kellan. He's doing everything he possibly can."

She wanted to feel hope. She wanted to believe that everything would somehow work out and that, by some miracle, she and Kellan would come out of this terrible situation as one, together. But dread was a cold weight in the center of her chest.

"I can't talk anymore," she murmured, already backing away from the open door and Nathan's concerned expression. "I have to go. I thought there would be more time. I have to see Kellan before he goes in front of the Council."

Nathan gave a slow shake of his head. "There won't be time for you to see him before he's brought to the hearing. The Council is assembling to meet him there within the hour."

"No." She swallowed, her throat gone dry. "No, this can't be happening. We need more time . . ."

Words began to fail her, fear swamping her. She edged farther into the bedroom, holding Nathan's apologetic, regretful gaze. She closed the door on him and sagged against it, her forehead pressed to the cool wood panel.

She had to see Kellan. And there was no way in hell she'd let him stand before that Council assembly without her there to help defend him. To fight for his freedom, with blood and blades, if it came down to that.

Tossing her dagger onto the bed, Mira headed into the bathroom and turned on the shower. She undressed and stood before the mirror, staring into the face of the woman she'd become.

Blood-bonded, in love.

Never so terrified in all her life.

She knew the reflection would be cruel, even before she removed her purple lenses and lifted her gaze to confront the gift of her Sight.

The vision appeared in no time at all. The same terrible outcome, playing before her eyes.

Kellan, dead on the floor in front of her.

She, weeping in grief-stricken anguish over his lifeless body.

Mira stared, horrified and heartsick, until the steam of the shower filled the room, breathing a thick fog across the awful vision she couldn't seem to escape.

Kellan knew, when the phalanx of heavily armed JUSTIS officers—four Breed and two human—came to retrieve him from his cell just before noon that day, that he couldn't be heading into anything good.

But the full impact of that suspicion didn't hit him until they led him into a cavernous, private hearing chamber at the GNC's headquarters building. There he found himself staring at a panel of all sixteen Council members, seated on a dais behind a broad U-shape judicial bench. At the center of the assembly was Lucan Thorne, looking grave in his role as chairman.

Most of the Order's elder members were present as well, the warriors and their mates seated on rows of benches below the dais.

But the thing that really put a jangle of alarm in Kellan's veins was the sight of Mira standing directly in front of the Council. Outfitted in black fatigues and combat boots, her long blond hair woven into a tight braid that snaked down her back, she was dressed for the hearing as though she'd come prepared for war.

What the hell was she doing?

Kellan nearly shouted it to her, but then she pivoted around to face him as his guards shoved him forward into the room. Her cheeks were flushed, eyes rimmed with red as she looked his way.

Her eyes . . . *ah, Christ.* Her eyes looked straight at him, no longer milky and unfocused, but bright behind the violet contact lenses and fixed squarely on him.

She'd been healed.

She could see.

He'd been afraid to trust the bond that told him earlier that day she was whole again, but now he felt a surge of elation—of bone-deep relief—to see for himself that either Tess or Rafe had been able to do for Mira what he'd been unable to with his blood.

Now he wanted to run to her and sweep her into his arms. He would have, if he didn't suspect his sudden break would invite the JUSTIS officers walking him into the hearing room to open fire on him and possibly Mira in the process.

The guards guided him forward, a pair of Breed males on each side of him, the two humans at his back. Kellan didn't miss the grim faces of the Order and their Breedmates nor the disapproving glowers of the majority of men and women seated on the dais. He was there to be judged—here and now—his guilt perhaps already determined, if the pall of heavy silence in the room was any indication.

And there was Mira, facing the Council on her own.

Even without the foreknowledge her vision had given him, Kellan understood Mira's presence in the hearing room. She'd come to plead her case before the judges. For him.

His beautiful, stubborn Mira.

His steadfast mate, standing with him even though he knew he'd broken her heart by turning himself in.

Pride and humility tangled inside him. He hadn't wanted her to be a part of this. And yet he knew there would have been no keeping her away.

As she looked at him now, her face collapsed in distress. She pivoted back around to Lucan and the Council members. "No, wait! Please, hear me out. Kellan is no killer. He was trying to save lives—to prevent a dangerous technology from being released. That's why he took Jeremy Ackmeyer. I'm not trying to excuse what he did, I only ask that you consider why he did it."

At the far end of the dais, an elderly human with sunken eyes and an unhealthy pallor cleared his throat. "The Council has heard your argument. All factors will be evenly weighed as the Council makes its determination in this matter."

"Director Benson," Mira implored, turning to face the old man directly. "I realize that this hearing is personal for you too. Jeremy was your nephew. He was a good man, an innocent man. I am truly sorry for your family's loss. I want you to know that Kellan tried to save him. After he realized the truth, Kellan did everything he could to find Jeremy. He tried to correct his mistakes, but it was too late—"

"Enough!" The old man's outburst shot through the assembly like gunfire. His heavy-lidded eyes were sluggish as he looked around the chamber, his gray head drooping between his slumped shoulders. "I've heard . . . quite enough. Please, let's have done with this."

A look from Lucan brought Nikolai out of the audience to collect Mira. She struggled at first, throwing a worried gaze in Kellan's direction as Niko led her back to her seat.

Kellan felt her distress echo through his veins as the armed guards directed his approach to the dais. They brought him to a halt before the Council, and Lucan's sober eyes settled on him.

"Kellan Archer," he announced to all those gathered. "Because of the unique circumstances of your case as a former member of the Order, the Council has agreed to a private hearing of the charges against you and a determination of your sentence by majority vote today. We have reviewed the crimes you stand accused of and have heard statements delivered on your behalf. These are serious crimes, calling for serious punishment. Guilt on any one of the charges carries a penalty of death."

"I understand," Kellan replied, taking in the solemn faces of the men and women who would decide his fate. He saw little mercy in any of them.

Then again, he'd expected none.

He listened as, one by one, the charges against him were read, then he gave his response to each of them. He hardly registered the words. All of his thoughts—all of his senses—were trained on the only person in the room who mattered to him.

Mira stared from her seat beside Niko and Renata, her eyes swimming with tears, fingers pressed to her lips. It killed him that she had to know this fear, this dread. This damned feeling of helplessness as they waited for the Council to begin delivering its verdict.

And then that moment arrived, and Kellan steeled himself to face the end of a path he'd been trying to avoid for the past eight years of his life.

Lucan soberly addressed the Council, instructing them to state their individual votes one at a time, calling for either incarceration for life or a sentence of death. "As chairman, my vote customarily would be heard last," he said. "However, as a condition of this private hearing—because it concerns a former warrior under my command as leader of the Order—the Council has required me to recuse myself from today's proceedings. I will not vote on sentencing, and the Council's decision will be final."

Kellan nodded his acknowledgment, then stood at attention as the voting began. There was little deliberation. Each Council member announced his vote, arriving at a surprisingly split tally across the GNC's human and Breed members.

Seven votes, representing both races, cast for his incarceration.

Eight others called for death.

One vote remaining.

The hearing would either end in a tie or a firm decision for Kellan's eventual execution.

It all came down to the councilman slumped at the end of the dais, Jeremy Ackmeyer's uncle. Kellan peered at Benson, sensing something more than simple grief or vengeance in the old man's troubled gaze. He'd been drinking, Kellan suspected now, noting the boneless sag of his shoulders, the glassy redness of his eyes.

"Director Benson," Lucan prompted, sending a glance over at him. "Are you prepared to state your decision?"

The old man grunted, lifted his head to glare in Kellan's direction. When he spoke, the word was blunt, final. "Death."

Kellan heard Mira's sharply inhaled breath. He felt her stricken reaction course through him, jolting his pulse like an electric shock as her worry shot into him through their blood bond.

"No." Her voice in the seated assembly behind him sounded broken, choked with tears. "No! He didn't kill your nephew, Director Benson.

He had nothing to do with the fire at Jeremy's lab or his death. You have to believe that! Do the right thing here. You have to show him mercy—"

"Mira, don't." Kellan pivoted to look as she flew out of her seat and started to rush forward in his defense. Alongside him, the four Breed guards went tense. He felt their alarm roll off them, noted they were all readying to draw their weapons.

"No!" Mira cried. "Lucan, don't let this happen, please!"

Kellan saw Lucan's grim look. Understood that the Order's leader had already done all he could. There was nothing more that could be said or done to spare Kellan.

"No," Mira sobbed, dropping her face into her palms.

Her anguish twisted his heart in a stranglehold. He hated that he was putting her through this, just as he'd dreaded all the years he'd stayed away, hoping to avoid this very moment.

At the far end of the chamber, Benson was shaking his head, muttering under his breath. "It's all gone too far," he slurred, his head hung low, face drooping as he spoke. "Too far now. I finally see that, when it's too late to make things right."

Kellan listened, curiosity prickling to attention as Benson rambled, morose and cryptic. There was remorse in the old man's voice, that much was unmistakable. And there was something else, something that made Kellan's blood pound in his temples.

"Too late for Jeremy," Benson murmured, thoroughly swept up in his own private misery. "Such a brilliant life, cut short. He was a pure soul, that boy, incorruptible. A true light-bringer who could've changed the world."

Light-bringer.

An unusual phrase. The very one Ackmeyer had used to describe his unreleased UV technology project.

Holy hell.

Benson was the one who stole the prototype. The realization sank in like talons in Kellan's gut. His blood froze, then immediately spiked volcanic with rage.

"Morningstar," he growled, all of his fury locked on the old man at the end of the Council assembly. Benson's drink-glazed eyes flew wide with guilt and terror. "You son of a bitch. It was you."

On a furious roar, Kellan lunged.

He felt the sudden rush of moving bodies behind him as he sprang airborne for the end of the dais. He heard Mira's scream. Heard the rapid explosions of gunfire going off in his wake.

He felt the sudden hail of pain, an unending volley of rounds, ripping into his torso and limbs as he came down on top of Benson and took the corrupt councilman to the floor.

Mira's voice was a heartrending shriek of anguish. "Kellan!"

He knew she felt the echo of his body's injuries and rage. Her terror merged with his own emotions, but he was too far gone to rein himself in. He gripped Benson around the throat. "Tell me who you gave the tech to, you goddamned bastard. Tell me!"

The human wouldn't talk. He clamped his molars together, drunken eyes fearful, though more for an unseen threat than for the vampire currently choking the life out of him. Kellan's heart thundered in his ears, so loud and labored, it was all he could hear as his blood pumped out of him, pouring from the countless holes perforating his body and limbs. The damage was total; the blood wouldn't stop.

He was dying.

The thought came at him, swift and certain, cutting through the chaos erupting all around him as time raced by in speeding instants.

He shouldn't have been surprised, given everything Mira's vision had predicted. But damn it, the shock of what he was feeling went through him like poison.

"Who killed him? You sold out your own flesh and blood—tell me who you did it for, Benson." With a snarl, he struggled to keep his hands wrapped around the human's neck as his strength began to seep out of him. He had to know, couldn't die like this without giving the Order something to go on after he was gone. If the human refused to choke out the answers Kellan demanded, then he would drag the truth from his mind.

Kellan read regret in the old man. Remorse for what he'd done, bringing about the murder of his nephew and soon the deaths of countless others. So many deaths to come, all under the guise of peace.

Kellan's grip started to slacken. He couldn't hold on. Not even when Benson scrabbled out of his reach and was swept away by GNC and JUSTIS guards. He rolled onto his back and found himself staring up at the hazy shadows of Lucan and the rest of the Order. He tried to speak but only coughed, sputtering blood as pain lanced through every inch of his body.

More than one warrior breathed a low curse as they looked down on him.

"Someone go after Benson," Lucan growled. "Goddamn it. Bring that son of a bitch in for questioning. Now."

"Kellan." Mira's voice was shattered with tears and anguish. She pushed through the warriors and dropped to her knees beside him. She grabbed his hand, clasped it against her breast as a sob racked her. "Oh, Kellan. No!"

Mira folded herself over him, weeping with a raw grief that destroyed him, even more than the bullets or his many past failures. He wanted to tell her he was sorry. He wanted to tell her that he loved her. That he always had, and always would, no matter what waited for him on the other side now.

But she knew that.

She looked into his face and nodded through her tears, her fingers light on his brow, trembling as she wiped the blood from his mouth and bent to kiss him.

Kellan wanted to tell her the words anyway, but there was something else she needed to hear. Something all of the Order needed to hear.

"Opus Nostrum," Kellan murmured, barely a whisper, fighting with all he had for the breath to speak as the space between one heartbeat and the next stretched longer every second. "Stop Opus Nostrum."

25

NO.

Oh, God . . . no, this couldn't be happening.

"Kellan." Mira squeezed his hand, felt the strength leach out of his grasp as his eyes fell closed. "Kellan? Oh, no . . . No, Kellan, please, stay with me. Don't let go."

But he was already drifting away from her, being pulled by unseen hands that wouldn't release him. She felt their blood bond stretch tight, thinner and thinner, a gossamer strand that couldn't be reeled back in, no matter how hard she willed it.

And then it broke.

She felt the pluck of shock as the connection severed. Felt her heart go numb and empty, set adrift in her breast.

Oh, God. She'd lost him.

Lost him all over again.

"Kellan, no," she cried, choking on hot, stinging tears. "No!"

She couldn't hold back her sobs. Her grief tore out of her, jagged and raw, as she collapsed atop his lifeless body and wept.

Kellan was gone.

Dead.

Just like her vision had shown her.

She wailed his name over and over again, out of her head with sorrow and soul-shredding anguish. She didn't want to believe that he was gone, but his hand was limp in hers, his strong body motionless, drenched in his spilled blood. So full of grievous, terrible wounds.

They'd killed him.

Her love.

Her mate.

Her best friend, her partner . . . her everything.

Gone.

Mira barely registered the hands that came to rest lightly on her shoulders as she clung to Kellan's lifeless body, bereft and sobbing. She barely heard Nikolai's low voice, his careful, quiet tone making the horror of it all seem even more real. "Mira," he said gently.

Renata was with him too, both of them trying to give her comfort. Rennie's fingers caressed the back of her head. "Come on, Mouse. Let him go, sweetheart."

"No," she growled, batting away the hands that had always provided her so much comfort as a child. Niko and Renata had always been able to make things better for her when she was a little girl. They were her parents in every way that mattered, the strong shoulders and loving arms she could forever count on whenever she needed them. But not today. Not now. They couldn't fix this, couldn't make it go away.

"They killed him," she murmured, miserable with despair. "Oh, God . . . They killed him."

She swung her head around to look up at Nikolai and Renata. Lucan and most of the Order were there too, the warriors and their Breedmates gathering solemnly around Kellan's body. Silent, shocked, everyone at a loss for words.

And behind them all, gaping in morbid curiosity, the members of the GNC—most of whom had needed no convincing to call for Kellan's death. They stared now, Breed and human alike, bobbing heads jockeying to get a glimpse of their reviled villain's body. Mira felt venom seethe through her veins at the sight of the Council members. They were as much to blame for Kellan's death as the JUSTIS guards who opened fire on him.

Contempt boiled up inside her, erupting on an anguished roar. "Get out of here," she snarled at the Council. "Get away from him, all of you!"

She launched herself at them, but Niko caught her in a sure grasp, held her back when every cell in her body was screaming for vengeance. Her despairing wail sounded animal, even to her own ears. She sagged into Nikolai's arms, tears flooding her vision.

"Take her back to headquarters," Lucan told Niko and Renata, his deep voice grave but low with sympathy. "See that she's comfortable. Whatever she needs."

Mira couldn't fight the arms that drew her away now. She had no strength, no will. No feeling at all.

Her chest seemed as though it were cracked open and filled with a cold, numbing wind.

Kellan was dead.

Mira walked woodenly, not even sure she was breathing anymore, as Nikolai and Renata led her out of the silent chamber.

Lucan threw a glower at the gawking GNC members as Mira was taken away from the scene. His vision was hot, sparking amber. His fangs felt sharp against his tongue when he spoke, his voice vibrating with lethal rage. "Show's over. You got your pound of flesh. Now get the fuck out of here."

The group scattered, silent and afraid. As they fled the chamber, Dante came in from the back where Benson had escaped. "The director's dead, Lucan. Found him in the rear corridor just now. Shot three times, point blank in the head. No sign of the JUSTIS officers who followed him out."

"Son of a bitch." Lucan raked a hand over his scalp. Benson had known something about Ackmeyer's UV technology. He'd practically confessed as much in the seconds before Kellan leapt at him. Benson had apparently known enough about Morningstar, and whoever now had their hands on the tech, for someone to make sure he didn't get the opportunity to say anything more. But who, and why?

And just how far did this conspiracy reach?

Now there was another question that needed swift answers as well: Who, or what, was Opus Nostrum?

Lucan glanced back at Kellan, at the dozens of gunshot wounds that took the young male down. "It didn't have to go like this, goddamn it. He deserved better. He deserved a chance at something more—he and Mira both."

Dante nodded grimly. "Maybe there's a way to make it right."

The warrior sent a meaningful look to his Breedmate, Tess, who stood with the rest of the Order and their mates. Before either Lucan or

Dante could say another word, Tess was in action, picking up on the thought and dropping down beside Kellan to run her healing hands over him. "His blood's still warm, but his heart is stopped."

"Can you jump it?" Lucan recalled an event Dante had described to him from Tess's life before she met her warrior mate. As a young woman, she'd once revived someone who'd passed suddenly from heart failure. Later, in her work as a veterinarian, she'd even cured a sickly little mutt of its cancer and other ailments using her extraordinary Breedmate talent.

God knew, the female had repaired more than her share of combat injuries for the Order over the past two decades.

But now Tess seemed less than assured. "I can restart his heart," she said, "but I won't be able to stop the bleeding and repair all the bullet wounds at the same time. I can revive him, but he could bleed out faster than I can fix him."

"Let me help you." Tess and Dante's son, Rafe, hunkered down next to her. The young warrior's face was solemn with purpose, his eyes—the same aquamarine shade as his mother's—intense with a determination Lucan had seen him display in equal measure on the field of combat. Rafe placed his palms on two of the bullet wounds, then gave his mother a nod. "You kick-start his ticker. Leave the rest to me."

Tess smiled, her face full of maternal pride as the pair of healers went to work on Kellan.

Lucan wanted to know as badly as anyone else gathered around the scene if the Order would have a miracle here today or a loss that would send the body of one of their own—one of their kin—up to meet the sun tomorrow morning in a funeral ritual.

But regardless of in what condition Kellan Archer returned to the Order's headquarters, Lucan and the other warriors had serious problems of their own to contend with now.

Problems that only became more urgent with the execution-style slaying of GNC director Benson a few minutes ago.

Lucan sent a glance at Gideon, Tegan, Dante, and the rest of the Order's elders. "Opus Nostrum," he said grimly, a question in his dark tone.

Gideon shook his head, as did the other warriors. "It's Latin. Means 'our work.'"

"Any idea what it refers to or, more important, how it might relate to Ackmeyer's Morningstar project?"

"First I'm hearing of it," Gideon replied.

Tegan inclined his head, gaze flat and cold. "I'll get a team together and run some recon. We can have boots on the ground at sundown."

Lucan nodded. "We're gonna need whatever you can gather. Leave no lead unturned. Report back to me on everything you find."

Tegan pivoted, signaling to several other warriors to join him.

"What about the summit reception?" Dante asked. "You want to step up security, put more heat on display, in case anyone's got ideas about doing something stupid tonight?"

Lucan considered for a moment. As tempting as it was, the last thing he needed to do was storm into the peace summit with an army of Breed warriors decked out in full-scale combat gear and heavy firearms. In fact, doing so could play right into the hands of anyone who might harbor a private wish to see the truce between mankind and Breed disintegrate.

What better place to incite a war than at a peace summit?

At the reminder of Darion's words, Lucan glanced over at his son. Dare's observation from several days ago, before all of this chaos began, had been troubling enough to consider then. Now it seemed all too possible that his son's keen head for tactics and strategies had predicted it right.

What if someone wanted to disrupt the summit gala tonight?

What if someone wanted to undo all the strides that had been made since First Dawn twenty years ago and set back the clock to a time when there was no peace? Or make sure there never could be any going forward?

To do so, they would have to get through the Order first.

Lucan looked at Dante, gave a curt shake of his head at the question of putting on a very public display of the Order's might. "Let's not tip our hand tonight. If something is in play, let the bastards get comfortable. Let them show themselves first. We'll be ready for them. Meanwhile, no one is above suspicion."

26

MIRA CAME AWAKE ON A GASP, LIKE A FISH TOSSED OUT OF THE ocean and onto dry land.

Shocked.

Confused.

Slapped into a sudden, harsh new reality.

She shot bolt upright in bed, breath heaving. Her heart was pounding fast and hard, as though it wanted to burst out of her breast.

She was back at the Order's headquarters, alone in a darkened bedroom. Nothing but silence all around her. She hardly noticed her surroundings, hardly cared how she'd gotten there or how long she'd been unconscious.

She vaguely remembered Nikolai trancing her after they'd left the GNC building. She couldn't blame him for putting her under a hypnotic sedation. She'd been inconsolable, hysterical with grief.

It all seemed like a nightmare—horrible and wrenching. But no, it had been real. She still had Kellan's blood on her clothes.

He had been shot.

Kellan was dead.

And yet . . .

She rubbed her chest, felt the steady beat of her heart, heavy and strong, beneath her palm. Her blood was thrumming in her veins. All of her senses honed on one pure point of awareness.

Kellan.

She felt him with every particle of her being.

She felt his pain, his struggle to cling to something that until now kept slipping out of his grasp.

Life.

She felt him reaching for it. She felt him fighting for each breath, forcing each heavy beat of his heart to push more blood into his veins. She felt his mind searching for her. Felt their bond reconnecting, giving him much-needed strength.

Oh, God . . .

Kellan was alive.

Mira swung her feet to the floor and stood up, just as Renata entered the room.

"Kellan?" Mira blurted, both a question and a prayer.

Renata smiled, relief written across her face. "Yes, Mouse. He's not out of the woods yet, but Tess and Rafe—"

Mira was too elated to let her finish. She let out a cry of disbelief and threw herself at Renata in a fierce, overjoyed hug. "I have to see him."

She raced through the mansion, following the thin tether of the blood bond she shared with him. It led her down the stairs to the main floor, then down again, to the underground wing of the headquarters' tech center and the double doors of the infirmary down the hallway.

Kellan lay in a hospital bed inside one of the half-dozen medical rooms. Tess and Rafe were with him. Nikolai, Dante, and Lucan stood off to one side of the bed. And Nathan was there, standing as rigid as a sentry on watch, flanked by his squad of warriors and Mira's too.

The teams she'd trained with, laughed with, rode into battle with, all gave her nods of greeting and support as she entered the room. As for Nathan, despite his carefully schooled posture, there was no mistaking the concern in his dark-fringed eyes as he pivoted his head and met Mira's gaze. He'd been worried about Kellan too.

Mira went to the side of the bed, not realizing she was holding her breath until she saw Kellan's chest rise and fall, and her own lungs expelled a ragged sigh.

She whispered his name, reaching down to smooth his coppery-brown hair off his pale brow.

"He's weak right now," Tess said gently. "He's lost a lot of blood."

"He's alive," Mira said. It was all the hope she needed. She kissed his mouth, tasted her own tears as she wrapped her arms around his bulky shoulders and let her relief pour out of her.

It took her a long moment before she could release him. She turned away, walking over to Tess and Rafe, her personal miracle workers. She embraced them both but held on to Tess with a gratitude that defied words.

Just that morning Tess had told Mira her vision had given her a gift she could only hope to repay. Never had Mira imagined how much she would need Tess's extraordinary power. How could she ever express the depth of her indebtedness?

"Tess, I . . ."

The other Breedmate merely smiled and squeezed Mira's hand. "I know. Now, go to him. Kellan needs you, more than anything else we can do for him."

Mira went back to his side and took his hand. His skin was warm. His fingers twitched in her grasp, then tightened. He could feel her. He knew she was there with him.

"His heart is very strong," Tess said. "He's been fighting very hard to come back. He didn't want to let go."

Mira couldn't hold back her little sob. "You came back to me," she murmured, leaning in close to him as she caressed his handsome face. "Now you're stuck for good, Kellan Archer. Do you hear me? Don't you ever let go again."

Tess's hand came to rest lightly on Mira's back. "I'd like to check on him a bit later, make sure he's in the clear. But right now, his healing will depend on you. Your blood will do the rest for him, Mira."

She nodded, noted that as Tess stepped away, she had placed a slender scalpel atop some folded clothing on the bedside table.

Mira's relief that Kellan was alive couldn't have been more complete, but she couldn't help feeling the dark gravity of Lucan's presence in the room. Kellan had been given the chance to defy the gunshot wounds that killed him in front of the GNC, but where did that leave him with Lucan and the rest of the Order?

"What happens now, Lucan? If Kellan wakes up—*when he wakes up*—where will he go from here?"

Lucan's grim expression gave nothing away. He stared at Kellan, then brought his stern gray gaze back to Mira. "None of this changes what's already come to pass. Dead or alive, he was still found guilty by the Council. He can't return to the life he was leading before. Neither of the lives he once led."

Mira knew her disappointment must have shown on her face. She'd been hoping for some kind of absolution from Lucan. Some reassurance that Kellan would be welcomed back into the fold and that life would go on as it once was. Better than it ever had been.

She was hoping for a miracle. And she had it, didn't she? Kellan was alive. The rest they would simply have to figure out later. They would figure everything out together.

And if that meant she had to leave the Order to be with Kellan?

She tried to ignore the twinge of hurt that notion brought with it. The Order was her family. Her purpose in life. Her home.

She glanced away from Lucan, to Renata, beautiful and heavy with child, nestled under the protective wing of Nikolai's strong arm. She looked next to Nathan, her dear friend. Kellan's friend. And to the trio of Breed warriors who had long ago become more than simply comrades. Everyone gathered in the room and under this roof was part of Mira's life.

For all her attempts in the past days to convince Kellan that they should run away together, abandon everything and try to outrun the destiny he'd seen in her eyes, she realized only now how steep the price would have been.

But Kellan had known.

Even with the prospect of his own death hanging over his head, he hadn't allowed Mira to turn her back on everything she loved for a life of exile and hiding with him. He'd chosen to face a fatal destiny in order to make certain she found her way back to where she belonged.

She loved him more for that sacrifice now than she had loved him at any other time.

Mira took the scalpel from the table beside the bed. She made a small incision in her wrist, then held the bleeding wound against his slack mouth. She stroked his hair, his cheek, softly encouraging him to drink. Her blood welled on his tongue, deep red, the coppery tang of it laced with the trace fragrance of lilies, her unique blood scent. Kellan responded after a long moment, his throat working slowly as the blood slipped to the back of his mouth.

"That's it," Mira whispered. "Take some more of me, Kellan. Take all you need."

His lips moved to get a better purchase on her vein. Then his tongue pressed against her skin, warm and searching. He took another swallow. Then another.

Mira caressed him as he drank from her, feeling his strength begin to renew through their bond. "Keep drinking," she told him gently. "Come back to me."

She hardly noticed the others in the room now, all her focus locked on Kellan. On making him better. Making him whole.

"Let's give them some time alone," Renata said. She led the group of warriors and their mates out of the room, pausing to send a caring, tender smile in Mira's direction. "I love you, Mouse."

Mira nodded, gave her a wobbly smile. "I love you too, Rennie."

She loved them all, the only family she'd ever known. And she loved Kellan, the man who had held her heart from the moment she first laid eyes on him.

She didn't want to choose. She wanted both.

Selfishly, desperately, she wanted both.

Four hours later, Lucan Thorne stood beside his Breedmate, Gabrielle, in the middle of the peace summit gala, dressed like a freaking undertaker in his black suit, black button-down shirt, and polished black shoes.

The rest of the Order on duty at the reception was similarly outfitted, a nearly twenty-man security detail garbed in finely tailored suits and tactfully concealed weapons. Not that they blended in, exactly. Hard to miss the presence of six and a half feet of muscled Breed might and darkly sober menace stationed in all corners of the glittering reception hall.

Precisely the point Lucan had wanted to make to the upward of a thousand human and Breed dignitaries and heads of state in attendance from various parts of the world.

The Order was on-site and vigilant.

They didn't need an arsenal of weapons to prove their point. It was evident in each warrior's stride. In his steady eye and stern jaw. And in the preternatural power that radiated off every one of Lucan's warrior brethren, even at rest. They were deadly cool and on the watch.

But they were there to maintain peace, not fan the flames of unrest or mistrust.

More than he could say for the thirty-plus cowboys swaggering around in Crowe Industries uniforms, each with a pair of sidearms bobbing at his hips. Lucan glowered as the preening peacock in command of those clueless yahoos started strutting toward him from across the wide floor of the crowded reception.

Next to him, Gabrielle put her hand on his arm and casually leaned toward him, speaking through her pretty, diplomatic smile. "Try to be nice. This is a party, remember?"

Eyes on Reginald Crowe, Lucan lowered his head and growled.

Filthy rich and oily with a born salesman's ready grin, Crowe strolled over in his black tux and white shirt, a slender flute of bubbling champagne caught between the fingers of his left hand. He was tall and fit, carried himself with an air of entitlement—of ownership of all he laid eyes on—that made Lucan want to punch the arrogance out of him on sight. Crowe's thick yellow mane held the golden glint of a Krugerrand, slicked back tonight, making his broad grin seem to take up even more of his Mediterranean-baked face.

"Chairman Thorne," he said, that grin seeming even tighter, far less friendly, up close. "Good evening to you."

Lucan had little choice but to take the offered hand and give it a firm shake of greeting. But he didn't have to curb his glare as Crowe's gaze shifted to Gabrielle. He looked her over from head to toe, stunning in her simple dove gray sheath and delicate heels. "I don't believe we've had the pleasure."

"My mate," Lucan snarled. "Gabrielle."

She gave a polite nod of her head and Crowe's face lit up with appreciation. "Enchanted, to be sure." He bowed slightly, then gestured with his champagne glass. "May I get you a cocktail or some hors d'oeuvres? It would be my pleasure to serve, Lady Thorne."

Gabrielle's smile went a bit strained at the unwanted attention. "No, thank you."

"What do you want, Crowe?"

Crowe swung his head back to Lucan. "Actually, I wanted to commend you on the decision to move forward tonight with the gala. Director Benson would've wanted that, I have to believe. He and the rest of the GNC—yourself included, of course—have done so much to make this summit happen. It would've been a shame to see it fall apart at the last minute."

Lucan grunted in acknowledgment. "Especially after you've obviously invested so much into the event personally."

Everywhere he looked he saw Crowe Industries' stamp on the party: from the security staff to the catering service and video crew broadcasting the reception for the rest of the world. For crissake, even the ten-man orchestra at the back of the lavish hall played under a digital banner bearing Reginald Crowe's smirking image.

And then there was the centerpiece of the man's ego—the crystal sculpture he was to dedicate to the GNC tonight in commemoration of First Dawn and the summit's mission of securing true peace—situated in the center of the grand hall. At least this wasn't a blatant ode to Crowe's arrogance. Not the life-size likeness of the man that Lucan had half expected but a tall obelisk carved of glittering, multifaceted crystal. The ten-foot sculpture tapered at its peak, on top of which sat an orb that gleamed as flawless and cool as a diamond but glowed faintly at its center in palest shades of peach and gold.

It was, Lucan had to admit, if only to himself, a stunning work of art. Most of the mingling dignitaries agreed, crowds drawn to the obelisk like a beacon in the middle of the sea of formally attired attendees.

Crowe took a sip of his champagne, surveying the reception he'd bought with what had to easily have been millions. He exhaled a beleaguered sigh and slowly shook his head. "A pity, really. This evening was supposed to have been a celebration of all the good things still to come. A recognition of all the promise the future holds. To have lost one of the world's most brilliant scientific minds and a respected statesman, both to violence in the same week . . ." Crowe clucked his tongue. "Well, it's unthinkable. Such a tragedy."

"Indeed," Lucan replied.

Crowe's gaze locked on him, as shrewd and sharp as a bird of prey. "And the Order must be in shock as well, not without its own losses this week. Terrible business, learning one of your flock has turned traitor. A former warrior, gone to the dark side to collude with the rebels . . . astounding." Crowe peeled his lips back in a cold smile. "I hope you'll forgive me for saying that's one death today for which I did find cause to celebrate."

Lucan gave a careless shrug, refusing to let the human goad him. "Apparently he wasn't the only one involved in conspiracy. Benson's murder by JUSTIS officers today obviously means the director had secret enemies of his own."

Crowe frowned as if to express regret, but the emotion didn't quite make it to his eyes. "We live in dangerous times, I'm sure you'd agree. And I have to say, I'm surprised at the lack of security response after the violence at today's hearing. I would've guessed the Order to come in tonight like a battalion on the march."

Lucan grunted, cool and unfazed. "This is a peace summit event, not a combat zone. Your men must've missed the memo."

Crowe chuckled, looking around at his uniformed guards who patrolled the party like a SWAT team.

"Makes me wonder whose interests you're protecting more," Lucan added. "The summit, the attendees . . . or your own."

Now the magnate's humor vanished, and his smile was anything but pleasant. "I happen to view those things in equal importance. Especially after the Order allowed someone like Jeremy Ackmeyer to be abducted under their watch—by one of their own fallen members, no less. I'm of the opinion we can't be too careful when it comes to protecting the interests of our future, Chairman Thorne."

"On that we are agreed," Lucan replied stiffly.

Crowe lifted his glass and drained it in one long swallow. He glanced to Gabrielle, gave her a gallant nod. "If you'll excuse me, I have guests to greet."

He didn't wait for a response. Spotting a Breed ambassador from South America arriving with his attractive blond mate, Crowe glided smoothly away, vanishing into the throng of tuxedos and evening gowns.

Gabrielle stared after him, then scoffed under her breath. "What an asshole."

Lucan grunted and drew her close to his side. "He is that, all right. And he's up to something. I can smell it on the son of a bitch."

He sent a glance to Tegan and Dante across the room, then a meaningful nod in Crowe's direction. They would be watching the human closely tonight.

And if any of the Order got so much as a whiff of cause to be concerned, the bastard was going to be taken down—whether the whole world was watching or not.

27

KELLAN WAS DREAMING OF LILIES.

Their sweet fragrance wreathed his senses like a silken ribbon. Pulled him gently to the surface, out of a dark, heavy slumber.

He was alive.

He opened his eyes. Blinked slowly as he focused on his surroundings. He was in a bed. A hospital—no, the Order's D.C. headquarters infirmary. He knew this place, had landed there after combat more than once in his distant past. But never like this.

And never with Mira nestled against him.

A rush of emotion swamped him.

He was alive.

And yet he knew he'd been dead. He remembered the moment when the blackness closed in and he lost his grip on the corporeal world. He'd tried so hard to hold on. He hadn't wanted to go. Hadn't wanted to leave her. He could still feel the sense of panic, of marrow-deep loss, as his connection to Mira thinned and stretched . . . then snapped, sending him drifting away from her, unmoored, lost in a sea of darkness.

He had died.

He understood that.

Yet here he was, given another chance to live. Tess and Rafe, he realized now. It was their hands that healed him. Their voices that told him to hang on, to reach for the line they were throwing to him.

And then there was Mira.

She'd saved him too. He could still taste her lily-sweet blood on his tongue. It had found him, healed him, just when he needed it most. Her strength, her power, her love.

Their bond had defied death, and he had never felt so humbled by anything before in all his days. He loved this woman—*his* woman, his eternal mate. He needed her more than air, more than anything else this life could give him. His heart swelled with love for her, reborn and re-newed, beating as hard and strong as a drum.

Mira stirred beside him, coming awake on a soft sigh. She wore the same black fatigues she'd had on when he last saw her, but they were bed-rumpled now, stained in places with his blood. Her blond braid was a wreck, more loose than not, pale hair framing her face in wispy ten-drils. He'd never seen a more welcome sight.

She lifted her head, sucked in a shallow gasp as she looked at him and saw his eyes open, gazing back at her. "Kellan . . . Oh, God. You're awake. You came back to me." He smiled but had no chance to speak before Mira crushed his mouth in a fierce kiss. She drew back and stared at him, her eyes dancing behind the purple veil of her lenses. "You're really here with me."

He managed a nod before she kissed him again, more tenderly this time, her hands cupping his face. She kept looking at him, searching his eyes, drinking him in with open joy and affection. Then she scowled, hissing a dark curse. "Don't you ever leave me again, Kellan Archer."

"Never," he vowed, his voice thick and rusty.

Her scowl deepened. "If you do, I promise you, right here and now, I will hunt you down and kill you myself. Do you understand?"

He smiled and pulled her closer. "Yes, ma'am."

His body was already back online, blood pumping robustly through his veins. Under the sheet that covered his naked body, his muscles flexed, rejuvenated and ready to be put to use. Something else was ready too, and it took Mira only a second to notice that every bit of him was awake and alive.

"You're unbelievable," she murmured, but there was humor—and no small amount of interest—in her eyes. "You have at least two dozen bul-let holes in you, in case you didn't realize that."

He didn't, and, in fact, he hardly felt the bandaged wounds now. All he felt was his Breedmate, his precious Mira, warm and sweet in his arms. He ran his hand down her back, to the firm curve of her behind.

He groaned, rejoicing in the feel of her under his hands, and pressed up against the length of him. "One of us has too many clothes on."

He wanted to lighten the moment, and, yeah, he was glad as hell to be alive and breathing again—best of all, to be doing it lying next to the woman with whom he hoped to spend a good long eternity. So glad he could think of no better way to celebrate the occasion than burying himself deep within the haven of Mira's delectable body.

But she was having none of it right now. She levered herself up on one elbow beside him, all serious. Her gaze was sober, her breath shaky as she let out a quiet curse. "I thought I lost you today, Kellan. I watched you die. I felt it." A crease formed between her light brows, eyes lowering as she slowly shook her head. "I wanted to hate you for surrendering yourself back at the Darkhaven in Maine. I think I did hate you for that, just a little. I wanted to make our time together last, and you took that away from me. From both of us."

He caressed her face and silky hair, swallowed on a dry throat. "I didn't mean to hurt you again. I didn't want to see you throw away your past—throw away your family—the way I had done. I didn't want you to face the same kind of impossible decision I did. I didn't want you to make my mistake."

"I know that now," she said, lightly stroking her fingers over his wounded chest. "It took almost losing you for good to understand what you'd done for me that night." She glanced back up at him, mouth twisted wryly. "That doesn't mean I'm not still pissed, by the way."

He arched a brow, let his hand drift down her arm, then along the swell of her breast. "I look forward to making it up to you." Then, tenderly, he lifted her chin and kissed her, unrushed and reverent. "You're mine, Mira. I love you. I should've told you that a hundred times before. I'm not going to blow that chance again. I have a second chance, and I'm going to make it right."

"We do have a second chance," she murmured softly. "But where will we begin? You're dead, Kellan. You and Bowman both. It's been reported all over the country, probably all over the world. The public wanted their vengeance, and the GNC was all too eager to tell them justice had been served."

He considered for a long moment. "Candice and Doc and Nina . . . ?"

"Lucan released them this morning, before you were brought in front of the Council. They would've heard by now that you were shot and killed." She stared at him, a fierce intensity in her eyes. "No one outside the Order can ever know any different, or your life will be in danger all over again. I can't bear that kind of worry. Not ever again."

"I won't ask you to," he said, smoothing away the tension around her pretty mouth. He exhaled sharply, sardonic. "Do you think you can love a ghost?"

"I loved one for eight years."

"So you did. Thank God you did." He caressed her cheek, the desire he felt for her flaring even brighter when he thought of how faithful she'd been to him. Steadfast and strong. She'd been his partner always, in every way. After all they'd been through, he wasn't about to let a little thing like death stand between them and their future together.

And he wasn't about to let anyone hurt Mira or the others he cared about. Which meant his new mission had become doing whatever he had to in order to bring down Benson and uncover the truth behind the name that the corrupt councilman had given in Kellan's final conscious moments at the hearing.

Opus Nostrum.

Kellan sat up, his blood pounding at the sudden recollection of Benson's guilt.

"What's wrong?" Mira asked, rising with him. He swung his legs over the side of the bed and she crawled behind him. "What are you doing?"

"I need to talk to Lucan."

"About what?"

"Benson." He stood up, expecting to feel weak or wobbly, but his legs held strong, bolstered by his Breedmate's blood. Even his wounds felt insignificant. He peeled one of the bandages away and found the bullet hole healed over, puckered and pink but already growing new skin. Kellan unwrapped the rest and tossed the dressings into a nearby trash bin. Someone had left a pair of sweats and a T-shirt on the table beside the bed. Kellan hastily put the pants on. "Lucan needs to hear what I found out from Benson today."

"You told him," Mira said. She came around in front of him and carefully smoothed her fingers over his healing wounds. "If you're talking about Opus Nostrum, whatever that is, Lucan is already looking into it. You gave him that intel just before you—"

"There's more, Mira. We need to bring Benson in. He's got information about some kind of attack that's being planned, one that involves
Ackmeyer's Morningstar technology. We need to interrogate the bastard ASAP."

She gave him a funny look, then shook her head. "Benson's dead. He
was killed by the same JUSTIS officers who shot you. They murdered
him execution style in a back hallway of the GNC building when he was
trying to get away."

Ah, fuck.

Kellan grabbed the T-shirt and shrugged into it. "Lucan needs to
know what's going on. I have to see him right now."

"You can't." Mira shook her head. "He's gone. He left with Gabrielle
and the rest of the Order and their mates some time ago. Everyone's at
the peace summit gala tonight."

The peace summit.

Realization sank in with sharp, icy talons.

"It's going to happen at the gala," Kellan murmured. "When I read
Benson, his guilt was over the fact that Opus Nostrum had killed Ackmeyer because of his UV technology and that many more people were
going to die because of it too—all under the guise of peace. They're
going to use Morningstar as a weapon at the gala tonight."

Lucan's grip was tight on his comm unit as he ended the call with Mira.
His curse, vicious and nasty. It drew an aghast inhalation from the
Breedmate of a visiting ambassador, who'd been blathering on endlessly
to Gabrielle and Gideon's mate, Savannah, for the past twenty minutes
about her latest art acquisitions. The female gaped at Lucan, who returned the look with a dark scowl, too distracted by troubling news to
be bothered with playing the pleasant party guest.

As the woman made her excuses and scurried away, Gabrielle turned
a wry look on him. "Thanks for the rescue. What did Mira want? Nothing's wrong with Kellan, is there?"

"He's fine. Already on his feet, in fact. But he remembered something more from his read on Benson." Lucan's blood ran a bit colder as
he took in the sea of people in attendance at the gala. He glanced to
Gideon, who stood talking with Darion on the other side of the two

Breedmates. "Kellan says Benson was aware of an attack being planned by Opus Nostrum. Something big, involving Ackmeyer's UV technology as a weapon. He believes it may be set to take place tonight."

"Here, at the gala?" Gabrielle whispered. "You don't think that's possible, do you?"

Gideon grunted, his blue eyes dubious over the rims of sleek, silvery-lensed glasses. "Between the Order and Crowe's security detail, this place is locked down. Someone would have to be insane to think they could get in here and wage some kind of assault."

"Unless they're already inside," Dare suggested.

Lucan felt a scowl tighten his face as he considered his son's all-too-probable scenario. With a tilt of his chin, he motioned Tegan, Nikolai, and Hunter over from across the room. "Everyone in here went through metal detectors and weapons scans, yeah?"

Tegan gave a grave nod. "Can't get into any government building these days without a full-body X ray. Everyone was scanned on entry."

Niko grinned. "Think it's too late to recommend Crowe for a cavity search? Nah, on second thought, he might enjoy it."

Crowe was currently working his way toward the lavish stage at the head of the large reception hall. He pumped dozens of hands on his approach, chuckling and backslapping with the dignitaries while leering at their wives and basically acting like he owned the damn place and everyone in it.

Lucan lowered his head and glared in Crowe's direction. His voice was a deep, rumbling growl. "He reeks of something more than just arrogance tonight. What if Crowe's got his hands on the Morningstar technology? Everyone went through metal scans on entry to the building, but did anyone check the rounds Crowe's security detail is packing?"

"You think they could be UV?" Niko, the Order's personal weapons expert and gearhead, blew out a low whistle. "Only one way to find out. Who's up for a round of show-and-tell?"

Tegan met his look. "We have to keep it quiet. Take his detail off the floor, bring them somewhere out of sight where we can search them one by one. Between the twenty of us, we can get this done in a few minutes."

Hunter nodded. "There are empty conference rooms on the west corridor outside the reception hall."

Niko grinned. "What are we waiting for?"

"Make it quick," Lucan said, "but keep this shit covert. Hit them with a trance on the way in, mind scrub on the way out. And if you find anything that raises suspicion, this whole party goes on immediate lock-down."

The three warriors acknowledged the command, then took off to alert the others on watch of the plan. Darion started to go with them, but Lucan held him back, a hand clamped tight on his son's muscled shoulder. "Stay close. I want you nearby to look after your mother if the situation calls for it."

Dare's brows lowered, his mouth flattening into a hard line. But he acquiesced with a nod and hung back, watching as the rest of the Order began discreetly carrying out the search on Crowe's security detail.

As for Lucan, his sights were fixed on Reginald Crowe, currently onstage and basking in thunderous applause from the crowd spread out below him. Crowe ate it up with unabashed pleasure, puffed up and pompous, a golden king about to address his lowly peasant subjects. When the adoration finally subsided, Crowe took the microphone to officially open the summit gala and to welcome the dignitaries as his personal guests.

Lucan tuned out the self-preening to survey the warriors' progress with the catch-and-release operation under way on the floor of the reception hall. Nikolai was casually guiding one of Crowe's security men out of the room, while Tegan had just returned to let another of the uniformed guards loose into the gathering. He met Lucan's gaze and gave a grim shake of his head. Nothing.

One by one the Order led Crowe's men out of the room. And one by one they were all returning without anything to report.

Maybe Kellan had it wrong.

Maybe the attack Benson was privy to was set to occur somewhere else, at some other time.

And yet every one of Lucan's battle instincts prickled with the certainty that something was off tonight. Something wasn't right, and he was willing to bet that something had everything to do with Reginald Crowe.

Onstage, Crowe's demeanor had sobered as he paused to express his shock and grief over the tragic loss of both Jeremy Ackmeyer and GNC director Benson. "Two great men, visionaries, both of them," he said, his voice carrying over the silent crowd. "One committed to advancing our world through science and innovation. The other devoted his life to ensuring a safer future for us all . . ."

Lucan tuned out the brief eulogy, instead watching as still more Crowe Industries guards were searched and released by Tegan and the other warriors.

Crowe, meanwhile, was gaining steam again. "To have lost two brilliant champions of our future at a time when we were gathering here to celebrate peace between mankind and the Breed only demonstrates the work still left to be done. Peace is our dream. Peace is our goal."

As the throng applauded and murmured their agreement, Crowe directed their attention to the center of the reception, where his glittering crystal obelisk shone like a beacon under the soft lights of the hall. "Tonight I give you a symbol of my vision for the future of our world. Tonight I propose a future of true peace. Not First Dawn, but a New Dawn."

Crowe's words put a sudden chill in Lucan's veins. He glanced at the obelisk again and noticed that the crystal orb crowning the sculpture had begun to glow with more intensity than before. Now the light inside the sphere pulsed with energy.

Holy shit.

It wasn't UV bullets they needed to worry about after all.

"Peace is our vision," Crowe was saying now, his gaze panning the crowd as he spoke. His eyes found Lucan and came to a stop. "Peace is our work. *Pax Opus Nostrum.*"

Morningstar.

Crowe had smuggled it in right under their noses.

"Get down!" Lucan bellowed. He pushed Gabrielle into Dare's arms and motioned for them to move the hell out of the room. As all eyes turned to him, Lucan drew his 9-mm semiauto from under his suit coat and aimed it at the obelisk. "Everyone down now!"

The light within the orb was growing stronger by the second, threatening to blow.

"UV bomb in the orb," he shouted to the other members of the Order. "Get the Breed civilians out of this goddamned room now!"

The crowd started screaming, even before Lucan fired the first shot.

Chaos erupted, humans and Breed scattering in a stampede of confusion and terror.

The crystal orb cracked with his bullet's impact, but the light didn't dim.

The other warriors rounded up the dignitaries as best they could, the tangle of panicked bodies making it next to impossible to see anything but the rush of men and women, dodging in all directions as the gala dissolved into mass hysteria.

Through the fleeing crowd, Lucan spotted Crowe as he leapt off the stage and headed for the shadows in the back of the reception hall. He wanted to pursue the bastard, but all of his focus—all of his savage purpose—was fixed on destroying the tower of deadly art now glowing with greater strength at the center of the gathering.

28

ALTHOUGH HE KNEW IT WAS THE LAST PLACE HE SHOULD BE—
and the dead last place he wanted to be with Mira alongside him—
nothing could have stopped Kellan from heading to the peace summit
gala once he realized there was a chance Ackmeyer's UV technology
could be unleashed on the Order.

As he and Mira pulled up to the curb in one of the Order's vehicles,
Kellan realized the situation was even worse than he'd anticipated.

Much worse.

Hundreds of people—humans and Breed alike—poured out of the
GNC building and into the night, fleeing on foot, screaming in utter
terror. Men in formal wear, women in shimmering evening gowns and
high heels, scattering in all directions.

Sheer chaos.

"Oh, my God," Mira breathed, coming around the sedan to meet
Kellan on the other side. She was dressed as he was, head-to-toe black
combat gear, sidearms loaded and ready for action. The hilts of Mira's
twin daggers, riding at her hips, glinted under the pale moonlight overhead. She stared at the scene of confusion, her expression slack with
alarm. "It's already happening. Kellan, what if we're too late?"

He glimpsed several of the warriors ushering Breed dignitaries to safe
ground, far away from the building. "We still have time. Come on."

Mira jogged after him, up a broad flight of stairs. They had to dodge
the flow of escaping party guests, who crashed toward them like cattle
swept up in a blind stampede. Kellan spotted an open side door, away

from the mad throng pushing and shoving out of the main entrance. He took Mira's hand and ran with her, ducking inside the building with her.

The scene in the lobby wasn't any more sane. Thick with scores of fleeing people, it was almost impossible to push against the current. Kellan saw Rafe up ahead, his blond head and broad shoulders towering over most of the humans racing past him. The warrior glanced over and his aqua eyes flashed with intensity.

"What happened?" Kellan called to him.

"Crowe," Rafe snarled over the tops of the fleeing throng. "Son of a bitch planted a UV bomb in the middle of the damn reception. Lucan's trying to shut it down. He wants a total evac."

Ah, Christ.

Even worse than ultraviolet rounds, a bomb utilizing that kind of technology could wipe out not only the Order but every Breed dignitary in the place.

Which was exactly Opus Nostrum's plan, he realized now.

"Kellan, look." Mira nodded toward the far end of the lobby. "At the elevators."

Reginald Crowe, flanked by a pair of uniformed security personnel, was rushing into a service elevator while the rest of the lobby swarmed with total chaos. Before Kellan had a chance to flash across the distance and stop the bastard, the doors slid closed. Crowe was gone.

"Fuck," Kellan growled as he and Mira ran up on the sealed doors. "He's heading for the roof. Stay here. Stick close to Rafe and the other warriors."

"Let you go after him alone?" she said, not even close to a question. "Like hell I will."

He didn't like it, but he didn't have time to argue with her, especially the way her chin hiked up as she spoke. And besides, Crowe was only human. The two guards with him weren't Breed either, which meant the three of them together would pose little problem for Kellan. Add in Mira's lethal skill with her blades, and Crowe's escape attempt was futile even before it began.

Kellan shot a glance at the service stairwell. Using the speed his Breed genetics gave him, he could be up to the roof in mere seconds. "I'm going up on foot. You take the second elevator."

She nodded and he took off, racing up the several flights to the service access door on the rooftop, just as Crowe and his security detail were taking their first steps across the asphalt. A helicopter waited a dozen yards away, a human pilot seated behind the controls. The engine whined to a start as Crowe strode swiftly toward the aircraft.

Kellan wasted no time. He put a bullet into the back of each guard's head, dropping the pair like bowling pins. Crowe drew up short as his men hit the ground.

"Don't move," Kellan growled. "Don't you fucking move, or you're dead next."

Crowe put his hands in the air and slowly turned around. His golden brows rose in surprise. "Well, this is an amusing development. The rebel leader formerly known as Bowman. I never expected to see a dead man staring at me over the barrel of a pistol this evening."

Kellan grunted. "Funny, I'm looking at a dead man too."

Crowe smiled. "You can't kill me. We both know that. You need me. You need information only I can give you. You want to know about Opus Nostrum, don't you?"

Kellan kept his aim steady on the center of Crowe's head. "I know all I need to know."

"Do you?"

Kellan held the man in a dark glower. "Let me summarize. You and Benson had plans of killing the Order tonight to clear the way for you and your twisted need for power. But you weren't capable of pulling off something like that on your own. You needed Jeremy Ackmeyer's technology to accomplish it. You needed a weapon capable of instant, mass murder. Morningstar was your answer."

Crowe smiled, seemingly amused.

"Benson stole the prototype from his nephew, but you decided Ackmeyer needed to die. No loose ends would be my guess. Lucky for you, his kidnapping provided the perfect opportunity for you to strike. You were able to kill him and blame it on rebels, ending the life of a pawn you always intended to sweep off your board."

Kellan heard the access door on the rooftop service building open behind him and Mira quietly announced herself. She drew up next to him, blades in her hands, looking fierce and formidable. Sexier than he wanted to notice in that moment.

He centered himself back on Crowe and the contempt he had for the man. "Benson wasn't on board with his nephew's killing, was he? That's why he showed up drunk at the hearing today. He said too much, so your spies had him executed on the spot."

Crowe chuckled. "You think you have it all figured out. You're not even close."

"I think I am. When I touched Benson, his mind told me what Opus Nostrum had planned here tonight."

"Opus Nostrum isn't the worst of your problems," Crowe replied. He lowered his hands, letting them fall slowly to his sides. He started walking toward Kellan and Mira.

Kellan raised the gun, prepared to fire a shot straight between Crowe's amused eyes. "Stop right there, asshole. Or your next step will be your last."

But Crowe didn't stop. He came forward another pace.

Kellan pulled the trigger—once, twice. Two direct hits, right between the eyes, a dead-on shot into the bastard's skull.

The bullets didn't so much as make him flinch. The blood seemed to evaporate on the spot, skin healing over even faster than one of Kellan's kind.

Mira sucked in a sharp breath. "Oh, my God . . ."

"What the fuck?" Kellan muttered, shocked and confused. "You're not human. Not Breed either."

Crowe grinned. "Now you're getting the picture."

Kellan emptied his weapon at him, but Crowe dodged most of the bullets with superhuman agility. Kellan reached for his second sidearm, but Mira was already in motion. She let her daggers fly on a battle roar, planting one blade in the center of Crowe's chest, the other driven deep into his throat.

Crowe cocked his head at her, a cruel, animalistic gleam in his eyes.

As if the grievous wounds were of no consequence at all, he plucked out the daggers and dropped the bloodied weapons to the ground.

The rising glow drew Nathan back into the reception hall as the crowd of screaming gala attendees continued to pour out to the lobby in wave after wave of mass hysteria.

Lucan stayed behind, attempting to disable the crystal obelisk and its illuminated orb. As Nathan stepped back into the hall, Lucan was discarding his empty 9-mm magazine and feeding another into the weapon. The orb was chipped and shattered but not broken.

"It's getting brighter." Darion Thorne had come up beside Nathan. "Gunfire isn't enough to destroy it. What the hell is that thing made out of?"

Nathan shook his head. He didn't know, but he had another weapon in his arsenal—one inherited from the Breedmate who was his mother. He tossed both of his guns to Darion. "Light that fucker up. I'll be right behind you."

Dare nodded and stalked across the emptying floor to meet his father in front of the obelisk. He opened fire in concert with Lucan, a 9-mm in each hand, squeezing off rounds with each long stride.

Nathan focused on the din of thunderous shots and the echoing screams of the crowd. He gathered the noise, summoning his Breed ability to bend sound waves and either amplify or mute them. He built up the cacophony, tumbling it into a ball of sound and energy.

Lucan glanced to his son, then to Nathan, giving both warriors a nod of approval. Of solemn respect and gratitude.

Together Lucan and Darion blasted into the orb, creating deep fissures in the glowing sphere of light. Nathan gathered more sound, until the vibrating collection of energy was almost too much for him to contain.

On a roar, he let it loose.

The air rippled as the sonokinetic blast arced toward the cracked obelisk.

Lucan and Dare leapt out of the way, both warriors still shooting at the sculpture as they tumbled away just before it shattered.

Light erupted from the orb, but it lasted only an instant. The pebbled crystal of the obelisk and its crowning sphere exploded in all directions, raining down onto the reception hall floor like thousands of tiny diamonds.

Morningstar had been neutralized.

Lucan glanced at Nathan, then his son. "Good work, both of you." His gray eyes flashed with hot amber sparks. "Now let's go find Crowe and finish that bastard."

29

MIRA GAPED IN ASTONISHMENT AS CROWE'S PUNCTURED THROAT and chest repaired themselves in a matter of instants.

Who—*or what*—was he?

Whatever the answer, there seemed to be no stopping him.

But that didn't keep Kellan from trying.

He launched himself at Crowe, a full-body assault that sent both males slamming into the side of the stairwell door of the service building on the roof. The heavy steel panel crushed inward with the impact, groaning on its industrial-grade hinges.

Crowe chuckled. "Not used to being beaten by someone lesser than your own Breed, are you, warrior? That would be your mistake, assuming I was anything less than your equal."

Kellan went at him again, throwing Crowe into the side of the rooftop building. For all the good it did. Crowe wheeled around in mid-air, taking Kellan with him. He thrust forward, propelling them both into a frightening tumble across the wide plain of asphalt, nearly to the edge.

"Your kind is an abomination. Bastards, born of mixed blood between the ones you called Ancients and the female halflings spawned by humans and the profane defectors of my own race. The Breed does not deserve to inhabit this planet, no more than the humans do. Your Ancient forebears thought they'd defeated us when they drove us from our own world, down to this crude rock. They thought they'd won again when they hunted us here and destroyed our perfect Atlantis, forcing our queen into exile. But we've only been waiting for our chance to rise again. We will have it, and soon. The wheels are already in motion."

Mira listened as she scrambled for a way to help Kellan defeat Crowe. She'd heard the theories over the past couple of decades that Breed-mates like her were the offspring of an immortal race who'd built a civilization human legends would eventually call Atlantis. Jenna's journals back at the Order's headquarters archives were filled with entries about that stunning probability. But no one had ever knowingly been face-to-face with an Atlantean until now.

The things Crowe was saying, the revelation that his kind had not only survived the destruction of Atlantis but were flourishing in secret, plotting their own war, was astonishing. It was terrifying. The prospect of war with another immortal race put a marrow-deep shiver in Mira's bones.

But her more immediate concern was keeping Kellan alive.

Her blades were of no help in slowing Crowe down, so Mira grabbed for her pistol. She knew bullets were hardly a sure thing in this fight either, but it was all she had.

If only she could find a clear shot.

Kellan and Crowe fought hand to hand, alternating between bone-crushing fists and violent body slams. They moved so fast, each gifted with a speed that was nothing close to human, Mira could hardly track them, let alone get a decent opportunity to fire on Crowe. She couldn't risk hitting Kellan. She'd seen him shot already today. She didn't have the heart to be the one pulling the trigger if he was in her line of fire.

After several aborted aims, she realized there was nothing for her to do but join in the fray.

She jumped on Crowe, tried to get her gun flush and steady against his head. One bullet into his head hadn't slowed him down, but she was prepared to squeeze off the entire magazine if he'd hold still long enough for her to attempt it.

She didn't get the chance to pull the trigger.

Crowe reared back and threw her off. He dropped his hold on Kellan, shifting around to face her as she fell to the rough asphalt of the rooftop and her gun clattered out of her grasp. Crowe fumed now, his features seeming to tighten across the bones of his face.

He looked utterly inhuman. Unearthly. She realized only now how true that observation was.

With a snarl, Crowe seized her, yanking her up off the ground and bringing her around in front of him like a shield. Kellan had her gun raised on Crowe, but somehow Crowe had acted equally fast, having retrieved a weapon off one of his fallen security detail before Mira had even registered his movements.

He put the cold nose of the pistol against Mira's temple as he started backing toward his waiting helicopter.

"Put her down," Kellan commanded.

"Oh, I don't think so." Crowe kept retreating, edging closer to the aircraft. The breeze off the slowly rotating blades stirred Mira's hair, sent wisps loose from her braid and blew them across her face.

She stared at Kellan, imploring him with her eyes, hoping he'd see that she wanted him to take his shot. Hoping he'd feel through their blood bond that she wasn't afraid. She trusted he could hit Crowe.

Do it. Take this bastard out before he reaches that bird.

She saw Kellan's finger tighten on the trigger. Felt his pulse kick with fear of harming her and the icy need to kill the one holding her. But at the last moment Kellan shifted his aim, shooting past Crowe and hitting his pilot.

The human rocked back in his seat with the impact before slumping down over the controls. The engine choked, and the blades lost some of their speed.

Crowe barked a laugh, unfazed. "You think after a few thousand years on this chunk of stone I haven't learned to fly your crude machinery? Please." He was still backing up, preparing to make his escape and keeping a firm hold on Mira the whole way.

She couldn't do much to get loose. His grip was iron around her middle. The metal nose of the gun bored into her right temple like ice. She swallowed her mounting panic as her ears filled with the steady *chop-chop-chop* of the rotor coming closer.

"A pity I'll only get to kill one of you before I have to go," Crowe taunted at Kellan. "I guess it'll have to be you."

Mira felt Crowe's muscles twitch nearly imperceptibly as he readied to take aim on Kellan. The instant the pressure eased from her temple, Mira broke loose from Crowe's hold and knocked his arm up, twisting out of his reach at the same time. She felt the sudden force of something heavy hitting him. Heard the low crunch as the propeller blade took his hand off at the wrist.

Crowe staggered, mouth slack as he gaped at his severed limb.

Then he looked back to Mira.

Something strange crossed his features as he stared into her eyes. He no longer seemed to notice the terrible wound that wasn't healing itself. His lost hand lay on the asphalt next to his gun, blood pumping down his forearm and onto the black rooftop. And yet Crowe stared at her eyes, utterly transfixed.

Her eyes . . .

She felt the tickle of one of her lenses where it clung to her cheek. It must have popped out during the struggle, unveiling the hypnotic mirror of her iris. Crowe didn't seem able to tear himself away from her gaze.

But he was still drifting backward, his steps sluggish now that he was caught in the power of her visions.

She didn't know what he saw.

She didn't think she'd want to know.

And in that next instant, it no longer mattered.

Crowe—or whatever his true, Atlantean name was—stumbled back on his heels. He was too close to the blades. Too tall, when the slowing rotors had started to droop with their loss of momentum.

Crowe turned his head then, almost as if some stronger part of his subconscious recognized the threat his waking mind couldn't see under the spell of Mira's gaze. He glanced behind him . . . just as the helicopter blade swung toward him, cleaving his head away from his neck.

Mira averted her eyes, but it was impossible to shut out the horror of what just happened.

Then, as Crowe's body crumpled to the ground, a bright light began to swell inside him. It rushed through his limbs and poured out of his neck, intense and pure and otherworldly. And in the center of his intact palm, a symbol began to take shape, illuminated from within.

It was in the shape of a teardrop falling into the cradle of a crescent moon.

The same symbol Mira and every other Breedmate bore as a birthmark somewhere on their bodies.

There could be no doubting it now.

The Atlanteans were real, the otherworldly fathers of the Breedmates.

The Atlanteans were alive, an unknown number of them, hiding in secret with their banished queen. Lying in wait for their chance to rise up against the Breed and mankind.

They were immortal and deadly.

They were the enemy.

Lucan crashed through the battered door of the rooftop service stairwell, Darion and Nathan right behind him. It seemed the only feasible place for Crowe to have fled, but the situation that greeted Lucan at the top of the GNC building was nothing he would have expected.

Mira and Kellan stood together in the darkness, she wrapped tightly around the Breed male, her blond head nestled into his chest, his muscled arms holding her close.

Two of Crowe's uniformed security men lay dead on the black asphalt in front of him. Across the way, a helicopter idled, its pilot slumped forward in his seat, engine winding down to an unmanned stop.

And lying under the slowing rotor blades, the headless body of Reginald Crowe.

Lucan stared, uncertain if he was seeing right, as a glow that seemed to light Crowe's limbs and torso from within now faded away before his eyes.

Behind Lucan, both Dare and Nathan murmured their disbelief.

Lucan glanced back to Mira and Kellan. "What the hell just happened?"

As the pair began explaining, more of the Order arrived behind Nathan and Dare. The younger teams, and the warriors who'd been with Lucan nearly from the start of the Order's founding. Gabrielle and the other Breedmates soon arrived as well, until Lucan found himself surrounded by the kith and kin who meant the most to him.

They all listened in silent astonishment as Mira and Kellan described what Crowe had done, who he was . . . and the things the immortal had revealed in his final breaths.

That Mira and Kellan had defeated Crowe by themselves was commendable, even if the leader in Lucan wanted to take the pair to task for the maverick move undertaken without his knowledge or permission. Perhaps that was the rebel in Kellan, the leader unafraid to charge to the head of any battle. God knew, Mira had never been known for her willingness to color within the lines.

Tonight they had been a united front. A team of two, stronger to-gether. It felt right, seeing them joined as a mated couple. A partnership that had been tested more than most, and hard-won.

Lucan walked over and extended his hand to them, first to Mira, whom he couldn't resist dragging into a brief embrace, feeling fatherly and proud of the little girl who had become such a valuable member of the Order's team. As they drew apart, Lucan clasped her hand in his firm grasp. "You honor us well, warrior."

To Kellan, he gave a nod of gratitude as he shook the Breed male's strong hand. "You as well," he said. "Maybe there's a place for a rebel ghost within the Order's ranks after all."

Kellan grinned, drawing Mira a bit closer to his side as he nodded in acceptance of Lucan's offer.

Lucan looked at them, then at his son and the younger warriors sur-rounding him. He was looking at the shape of the Order's future. A new generation, already stepping up to the plate.

And they would be needed, all of them.

Lucan glanced down at Reginald Crowe, realizing he was looking at something new there too: an enemy the Order had never confronted before, one that was clearly playing by its own set of rules now.

"What happened here tonight marks a new beginning," he told the men and women of the Order standing with him under the dark night sky. "This marks a new war . . . one we must win."

A round of agreeing voices answered him, grim faces filled with de-termination and fire.

Lucan met each fierce gaze, man and woman alike. "From this mo-ment forward, we play by our own rules. Whatever it takes, whatever the cost. Our new mission begins now."

Epilogue

THE GNC SUMMIT WENT ON AS PLANNED THAT NEXT DAY. LUCAN had announced to the world that there was no better time to gather for serious conversations about the future than in the wake of an assault that might have set the peace efforts of mankind and Breed back centuries.

Reginald Crowe's death had exposed him as the mastermind behind the attempted bombing at the gala. That he was something more than human was a fact Lucan and the rest of the Order agreed would only make an already skittish population even more uneasy. To the human and vampire nations around the world, Crowe was merely a would-be terrorist and a member of a clandestine cabal the Order had now made it their public mission to root out and eradicate.

In private, the Order's mission was something far more urgent.

A mission that would involve every District Command Center and warrior team posted in all corners of the globe.

The Atlanteans and their queen had to be found. They had to be stopped.

Mira had never known Lucan Thorne to be so serious about a mission objective before—and given the many wars and battles he'd fought in his more than nine hundred years of living, that was saying a hell of a lot.

She almost felt guilty about the respite Lucan had granted Kellan and her after their defeat of Reginald Crowe. Then again, it was hard to feel anything but grateful—not to mention, blissfully exhausted—when she was sprawled atop Kellan's naked body, the two of them having just made love in front of a crackling fire in the remote Darkhaven nestled deep in the northern Maine woods.

They were three nights into a week of alone time, a break they were doing their best to make the most of, in and out of the bedroom. Tonight, after a long walk in the woods where they used to play war games and wage snowball fights as kids, they'd forgone the bed in favor of the fluffy sheepskin rug in front of the fireplace in the Darkhaven's great room.

Kellan's fingers made little circles on the small of her back where he held her close to him. His body was warm and strong beneath her, his heart drumming against her ear. She thought he'd been sleeping— assumed he'd have to be, after their workout for the past hour. But he was awake. Awake in every way. Inside her, she felt him growing thicker, already pulsing against the tender walls of her body.

Mira lifted her head to look at him, incredulity tugging at her mouth. "You can't be serious."

His grin was slow and wicked. "Do I feel serious?"

She laughed as he tumbled her over onto the soft animal skin, his hips wedged deliciously between her parted thighs, his fists planted on either side of her, supporting his weight above her. "I'm so happy, Kellan. My heart has never felt so full."

He smiled and kissed her, moving against her in a deep, slow thrust that made her veins go bright with electricity and heat. "Do you know how much I love you?" he asked, even though he'd shown her a hundred times in the past few days, told her with every tender glance, every hot touch and possessive, claiming kiss. "I love you, Mira . . . my mate. My life. You're my everything."

She reached up to him, caressing his face as he stared down into her eyes. When instinct made her flick her gaze askance, Kellan lowered his head and kissed her. "Let me see you," he said, bringing her back to face him once more. "So beautiful. You never have to hide your eyes from me again. I'm not afraid of what I'll see. Not anymore. We've already been through the fire."

"We came out of it together," she said, her love for him a sweet ache in her chest. "We'll make it through anything now."

He nodded, his rhythm getting stronger, more intent. "You're mine, Mira. Mine forever."

"I always have been." She smiled, knowing he could feel the depth of her promise in the blood bond that wove them together, heart, mind, body, and soul.

He covered her with his body, with his strength and heat and the passion that she knew would always take her breath away.

He loved her, even the part of her that had nearly destroyed him.

Kellan kissed her again, deep and slow and thorough. As if to let her know their love had all the time in the world. "You're mine, Mira," he purred darkly. "And I'm not ever letting you go."

About the Author

Lara Adrian is the *New York Times* and #1 internationally bestselling author of the Midnight Breed vampire romance series, with more than 2 million books in print in the United States and translations licensed to more than 18 countries. Her books regularly appear in the top spots of all the major bestseller lists including *USA Today*, *Publishers Weekly*, IndieBound, Amazon.com, and Barnes & Noble. Her debut title, *Kiss of Midnight*, was named Borders Books bestselling debut romance of 2007. Twice her novels have been named among Amazon.com's Top Ten Best Romances of the Year and twice nominated for Goodreads Choice Awards for Best Romance of the Year. Reviewers have called Lara's books "addictively readable" (*Chicago Tribune*), "extraordinary" (Fresh Fiction), and "one of the best vampire series on the market" (*RT Reviews*).

With an ancestry stretching back to the Mayflower pilgrims and the court of King Henry VIII, the author lives with her husband in New England, surrounded by centuries-old graveyards, hip urban comforts, and the endless inspiration of the broody Atlantic Ocean. She is currently at work on the next novel in the Midnight Breed series.

Visit the author's website and sign up for new release announcements at www.LaraAdrian.com.

About the Type

This book was set in Berling. Designed in 1951 by Karl Erik Forsberg for the Typefoundry Berlingska Stilgjuteri AB in Lund, Sweden, it was released the same year in foundry type by H. Berthold AG. A classic old-face design, its generous proportions and inclined serifs make it highly legible.